ENEMIES OF THE STATE

THE EXECUTIVE OFFICE #1 - SPECIAL EDITION

TAL BAUER

Second Edition
10 9 8 7 6 5 4 3 2
ISBN 9781520921679
Copyright © 2016 – 2019 Tal Bauer
Cover Art by Natasha Snow © Copyright 2017
First Published in 2016
Second Edition Published by Tal Bauer in the United States of America

To all victims of terror & hate worldwide.
May we always work to make the world better in your name every day.

THE EXECUTIVE OFFICE CAST

White House

Jack Spiers: *President of the United States*
Ethan Reichenbach: *Head of Presidential Secret Service Detail*
Scott Collard: *Presidential Secret Service Detail Agent*
Levi Daniels: *Presidential Secret Service Detail Agent*
Luke Welby: *Presidential Secret Service Detail Agent.*
Elizabeth Wall: *Secretary of State*
Jeff Gottschalk: *Chief of Staff*
Pete Reyes: *Press Secretary*
General Bradford: *Chairman of the Joint Chiefs*
General Porter Madigan: *Vice Chairman of the Joint Chiefs*
Lawrence Irwin: *Director, CIA*
Peter Stahl: *Director, Secret Service*
Lieutenant Adam Cooper: *Leader of USMC Special Operations team*

Russia

Sergey Puchkov: *Russian President*

Saudi Arabia

Prince Faisal al-Saud: *Royal head of the Saudi Intelligence Directorate*

China

Colonel Song: *Central Military Commission, People's Republic of China*

PROLOGUE

The Near Future

Washington DC

EARLY MORNING in Washington DC was the time for ghosts, especially in winter.

Fog shrouded the city, encasing the capital in a fragile stillness. Darkness clung like damp silk. Bare branches littered with icicles jutted across roadways, skeletal and scratching against the night. Few cars moved through the city, drivers staying away from the slick streets.

One lone SUV crunched across the snow, briefly skidded out, and came to a stop outside the National Mall.

General Porter Madigan, Vice Chairman of the Joint Chiefs of Staff, waited behind the Lincoln Memorial. Across the Potomac, Arlington National Cemetery seemed to gleam, white headstones catching and holding on to the fractional light filtering through the fog-drenched city. Faint, the glow was just enough to touch the general's soul.

So many fallen. So many who had sacrificed to bring the world along to *this* place. He could feel the ghosts of the dead hovering in the mist, pressing in on him.

He wouldn't end up in the frozen earth, forgotten by everyone. He wouldn't go out like that.

Snow crunching beneath boots, coming up on the right from the Korean War Memorial, had him walking to the shadows of the Lincoln Memorial. He could still feel the heavy weight of Arlington's gaze lingering on his spine.

"General." His visitor nodded, striding across the memorial's plaza until he was standing behind one of the massive colonnades, hidden from view. His visitor tucked his face into the upturned collar of his parka and shoved his hands in his pockets.

Smirking, Madigan joined him. "Cold?"

A hard glare. "You know I spent too much time in the sandbox. Anything below eighty and I freeze."

Madigan shifted back to his stern professionalism. "Did you make contact with Al-Karim?"

"Yeah." His visitor nodded into his parka. "This morning, Karim's local time." The middle of the night in DC.

"And is he back on track with the plan?" Madigan's voice ground over his syllables, almost growling.

"Yes, sir."

"Does he need to be reminded again of his place in the universe? *My* universe?"

A shake of his visitor's head, though it could have been a shiver. "I don't believe so, sir. Our last drone strike took out one of the refineries he and his forces controlled. He wasn't pleased."

"I'm not pleased when he thinks he's got free rein to do as he pleases in *my* Middle East. I didn't raise this goat-fucker up out of Abu Gharib to be his own man. I pulled him out of that shit so he could be *my* man."

Al-Karim left Abu Gharib one sunny day in Baghdad, thrown from the back of a pickup truck into the desert. A year later, he emerged in Libya, recruiting fighters for his jihadist rebellion against Libya's government. When Libya fell, Al-Karim reemerged in Syria, recruiting Syrian rebel factions into his jihadist movement. The years rolled on, and Al-Karim moved up in the ranks, commanding a wing of the surging Islamic Caliphate. Al-Karim had personally led the Caliphate's attack on Tikrit, capturing the former home of Saddam Hussein. He'd dispatched Caliphate soldiers on other global operations.

And all of it, every single thing, had been done under the general's explicit orders.

Occasionally, though, Al-Karim had to be reminded who kept him alive. "His orders come from *me*."

"He understands, sir."

"Good." Madigan studied his visitor. "We're ready to begin the final phase. Are you good to go?"

"Yes, sir." No hesitation. No wavering. If there was anyone who could have been the weak link, Madigan had always suspected it would be him. The kid had nurtured a level of hero worship toward Madigan over the years, but he'd worried that could cool, or transfer to someone else. Apparently, his worry hadn't been necessary.

He really should have had more faith in the kid. He'd personally recruited him, after all, plucking him out of his original assignment in Iraq and dropping him into his command. Twenty years, and even though the kid now wore civilian clothes and didn't officially work for the Army anymore, he still reported directly to General Madigan.

"Excellent. Deliver the orders for our weapons shipment. Target the delivery for six months from today."

"Yes, sir." The kid was shivering again, wrapped in his parka. It almost made him want to ruffle his hair. It wasn't quite fair to call him a kid, not when he was pushing his forties. He was still a kid to the general's mid-sixties, though.

To Madigan, he always would be that baby-faced soldier lost and scared in the backwater of Baghdad, filled with unrecognized potential.

"Get out of here." Madigan waved him away. "Go home. Get some rest. You're going to need it." He tried to grin, but barely managed a sly curve of his mouth, toothy and lined, lips chapped from the cold. "The biggest job of your career starts in three weeks."

CHAPTER 1

Texas

AUSTIN WASN'T as frigid as Washington DC at Christmastime, but it still had a bite to the night air. Cold wind snaked around Special Agent Ethan Reichenbach as he stood on President-elect Jack Spiers's balcony overlooking Austin's downtown at the intersection of Sixth and Congress. Sixth Street, Austin: a vibrant, garish strip of neon bars, thrumming music lounges, country pool halls, and late night tattoo parlors pulsing with the laughs and shouts of college students, locals getting down, and hustlers. Christmas Day, and the parties still raged.

Ethan shook his head, eyeing long lines of smooth legs stretching down from miniskirts and sequined cocktail dresses. The girls shivered, huddling close together.

He'd never understand women. Instead, his gaze drifted to a group of men, college age by the looks of their clothes and lack of fashion sense. Faded jeans, T-shirts and flannel overcoats, and loose beanies crammed on their heads. He could just make out the cut of their jaws, the curve of some of the guys' biceps. Some smoked, and others stood with their hands in their pockets, bouncing from foot to foot to try to stay warm.

Ethan smiled. He'd been young like that once. What was it, almost twenty years ago? His twenty-first birthday, he'd gone out to downtown Fayetteville to get ripped, and—for the first time—didn't have to hide in the trunk when he and the rest of the guys drove back onto base. Fort Bragg's military police loved to bust underage drinkers, and he'd spent countless weekends crammed in the trunk, hugging the spare tire and Corporal Lawson's crap as he was ferried in and out of the base.

Ancient history. Ethan sucked in a deep breath, letting the cold fill his lungs. Texas's capitol dome caught his eye, gleaming over downtown. The Texas flag proudly flapped in the night breeze, beneath the American flag.

Here we go again. Another president, another four—or eight, if Spiers could crack the steely wariness of the American electorate —years.

After twelve years in, he was a veteran of the Secret Service. He'd started his career in the Army, still with baby fat on his cheeks, enlisting straight out of high school. Ten years into the Army, and he'd needed a change. It had been too stifling, hiding who he was or changing pronouns when he met up with a guy. He got tired of making up excuses for why he didn't want the guys to hang out with him when he needed to go out and find some guy to screw all night long.

The federal government was much more lenient than the military, and he'd applied to every agency he could, all of the alphabet soup agencies and administrations there were, and a few he hadn't known existed. The United States Secret Service called him back first.

Twelve years and three presidents later, Ethan was the new Senior Special Agent in Charge of President-elect Spiers's protection detail, and had been handpicked to lead the president's Secret Service detail back in Washington. Headquarters put him with Spiers's campaign when it became more and more obvious that the senator from Texas was set to win the general election.

Another one-term president, the third in a row, was bumped from office in another display of the American public's disgust of Washington. Spiers was in, the easy-going pretty-boy sent to clean up DC. Unease hung in the air in the nation's capital, as if everyone in office had a timer on their back ready to pop, or a hook just out of sight waiting to pull them off stage.

Presidents came and went. To Ethan, Spiers was just another protectee. Just another job. Spiers was a promotion, a new face, and new routines. A new boss to get used to.

The Secret Service didn't get involved with their assignments. They never got attached, or friendly with their protectees. They were invisible, silent sentinels standing their watch.

Behind Ethan, the glass door to the balcony slid open. President-elect Jack Spiers poked his head out.

Frowning, Ethan turned around. Why was the president-elect zipped up in his jacket, and why were his shoes on? He was supposed to be reading briefs in front of the fireplace, where Ethan had left him, feet up and a beer in his hand. "Sir?"

"Hey, I'm going to pop on down to Sixth Street and mingle a bit." Spiers nodded, as if that was that, and tried to close the door.

Ethan grabbed the frame, stopping him. "Sir, no, you're not."

The president-elect pulled a face. "Look, this is my home state. This is my *home*, in fact. I've gone down to Sixth Street every Christmas. It's a tradition. I mingle with the people, we share stories, I listen to them, and we all have a great time. I can't stop now."

"Sir, it's not possible for you to go down into the crowds. No one has been vetted. The crowd hasn't been monitored. We haven't secured any of the locations on the street. It isn't safe for you to mingle, Mr. President-elect."

"It's fine. Really." Spiers tried to force the sliding door closed, against Ethan's hand.

Ethan pushed back, opening the door and striding forward, making President-elect Spiers step back. Jack Spiers wasn't a short man; no president ever was. He was just under six feet, but he was nerdier looking than the other presidents. Younger, too. Mid-forties, with blond hair streaked with gray from a lifetime of politics. He had a taut face, a slim jaw, and a lean swimmer's build. Black-rimmed reading glasses framed cornsilk-blue eyes—eyes that had turned hard and were glaring at Ethan.

"Sir." Ethan paused, breathing deep. It wouldn't do to piss off his new boss before Inauguration Day. That would be a new record, even for him. "It isn't safe for you to go out and 'mingle' like you used to do. Things are different now. You can't move around without a protective detail, and you can't wander unprotected into crowds." He exhaled. "Sir, all presidents go through this. It's tough, getting used to these changes. Constant protection, security, and surveillance."

President-elect Spiers turned away, his back to Ethan. His hands landed on his hips. "It's like being a rat in a cage." Spiers glared over his shoulder. "Don't you have agents here who can provide crowd protection? Where's the rest of my detail? Aren't they supposed to be on-call?"

Ethan's stomach sank. His promotion, and the warm smile Director Peter Stahl had given him, flashed in his mind. He swallowed. "Sir, I confirmed with your chief of staff that your plans this holiday evening were to stay in your home and have a quiet night in."

"What's Jeff got to do with this?"

Jeff Gottschalk, the president-elect's chief of staff, was a quiet man, serious and dedicated to his service to the president. He was a man normally too busy for anyone else's questions, but he'd given that much of the president-elect's plans to Ethan. Perhaps he shouldn't have trusted Gottschalk's information. "Sir, based on your chief of staff's information, I decided to give the rest of your personal detail the holiday evening off." Ethan held President-elect Spiers's gaze. "This is the last Christmas they'll spend with their families for the next four years. Maybe even the next eight years."

Ethan watched the president-elect take a deep breath in, holding it in his lungs. Those blue eyes, so hard and frigid moments before, softened. He pulled his glasses off and pinched the bridge of his nose as he spoke. "My personal detail. Those are the guys who have been on the campaign, right? With you? I mean, they're all coming to Washington with me? With us?"

"Yes, sir. Agents Levi Daniels, Harry Inada, and Scott Collard. We've all been by your side since the Republican nomination." Agent Scott Collard was like an older brother to him, and they'd propped each other up with bullshit and good-natured harassment through the bitter end of the presidential campaign. When Spiers had won, they'd toasted to the loss of their social lives for the next four years with gas station vodka downed from chipped motel coffee mugs.

President-elect Spiers unzipped his jacket and shrugged it off his shoulders. He tossed it on the back of his couch. A spread of binders and spiral-bound reports, all covered in official red seals with "CONFIDENTIAL" or "TOP SECRET CLEARANCE" borders and stamps littered the couch cushions. "Well," Spiers sighed. "Looks like I am staying in tonight."

Relief swept through Ethan, unclenching his stomach. "Yes, sir."

Chuckling, the president-elect collapsed into the corner of his couch and reached for one of the binders. He sighed, long and loud, and pushed his glasses back on his face.

That would be his cue to leave. Ethan turned away. He wasn't going far—maybe to the kitchen to scrounge up some food—but he didn't need to be hovering in the same room as the president-elect. Jesus, he was going to see enough of the guy over the next four years. He was going to be closer than Spiers's own shadow.

President-elect Spiers's voice made him pause. "Agent Reichenbach, that was a good thing you did tonight for your men. They've done a fine job on the campaign, and I know they'll be excellent in Washington, too. They deserve a night off." He tossed a glance over the back of the couch. "And so do you."

Ethan managed a tiny smirk. "The cat stays and works while the mice play, sir."

"I think that goes a little differently." Now President-elect Spiers was smiling. Some of his stiffness leached away.

"I'm the loner of the bunch, sir. They've got families and loved ones. I don't." No partner, no lover, no long-term relationship. A few guys had tried, but he'd put an end to that quickly. He wasn't the man for long-term relationships. He didn't have that kind of life. He didn't have that kind of heart.

President-elect Spiers's smile turned sad. Ethan kicked himself inside, forcing himself not to grimace. But his eyes darted to the folded flag encased in a memorial box on the mantle, right beside a picture of the president-elect's deceased wife, Army Captain Leslie Spiers.

The year of her death was printed on the memorial case. Fifteen years prior, in the height of the Iraq War.

Ethan had been lucky. He'd lived through the war. The president-elect's wife hadn't.

"I'm sorry, sir," Ethan said quietly.

"Would you like a drink?" Standing, President-elect Spiers gestured for Ethan to join him on the couch, and then to the small drybar in the corner of the room. The sadness was gone from his eyes, replaced by a hard kind of pleading. A wish to not be alone.

Disappointment crawled over Ethan's skin, sliding uncomfortably close to unease. "I can't, sir. I can't drink on duty." Not to mention he wasn't supposed to socialize with the president-elect, or any protectee. Nothing personal. No friendships. *He's just a job.*

But he was also a human being, a *lonely* human being, and Ethan understood that better than most. "I... have some reports to do. I could bring my laptop in here?" God, he hated how his voice rose at the end, uncertainty dripping from his words.

President-elect Spiers grinned. "Sure. Plenty of room." He pushed three binders from the DOD and one from the CIA onto the carpet, opening up the end of the couch and coffee table for Ethan.

Ethan grabbed his laptop and fumbled plugging in the power cord—first unplugging the Christmas tree lights—but then they were both sitting down, almost side by side and absorbed in their own work. Quiet descended over the pair.

Restlessness clung to Ethan, but it slowly dissipated as he buried himself in his reports. Still, with every turn of the page President-elect Spiers made, and with every shift on the couch, Ethan was uncomfortably aware that there was a line here that he was very seriously bending.

Not the best way to begin his new position.

———

PRESIDENT JACK SPIERS'S INAUGURATION CHEERED BY MILLIONS

President Jack Spiers's Inauguration was cheered by millions of Americans as they crowded along Pennsylvania Avenue. Others packed themselves in front of the Capitol, watching the President take the Oath of Office and deliver his Inaugural Address. In the address, President Spiers reiterated much of what his campaign had centered upon: America's strength, tempered by her commitments to her allies in a dangerous world, the perils presented by the increasing powers of the renegade Islamic Caliphate, and his commitment to strengthen America's response to the shifting, uncertain political and military landscape. The president spoke about his commitments to NATO and America's European allies, especially in the wake of the refugee crisis of the past decade and the increasing number of terror attacks within Europe's major cities.

Much of President Spiers's popular support comes from a broad base. "The party leadership looks at President Spiers as a unifier," RNC Chairman Rick Smith said. "He's a likable guy. He delivers on his promises. He believes in America, and he wants what's best for everyone."

President Spiers has enjoyed one of the highest popularity ratings of any recent candidate, but whether those numbers will translate into approval ratings is anyone's guess.

Some wonder how much President Spiers's deceased wife, Army Captain Leslie Spiers, who was killed during an ambush in Iraq during the War in Iraq, may have impacted his campaign. "Certainly his wife's death impacted [President Spiers's] life," Chairman Smith said. "He never would have gone into politics had she not been tragically killed in action. He was a private practice lawyer in Austin, and she worked at Fort Hood. Then she was killed, and his whole life pivoted. He dedicated himself to serving active duty soldiers and veterans, and ran in Texas on a platform to better our armed forces and provide better support to our veterans. In the Senate, he served on the Intelligence Committee and the Armed Services Committee, two committees deeply entwined with America's military efforts. He's shown nothing but the strongest commitment to our nation's heroes, and I fully believe that stems from the love he has for his wife, and how he honors her memory."

CHAPTER 2

Washington DC

WHEN ETHAN finally made it back to the White House after the Inauguration Parade, all of the snow had melted from DC's streets, and the temperature was a blustery seventy degrees. The calendar on his desk said "March."

"I still can't believe you got taken out by a bunch of punks." Agent Scott Collard, Ethan's best friend, swiveled in his desk chair, grinning like a madman.

Ethan chucked a pen at his head as he leaned against Agent Levi Daniels's desk. He flexed his leg, straightening his knee, and then kicked Scott's chair. Scott scooted away just in time.

"I didn't see you brawling on Inauguration Day. Where was my backup?"

"You're the one who wanted to walk around in the crowd with the intel dorks." Scott shrugged. "Why you weren't walking on the route with us is your business."

"We had credible intel that there was going to be an attempt to jump the perimeter and attack the Beast." The Beast was the unofficial code name for the presidential limo.

"And by attack, they meant pelt it with tomatoes."

"It's still an attack."

"You got your ass kicked by vegan vegetable throwers."

Ethan loomed over Scott's chair. He was trying to be intimidating, but he knew his grin was ruining it.

Scott snorted. "You had tomato dripping from your nose and hair."

"What if they had hidden something in one of those tomatoes? You wouldn't be making fun of me then."

"I'm giving you a new codename. Salad Reichenbach." Scott spun in his chair, shouting out to the agents scattered around the office. "You all hear? Quarterback is now Salad. Copy?"

Laughs and nods floated back to the two men. Ethan shook his head. He put his foot on the edge of Scott's chair and pushed, sending his friend wheeling away, down the rows and rows of desks and toward the lockers where the agents at the White House kept their spare clothes, extra suits, and even their tuxes.

They were in the Secret Service White House command post, codenamed Horsepower, situated directly beneath the Oval Office. Rectangular and the size of a soccer field, the agents used the command post as an all-around everything office. Bunk beds were pushed against a far wall near the lockers, and desks lined the front half of the room. Mirrors on the back wall helped agents dress smartly in their suits and tuxes, and large screens at the front displayed real-time intelligence, constantly updated and fed from Secret Service Headquarters on H Street. When the detail agents didn't need to be surrounding the president, or when they weren't standing post, they spent their downtime in Horsepower.

"Hey, how's Agent Welby doing?" Ethan headed back to Daniels's desk and perched on the edge again, crossing his arms.

Daniels cast him a droll stare, barely looking up from the email he was typing. "Welby's a'right," he drawled. His eyebrows rose, nearly off his forehead, as he fixed his gaze on Ethan. "Stick up his ass, but he's a'right."

Ethan smothered a grin. Agent Welby had come in to replace him as presidential detail lead while he was out, recuperating from his busted knee after the brawl during the Inauguration Parade. Welby had seniority on Scott by one year, and it drove Scott crazy. Scott had texted him almost daily, bemoaning Welby's mulish, boring attitude and his laugh-a-minute personality.

"You coming back in as lead?" Daniels's eyes shone, hopeful.

"Got to go through a few more stacks of paperwork first, but yeah." Ethan winked at Daniels and stood, stretching. He tried for casual, speaking as he rolled his shoulders. "How's the president?"

He failed. Daniels's eyebrows shot high again. "How's the president?" He stared at Ethan as if he'd just claimed he was a prince from the planet Saturn.

"Yeah. How's he doing?" No way to back out of it now. He might as well try to blunder his way through, as if asking after a protectee were the most natural thing in the world.

Daniels frowned. "I try to stay out of his way, and I make it a point to not listen whenever I'm in the Beast. I don't want to know how his negotiations are going with Congress on the educational bill, or if he's banging any aides in the West Wing."

"Is he?" Ethan frowned.

"Nah, man, the guy's legit. Straight shooter." Daniels's wide smile broke over his face, and he laughed, pushing on Ethan's shoulder. "But seriously, man, I stay out of it. Keep my distance, just like you taught us. Like you drilled us." Daniels peered at him. "This a test?"

Snorting, Ethan clapped Daniels on the arm. A way out, and he took it with both hands. "You passed. Good job, Daniels."

The look in Daniels's eyes said "fuck you," and he buttoned his suit jacket as he stood from his desk. "I need a cup of coffee from the Press Corps bullpen."

"The White House Mess is six feet to the right." Beneath the Oval Office, on the basement level of the White House, the Secret Service command post shared space with the White House Mess, the Situation Room, the National Security staff, and Homeland Security's White House Control Center. It was an odd mixture of Top Secret clearances and Navy stewards and chefs, but at least the coffee and chow were always close at hand. Agents went on fridge raids at all hours, and the Situation Room hosted impromptu slumber parties at the drop of a Predator missile strike.

Smirking, Daniels led Ethan out of Horsepower. "Yes it is, but, the Mess doesn't have Annie Perkins working down there."

"Annie Perkins?"

They strolled up the stairs to the first floor of the West Wing, to the hallway between the Oval Office and the Cabinet Room. Daniels filled Ethan in on the voluptuous beauty that was Annie Perkins, reporter from the Tribune and a current project of Daniels's. Ethan chuckled, already well ahead of Daniels in the script. Hell, he used the same playbook... just not with women. And never for more than a night or two.

He'd seen this particular story play out time and time again. Daniels could woo the ladies in droves, and he stayed with them for a couple of months before cutting them loose and playing the field again. Mixed in were one-night stands and nights of debauchery, and several memorable nights where Daniels had chanced to go with Ethan out to the gayborhood. Ethan had told him the secret of picking up chicks in gay bars—nearly all of them were straight, and they would swoon for a straight man confident enough to chill at a gay bar with his gay friend. Daniels never left alone.

"Have you asked her out yet?"

"Patience, man. Patience." Daniels held up his hands, trying to slow Ethan the hell down. He smirked, shaking his head at how hard-charging Ethan was. This was an old argument of theirs. Daniels played the long game and enjoyed dating his lady for a few months. Ethan liked his men hot and their encounters short. He was gone by morning.

Ethan shook his head, retort on the tip of his tongue, when a voice down the hall called out his name.

"Agent Reichenbach!"

Daniels's eyes grew comically huge, and he snapped to attention in a smart second, wiping the smirk from his face and hitting "professional" just as President Jack Spiers broke away from his chief of staff and strode down the hallway to the two agents.

President Spiers held out his hand to Ethan.

Ethan shook it, stunned. "Mr. President. How can I help you, sir?"

"They told me you were injured and recuperating. I didn't know you were back on duty." The president was beaming at him, a radiant smile that went all the way to his eyes. The press had endlessly dissected that smile on the campaign.

Ethan suddenly understood why President Spiers had locked up the soccer mom voting bloc.

"First day back, sir." Ethan let go of the president's hand and stepped back. "I'm working over at Headquarters for now."

President Spiers frowned. Behind him, Jeff Gottschalk cleared his throat, a polite reminder to the president to hurry it up.

"Listen, I've got a meeting right now. Can you swing by my office in an hour?" The president waited for Ethan's single nod before he flashed his brilliant smile again. "Great. We'll talk then."

And then he was off, striding down the hallway and into the cluster of his staff. He reached for file folders and a binder and pulled out his smartphone all at once. His reading glasses slid down his nose, and he absently pushed them back up with one finger as he scrolled through his phone.

When Ethan turned back to Daniels, the younger agent's incredibly unimpressed face stared back at him, his eyes narrowed.

"That was nothing."

"Should I ask *you* how the president is doing?"

"Shut up."

An hour later, Ethan stood stiffly in the Oval Office, alone, his feet shoulder width apart and angled at a perfect forty-five degrees, hands clasped behind his back, spine straight, knees unlocked.

His gaze darted around the office, taking in the changes President Spiers had made. His predecessor had thrown the Oval Office back to the "good 'ole days" as a physical reminder of what his campaign had been all about, and heavy red curtains had hung from the windows while the carpet had been replaced with a deep navy plush, making the presidential seal in the center of the rug stand out vividly. Red and white striped couches had been added to the room, and the whole office had looked like a Fourth of July parade had exploded within.

President Spiers, on the other hand, preferred a more stately and refined look. Gone were the heavy curtains and the blue plush rug. White gauze hung behind the Resolute desk, and a cream and beige sunburst carpet stretched out around the presidential seal. Ivory and butter yellow stripes lined the walls above the wainscoting, encasing the office in an almost serene feeling. The couches were Revolutionary Americana, striped in white, pale blue, and tan, and with polished mahogany arms carved in a delicate spindle.

Ethan stared at the picture of George Washington over the fireplace mantle, a staple of the Oval Office for every president. *What the hell am I doing here? Why does he want to talk to me? I'm just a detail agent. Shit, was it something Welby did? That fucker.*

He bounced on his heels, and his eyes tracked the sweeping minute hand of the nautical clock perched on the edge of the fireplace mantel. President Spiers was late. Not much of a surprise. The world moved for the president. Time was something that happened to other people.

When President Spiers breezed in—entering through his study and the private hallway on the left—Ethan jerked back to attention.

The president didn't notice. His head was buried in his phone as he spoke. "Agent Reichenbach, sorry I'm late. Congressional leadership was here with an update on the education reform bill. They know how to talk." He dropped his phone onto the Resolute desk with a clatter, sighed, and then smiled lopsidedly at Ethan. "I was one of them, and I'm still amazed at how much they can talk around a subject." He waved Ethan closer. "Please, relax. This is informal. Totally off-the-books. Just a catch-up chat." He crossed his arms and leaned one hip against the desk. "How are you doing, Ethan? Can I call you Ethan?"

"Uhh, yes, sir, you can if you'd like." Ethan frowned. "Is there something I can help you with, Mr. President?"

President Spiers tried to wave him off, squinting as he scrunched up his forehead. "Please, please, no need for the formality. Like I said, I just wanted to catch up with you. See how you were doing. See when you were hopefully coming back?" That last sentence ended on a higher note, a question, and the president's eyebrows rose.

It is fucking Welby. "I still need to take care of a few paperwork hurdles before I'm cleared to return to duty on the detail, sir."

"But you'll be back? You're good? No long-term injuries, no pain, nothing wrong?"

"I'm fine, sir." Ethan grinned. "Someone got a lucky kick in while we were subduing some miscreants during the Inauguration Parade. Nothing life-threatening. My leave has been mostly boring."

President Spiers smiled. "Glad to hear. And if it will help, I'd be happy to call over to the Secret Service and request your reinstatement as detail lead."

Damn, Welby, what the hell did you do? "Is there something wrong with your current detail lead, Mr. President?"

A long sigh, and President Spiers looked away, squinting through the glass-paned door leading to the West Colonnade and the Rose Garden. "He's a great agent. He's solid, he knows his stuff, and he's reliable."

"But?" Ethan waited for the shoe to drop.

President Spiers winced. "He's... a bit stiff. He's... a little like a jailer."

"Agent Welby is a fine agent. And he sounds like he's being a textbook Secret Service agent to me. We have rules to follow, Mr. President, rules that keep you alive." He frowned. "Do you expect I'll be different?"

President Spiers's eyes met his. "I think you can see the bigger picture when you need to."

Ethan shifted, his gaze darting to the windows for a moment. Christmas flashed through his mind. He'd never told anyone what he'd done, or about how the president could have handed him his ass that night, but instead that they'd sat side by side and worked until the wee hours of the morning.

"You're standing here talking to me now, Ethan. Not many other agents would do that."

"We're not supposed to talk, sir. I am supposed to be your oppressive shadow. And, a little bit of a jailer."

President Spiers threw back his head and laughed. He reached for his phone, clattering on the desk. A quick scroll, and then he frowned, a single line creasing the space between his eyebrows. "I just want you to know that I'm looking forward to your return, Ethan." He smiled and then waggled his phone. "I'm sorry. Duty calls. But we can catch up when you're back on the detail." He grinned. "Right?"

He shouldn't be doing this. God, he shouldn't be doing this. This had bad decision scrawled all over it. Even the slightest hint of friendliness with an agent's protectee was deeply frowned upon.

But he smiled back, nodding. "Mr. President."

Excusing himself, Ethan slipped into the hallway, leaving the president scrolling through his phone.

CHAPTER 3

Washington DC

THREE WEEKS LATER, Ethan was back as presidential detail lead, working alongside Daniels, Scott, and Harry Inada on the main detail team. There were over three hundred agents on the presidential detail alone, spread out to cover every shift and hold down posts in the White House offices and the Residence. They all traded barbs with the vice president's detail and shot the breeze in Horsepower together, but the four main guys, the closest protective detail assigned to the president, were Ethan and his team.

Ethan had tactical command over the whole detail, and he managed the agents' shifts and assignments, kept up with intelligence from H Street, and reviewed all of the squeal sheets—reports of all incidents and threats to the president from the past twenty-four hours. He moved with President Spiers when the president left the White House, staying by his side in the crowds and riding in the front seat of the Beast. And, when he wasn't with the president, and wasn't working in Horsepower, he helped train the junior agents on the detail, shadowing their posts and giving them pop-quizzes over coffee he personally delivered.

He thought things were going well. He'd set the Beast's radio to the president's favorite stations and asked him if he saw the recent game—golf, basketball, or hockey, since it was spring. Then he'd shut up, monitor the radios, and advise Inada in the driver's seat while the president scrolled through his phone or flipped through his padfolio of folders and briefs and memos.

The president hadn't asked to chat with him again, and Ethan was going out of *his* way to interact with a protectee, stepping out of the shadows to ask him a few meaningless questions. He was doing more, he knew, than Welby had done.

So, when Daniels cornered him in the White House Mess—in between reviewing intel reports, authorizing the presidential advance party to Turin for the G-7 Summit, and finalizing security provisions for the president's dinner out at the residence of the Speaker of the House—he was more than a little surprised.

"Hey, Ethan. Got a minute?" Daniels had a cup of coffee in his hand—from the Mess, not the Press Office bullpen upstairs—and was staring Ethan down.

With a look like that, he couldn't say no. "'Course. Here?"

Daniels shook his head. He jerked his chin for Ethan to follow, and they headed for the quieter area of the basement, tucked behind the stairwell. "It's about the president," Daniels said quietly, swirling a wooden stick through his coffee. "Something's up."

Ethan blinked. "What do you mean 'something's up'? Is this a security issue? Is it political? Or a personal issue? You know we don't get involved in anything political or personal." And, more often than not, if there was something on the president's mind—on any president's mind—it was either political or personal. They left security concerns to their shadows.

"He's canceled his morning workouts."

"Already?" Ethan sighed.

Presidents occasionally canceled their workouts when they were psychotically stressed—exactly when they should be hitting the gym more—but never this early into an administration. Was there a memo he'd missed about the next World War starting?

Daniels cringed. "And... I think it might have something to do with us."

"As in the Secret Service? His detail?"

"Yeah. He was trying to pal around for a while in the morning, in the gym, and then he stopped doing that. He kept asking us questions, but even that stopped. Last time he was working out, he just kinda stared at us and then told us to not worry about it anymore."

"Meaning he was canceling his workouts?"

Daniels nodded. Ethan pulled his phone from his pocket and called up the president's daily schedule. As part of the detail, he had President Spiers's schedule at his fingertips at all times. Today was supposed to be a buttoned-up day—a day entirely in the White House. That usually meant a packed day as well, full of meetings and phone calls.

But, right in the middle, he saw a window of opportunity. The president was eating lunch. Alone.

"Thanks for letting me know, D. I'll try to talk to him." Ethan shoved his phone back in his pocket, ignoring Daniels's raised eyebrows.

The president—all presidents—had to work out. It didn't matter what it was, but they had to do something. Anything. Even just walking, or worse yet, pacing. The stress would kill them if they didn't, and they needed an outlet from their duties.

"Thanks. Let me know what the guys and I can do." Daniels nodded and stepped away, heading back for Horsepower.

Inhaling, Ethan closed his eyes and dropped his head. How would he approach this? Telling the leader of the free world to get back on the treadmill wasn't the easiest thing in the world. And, he wasn't the most delicate communicator. He could delegate, pass it off to the president's chief of staff, or even his secretary. But if his agents had done something to piss President Spiers off, he should be the one to fix it.

He checked his watch. He had two and a half hours to figure something out.

THE PRESIDENT'S SECRETARY, Mrs. Martin, let him into the Oval Office ten minutes after the Navy steward delivered the president's lunch. "He's not expecting anyone," she warned, tsking Ethan with her eyebrows and the glare in her eyes.

He caught the president while he was eating, midchew as he looked up from the couch, hunkered over his chicken Caesar salad. Wide, shocked eyes darted to Ethan as he entered, and Ethan caught him sheepishly closing and tucking away the latest bestselling thriller.

Ethan grinned. "I've been meaning to read that one. How is it?"

"Good." President Spiers wiped his mouth with his napkin and chuckled. "It's good. I'm supposed to be reviewing the brief from Congress on their latest version of the education reform bill." He shrugged, blushing. "You caught me."

"Sir, if you're anything like the other guys who've held this office, you won't be the first to sneak in some personal time." Good for him. President Spiers had sometimes seemed buried on the campaign, immersed so deeply in running for president that he stopped being human. Always juggling his phone, his padfolio, and a dozen binders in between speeches and flights. And, there were always more binders and reports and files spread out on the floor of whatever hotel room he was in for that night.

Ethan hadn't been up to the White House Residence much since President Spiers had moved in, but he'd seen stacks of binders and Top Secret reports cluttering the coffee tables and countertops as he'd checked in on his detail.

President Spiers leaned back, and one long leg crossed over the other, his foot gently tapping in the air. A soft smile lingered on his face. "How can I help you, Ethan? I take it this meeting is off calendar?"

"And off-the-record." Ethan tried to smile back, but years of a beaten-in respect for authority and a bone-deep honor for the chain of command twisted his lips into a tight, thin line. His feet were rooted to the floor as he clasped his hands behind his back. "Sir, my men tell me you've canceled your workouts."

The president stared at him, his expression going blank.

Ethan swallowed. "Sir, physical fitness is important, especially with this job. You need a stress relief—"

"I didn't realize babysitting and tattling were part of the Secret Service's duties."

His hands clenched, made fists. "Sir, that's not at all what is happening. We are concerned for you, and for your health. We've all seen presidents who had meltdowns because they didn't have the right stress relief. Trust me. Working out is a great way to shake off this office when you need to."

Again, President Spiers was silent. He simply stared at Ethan, gazing into his eyes, and where there was friendliness only moments before, there was now a guarded wariness. "And what if it's my work-outs that are causing me stress?"

"Sir?" Ethan frowned.

President Spiers pushed himself to his feet and paced away from Ethan, heading toward the opposite end of the Oval Office. His hands disappeared into his suit pants pockets, but his back stayed ramrod straight, shoulders tight and tense. Ethan could see the seams of his jacket straining at his shoulders.

"Look, I'm not the most gregarious guy, but I'm not a shut-in either. My whole political career has been built on being a 'man of the people'." He paused in front of his desk, his head bowed, chin almost on his chest. "Suddenly I'm the president, and there's this impenetrable divide between me and everyone else."

There wasn't anything *sudden* about his presidency. Ethan remembered the long campaign, first from the endless news reports, and then the whirlwind cycle of small towns and big cities and plane rides that made up the last 180 days of the campaign, when he and his team—and so many other agents—were assigned to the major candidates in the election. "Sir, you're the president. You're the most important man in the world—"

"No I'm not." President Spiers chuckled, looking out of the Oval

Office windows to the Rose Garden. "I'm just a guy who wants to push his ideas on everyone else." He winked at Ethan, tossing a glance over his shoulder.

It was Ethan's turn to stay silent. He chewed the inside of his lip. Typically, appealing to a president's sense of vanity worked for him. At least, it had in the past when he'd needed to convince a president to listen to the Secret Service and follow their directives for safety and security.

"I had a group of guys that I ran with in Austin," President Spiers said, breaking the silence. "And in DC, a few years back, I had a group of people I hung out with at the YMCA where I went swimming. We weren't close friends. I lost touch with them when I started campaigning. Wouldn't even know how to reach them." He turned, leaned back against his desk, and gripped the edge of the carved wood. "But it was something, you know?"

"We can... invite members of Congress to join you on a run? Or hire a personal trainer for the White House weight room? Or, if you have associates locally, here in DC, we can vet them and run a background check, and if that passes, they could join you during your workouts?" Ethan scrambled, trying to come up with some kind of solution.

President Spiers laughed. "I don't know any members of Congress who would voluntarily run anywhere, even with the president." He grinned, but it faded quickly, and he shook his head. "And it's not about hiring anyone. I've got enough people working for me as it is. And don't you think it's a little depressing that anyone and everyone I've ever known has to submit to a complete background check to even see me, or take a jog with me? I'm going over to dinner at Bob's house, and the whole evening has become a three-ring government event."

"Bob" was Robert J. MacNaughten, the Speaker of the House of Representatives, and the entire evening was a *very* big deal to the Secret Service. Ethan stayed silent.

Sighing, President Spiers crossed his arms. "Ethan, I appreciate your consideration, and where the concern comes from. And I remember what you said at Christmas. I *am* having a hard time adjusting, I think. I'm like a goldfish in that gym. Your guys are out there standing guard, and I'm all alone in there, sweating it out under the spotlight. It's... weird." He shook his head. "I can't be the only president to have gone through an adjustment phase."

You're the only one who didn't love the spotlight. The adulation, and the sudden spectacle being made of himself. Ethan shook his head. "No, sir. But, Mr. President. Can you resume your workouts? I'll..." He trailed off. "I'll think of something."

Where had that come from? What part of his brain had misfired to say that? Think of something to help the president? Who did he think he was? If President Spiers had any brains, he'd laugh him out of his office. Heat pooled in Ethan's belly, heavy with embarrassment. Why was he always sticking his foot in his mouth around this president?

President Spiers smiled, big and broad. "I'd appreciate that, Ethan. You know, I do value your insight. You've seen my predecessors, and all of their foibles and faults. If you have advice for me, I'm all ears."

That was *not* what he'd been expecting. Swallowing, Ethan tried to find his tongue. "I'm... just your detail lead, sir."

"You are the kind of guy I'd like to call a friend."

And there it was, that invisible barrier President Spiers had bemoaned, slamming down between them with all the force of a guillotine. Ethan felt the physical push of the barrier against him, a klaxon blaring in his mind telling him to back away. This was dangerous, this path of familiarity and easiness. Where there was familiarity, there was laxity, and where things were lax, there was danger and risk, and breaches in security. He couldn't be a friend to this man, someone he was supposed to protect at all costs, even with his own life. How could he ever be objective if he got close to the guy?

Granted, it wouldn't be difficult to befriend President Spiers. He was unique, a man apart amid the political machine of Washington.

Someone who hadn't lost his soul or sold his morality to the devil. He was a man of compromise and of reaching across the aisle, and of kept promises, of easy smiles and warm laughs, and gentle blue eyes. Someone who ran with strangers in Austin so he'd have normal guys keeping him grounded in reality, and who just wanted to make the world a safer, better place, but who hated the isolated tower he'd been put in to do so.

The presidency is going to crush him.

That thought hit Ethan hard, a punch to his gut, and he wished, for a moment, that it could be different. That he could pal around with President Spiers, could give him some straight talk on how to fly right and not get lost in the quagmire that was the Oval Office. Or take him out for a beer when the stress got too high, or text him a video clip to make him snort coffee in the middle of a brief. Those were things friends did, and if there was ever a man who needed a friend, it was President Jack Spiers.

But not Ethan. It couldn't be Ethan.

Ethan pasted on a tight, fake smile, nodded once, and excused himself. "Mr. President. I won't take up any more of your time."

As he walked away, he caught the surprised light in President Spiers's eyes, and the way he failed to hide his sudden frown and the single line creasing the space between his eyebrows.

Ethan didn't stop walking as he made his way out of the president's secretary's office. He bypassed the Cabinet Room, ignoring the waves and nods he got in the halls. Down the stairs he went, to the ground floor and past the Situation Room and Horsepower, and then into the tunnels.

Beneath the White House Residence, tunnels funneled stewards and staff and agents to and fro, and the occasional golf cart or small flatbed loaded down with crates of food or laundry or binders full of briefs, or even fresh flowers. It could be anything beneath the White House.

He slipped out of the tunnels at the basement of the Residence and took one of the internal stairways up to the personal floors for the first family. The first family, at the moment, was a single bachelor, and most of the extra bedrooms were unused and unopened. Fresh flowers still sat in vases in all the lived-in rooms of the Residence, though. In the president's dining room, selections of state china were laid out, waiting for Spiers to choose his design. It was the responsibility of the first lady to pick the official state china, but in the absence of a first lady, the president had yet to select his pattern. Ethan swallowed.

He finally arrived at the White House gym, sidestepping stewards with laundry and vacuums scuttling about, keeping the Residence organized and clean—aside from the president's official clutter—while Spiers was in the Oval Office.

He hesitated outside the president's gym doors, gazing through the glass. Treadmills, ellipticals, a stationary bike, a weight machine, free weights, a couple of benches, and a wrestling mat for floor work filled the space within. Mirrors lined one wall. Agents had stationed themselves at the door and in the hallway during Spiers's morning workouts, watching in case the president needed anything.

He'd had a ludicrous plan banging around in his brain since he'd left the West Wing, and he'd spent the majority of the walk trying to convince himself that it was a stupid idea and that he was way out of line. That it would only end in disaster.

All of that was true.

And yet, the president's crooked smile and the tilt of his head stayed in the darkness behind his eyelids. He saw Spiers's smile with every blink, every footfall, like a knife to the brain.

Damn it. He was the president's detail lead. So this was just another part of the job. Keeping the president safe and sane.

If he repeated it enough, he might actually convince himself.

Ethan pulled out his phone and typed a quick memo to his detail. He didn't hesitate, and he didn't reread it. He just hit *send*. Leaning his head back, Ethan started counting the seconds until Daniels called.

Forty-two seconds. His phone vibrated. Daniels.

"Reichenbach," he growled as he answered.

"*You want us to what?*" Daniels couldn't have forced any more incredulity into that sentence.

Ethan closed his eyes, shutting out the president's gym. He leaned his forehead against the glass door. "Just be ready, all right? I'll take the lead. And I want to get a debrief from you. Meet me in Horsepower in five."

THE NEXT MORNING, Ethan, clad in crisp United States Secret Service workout shorts and a training t-shirt, tucked in tight, paced inside the president's gym. Two other agents were working out: one on the elliptical and one on the weight machine. He put them on the two machines the president—according to Daniels—never used.

Before this morning, Daniels had taken the lead on the early shift with the president in the gym while Ethan managed the detail's morning administration in Horsepower.

Today, they flipped.

Today, Ethan had apparently decided to lose his Goddamned mind.

He hadn't even told President Spiers.

God, he hoped the president would decide to work out today. This would all be an embarrassing show of his stupidity if President Spiers just ignored everything they had discussed yesterday. He kept pacing.

When the door to the gym pushed open, Ethan whirled, his chin held high, jaw clenched. Unconsciously, he stood at the ready, feet shoulder width apart, his linebacker's shoulders raised, fists held in a loose clench, almost like he was ready to brawl. He was a big guy, and regular workouts helped keep his strength primed.

He just normally used the Secret Service's workout room. Not the president's.

President Spiers stopped in the doorway, his mouth falling open as he saw Ethan and his agents working out in his gym. Spiers wore a ratty t-shirt from the University of Texas and baggy sweats with coffee stains on them. His eyebrows shot up as he slowly smiled. "So this is your solution? Invading my gym?"

Ethan's spine cracked as he straightened. His shoulders tensed. "Sir, I thought you would enjoy some company." And not just any company, like getting some congressmen in there to harass President Spiers on his workouts, or make Spiers wait while they vetted a friend —or flew in a friend from Texas, even—but regular Secret Service agents, men who were—when all the luster of the Secret Service was taken away—just regular guys living their life.

And who were top-level security cleared, with codename clearance access to the president.

President Spiers grinned as he padded over to Ethan, standing in the center of the wrestling mat. "So, what kind of workout do you have in mind for us?"

Across the gym, an agent's foot slipped out of his pedal, spinning the stationary bike's wheels in a frenzy. Ethan gnashed his teeth, but he held the president's gaze. "Whatever you'd like, sir. We can run laps and then move to the free weights, like your normal routine."

"I don't know whether to be creeped out or impressed that you know my routine."

"Part of my job, sir." Ethan flashed a quick grin. "If I don't know everything, then I've missed something critical."

President Spiers stretched, leaning over and bracing against his knee. "Army Special Forces?"

Ethan nodded.

"You'll have to tell me all about that. I love hearing from vets."

Ethan kept his mouth shut as he stretched alongside the president. Eventually, President Spiers shucked his sweats. He wore an old pair of running shorts that barely stretched to the top of his thighs. His legs were toned, long and lean, and dusted with light hair down to his ankles. Ethan glued his eyes to the ceiling.

"All right, let's do a few miles to warm up and then hit the weights. I'll spot for you if you spot for me? Though..." President Spiers trailed off as he studied Ethan's bulging biceps, straining the limits of his t-shirt sleeves. "I think I'd kill myself if I tried to lift what you are capable of."

"We could always do a push-up contest." Ethan clamped his mouth shut. Who was this guy who stole his tongue and spoke for him in front of the president? That asshole always said the dumbest things.

President Spiers laughed. He flexed, and his compact muscula-ture didn't stand a chance against Ethan. Where Ethan was buff and brawny, the president was lean and trim, a swimmer with a tight body. Even in his forties, the president was fit, with only a tiny cushion padding his midsection. Ethan hadn't boasted a washboard set of abs since he was in his twenties, but he had a flat stomach and a broad chest, and he'd never gone home alone. His arms, big as some people's thighs, pulled so many in.

"I'll sit on your back for a handicap. Then you can do push-ups." President Spiers winked.

Across the gym, the bike spun out again, and the agent cursed, covering up the slip with loud coughing.

Ethan set up his treadmill beside President Spiers's. He started slow, and let the president run at a faster pace than him. He wasn't a sprinter, but he could run for hours once he found his pace. A pace that was generally faster than President Spiers's. But he was doing this for the president, and that meant working out at his speed.

He kept telling himself this was all part of the job.

Seeing that smile on President Spiers's face didn't hurt either.

"So, Ethan?" The president grinned, his face nearly split in two.

"Yes, Mr. President?"

"I was thinking of taking up kick boxing. Want to spar?"

"Don't push your luck, sir. I'm already off the grid doing this. I'm not throwing a punch at you, Mr. President."

Laughing, the president threw him a wry smile. Ethan shook his head, but smiled back. Jokes. Now they were doing jokes and teasing each other. Christ, he was in trouble.

"Since we're working out together, you really can call me Jack." This time, President Spiers wasn't joking. He could see it in his eyes.

"Yes, Mr. President."

Neither was Ethan.

They ran in silence for the next twenty minutes, until President Spiers slowed to a jog, and then a walk. After cooling off, they moved to the free weights.

Ethan felt the burn of his agents' stares on his back for the entire morning workout.

———

PRESIDENT SPIERS VISITS ARLINGTON NATIONAL CEMETERY FOR MEMORIAL DAY

President Spiers visited Arlington National Cemetery today to pay his respects as Commander in Chief to the nation's fallen military heroes. He participated in a wreath-laying ceremony at the Tomb of the Unknown Soldier before making his way across the memorial on a personal visit.

Fifteen years ago, Spiers's wife, Captain Leslie Spiers, was killed in combat during the War in Iraq and was laid to rest in Arlington National Cemetery. The president spent half an hour in silence at her headstone, in private, with only his detail nearby.

ISLAMIC CALIPHATE ATTEMPTS
TO SHOOT DOWN COMMERCIAL
AIRLINER OVER IRAQI AIRSPACE

The Islamic Caliphate attempted to shoot down a commercial airliner on a flight from India to Berlin yesterday. Caliphate fighters fired anti-aircraft missiles, stolen from the Iraqi military and the former Syrian government, at the passenger jet as it cruised at 31,000 feet. The pilot evaded the missile, putting the passenger plane into a dive before diverting the plane into Azerbaijani airspace.

CHAPTER 4

Camp David

SPRING AND SUMMER meant travel at the White House. It was a rule, along with "don't touch the cookies baked for the president" and "never trust that a microphone is ever truly off".

First up was the G-7 summit in Turin, Italy. Ethan had already dispatched the advance team and everything was set for the president to arrive Monday evening. That just left the packing.

President Spiers—*Jack*, a traitorous voice inside his head insisted —wanted to go to Camp David before the summit. Ethan gave Inada and Scott the weekend off to spend with their families and drove with Daniels and the president up to Camp David, along with 300 other agents and staffers in a convoy. A weekend in peace was what the president might have wanted, but Washington came with him.

Still, Camp David was a world away from the pressure cooker that was DC. Ethan loved it there, especially when he had to deal with presidents he hadn't liked. He'd take shifts in the woods, walking the perimeter or standing post in the forest and solitude, enjoying the silence for once. It was only an illusion of being alone, but it helped. Kept him grounded when it was back to the concrete jungle and the frenetic pace of Washington.

Driving up with President Spiers for the first time, Ethan closed his eyes and leaned his head back, taking in the fresh scent of pine and crisp mountain air, of kicked-up dust and meadow grasses, and spring flowers bursting free from winter's ground. Memories bubbled up in his brain, days as a child running in the backwaters of Wyoming, fresh pine logs crackling in fire pits, and fingers sticky with tree sap grasping at the rusted handles of his single-speed bike.

He opened his eyes, a grin lingering on his face, and froze.

From the backseat, President Spiers smiled at him in the rearview mirror. The rear partition was down. It was down an unusual amount for President Spiers. "Love the woods, Ethan?"

"Mr. President, Camp David is definitely one of my favorite places. You're going to love it up here."

Part of him twanged, a banjo string suddenly breaking at the thought. Those weren't just words. The president—*Jack*—really was going to love it, and Ethan knew him well enough now to say that with certainty.

Morning workouts had become a regular occurrence almost by accident. Neither he nor President Spiers spoke up about changing the routine or the schedule, and Ethan just kept showing up. He let the other agents go, though, and it became just the two of them —*alone*—in the early mornings. President Spiers was always there, always smiling. Some days they pushed each other, racing in sprints or trying to rack up more miles in a competition, and other days they took it easy, jogging slow and trading stories from their pasts.

Ethan now knew an uncomfortable number of truly blackmail-worthy stories of Congress from the president's—*Jack's*—days there.

His traitorous brain had never let go of President Spiers's request to call him by his first name. Now, it was a struggle to refer to him by his title even in his own mind. He felt himself returning smiles offered freely and wanting to laugh with the man, heard himself share jokes and stories from his own past as they jogged together. And then, later, he'd berate himself in silence, whip himself in his own mind, reminding himself again and again about the rules, the regulations, the reasons why he couldn't do *exactly* what he was doing.

Damn it, he was at war with himself, trying to hold back from President Spiers's overtures of friendship, fighting and hating that restraint with every breath.

"I can't wait. Are there running trails? Think we can go out for a jog, Ethan?"

Ethan inhaled, ignoring Daniels's sidelong glance. He heard what President Spiers didn't say. *Think we can go out for a jog together?*

"We'll send a team out and check the trails," Ethan punted. "See if they're in good order for you. Safe for running."

The president—*Jack*—nodded and leaned back.

President Spiers had been doing *that* more and more, too. Instead of pushing, he'd close up, go silent. On the drive, he'd spent most of his time looking out of the SUV's windows, watching the concrete jungle fade away, replaced by rolling fields and meadows and eventually the pine forest surrounding Camp David. For the normally friendly president, the silence stood out.

Ethan's gaze lingered on President Spiers in the mirror. He forced himself to look away.

Arriving at Camp David was an exercise in orchestrated madness. The staff and military personnel at Camp David took over, Navy stewards and military officers bustling the president around on a grand tour. They showed him the presidential lodge, the master bedroom suite overlooking the pristine forest, and the great room with a fireplace that took up an entire wall. Next, the porches and the back patio, the fire pit and the pool deck, and then they loaded him up in a caravan of golf carts to drive him around the grounds. There were two chapels, tennis courts, a golf range, hiking, biking, and jogging trails, and even an animal preserve at the retreat, all for the president's pleasure.

Ethan didn't have to stick by his side at Camp David. The detail was almost superfluous there, secluded as they were on one of the most secure military installations in the United States. Being at Camp

David was almost a pseudo-vacation for the agents as well. They weren't the sole layer of protection for the weekend.

He watched from the porch steps as the president—*Jack*—was escorted around, and smiled back, shaking his head, when President Spiers invited Ethan down join him in his golf cart for the rest of the Camp David tour.

Daniels's eyes burning into his shoulder blades held him back, as did his self-castigating conscience.

Ethan and Daniels watched President Spiers's golf cart caravan drive off, kicking up dust as the tiny engines whined and almost a hundred sets of wheels sped away. Finally, there was silence.

"Gonna go check the trails?" Daniels eyeballed Ethan.

"Yeah." Ethan hesitated. "Want to take a walk?" He hadn't spent much time with Daniels outside of their duties, and when they were on, they were on. There wasn't much room for small talk. Catching up with Daniels would be good. "I haven't heard about Annie Perkins in a while."

"Man, she's ancient history." Daniels smiled as he sauntered down the steps, shaking his head and his long arms, seemingly shaking DC out of his system as he took a deep breath of fresh air. "I'm enjoying the single life again."

Ahh, one of those times. Ethan chuckled, and they set off down the main dirt road before turning out at the first trailhead. They'd worn boots and cargo pants for the drive up, ditching their suits back at the White House.

Daniels kept quiet for the first mile.

Ethan's spine uncoiled as they walked, losing its rigid, almost frantic clench. His shoulders loosened, his muscles seeming to relax for the first time in months as damp earth squished beneath his boots, and fallen pine needles and spring buds filled the trail with spring's clean scents. Fresh grass and blooming flowers tickled his nose, late spring in full bloom. *This* was what he loved. Simplicity, quiet. No presidents around to make his head spin. Nothing nearby that tried to pull his attention, divert him from what he needed to do. Who he needed to be.

He knew the quiet was too good to last.

Daniels finally spoke up. "Why are you getting all buddy-buddy with this president, Ethan? You've been the iceman for the past three guys. You *taught* us distance and non-interference when we joined. Now you're working out with the guy on the regular?" Daniels shook his head. "I don't get it."

"The iceman?" Ethan stalled.

"'Iceman Reichenbach.' That's what they called you when they told me I was gonna be working with you." Daniels watched Ethan as they turned down one of the side trails.

Swallowing, Ethan shook his head. "It's nothing, Levi." He put one foot in front of the other, wet leaves and flower petals sliding beneath his boots. "And you're right. Distance is important. Critically important. You can't be objective if you're involved with the protectee."

"You telling me you're 'involved' with the president?"

"No," Ethan answered quickly. "I'm the detail lead. And, as part of my job, I'm trying to keep him safe and sane. Making sure he works out. I'm keeping him grounded. That's all."

"That what you're telling yourself?"

Ethan let out a long breath. "He's a good guy. Better than the last three. I'm not talking about politics or anything. I mean, he's a good *man*. A good *person*."

Silence. Then, "Are you attracted to him? Like, think he's more than just a hot dude?"

"*What?*" Ethan shot Daniels a horrified glare. Panic slicked up his bones, heat burning him from the inside, searing his blood. He wanted to dive into the bushes, disappear like he was in a cartoon and could pull himself out of the frame. "What the *hell*, Levi? What kind of question is that?"

"I'd ask any female agent, or any male agent who is attracted to men, the same question if they were spending time with an attractive male protectee. President Spiers is a good-looking guy, Ethan. I'm not into men, but I ain't blind. And, like you said. He's a decent man." Daniels's eyes were kind as he gazed at Ethan, trekking beneath the cypress and spruce. Holly bushes bracketed the sides of the trail, berries in ripe, vibrant bloom. Above, bird calls split the air, twittering and warbling between the branches.

"I'm a professional," Ethan snapped. "That's *out* of bounds."

His brain screamed at his heart, calling him a liar and a scoundrel, hurling insults from the dark corners of his mind.

Daniels had called him out on it, had really called him out on the one thing he was trying to hide and bury and escape from. His insides squirmed, his stomach twisting as he tried to swallow past the lump lodged in his throat. Daniels's eyes stayed on him, watching.

Physical attraction was one thing. He'd dealt with that before. But was this *just* attraction? Just physical lust? All this time, he'd been yelling, chastising, and berating himself for wanting to call the man "Jack" in the privacy of his own mind, and running up against the shackles of his own training, his decades-long, ingrained respect for authority.

Falling for a protectee was part of Secret Service Agent 101 training, and summed up in one word—*don't*.

Why would he be interested in the president, in Jack Spiers? Was it his somewhat nerdy appeal? That long, lean body? The stormy eyes and his Roman features? He had the look of a military man, cleanly trimmed, and that had always attracted Ethan, but he'd seen attractive men before and hadn't compromised his professionalism. The attachés to the Joint Chiefs were some of the hottest pieces of ass on the planet, especially in their dress uniforms, but Ethan wasn't panting around the Situation Room for prizes they'd toss his way.

Was it, instead, the president's—*oh for fuck's sake, Jack's*—character, then? Those indefinable attributes that made him *him*? His quirky smile and the way he loved to poke fun at Ethan? His wry sense of humor, coming out when they were alone and always managing to get Ethan to laugh? How he lit up when he thought he'd made a human connection, and how lonely and alone he'd seemed those first few months after Ethan had taken over the detail?

No. No, he wasn't thinking about this. He wasn't going to allow himself to. So what if he popped a boner for President Spiers every once in a while? It stopped there. No further. He wouldn't allow it.

"I'm just trying to help the guy," he finally grunted. "He's having a hard time adjusting to a full-time protective detail. I'll pull back when he's got his legs under him. I'm just trying to..." His gruff voice faded away. "Be friendly, I guess."

"All right, Ethan. Sounds good. Lemme know if you need any help when you need to pull back." Daniels slapped one hand on Ethan's shoulder and let it linger as they walked the last of the trails back to the lodge.

A LITTLE AFTER MIDNIGHT, when the moon hung fat and low, and the pine trees carved dark pyramids against the star-littered sky, Ethan restlessly wandered the main lodge at Camp David. His thoughts kept skipping, lingering on memories of the president—*Jack*—from their workout that morning, before they left the White House, and from the evening before, when he'd walked President Spiers—*Jack*—from the Oval Office to the Residence.

The president had carried his suit jacket over his shoulder, hooked on a finger, and his sleeves were rolled up, showing off his arms. Ethan's eyes had wandered over the skin below his elbow.

He couldn't get the memory out of his mind.

Smooth and soft, the curve inside a man's elbow was a place where he loved to linger with his lips, peppering his lover with kisses as he traveled down his body. A kiss to the inner elbow, a hand on a lover's hip, stroking, and he would roll in Ethan's arms, surge against Ethan's body, wrap his legs around Ethan's hips. He'd sweep his lips across their chest, press his face against hard abs. Slide lower, drop down, until—

If he closed his eyes, he could practically feel it. Taste it. Taste *him*, even. What did President Spiers taste like?

No. He wasn't going there.

Ethan slumped against the kitchen wall. It had been too long.

That's what was going on. That was why his libido had taken control of his brain. That was why he was acting so ridiculously, utterly stupid. He hadn't gotten laid since before the Inauguration. A quick, hot fuck during the waning days of the campaign had been his last one-night stand, a Midwest campaign stop and an overnight reprieve from the stress of being an agent while Scott took over for the night.

He hadn't meant for his dry spell to go this long. That wasn't his usual procedure. He never wanted for a partner, never. Regular sex, anytime he wanted it, with just a few hours out at the bars. Was this what happened when he went too long? Was he really this much of a sex fiend that he'd pant after the president? After *Jack Spiers*?

For God's sake, Daniels had called him out on it today. It wasn't just something he was struggling to contain on his own, with uncomfortable dreams and suppressed boners and quick jerks in the shower. This was something that others could see, too. Christ. Could the president?

Firelight from the great room caught his eye, flickering over wooden paneling along the lodge's back wall and over the exposed beams crisscrossing the ceiling. Echoes of the flames danced across the bay windows overlooking the lodge's back patio. Outside, soft ripples from the wind caressed the surface of the lit pool, and beyond, the pine forest whispered with midnight's gentle breeze.

He slouched again, staring outside. If he could capture some of that peace, some of that serenity out in the woods, and bring it into his soul, he'd be a much better man. He could get a grip on this horniness, control his wildly inappropriate thoughts. Camp David had always been a place of solace for him, one of the better perks of the job, and, God, he desperately needed that now. His eyes traced the shiver of a pine, watched the flutter of branches against the stars. *Get a hold of yourself, Reichenbach. Don't be a jackass. Don't throw everything away because of your cock. You're better than this.*

"Ethan?"

His throat closed. Flaming heat raced over him, shame and want and mortification all rolled into one. *Walk away. Walk away now.* His eyes slipped closed. Guilt, heavier than lead, sank in his soul, pulling on his tongue and stilling his words. What mockery was this, as he was pleading for strength, to have temptation reach out to him?

Exhaling, Ethan pushed off from his slouch and padded into the den. The president—*Jack—Oh for fuck's sake, fine. Jack. I'll just call him Jack in my mind. Fuck me!*—was sitting on the couch, his head thrown back on the plush cushion, looking at Ethan heading toward him from his upside down view. A lopsided grin stretched across his face, the same grin that melted Ethan's spine whenever it was given to him and haunted the edges of his dreams.

Something depraved inside Ethan took him to the back of the couch, until he was leaning over Jack, staring down at him from above. He rested his hands on either side of Jack's head, gripping the cushions with sweat-slick palms.

Inside, he was shouting, barking orders at himself to turn and walk away, to push back against this yearning, to fight these desires.

Ethan smiled down at Jack. "Mr. President," he said softly. His voice had dropped an octave, almost purring over the syllables. The hair on the back of his neck stood on end, shivering in the night.

Jack's reading glasses were off, lying on the coffee table on top of an open brief. Scattered papers cluttered the table's surface, and Ethan caught the words "China," "Taiwan," and "backchannel" before he looked away, back into Jack's eyes. By the light of the fire, the grey around Jack's temples was almost a liquid silver dancing through his short blond hair all over his head. The arches of his cheekbones seemed to glow, catching on the flickering flames, leaving the flat planes of his cheeks and his five o'clock stubble shrouded in shadow. Plump, smooth lips held laughter in the curves of his smile.

Ethan hadn't had a single drop to drink, but his knees were weak, as if he was about to be pulled under, and his head swam, lost in the fog of a delirious buzz.

He couldn't have stopped the slow smile from spreading across his face if he had tried. He didn't try, though, and that was just another thing to be upset with himself over, later. Later, he'd berate himself. Now, he'd take this. He'd drink this moment in and then lock it away, burying it and these feelings where he could never reach them again.

"You're up late." Jack held Ethan's gaze, still looking up at him from his upside down vantage.

"As are you."

"President's prerogative. No bedtime." Jack winked.

Chuckling, Ethan stepped to the side and crouched down, crossing his arms over the back of the couch and laying his chin across his wrists. He was suddenly on the same level as Jack, bare inches from the warmth of his skin. Jack's scent—sharp pine, clean and crisp—teased Ethan's brain. God, why did he have to smell like pine? Was it just the place, Camp David suffusing everything and everyone? Or did Jack truly smell like a slice of Ethan's heaven on earth?

"Can I ask you something?" Jack rolled his head sideways, staring into Ethan's eyes. He tucked one hand around his knee and waited.

Guilt-tongue was back, flooding Ethan with shame. God, what could Jack be asking? *What's going on here? Why do you look at me like that? Don't you think we should keep this more professional, Agent Reichenbach?* Heat burned through him, searing the inside of his skin. *Here it comes.* Castigation, repudiation, demotion.

Ethan nodded, trying to steel himself for the blow. His gaze wandered over Jack's face one last time, trying to hold on to the beauty.

"What do you think about China?"

Ethan blinked. He didn't breathe, simply stared at Jack. He blinked again. "Excuse me?"

Jack pushed up from his slouch with a groan, dragging himself to the edge of the sofa. He rested his forearms on his knees and jerked his chin at the piles of paper spread before him. "China. Their whole mess, and the nightmare we've got going on between them and Taiwan, courtesy of my predecessor." Jack shook his head, pinching the bridge of his nose. "When China invaded Taiwan eighteen months ago, my predecessor had drawn the US military down to such a level that we couldn't respond to help Taiwan without opening ourselves up somewhere else. And with the bombings all across Europe and the threats rising against the homeland, very few in Congress were willing to authorize a military mission to Taiwan, despite our obligations under the Taiwan Relations Act. China took Taiwan without so much as a peep from us." Jack shot Ethan a rueful glare. "So much for us being a strong partner and ally."

"They invaded because of the Caliphate attack on the capital. The one that destroyed the parliament building in Taipei." Ethan remembered the frantic energy of that day, and the distraught look of failure that haunted the former president's eyes. The president knew, that day, that he was done. He couldn't respond to an ally, couldn't answer China's invasion—shrouded in a military aid mission to help the besieged Taiwan—and he couldn't fight back from the damage that did to his presidency. It had been like watching a wounded gazelle get stalked on the savannah by fourteen different kinds of predators.

"Exactly." Jack leaned back, crossing his arms behind his head and slouching into the couch cushions. His back was straight, his stomach flat. Ethan tore his eyes away from the stretch of his shirt across his chest. His memories betrayed him, calling up flashes of skin he'd spied when Jack had wiped his face with the edge of his t-shirt, revealing his tanned stomach and light hair disappearing into his waistline.

Ethan dug his fingernails into his palms.

"I've been reviewing the intelligence on that attack. The Caliphate hasn't been able to get any foothold in East Asia, despite its best efforts. China has been ruthless with any hint of Caliphate activity. There's no religious freedom of expression there."

Whatever Ethan had expected when he walked in, chatting with Jack about the United States's tangled foreign policy with China and Taiwan wasn't it. He slowly stood, pushing himself up, and paced around to the front of the couch. There was a chair with Jack's suit jacket lazily thrown across it and an empty space next to Jack. Ethan hesitated.

Jack gestured to the couch, beside him. "Please, sit. I want to hear your thoughts."

Swallowing hard, Ethan sat, looking anywhere but at Jack. "Sir, I'm not qualified to speak on this subject. I am not one of your Cabinet members, I'm not a foreign policy expert, I'm not—"

Jack cut him off, reaching over and laying a hand on his arm. "Ethan, relax. I don't want a wonk or a policy expert on this. I want someone I can trust, someone I can just vent to and bounce ideas off. Someone who is..." He smiled, leaned back, and shrugged. The fire caught on his eyes as he tilted his head. "Normal," he finished. "I need to get back in touch with normal America."

"And you think I'm normal America?" Ethan snorted and shook his head.

"You're far more normal than anyone in my Cabinet. You're grounded. You have a sense of reality. Sometimes I wonder how my advisors even get into the office on their own."

"They don't. Everyone has Secret Service protection, which includes a driver."

"I knew it." Jack winked. "I just keep going over my options. The wonks have their opinion. My Cabinet has a different opinion. I have my own opinion. Do you have a minute to chat? Help me bounce ideas around?"

Ethan shrugged, throwing his hands wide. "Just... don't listen to me if I advocate a nuclear strike."

Jack smiled. He grabbed his beer bottle from the table, rolling it between his palms as he spoke. Ethan stared at the beer, desperately wanting to be the bottle in Jack's hands.

"I don't understand how the Caliphate found a foothold in Taiwan, much less Taipei. China's secret police should have stopped that attack. Somehow, they didn't, and the devastation was enough to push Mainland China into invading Taiwan. Taipei fell, China took over the island, and we were left out in the cold with no options. It was a bad day for America."

Ethan nodded, following the narrative with his own memories of the former administration, and with the former president's ferocious anger, lashing out at anything in the aftermath of Taipei's fall. His wrath at how he'd boxed himself in had been legendary, and his fall in the approval ratings astonishing. "Are you... planning on invading Taiwan?"

Jack shook his head. "No. We still don't have the manpower in the military. Not with everything that's been going on around the world. Europe's under constant alert against more terror attacks, and the Caliphate has been moving against all of our allies in the Middle East. Besides that, I don't want an all-out war with China. I don't want war at all. I want peace, and I want security."

Peace through a strong military and an aggressive defensive posture in the world, and firm commitments to allies. Ethan remembered the campaign.

"Since that day, we've cut off official diplomatic ties with China. We don't have direct communication with their government. We put tariffs on their imports, but we can't do much more, not without torpedoing the global economy. It's not like trying to sanction Iran, who we could effectively isolate. This is a major global economic player." Jack took a pull from his beer and set the bottle down on the rug, tucked next to the edge of the couch. He leaned toward Ethan with burning eyes. "But... we'll have a backchannel to China during the G-7 Summit in Turin," Jack said slowly. "*They've* set it up. *They're* reaching out in an overture." He paused. "So. Do we engage them? Or do we keep them on ice?"

Ethan's eyes widened, growing large as Jack stared at him. Jack was asking for Ethan's opinion on foreign policy? And not just trivial foreign policy, like would the prime minister of Great Britain prefer golf or polo during their visit, but world-shaking decisions. Ethan wasn't the guy for this. He wasn't someone a president should listen to about what to do regarding China. "Sir, I'm *really* not qualified—"

"Please, Ethan. I just need to chat it out with someone. I think my mind is made up, but I want to be sure." Jack smiled. "And you really can call me by my first name."

"Mr. President." Ethan licked his lips and looked away. His thoughts spun on, swirling as he stared into the fire. He tried to focus on China, on Taiwan, on the dangers of invasion and the complications of icing out a global player in the world economy, but all he could see in his mind's eye was the curve of Jack's lips and the dimple in his cheek when he grinned lopsidedly at Ethan. Pine floated to his nose, and Ethan's eyes closed as he took a breath, greedy for the scent.

He was in so much shit. So much deep shit.

Ethan leaned forward, clasping his hands between his knees. "I told you I'm not a politician. My specialties are military tactics and protective details. This isn't either of those things." He shook his head, trying to convert global politics into round numbers, something more familiar, more like what he was used to. "Whatever we do, it's not going to be exactly what China wants. What they want, what they've always wanted, is equal footing and equal status. They want to be a co-world power. They always have. But we won't give them that."

"They're not a world power. They're a world influencer." Jack's interruption was smooth.

Ethan nodded. "Just their human rights issues alone knock them out of that race. So they try to force our hand. Take Taiwan. Surely, we'll have to deal with them as equals now, right? At least in their mind." Like a bully making noise, shouting threats that they demanded be taken seriously.

"So, the choice is to engage as equals or walk away entirely?" Jack waited for Ethan's response.

"Middle grounds can be dangerous. Sometimes they're just... holding zones to worse places." Ethan cringed. He should know. He was stuck in the middle ground, and it was only getting more slippery. "Look, I'm not good at this stuff—"

"No, you're better than you think you are." Jack hitched his leg up, tucking one foot beneath his thigh. "Give yourself more credit. And you're right. I don't want to engage them on equal footing. I don't want to give them that satisfaction. They invaded our ally. Seized Taiwan. Now, they want to go back to what we were before all of that? No, not while Taiwan is under Chinese occupation. I want to keep China on ice for now." He frowned. "But something still isn't adding up for me. Why invade Taiwan and then go dark? They haven't tried to make a spectacle of the invasion. When Putin invaded Ukraine, it was years of posturing. With China, it's like they want to be forgotten, and have the world forget they invaded Taiwan. But now this overture?"

Ethan's eyes narrowed. All his years in the Army, in the Special Forces, were sending warning signals to his brain. "I agree, sir. Something isn't right. Could they be biding time? Saving up their energy for something bigger? Is this just a distraction?"

"Possibly. But there's no indication that they're making any moves like that. They've all but stopped trying to incite Japan into a conflict over those damn islands. And, they've beefed up their aid projects in Iraq. Building new hospitals, and four new oil pipelines. But they haven't scheduled any new military maneuvers, no exercises in the South China Sea, or anywhere near our fleet. They're just... silent." He exhaled. "Until now."

"So do you see what they have to say, or do you keep giving them the cold shoulder?"

"They haven't given me any compelling reason to engage with them. As it stands right now, this is practically a summons."

"The president of the United States is summoned by no man and no nation."

Jack smiled. "No, the office certainly isn't. The man, Jack Spiers? I can be humble." He scrubbed his hands over his face. "Is there anything to this, or is it just them posturing and jockeying for acknowledgement? For equality?"

"I don't know." Ethan's thoughts swam, tumbling around each other. "I'd play it cautious. If they haven't given a compelling reason to engage, then they might just want to leverage this meeting as international acknowledgement, or worse, spin it as an acquiescence. They could leak the details to the press, and then it looks like we're meeting the invaders in secret."

"My thoughts exactly. There's a lot of risk with accepting this overture."

"And what do you lose if you don't accept?"

Jack shook his head. "Unknown."

Silence, for a moment. The fire crackled as a log shifted, resettling in the grate. Ethan held Jack's gaze. His heart beat faster. "What are you going to do, Mr. President?"

"I'm not going to accept." Jack nodded, once. "I'm not going to." He leaned back, watching Ethan, seemingly appraising him. "Thoughts?"

God, he shouldn't be here. He shouldn't be having this conversation. It was all kinds of wrong, six different kinds of illegal, and had tragic implications for his career. Still, he smiled. "You're more decisive than your predecessors, sir. It's admirable."

Jack grinned. "You know, I'd love to hear your insight into my predecessors someday. Must be good stuff."

"Honestly, sir, not really. I try to tune most of it out. I'm not a politician. The sausage-making part of politics doesn't interest me."

Jack opened his mouth, ready to speak, when the lightbulb in the kitchen clicked on. Ethan leaped to his feet, hovering over Jack on instinct, and reached for his holster. One hand dropped to Jack's shoulder, steadying him.

As if there'd be an intruder in Camp David's lodge kitchen. Still, the urge to protect was too ingrained, the need to act bone-deep within him.

Jack stared up at Ethan, smiling.

A moment later, Daniels ambled out of the kitchen, freezing in the doorway. "Sir," he said, addressing Jack and standing straighter. His eyes darkened as he turned to Ethan. "Agent Reichenbach?"

Ethan tried to relax, but having Daniels catch him alone with Jack was almost as nerve-wracking as facing an intruder. "Agent Daniels." He dropped his hands, letting them hang limp and useless in front of him. They felt like gorilla paws, useless and sweaty, and he shoved his hands in the pockets of his cargo pants. "I was just doing a final check before turning in."

Ethan glanced down. Jack was watching him, his stormy eyes seeming to smolder beneath the crackling flames of the fire. Were those embers in his eyes a reflection, or was there something burning deep within? And that heat—that couldn't be coming from Jack, could it?

Inhaling—*and damn that pine scent wafting from him!*—Ethan pulled away, tearing himself from Jack's side. He was seeing things, imagining something that wasn't there. He might want to believe Jack looked at him with something other than just a hint of friendship, but that wasn't reality.

In reality, he was way, way out of line, projecting his desires inappropriately on his protectee.

"I'll walk back with you." Ethan crossed the great room to Daniels, leaving Jack behind. "Good night, Mr. President," he called out, turning at the kitchen doorway.

Jack nodded back, waving. "Night, Ethan. See you tomorrow."

Daniels was silent the whole walk back to the Secret Service guesthouse. He gripped Ethan's shoulder, squeezing once, and then left him to his thoughts.

JUST AFTER DAWN, knocking broke the serenity of the only morning Ethan and Daniels had to sleep in, shattering their day of rest and relaxation within the confines of Camp David. Banging echoed through the Secret Service's guesthouse.

Ethan jolted awake, and then padded to the door in his boxers and T-shirt as Daniels stayed in his bedroom, groaning and cursing loudly through his door.

Grumbling, Ethan threw open the door with a glare. If whoever it was wanted to be a dick and wake them up like this, on their day off, then they could deal with his grumpy ass.

He froze when he saw Jack on the guesthouse stoop, clad in running shorts and a long-sleeved Dallas Cowboys shirt, stretching out his calf muscles.

"Great morning for a run!" Jack said with a smile. "Want to head out?" He frowned a moment later, seeming to catch Ethan's bedridden, just-awoken state. "Did I... wake you?"

Ethan scrambled for something to say. Sleep and shock stilled him, blanking his mind. Seeing Jack so unexpectedly, and in his domain, sent his heart into a wild frenzy and his throat into the grips of a vise. "Mr. President," he choked out. "We were planning on taking the morning off. Naval security and the Marines were going to pull shifts today." It was considered a professional courtesy to both sides; the Navy and the Marines got the prestige of pulling personal security for the president, and the Secret Service took some much-needed time off.

"Shit. I'm sorry, Ethan." Jack backed away, his eyes full of embarrassment. "I didn't know. I'm sorry. I shouldn't have just barged down here like this."

No, you shouldn't have, but that's my fault for letting you think that any of this is all right. Sighing, Ethan thunked his forehead against the door, cursing under his breath as he watched Jack walk away. "Mr. President, I'll be ready in just a minute."

He shut the door on Jack's "are you sure?" and raced back to his room. Daniels was cursing from behind his door, cussing out whoever had woken him up, and at Ethan for not telling them to go fuck off. Ethan ignored his grumbles as he stripped, pulling out his running shorts from his duffel bag and throwing them on. He left his t-shirt on and grabbed his hoodie, pulling it over his head. Nothing to do for his hair. He grabbed his Secret Service ball cap and plunked it on his head. Socks and sneakers later, he was back outside, rolling his shoulders next to Jack.

"Shall we?" he grunted.

Jack was quiet as they took off. Guilt poured off Jack in waves, amid sidelong glances and pinched frowns sent his way. Ethan stayed quiet, unnaturally so compared to the ribbing and teasing they usually batted back and forth in the White House gym. He kept his eyes forward, staring at branches and the wet, needle-covered ground winding before him.

He couldn't keep this up. This had to end. Whatever longing and sexual fascination he'd developed for Jack, he had let it get too far. Jack couldn't be seeking him out like this. He just couldn't. It wasn't right. It wasn't appropriate, and he'd be lucky if he got off with a write-up and a reassignment.

And, last night? The president asking him for advice about foreign policy? That was dangerous in the extreme.

He'd stayed up nearly all night, tossing and turning as moonlight crept in through his guesthouse bedroom window. Self-castigation turned to anger, which morphed into shame as the clock struck three AM.

Jack had been lonely, seeking out a friendship and some regular male bonding, and he'd perverted the situation, turning it into his own twisted fantasy. He'd taken advantage of Jack's want of a friend, and he'd inserted his own desires. He could barely be around the man without imagining something else. Something hotter. A little more horizontal.

This was why objectivity, distance, and non-involvement were so important. He couldn't let anything get in the way of his duties, and holy shit, was this hugely blowing it.

He'd resolved to put distance between them. A Grand Canyon's worth of distance. A chasm, in fact, furrowed deep into the earth. Daniels could take over the morning workouts. He'd promote Scott into the lead on the president's detail and take on more of the administrative role. He'd stay back, stay way, way out of Jack's orbit, and let this—whatever it was—die. He had to be ruthless. He had to be quick. Kill it entirely. Take out the threat and go back to normal operations. He'd excise Jack from his life.

And he'd go back to the bars, pull some fresh piece of ass, and pound this out of his system.

He'd decided all of that as the clock struck four AM, and he'd finally been able to get to sleep a little while later.

So why was he running at eight thirty in the morning with Jack?

Anger clung to his bones, made his feet hit the dirt harder than normal. He ran faster, pushing his body in a physical exorcism. Beside him, Jack breathed hard, but stayed by his side. Worried glances burned onto Ethan's profile, Jack's eyes tracing over his skin every so often.

Jack would eventually realize this was crazy. That this whole morning was weird, and awkward, and not right. He'd pull back, too. He'd have to. This just wasn't normal.

Ethan worked hard to convince himself, repeating his decision inside his head like a bassline drumbeat, pounding it into his brain with each slap of his feet against the ground. By the time they rounded the last bend of the trail and headed down the final stretch, he couldn't think of anything else other than getting as far from Jack as he possibly could.

They slowed to a stop, breathing hard, and stretched in the clearing behind the lodge, beneath the pool deck and near the guest-house parking area. Jack doubled over, hands on his knees, sweat dripping from his temples and the ends of his blond strands. He gazed up at Ethan from his slouch, a question buried in his eyes.

Ethan turned away. His stomach clenched. He swallowed, but he couldn't shake the guilt lodged in his throat.

"I'm sorry, Ethan," Jack said between breaths. "I shouldn't have bothered you."

It wasn't a bother, sir. Always happy to run with you, Mr. President. I'd do this every day if I could, Jack.

Ethan shut his eyes against his rebellious mind, throwing his decision in his face as his desire flared. He wanted to comfort and soothe, reassure Jack that it was all good, it was fine to spend time together, in fact, they should go back out for a more private explo-ration of the trails, and of Jack's body. He'd start at the top and work his way down, licking sweat from his neck and stroking his skin. Seduction 101, his usual game. Seduce and sweep him off his feet, a whirlwind of sexual delight.

He squeezed his fists until his nails bit into his palms. "If you need anything security-wise, Mr. President, the Navy and the Marines will be able to assist you until tomorrow morning. We'll take over for the drive back to DC." He nodded once, briefly meeting Jack's eyes.

Jack nodded. He looked down, staring at the dirt as a bead of sweat rolled down the tip of his nose.

Ethan wanted to lick it off.

"Understood, Agent Reichenbach. Have a good day." Straightening, Jack headed back for the lodge, his shoulders square, back straight, and head held high. He never looked back.

Ethan watched him until he disappeared into the lodge's back door.

He trudged to the guesthouse, slipping between the parked SUVs around their door.

Whirling, he slammed his fist against the reinforced steel plating on the president's backup SUV. It didn't dent, and the pain tore through him, rocketing up his arm as the skin across his knuckles split. Blood welled and slipped to the gravel beneath his feet.

He *had* to cut this out, excise this fascination, this obsession. *Jack.*

It just sucked to do so. It hurt, far more than it should.

RUMORS OF AMERICAN— CHINESE COMMUNICATIONS CHILLED AT G-7 SUMMIT AMID REPORTS OF INCREASED CHINESE AID TO IRAQ AND AFRICA

Rumors swirled at the G-7 Summit in Turin, Italy, regarding conversations between American diplomats and Chinese envoys chilling, perhaps even freezing altogether.

China, while not a member of the G-7 summit, sent envoys to the world event, as did other nations on the periphery of the G-7 nations. According to one unnamed source, China attempted to reach out to American diplomats at the summit but were dismissed and denied an audience. "China demanded to speak with top-level American diplomats," the source claimed. "But China doesn't have that kind of pull anymore." When asked if there were any meetings at all between the Chinese and any American diplomats, the source refused to comment.

Rumors of a Sino-American freeze come amid the Chinese government publishing reports confirming increased aid packages to Iraq and East Africa. Totaled at two billion US dollars, the aid packages include the construction of hospitals, schools, and increased infrastructure, including roads, oil pipelines, and shipping ports.

CHAPTER 5

Dubai

THE AL MUNTAHA RESTAURANT, located in the Burj Jumeriah—the world's first six-star luxury hotel—attempted to redefine destination fine dining for the global elite. Perched at the top of the Burj Jumeriah, the glittering city of Dubai, the man-made Palm Islands, and the Persian Gulf stretched out beneath the floor-to-ceiling windows, sparkling in the dusky colors of the Middle Eastern twilight.

On other evenings, *Al Muntaha* would be filled with the soft rustle of napkins and the clink of silver and gold flatware, and the whispers of crystal slipping against linen tablecloths as soft laughter and fourteen different languages bantered over seven-course meals.

Tonight, however, only two diners sat in the restaurant against the windows overlooking the Gulf.

Neither man noticed the view.

Colonel Song Jian-Heng, a mid-ranking officer with no distinctive pomp or circumstance, or fancy add-on to his title, held a vague position within the Central Military Commission in the People's Republic of China. His obscurity seemed to help his obfuscation, almost as if he was hiding how close a connection he actually had to the ruling powers within the People's Republic.

Prince Faisal al-Saud, royal head of the Saudi Intelligence Directorate, never underestimated Colonel Song's import. This was a man who had phoned him directly, out of the blue one day, bypassing all of his security. But what was it to one of the chief spies of the People's Republic to find the personal cell phone number to the little known —but favorite—nephew of the Crown Prince of Saudi Arabia?

Colonel Song flipped shut a manila file folder, resting on the edge of the dining table. A full glass of wine shivered as his hand drew back. "How did he die, again?"

"During questioning," Faisal demurred. Saudi interrogations were renowned for their efficiency, and for their brutality. When Hu Xeng-Chen died in the basement of an unmarked Saudi military base, soaking wet, battered, bleeding, and broken, he'd revealed everything —absolutely everything—he had ever known. "We are confident he spoke the truth."

Faisal tried to nibble on honey-coated *luqaymat* while Colonel Song studied the plain manila folder. Faisal was almost two decades younger than the colonel. He swallowed, watching his guest carefully. He still couldn't get a read on the colonel.

He had to make this work. He had to have a success again, for his own sanity. For months, he'd been stagnant, his intelligence dried up, ever since—

No. Do not think about it. About him.

If he could impress his family again, then perhaps he could work his way back to their confidences. Maybe one day he would no longer be discarded as the familial nuisance they had to endure.

"And Mr. Hu had no knowledge of why you detained him?" Colonel Song's dark eyes pierced Faisal suddenly, flicking to him faster than a blink.

Faisal swallowed. "None." He licked his lips, tasting honey. "He had never heard of the account in his name at HBCC Banking. He didn't know any of the account details. His reasons for traveling abroad on the dates in question were for construction contracts and arbitration meetings."

"He was framed." Colonel Song wasn't asking a question.

"Someone worked very hard to make it appear that Mr. Hu was involved in money laundering for the Islamic Caliphate."

"Someone?" Colonel Song's eyebrows rose. "I think you are smarter than that."

Faisal's chin rose. He stared at Colonel Song. Silence stole over the restaurant. In the corner of Faisal's eye, he saw one of his bodyguards shift, eyes darting over Colonel Song.

"This reeks of the Americans," Faisal finally said.

Colonel Song murmured under his breath. "The Americans." He reached for his wine glass, swirling the burgundy liquid before taking a sip. "Except, Mr. Hu was supposed to be the Islamic Caliphate's entry to Taiwan."

Faisal shook his head, frowning. "Mr. Hu had no connection to the Caliphate. He wasn't a part of their attack on Taipei. The account in his name funneled money to the Caliphate, but he was not aware of its existence, or how that account came to be. He was set up."

"Which, by extension, means that whoever set up Mr. Hu is also responsible for enabling the Caliphate's attack on Taiwan."

"Why would the Americans set up a Taiwanese national as a false front for funding the Caliphate to invade Taiwan?"

"The Americans are not known for their forward-thinking foreign policy. They armed the same people who turned on them years later. They want to play the world police, but lack the ferocity to do what is needed." Colonel Song spun the stem of the wineglass between his fingers. "I have seen them employ false flag attacks before. This, though..." He sighed. "They were honestly furious when we invaded Taiwan to restore stability to the province and banish the Caliphate."

Banish the Caliphate. Faisal forced himself not to react. The Chinese had swept through Taiwan, destroying and exterminating every Islamic Caliphate soldier on the island. No prisoners. No interrogations. Just elimination.

"If the Americans set up the Caliphate's invasion of Taiwan, what did they expect would happen?"

"They didn't expect anything. The invasion took them by surprise. They were completely unable to respond."

"So... why did they prop him up?"

"Because it wasn't the Americans who set up Mr. Hu." Colonel Song set down his wine glass in the center of the manila folder.

Faisal stared.

"It's not the Americans who are behind this. Not their government. This is obfuscation. Someone covering their tracks."

"Who is responsible, then? Is it the Russians? Trying to undermine America again?" His mind spun, possibilities swirling and tumbling around each other. Russia hated America, always had, and seemed like they always would. President Putin had wanted to bring the West down a peg—or a hundred pegs—and since they had successfully seized Ukraine a decade prior, they'd expanded their territorial rumblings. Saudi sold them oil in exchange for assurances they wouldn't destroy the Kingdom with their wild plots and ploys.

Colonel Song smiled. It wasn't a warm smile, or a friendly one. "That is what we have to figure out." He glanced at the manila folder. "Quietly. This is not something for the world stage, or for the western media. We must be silent in this search. We do not want whoever is pulling these strings to know we are onto them."

Faisal nodded. His stomach churned. Hu's death would leave questions when his puppeteers tried to use him again. "I'll do what I can to have Mr. Hu remain living. At least, in the financial world. Online."

"As will we." Colonel Song stood, buttoning his suit jacket. "I will be in touch."

Faisal stood as well, straightening his long *thawb* and heavy, gold-trimmed robe. "The news is reporting the Americans ignored your government at the G-7."

Colonel Song paused. He stared at Faisal.

"Are you sure it isn't them?"

Colonel Song reached for his wine glass for the final time. He swallowed the last of the burgundy liquid in one swallow. "After the G-7, I am more certain than before."

CHAPTER 6

Washington DC

As WAS tradition after the first overseas trip—to Turin for the G7—Ethan took his team out for dinner and drinks at the Capital Grille, just up Pennsylvania Avenue. Scott, Daniels, and Inada all piled into Ethan's SUV for the drive downtown, catching up with each other and finally relaxing.

Ethan gave Inada a one-armed hug when they all met up outside Horsepower before heading to the parking garage. Inada had ended up with the opposite shift from Ethan, and he hadn't seen much of the man for months. Even when they were at the White House together, inevitably they'd be in different sectors. Inada didn't stick around much after his shift, either. He had twin daughters in first grade, and when he wasn't at the White House or on the detail, Inada was at home with his family.

After sitting down in a corner booth, Inada whipped out his phone and streamed through his photos, regaling Ethan with pictures from the twins' last day of school, the start of their summer vacation, and their trip to the National Mall as a family on one of Inada's off days. Scott, father to a teenaged daughter, grinned as he saw Inada's photos. Moments later, he horrified Inada with tales of teenaged woe and parental agony—sneaking out at night, screaming matches over grades, and boyfriends who did not measure up at all. Inada put his hands over his ears and refused to listen, especially when Scott kept telling him he had a double dose of teenagerhood heading his way.

Daniels, the ladies' man, and Ethan, the men's man, chuckled on the sidelines, shaking their heads.

Scott egged Daniels into spilling the beans on his serial girl-friends. He laughed when Inada shot him a dirty look. "Hey! I'm married! I can't go shopping, but I'd like to at least hear the reviews of what's out there!"

Daniels talked through the appetizer and into their steaks, but then passed the ball to Ethan with a mischievous twinkle in his eye. "And how are things going for our other player? I'm not the only one to have a more active love life than you two." He waved his fork between Inada and Scott.

Ethan shrugged. "Honestly, nothing to report." He shook his head as Daniels scoffed. "No, really. A bum knee isn't the sexiest thing in the world, you know."

Scott mocked Ethan sarcastically as Inada, always the sensitive one of the bunch, nodded at Ethan, very sympathetic.

"But you've been back for months now. Surely you've gone out since?" Daniels frowned, just the tiniest bit.

It was the beer that did it. He was relaxed, and he didn't see it coming. "Nah," Ethan said, slicing into his steak and spearing a piece. "Funny thing, you know. Being detail lead is pretty time-consuming. Doesn't leave a lot of personal time. I go home, sleep if I'm lucky, shower, shit, and shave, and then I'm back at the office."

Daniels and Scott shared a long look. Ethan froze, his fork halfway to his mouth.

"Well, that's because of all the extra duty you're pulling," Scott said slowly. He had a teasing smile on his lips, but heaviness hung in his eyes as he looked at Ethan.

"You pulling extra shifts, Ethan?" Inada, totally out of the loop, missed the exchange.

Ethan chewed, scrambling for cover. He hadn't told Scott anything, not like he'd told Daniels. Scott would run him through, read him the riot act, and then force him to fly right. They'd been best friends long enough to call each other on their shit the hard way.

"I'm not pulling anything extra anymore," Ethan said, swallowing. "There was just an adjustment phase the president was going through. It's all good now."

Daniels smiled at him before turning back to his dinner. Inada dismissed the entire exchange, forgetting about everything when his wife texted him to let him know they were on the way home from their Girl Scout meeting and that he should head back now to see the girls before bedtime.

Scott's gaze lingered on Ethan.

Daniels made his excuses to head out shortly after Inada. He had a date with a lady friend at a bar, he said. When Ethan shook his hand and asked for her name, Daniels said he'd tell Ethan tomorrow, after he met her. A wink and a backslap later, Ethan watched Daniels saunter out of the restaurant, leaving him and Scott alone.

It felt like a trap. He hadn't missed the long look Daniels and Scott had shared as they said their good-byes.

Scott waited until the waiter cleared their plates and brought them another beer each. He held Ethan's gaze, staring at him other across the table in silence, small, knowing smiles playing over their lips.

Ethan looked down finally, playing with the corner of the table-cloth. "So Levi talked to you."

Scott nodded. "He did. He's worried about you, especially after Camp David."

"Look, I'm fine. There's nothing going on. He's got nothing to be worried about."

"Is that why you moved me into the lead position on the detail and took a back seat in Turin?" Scott cocked his head to the side.

Ethan took a pull from his beer, stalling. "We all knew President Spiers was different from the usual clown we get in office," he said, gesturing with his beer bottle. "He had a harder adjustment period than the others. He's not used to being isolated, and he definitely wasn't used to a protective detail. He was lonely, we were the only ones around him all the time. It was the perfect storm for a misunderstanding."

"A misunderstanding?" Scott's eyebrows rose. "On whose part?"

"The president wanted a friend." Ethan set down his beer bottle and leaned forward, elbows on the table. He stared Scott down. "I helped him get settled in his new routine of being president. But he knows that there is a line separating us. Separating protectee from Secret Service detail agent. There isn't a friendship. He knows that now."

Scott held his stare, not blinking.

Holding his breath, Ethan waited. He'd sold Scott his revisionist history. It was up to his friend to buy it.

After Camp David, Ethan had called Scott and bumped him up while Ethan took over the backend administration. He ran the command post during the trip to Turin, sitting at monitors and running with the advance teams while Scott, Daniels, and Inada moved with Jack throughout the G-7.

There were no morning workouts. There were no late-night conversations. There was no contact, of any kind, between him and Jack.

It hurt, the first few days. He rode back to DC from Camp David in a different SUV than Jack. He forced himself to not head for the Oval Office when they returned, not bump into Jack in the hallways to make small talk, or ask about the game. There were agents stationed in the Residence for Jack's protection, and if he needed a friend, then he could call someone he knew. The Secret Service wasn't there to be rent-a-friends. He'd forced himself to stay in Horsepower for hours, catching up on his paperwork as he bullied his feelings out of his system, as he'd buried his want and his desire.

If he'd watched Jack on the monitors, his eyes lingering on the man's face, he didn't have to admit that to anyone. Especially not himself.

They left for Turin the next morning, and it was a whirlwind, as it always was, of calculated movements and choreographed security scenarios, moving the president from one place to the other and keeping a constant watch on him during the event. Casual time, in the evenings after the summit, was the worst. Jack tried to relax in the hotel's lounge with the leaders of Europe, and the Secret Service had to jockey shoulders with all the rest of the world leaders' protective detail agents.

There hadn't been time to think, much less to feel, and Ethan had operated twenty hours a day on eight cups of coffee, keeping his agents on the protective detail perfectly coordinated and in sync. When they all boarded Air Force One to head back to the US, Ethan had racked out on a bunk below deck and slept through the entire flight.

Two days back in DC, and he still hadn't seen Jack. He was calling that a success. A painful success, but something that had to happen.

Different time, different place? Maybe he would have flirted a bit more. Pushed the limits a bit. Or, maybe not. He'd never been one for straight-chasing. That was just a headache, and not necessary. There were plenty of gay men around. Men who knew they wanted other men, who he didn't have to constantly search out signs and signals with, or try to divine meaning behind gestures or looks or turns of phrase.

No, this was for the best. He was a professional, and he wasn't going to let something like this interfere in his duties. There were a million fish in the sea.

And it wasn't like he was searching for anything in particular anyway. He wasn't one for long-term anything. If he had to put a number to it, the length of his relationships could be measured in hours—the length of time it took to rock and roll in bed, get dressed, and slip on out. There wasn't any point to spending the night after a hot horizontal humping if he wasn't interested in anything that came after.

Panting after Jack for a one-night stand was out of the question.

So, he crushed his libido, tried to kill his desire. It was a fantasy, nothing more. Where it came from, he would never know. But what was done was done. He'd washed his hands of the business.

Now, to convince Scott he was through and there was nothing to worry about.

"Did the president ask about me?"

Scott's eyes widened. Shit, that wasn't the way to convince Scott that he was over the man, or that Jack knew their boundaries. Ethan fumbled, stuttering. "I just want to know if he understood the boundaries, or if it needs more reinforcement?" God, he could be so fucking stupid sometimes.

"He never mentioned you once." Scott watched him closely.

Well, that stung. For some reason, no matter how much Ethan convinced himself he was done, through, so beyond Jack it wasn't funny, he'd find himself wandering right back to his memories, or getting stung by an offhand comment. *Maybe the start of that friendship actually meant something to you.*

"Good," Ethan said, forcing cheer into his voice. He grinned, slouching back in his seat, going for nonchalant. "That's great. See? Things are fine."

"You going to take over as point man again?"

He froze, his beer bottle hovering in front of his lips. "We'll see," he shrugged. "I'll play it by ear. See how things shake out now that we're back into our routine."

Scott was still watching him.

"Look, seriously. It's fine. It's all fine. There's nothing going on. The president is doing what he has to do. You're doing a great job as point man. I'm taking time to get familiar with all parts of this detail lead role, both point man and administration. It's all good, Scott. I swear."

Slowly, Scott smiled. He reached out with his beer bottle, holding the neck at an angle. Ethan tapped his bottle against Scott's and downed the rest.

"You really should go get laid again," Scott said as he set down his empty beer.

"You know, there are limits to this friendship." Ethan grinned, shaking his head.

"No, there aren't. You said once that the best part about being gay was the constant sex. If you're having a dry spell, then what the hell does that mean for me and my future?"

"Okay, your sex life goes over here," Ethan mimed putting something inside an invisible box. "In this box of things we don't talk about."

"You didn't have any limits when you were telling me about that flight attendant you banged."

"He was flexible." Ethan winked.

"Or the lawyer you picked up at that State Dinner two years ago."

"Scandalous and hot."

"Or the Georgetown doc you picked up on the National Mall out jogging. *Jogging*. Man, I look like a dying Basset Hound when I'm done with a run, and you can pick people up while jogging?" Scott threw his napkin at Ethan.

Ethan batted it away.

"Why didn't you pick up some nurse while you were out with your knee all busted up, saving the president from the vegans?" It was Scott's turn to wink.

Shrugging, Ethan leaned back, smirking at his friend. Why had this dry spell come over him? Until his libido had fired off over Jack, he really hadn't noticed the sudden change in his sex life, from full speed ahead to barely dog paddling. "Dunno. Maybe I'm just getting old."

Scott, predictably, snorted and guffawed all at once, an undignified kind of squawk that shook Scott's small belly. "Yeah, right. You're getting old. You're like a GI Joe doll. You gay guys are ageless."

"Don't hate." Ethan grinned. "I'd be happy to share the secrets with you, though."

"I'm good." Scott stood, along with Ethan, and dropped a hundred on the table. "I like grossing out my wife and daughter with my caveman ways."

"You blame your farts on the dog, don't you?"

"Nope. On my wife."

Laughing, they headed out, waving to the hostess as they ducked outside. DC summers were warm, even after the sun went down, and Ethan kept his suit jacket thrown over one shoulder. Scott had his fisted in one hand, wrinkling the collar.

"Hey man," Scott said, stopping next to Ethan's SUV. "Seriously. You can call me anytime. Anything you need." He grasped Ethan's hand, holding his gaze. "Anything, anytime."

Ethan pulled him close, wrapping him up in a one-armed hug. "Thanks, Scott," he said softly. "Really. But I'm good."

Scott pulled back, shuffling his feet and smiling in that uncomfortable way he did when he got too emotional. "You should come over again. We'll cook dinner for you. Liz can irritate the hell out of you with her teenage drama. We can get buzzed and yell at the TV. Stacy can roll her eyes at us. It will be great."

"Sounds like fun." Ethan laughed, beeping his car to unlock it. "Want a ride to the Metro?"

"Nah, I'll walk." Scott slapped his shoulder once more. "Have a good night. See you at the office."

Ethan waved as Scott headed off, ambling down the street to the National Archives station. He hopped into his SUV after Scott disappeared down the Metro stairs, but he sat, idling, and sighed, leaning back against the seat.

No, he wasn't going to do this. He wasn't going to remember the past few months, or think of Jack's smile, or his laugh.

Shifting the SUV into gear, Ethan pulled out into DC traffic and turned north on Pennsylvania Ave toward 12th Street. The White House passed by on the left, white marble gleaming across the lush lawns, fountain burbling in front of the Residence. He hesitated at the intersection of 12th Street and Massachusetts Avenue. A right on Mass Ave would take him to 18th Street and up to Adams Morgan, and his gay bars. He could go tonight. Find some hot guy to go home with—or not go home with, but slip into the back with—and break this dry spell.

Or, he could turn left on I Street and head for his condo in Foggy Bottom.

A car horn honked behind him.

Ethan turned left on I Street. Jack's smile stayed in the space behind his eyes.

HE WAS up ungodly early the next morning, still out of sorts from the trip to Turin. It was pitch black outside, and as quiet as Washington could get. Car horns honked as tires slapped against the pavement and engines hummed, the nightlife of the city dragging on. Too early to run, Ethan dressed in his suit and headed down to his condo's garage. It was never too early to start the day, and at this time, there'd be no traffic on his commute. Ethan shook his head at his own lame attempt at positivity.

The White House was quiet at four in the morning, but not empty. He badged through the gate, waving to the uniformed agents manning the guard shack, and parked in the garage. A cup of coffee, and then he'd hit the stacks in Horsepower. Maybe he'd even get ahead of the curve for once.

Whistling as he walked, Ethan spun his keys in his hand as he headed into the White House Mess.

He stopped dead, frozen in place, when he saw Jack leaning against the stainless steel coffee counter, hands braced in front of him, head bowed low. His suit jacket was off, tie undone and gone, left behind somewhere, and his sleeves were rolled up to his elbows, messy and undone. His eyes were closed as he breathed deeply, leaning over a cup of coffee.

"Mr. President?" Ethan inched forward, one eye on Jack and the other desperately searching for the detail agent who was supposed to be in the room with the man. Jack wasn't supposed to be wandering alone. He always had an agent with him, other than in private spaces. Where the fuck was his agent?

Jack snapped up, eyes wide and surprised, as if just waking. He stared at Ethan, and then frowned. "Ethan?"

"Sir? Are you all right? What are you doing here?" *And where the fuck is your protective detail?*

Jack blinked fast, reaching up to rub the bridge of his nose. "Damn," he sighed. "It's been a long evening."

Evening? "Sir, it's zero four thirty. Have you slept at all?"

Groaning, Jack shook his head. "That explains it. Nope, no sleep tonight. Been in the Situation Room since seven."

Shit. Ethan hadn't turned on the radio on the drive in, listening instead to his music. If another 9/11 had happened, he was woefully ignorant of it. "What's going on, sir?" He hesitated. "Are you sure you're all right?"

Jack finally turned to him. A small smile played over his lips, tired, but warm. "I'm fine, Ethan. Thanks for asking." He inhaled the steam from his coffee mug before taking a sip. "And what happened was—"

"Actually, sir, I shouldn't have asked." Ethan tried to wave him off. "That was a slip of mine. Please. Don't answer." So much for his professional boundaries. They were mocking him in the back of his mind.

Jack shook his head, dismissing Ethan's protests. "Nonsense. You know I value your input. I've wanted your advice about a few things, but haven't seen much of you around." Jack took another sip of coffee, and Ethan cursed himself for the rush of pride warming his belly at Jack's words, right in front of the curl of his intestines, cringing. "We put more ships into the Mediterranean, the *Freedom* and the *Coronado*, as part of a rotation with NATO to spot-check transports and cargo haulers. We're trying to stem the flood of piracy, human trafficking, and arms smuggling going across the sea, especially in the eastern Med. One of our ships stopped an unflagged cargo hauler with containers supposedly bound for the refugee resettlement zones in Germany, Austria, and France."

Ethan busied himself with filling up his own coffee cup. Jack didn't move, and Ethan ended up side by side with him, leaning back against the steel counter. "Let me guess," Ethan grunted. "Not food and blankets?"

"Assault rifles, RPGs, grenades, and machetes. And the Caliphate just issued another *fatwa*, urging immediate attacks against the West. French police took down a refugee with homemade dynamite strapped to his chest."

"Shit."

Jack nodded. "Another piece of bad news for the refugees." He sighed. "The Caliphate also says it has another six hostages, but won't release the names or the nationalities." Jack squinted at Ethan, his face scrunched up. "Paris and Berlin are shitting themselves. Europe as a whole is freaking out, asking how many crates of weapons slipped through that we don't know about. The counterterror teams from France and Germany are banging down doors and questioning everyone on their watch list. MI6 is flying to the continent now to share any intel they have."

Ethan whistled. "Any credible threats or actionable intel? Anything specific?"

"Not according to the CIA, NSA, and DOD. We've just got a big question mark right now, and that's what scares everyone the most."

"I get it. Had more than a few of those moments in the Army. The big question marks, where you don't know what will happen."

"Exactly." Jack smiled, nodding his head.

It was too easy to keep talking to him. "You think everything is good, and then you're clearing out a house during a cordon search, and all of a sudden, you're face-to-face with a bunker buster rigged to blow. Or a BCIED."

Jack's smile turned brittle. "You were caught in a Building Contained IED?"

Building contained improvised explosive devices, BCIEDs, had taken out more soldiers than Ethan could count. Giant IEDs rigged inside houses or buildings, set in the path of US military units clearing and searching houses and neighborhoods. "Not ever hurt in a blast. I defused the ones we ran into. Never was unlucky enough to get caught when they blew. Had good spotters on my team, good guys who knew how to track wires and find the bombs."

Jack looked down, deep into his coffee. Long lines stretched from his tired eyes, reaching for his temples. "Leslie was caught in a BCIED," he said softly, almost whispering. "It vaporized her unit."

Was there never going to be a moment where he didn't royally fuck up when talking to Jack? Maybe this was his punishment for even talking to Jack again. He was supposed to be distant, right? Instead, here he was, making an ass of himself, again. "Jesus," he stammered. "I'm sorry, sir. Shit, I'm sorry. I didn't mean—"

"It was a long time ago, Ethan." Jack rested a hand on his forearm, stilling his words. "It's all right. And I'm glad that you and your guys all came home."

Ethan's arm burned where Jack touched him, even through his suit. His gaze was glued to Jack's hand, to his fingers, and he could barely think, let alone speak. His tongue was heavy, his thoughts dizzy, as if his mind was full of helium. "Sir, I really am sorry..." he whispered. He didn't even know what he was saying.

"You don't have anything to apologize for," Jack breathed. A smile played over his lips, dimpling his cheeks. The moment stretched on as Ethan lost himself inside Jack's eyes, in his deep blue gaze, in the emotions that suddenly tore through Ethan. A bolt of want, of aching longing struck him straight in the heart. Ethan inhaled sharply, just a bit, and caught Jack's subtle pine scent. He nearly groaned, nearly whimpered as he held himself back. *Focus, focus! What the fuck is wrong with you? This is the president, and he's straight! He's talking about his dead wife, for fuck's sake.* His heart only burned hotter, trying to melt the ice flows in Ethan's veins.

Jack stepped away, pushing off the steel counter as he clutched his paper coffee cup. "I missed you in Turin. I don't think I saw you at all over there."

"Uhh, no, sir." Ethan fumbled his own coffee, spilling it over the back of his hand. He cursed under his breath, shaking his hand, and then grabbed a wad of napkins. "I was running the backend of the trip. In the command post."

"You did a great job. I'm still alive." Jack grinned. "Now that we're back, we might be able to see more of each other again?" Jack's voice rose, a question in his words. He swallowed, and Ethan's eyes fixed on the rise and fall of his Adam's apple. "Ready to kill me on the treadmill?"

I can't escape this man even if I tried. And God help me, but I don't want to try. Ethan licked his lips. The stench of coffee clung to him, but he could still sense the lingering hint of pine, and a deeper, warmer scent that was all Jack, hanging in the air. His heart pounded, almost beating out of his chest. Why this man, why this place, why now? *I can't, good God, I can't fucking do this.*

"Sure, Mr. President. How about tomorrow? I can come by at our usual time?"

Beaming, Jack nodded. "Sounds great." He headed toward the Situation Room, but paused at the door. "You know," he said, turning back to Ethan. "You really can call me Jack."

Ethan nodded. "Mr. President." He smiled.

Jack shook his head and walked out.

Heaving a gasp, Ethan collapsed backward against the steel coffee counter, barely setting down his cup before his hands flew to steady himself against the railing. *Fuck, fuck, fuck!* He was in such deep shit. What was his problem?

This was more than just lust. He wasn't dumb enough to deny that. But how? And why? He'd closed the door on this kind of thing years ago. He wasn't that man.

So why was he falling head over heels for *Jack?* For the *president?*

A sandy-colored head of hair poked into the Mess. The young detail agent spotted Ethan, and his eyes went wide. He swallowed, hesitated, and opened his mouth. Closed it again.

"Agent Beech," Ethan growled, straightening himself up to his full height. He towered over most people. "What is your post and duty?"

The younger agent's eyes went wide. "I traded my shift with Keifer and took his overnight. I was supposed to be standing post in the Residence, but then the president went down to the Situation Room.

I..." He hesitated again. "I fell asleep, sir. Have you... seen the president?"

Ethan closed his eyes and counted to ten, breathing deeply. If he murdered this young agent, he wouldn't ever get to see Jack again. "The president headed back to the Situation Room," he growled. "When your shift is over, and you've stayed awake for the remainder of it, come see me in Horsepower."

RUSSIANS FLEX MILITARY MIGHT
OVER REFUGEE ARMS CRISIS

Panic tore through Western Europe when news broke of a cargo hauler carrying freight containers filled with weapons bound for refugee resettlement zones in Germany, Austria, and France. Western European leaders questioned the NATO-led Mediterranean Inspection Fleet's effectiveness.

In response to the crisis, Russia issued a condemnation of the NATO-led Mediterranean Inspection Fleet and declared that their occupied lands in Eastern Europe would be guaranteed safety from any terror attacks thanks to the security of the Russian military and the Kremlin.

European leaders from Germany, Austria, France, and England will gather with President Spiers at Camp David at the end of this week in an emergency summit to address the continuing security concerns within Europe. Also on the agenda are Russia's military movements, both in Europe and in the Middle East.

CHAPTER 7

Camp David

THE NEXT TIME they headed up to Camp David, over two thousand people accompanied Jack, and it wasn't for a weekend vacation. The British prime minister, French president, and the German chancellor were all crammed into Marine One, along with their own protective details. The president, the vice president, Ethan, Daniels, and Scott all rode Marine One up as well. Inada had left the day before, taking a caravan of Secret Service agents to Camp David to prep for the emergency summit with the Navy and the Marines.

Ethan, Daniels, and Scott sat in the back of Marine One, alongside the other world leaders' personal detail leads. France's detail lead spent the flight shooting dark, heavy glares at his German counterpart, who pretended to ignore the Frenchman while tossing snide snorts back his way. The British detail lead spread the *Times* across his face and went to sleep. His snores filled the rear cabin.

Ethan watched Jack talk to the British prime minister, speaking fast and gesturing with his hands. They spoke over each other at times, heated discussions rising and falling. Laughter broke out every now and then.

Ethan relaxed into his seat, but kept his eyes on Jack while Daniels and Scott played cards.

Halfway through the flight, Jack looked up and met Ethan's gaze. He smiled, and it went right through Ethan, stabbing him in a way he both agonized and adored. He grinned back, even though his heart was aching and his palms were sweating, and he berated himself just a little bit more every single time this happened.

Jack went back to his conversations with the world leaders, and Ethan purposely stared out of the window for the rest of the flight. His ears picked out Jack's laugh, and though he couldn't make out the words over the din of Marine One's rotors, he still closed his eyes around the lilt of Jack's words and the warmth of his laughter.

When they arrived, Inada had already coordinated three full detail teams assigned to the German, French, and British envoys. The first few hours were a mess of moving people and personnel into place—the German chancellor and her team took one of the south guesthouses, the British prime minister and her team took over the guesthouse the Secret Service normally used, and the French president and his detail moved to the northern guesthouse. Golf carts zipped around Camp David, ferrying men in suits with radios and Marines with M-4s across the property.

He helped Gottschalk rearrange the lodge's great room and dining room, pushing together tables to the center of the room and dragging the couches to the far wall. Gottschalk's staff scurried in next, dropping binders and bound reports and classified folders stamped with "NATO EYES ONLY" in front of each seat.

Gottschalk motioned for Ethan to join him in the kitchen. They grabbed bottles of water from the fridge and downed one each in silence, eyeing the food laid out for the envoys.

"Agent Reichenbach, right?" Gottschalk said, wiping down his forehead. His hair was cut short, trimmed into a neat high and tight, and his hazel eyes were sharp as they stared at Ethan. He had his battered Army backpack slung over one shoulder, his version of a briefcase.

He nodded, swiping a cookie from the nearest tray. He broke it in half and offered a piece to Gottschalk.

Gottschalk raised one eyebrow. He didn't take the cookie. "You've been spending a lot of time with the president. Is there something I need to know about? Any security concerns?"

Ethan shoved both halves of the cookie in his mouth, taking his time chewing. Gottschalk was the president's right hand, his chief of staff, and someone Ethan had successfully managed to avoid... until now. There hadn't been an administration yet where the Secret Service and the chief of staff didn't come to verbal blows. Usually it was around midterms, or around reelection. Six months into the administration was early.

"Nope," he finally said, swallowing the cookie. "The president is fully secured."

Gottschalk frowned. "So why are you spending so much time with him?"

Ethan would take shit shoveled by Scott, and he was starting to take shit from Daniels, too. Those guys were his friends. He'd also take all the shit he could shovel on himself, all his midnight doubts and self-castigation.

But he'd be damned if he was going to take a single ounce of bull-shit from Gottschalk.

"He asked for a workout buddy," Ethan shrugged. "He needed a spotter." Straightening, Ethan angled his shoulders just so, showing off his broad shoulders. He looked like a linebacker. "Trust us. We know what we're doing. Physical fitness is an important stress relief for presidents in office."

Gottschalk surprised him. He laughed, the first time Ethan had ever seen him crack so much as a smile. He looked away, out through the kitchen windows and over the back patio. "Well, you are a good choice for that."

Ethan suddenly realized what Gottschalk was trying to hide, an emotion the chief of staff was smothering. *Jesus, he's jealous.* Of their friendship, perhaps? Did Gottschalk want to be closer to Jack? Know him as a friend, and not just a boss?

He cleared his throat, brushing cookie crumbs from his suit jacket. Now he felt like an ass. "I'm sure if you said you were interested, he'd enjoy working out with you, too." It hurt, to offer some of his sacred time with Jack to someone else. But it was the right thing to do, for so many reasons. Gottschalk would be a far better choice for a friend than Ethan.

Gottschalk smiled, but it was faint on the edges. "Thanks, Agent Reichenbach. I'm sure he sees enough of my face as it is." He slapped Ethan on the shoulder. "Thanks for taking care of him. I'm glad you're there. He needs it."

Ethan's smile was hollow as Gottschalk moved away. He was on thin ice, and it was only getting thinner.

———

THE FIRST EVENING of the emergency summit went long.

Jack, the German chancellor, British prime minster, and French president were joined in the great room by Jack's chairmen and vice chairmen of the Joint Chiefs, his national security advisor, CIA director, and the chiefs of staff from the German, British, and French administrations. Gottschalk sat next to Jack, scribbling notes and leaning back to whisper in his aide's ear every ten minutes. His aide would furiously type out messages on his laptop, and somewhere down the table, someone else would check their tablet.

Ethan watched through the glass windows on the pool deck, sitting with Inada while Daniels and Scott took a break inside. Their detail had been moved to the main house, and the four of them were sharing two bedrooms across the hall from the president's suite and just down the hall from the vice president's rooms. Marines stood post at every entrance and exit of the lodge, and inside at the protected hallways.

When the clock crept past midnight, Daniels and Scott switched with Ethan and Inada, taking over the watch for the rest of the night. Ethan slipped inside, his eyes tracing over Jack's profile before he headed down the hall to his and Inada's room.

He gazed at Jack's closed door. Visions played in his head, visions that made his blood run hot and his cock grow in his suit pants. He wanted. *Damn*, he wanted. Closing his eyes, Ethan turned away, to his own bedroom.

THE SUMMIT DIDN'T RESUME until lunch the next day. Ethan ran alone in the morning, jogging through the trails in the backwoods of Camp David. He spotted the German and French detail leads jogging together at a break in the trails, each of them arguing with the other in their native language. Ethan headed in the opposite direction, shaking his head.

He spent the day working on the patio deck, watching the summit proceedings through the bay windows. Everyone was more casual on the second day, dressed down in polos and khakis, and the German chancellor and the British prime minister wore knee-length skirts and cardigans. Jack was in jeans and a Cowboys polo. Ethan had a feeling his shirt would be untucked by the end of the afternoon.

He heard snippets of conversation as aides moved in and out of the lodge. Russia was on everyone's lips, as was the Caliphate. General Bradford, chairman of the Joint Chiefs, made a presentation to the group about the support the United States military could offer their allies. Ethan spotted locations identified in Europe for US troops to forward deploy, alongside their European counterparts, and an increase in boots on the ground at Ramstein, Landstuhl, Brunssum, and Aviano. A new naval fleet in the Mediterranean was proposed. Ethan saw potential drop zones for an airdrop into Syria, and even Western Iraq, Anbar Province. Maybe now the world was going to straighten Syria out. Finally.

The summit broke apart before dinner as each of the participants started going cross-eyed, pinching their noses and rubbing their temples. Aides buzzed, shepherding their people into convoys of golf carts as everyone headed back to their guesthouses to rest and refresh. On the pool deck, stewards began setting up a long banquet table.

Ethan was unplugging his laptop and stacking his files when Jack wandered outside. He had a crease down the center of his forehead. Exhaustion clung to him. As Ethan predicted, his polo was untucked, loose around his hips.

"Mr. President."

"My brain hurts." Jack stuffed his hands in his pockets. "Want to sit in for me in there? Do me for a spell?"

Ethan's brain went to all the wrong places, imagining everything he could do to Jack if only given half a chance. Coughing, he focused on rolling his laptop cord in a tight spiral. "I'd lead the world to the apocalypse," he chuckled. "You definitely don't want me in the driver's seat."

"Nuclear trigger finger?"

He mimed firing in the air. "If it weren't for that pesky fallout radiation…" It was black humor, but Jack grinned, and that was all that mattered. He sobered, gathering his laptop and files into his arms. "Looks like you got good work done in there." Not that it was any of his business.

"Yeah, I think so." Jack led the way inside, holding the door open for Ethan. It was all kinds of backward, and Ethan hoped no one would see. Of course, the first person he laid eyes on when he walked into the lodge was Gottschalk, staring at them. But Gottschalk just looked away, smothering a tiny grin.

Maybe he was wrong about the chief of staff.

Ethan shifted in front of Jack as they headed down the hallway to the president's suite and the Secret Service's rooms. Jack spoke again once they were alone, past the Marine standing guard. "We've got some options for preparing ourselves for all possible scenarios. Scalable responses. We're going to try to work with Russia, too."

"Work with Russia? Isn't that like asking a bear not to eat you?"

Jack snorted. "Yes, it really is. But the last thing we want them to do is provide material support to the Syrian Provisional Government while we're trying to support the rebels against the SPG. We'd have a brand new proxy war, this time in the world's nuclear powder keg. No one wants that."

They stopped at the end of the hall, outside Jack's suite and the door to Ethan's bedroom. Inada was somewhere on the grounds, and Daniels and Scott were probably still sleeping off their overnight shift.

They were alone, really alone.

Maybe it was the closeness of the hallway or Jack's casual slouch against the wall, a lopsided grin stretching his lips. Maybe it was the scattered forest light shimmering through the windows and sparkling off Jack's blue eyes. Whatever it was had Ethan transfixed. His skin suddenly seemed too small, his bones too large. He was floating, untethered from gravity, and at the same time, he was free-falling, screaming toward some chasm of the unknown. His tongue stuck to the roof of his mouth, thick and heavy and frozen. He scrambled for something, anything to say.

"Big dinner they're setting up out there." *Jesus*. Ethan could really kick himself sometimes. How could he pick up anyone he wanted at a bar, and yet fumble so stupidly in front of Jack time and time again?

"Yeah, they want to impress the visiting heads of state or something. I suggested a good old-fashioned barbeque. Chef voted me down." Jack hesitated, and Ethan saw wariness creep into his gaze. "Are you... free later? I mean, off duty? I didn't see you after we shut down last night."

Ethan swallowed hard, his heart lodged in his throat. "My shift ends at midnight, Mr. President," he grunted. "Your talks ran late yesterday."

"Too late." Jack scrubbed a hand over his face. "Tonight might go late again. In Turin, these guys liked to jawbone and throw back a few drinks. If you're around, can you stage a rescue for me? Maybe we can set up a signal..." Jack trailed off as Ethan laughed.

"What, you'll flap your arms like an eagle, and I'll swoop in for the rescue?"

"Something like that, sure." Jack grinned.

Ethan relaxed, the tension uncoiling from the base of his spine.

"I'll see what I can do, Mr. President. I'm with you all the way. I'm sure we can arrange a rescue. Though..." He hesitated. "Isn't that more your chief of staff's role?"

Jack shook his head. "Jeff would laugh at me. He leaves me to the political conversations and prefers to stay behind the scenes. He doesn't even talk to the press. I think he likes it when I squirm." Jack smiled, but it faded into a soft, wistful look. "Jeff knew Leslie and her unit. They served together. I didn't know him, but as soon as I found out they knew each other, I knew I wanted him on board, no matter what."

Now Ethan felt even worse. His stomach dropped, heavy with guilt. "Sounds like a good guy."

"I like good people around me. Makes me look better." Jack winked, and he reached out, squeezing Ethan's elbow.

Ethan reacted before he thought, reaching for Jack's hand and holding him in place. Warmth spread from his touch, blooming across Ethan's body. His heart beat faster as his fingers tingled. He licked his lips, his eyes darting down to Jack's mouth.

Confusion started to tangle with the light in Jack's eyes.

Across the hallway, Daniels's and Scott's door opened. Daniels stopped dead, his eyes going wide as his jaw dropped. "Mr. President," he said quickly, straightening. He was dressed down in cargos and a Secret Service t-shirt, a towel still around his neck.

Daniels's eyes dropped to Jack's and Ethan's hands, both still linked together and resting on Ethan's elbow. "Agent Reichenbach." He looked up, staring at Ethan with burning eyes.

Jack spoke first, pulling away from Ethan and shoving his hands in his pockets. "I'll quit bothering you, Agent Reichenbach. Remember our deal? You need to save me. It's your American duty."

"On my honor, sir." Ethan smiled as Jack nodded to Daniels and walked away, heading back down the hallway and past the Marine standing guard.

Ethan watched him go, not looking at Daniels. Finally, he turned to his friend.

Daniels leaned against his doorjamb, staring at him, his lips pursed.

"What?"

"I hope you know what you're doing."

DINNER RAN LONG, in the European style, descending into conversation over bottles of wine on the pool deck as the stewards cleared the table. Ethan hung back with Inada, Daniels, and Scott, eating leftovers in the kitchen with the other members of the international detail while the dinner party carried on outside.

Shortly before eleven, the heads of state stretched from the table and spread out around the pool deck. The German chancellor and the British prime minister both folded themselves down into pool chaise lounges with refilled wine glasses and stared up at the sky. The French president sat alone, smoking a cigar with his feet dangling in the water, his suit pants rolled up to his knees. The detail agents—Secret Service and foreign nationals—had moved outside, standing scattered around the patio and pool deck and watching their protectees.

Gottschalk sat with Generals Madigan and Bradford, vice chairman and chairman of the Joint Chiefs, sharing a bottle of whiskey. For once, Gottschalk looked relaxed—his tie loose, his shirt unbuttoned, and a tired smile on his face. It was good to see, and Ethan nodded as he met the chief of staff's gaze across the deck. Gottschalk raised his glass and invited Ethan to join them with a smile and a nod toward the table. Ethan shook his head, but part of him wanted to go over there and take a seat and forget about the gnawing worry chewing on the back of his brain.

A worry named Jack. Ethan spotted him standing on the patio above the pool deck, looking down at the smattering of foreign heads of state and political power.

Ethan moved in from behind, sliding alongside Jack soundlessly. "Are you in need of a rescue, Mr. President?"

"Thank God, you're here." Jack nudged Ethan with his elbow. "I really didn't want to go sit with the French president for another two hours. Quick, motion like you need me inside and I'll follow you in."

Smothering a grin, Ethan slapped his official don't-fuck-with-me face on and nodded to Jack, gesturing toward the lodge. He escorted him in a moment later, shutting the door behind them both with a quiet *snick*.

They weren't alone, though, not yet. A Marine still stood guard, and the chef and a few stewards puttered in the kitchen. Jack held his finger to his lips and nodded toward his suite. Ethan followed behind Jack.

He hesitated as Jack pushed open the door to the president's suite. He shouldn't be doing this. He shouldn't be doing *any* of this.

Jack held the door open for him with a smile, beckoning him inside.

Ethan followed, and he just knew he had that scrunched-up grimace on his face, the one Scott said made him look constipated. Great. Just what he wanted to look like in front of Jack.

"I never thought I'd say this, but I am ready to go back to Washington." Jack bypassed tables covered in reports and papers and headed for the mini-fridge tucked under the sideboard. "Ethan, can I open you a beer? I owe you a serious thanks for everything you've done for me. Sit with me, please. Let's hang out."

He couldn't breathe. Air wouldn't fill his lungs, wouldn't drag in through his clenched throat. His duty, his professionalism, and his career all screamed at him, shrieking that he turn away, that he say no. His heart squeezed painfully tight, wanting—yearning—just for a moment to be a different man. To be a man who could accept Jack's offer of a drink, even if it was only a friendly overture. To be a man who could accept Jack's friendship openly and honestly for what it was, and not try to twist it around, see things that weren't there, read meaning into Jack's actions that he wished for, but weren't really present.

As much as he wanted this invite to be a sign of something more, in reality, it wasn't.

That ached. The one man he'd gone and fallen for, and Jack was so many different kinds of off-limits. The first, and most important, of course, being that Jack was straight. And he was treading on the edge, the very, very edge, of being fired. He was going to lose everything if he kept going. He would lose Jack, whatever friendship they had, and his job, his career.

He shouldn't be here at all.

"Mr. President—"

"Jack, please," Jack interrupted, gently.

"Mr. *President*," Ethan repeated. "I can't. I'm sorry, but I can't." The hardness in his voice masked his sorrow. "I'm your detail lead, sir."

Jack huffed, his hands rising to his hips. "Well, when can I have a drink with you? Not until I'm out of office?"

Ethan stayed silent. "Never" hung in the air, unspoken.

It was like a switch had been flipped. One moment, Jack was watching him carefully, asking for something Ethan just couldn't give. And then, after Ethan declined, Jack straightened, squared his shoulders, and nodded once. "Okay, Agent Reichenbach. I... apologize if I've put you in an uncomfortable professional situation. It won't happen again." He nodded to the door. "Have a good night."

Ethan's jaw dropped, but Jack didn't see. Jack disappeared into his bedroom, shutting the door behind him.

He tipped his head back, and he cursed under his breath as his hands clenched into fists.

One step forward, ten thousand gigantic leaps backward.

CHAPTER 8

Camp David

ETHAN WAS as good as a ghost the next day.

Jack paid no attention to him, nothing more than he paid to any other agent on his detail. He was polite yet distant, saying a quick "thank you" whenever Ethan held open a door, but that was it.

Gone were the smiles, the quick looks, and the inside jokes. It was as if they had never been friends. It was exactly as it should have always been.

It felt like Ethan had scraped his heart raw with a cheese grater. His eyes lingered on Jack behind his sunglasses. No matter how much he told himself that this was how it was supposed to be, that this was how it *had* to be between himself and *any* president, the quiet, hopeful part of his heart—a part he'd tried to destroy, tried to bury—mourned in silent, searing agony.

Ethan begged off Marine One, putting Daniels and Inada in charge of the detail back to the White House while he closed down Camp David. Inada had to get back to his family, he said.

Even he didn't believe his excuses.

Scott seemed to sense something was off, and he volunteered to help with the post-summit wrap-up despite all of Ethan's protestations. Hours after Marine One lifted off, taking Jack and the rest of the summit back to Washington, Ethan and Scott piled into their armored SUV and began the drive back.

Silence filled the truck for the first half hour. Scott seemed content to let Ethan stew as he napped behind his sunglasses. Ethan's jaw clenched over and over, the muscles bulging outward in time with his pounding pulse.

"How do you know when a woman likes you?" Ethan finally broke the oppressive silence.

Scott slowly turned toward Ethan, pulling off his shades as he stared at his friend. "That is honestly the last thing I expected to come out of your mouth."

Ethan stayed silent.

"What's this about?" Scott frowned.

His hands gripped the steering wheel, kneading the leather. "Seriously. How do you know when someone is flirting with you? How do... straight people flirt?"

"Is there... a woman you're interested in?" Confusion strained Scott's voice.

"Scott, please," Ethan growled. "Just help me out here?"

"What the fuck is this about?" Scott's voice turned hard, cutting. "What the hell is going on?"

"I don't know how you straight people fucking flirt, okay?" Ethan exploded. "I can't tell when someone straight is trying to flirt with me, or if they're just being friendly, or whatever. In my world, when I want a guy, it's a lot simpler. I think he's hot, he thinks I'm hot, and bam, we're fucking." Exhaling, Ethan's knuckles went white on the steering wheel. "I don't know how straight people do things."

Scott stared at him, his eyes searing. "If they're straight, they're ninety-nine percent likely to not be flirting with you."

Ethan grunted.

"Someone you're interested in?" Scott asked, his voice carefully neutral.

Ethan didn't answer. He slammed down the turning indicator, jerked the SUV into the fast lane, and gunned the accelerator. "If someone was trying to spend time with you, *really* trying to be with you, and wanted your opinion on things, joked around with you, and then asked you out for a drink, would that be... something?" God, he sounded so fucking lame.

"If we're talking about a guy and a girl, then yeah, that'd be a pretty good guess. You could take that one to the bank." Scott hesitated. "But if we're talking about *you* and the *Goddamn president...*"

Ethan swallowed slowly.

"Jesus fucking Christ," Scott hissed. He whirled in his seat, leaning across the center console and jamming his finger into Ethan's face. "What the *fuck*, Ethan? You said this wasn't an issue. You said you had this bullshit under control!"

"I didn't ask for this!" Ethan shouted. "I didn't ask for him to flirt with me! I didn't ask for—" Ethan shut his mouth.

"For what? What the fuck else aren't you telling me?"

"Nothing."

"It's way past nothing, asshole!" Scott snapped. "You're so Goddamn compromised you're *beyond* firing. This is everything that we are never supposed to do." He started listing Ethan's sins on his fingers. "Losing objectivity. Becoming overly familiar with a protectee. Inappropriate behavior with a protectee. And *lying* about it," he finished with a roar. After a moment, Scott's head whipped back around, glaring at Ethan. "And what the fuck did you say about asking your advice? Are you talking to him about political business?"

"He wanted my opinion—"

"Oh, Jesus fucking Christ," Scott groaned again, falling back in his seat. His hands rose, rubbing over his face. "Ethan, Jesus fuck."

He hadn't thought it would be possible to feel worse than he did after Jack had ignored him that morning, dismissing him as if he were nobody special, but Scott's furious anger hit him like a wild punch. It had been safe living in his make-believe world, where only he knew about his fantasies, and only he knew about Jack's constant overtures of friendship. He was "handling it" to his friends and, behind their backs, reveling in the forbidden. Suddenly, on a sunny afternoon in an armored SUV, everything was all coming apart.

It felt like ice cracking, like a glacier fracturing deep in his chest. He inhaled against the pain and the frigid chill sweeping through him. His throat closed, and Ethan blinked fast behind his shades. *God, don't be this fucking stupid.*

"I didn't—" Ethan started, but stopped when his voice wavered. Scott stared at him. "I didn't ask for this," he finished through gritted teeth.

"You didn't do anything to stop it either." Scott wasn't shouting anymore, at least, but his voice was still hard.

"I didn't want to stop it," Ethan finally admitted. *I still don't.*

Scott sighed, bracing his elbows on his knees. The seat belt stretched long, whirring through the buckle, the only sound in the cabin.

"You know the president is straight, right?" Scott finally said. "I mean, he was married. To a woman. He's a widower."

Lots of gay men were married before, the traitorous part of his mind tried to protest. Ethan shut that down. He didn't need any more false hope. False hope was what got him to this place. "I know," he choked out. "And that's what's been driving me crazy. He's not..." Ethan hesitated. Was he really going to talk about this? "He's not giving me any signals like I'd expect if he were interested, or if he were gay. I mean, if he just wanted to fuck, we could have already done that a hundred times."

"Jesus Christ," Scott muttered. "Thank God for small miracles."

"What the fuck, Scott?" Hurt wound through Ethan's words.

"Oh, for God's sake!" Scott groaned again, closing his eyes. "I don't give a fuck that you're gay. You know I love you like you're my brother. But I am worried as hell about your career, and about your decisions right now. This *is insane!* We're talking about you freaking out wondering if the *president* is flirting with you? *Really?*"

"Is he flirting? Is that what he was doing?"

"Ethan..." Scott's tone held a warning as he exhaled.

"Scott, please. I'm going crazy."

"No shit!" Scott snapped. After a moment, he continued, "I mean, yeah, straight guys do all of that. How did you and I become friends?

We drank together, bullshitted together, laughed together. All of that. You weren't confused over me, were you?"

"No offense, man, but I never wondered about you." Ethan ground his teeth. *I never wanted you either. Not like I want—* He shut down his brain, gunning the engine to drown out his thoughts.

Scott sighed. "I've thought for a while that whatever you and the president were doing together was weird, even before Levi talked to me. Whatever you two are doing, whatever kind of bromance you've got going on, it's strange. And you're doing a shit job of hiding it."

Silence filled the SUV again, save for the slapping of tires against the road and the hum of the engine.

"What are you going to do?" Scott finally asked.

Wasn't that the real question? What was he going to do? What did he *want* to do? Had he even let himself think about what he wanted?

His heart surged and then sobbed. What he wanted was impossible.

He wanted *Jack.*

And not just in the physical sense. He didn't just want to fuck and run. No, not a one-night stand for him. For this first time, he wanted everything. The American dream, the apple pie life. He wanted the morning after, and seeing Jack slowly wake up in his arms. His hair, mussed and standing on end. His lazy smile, sleepy in the sunshine. He wanted to hear Jack talk about politics and the world and how he was going to bring order to a chaotic, desperate, deadly planet. He wanted to rub Jack's shoulders when he slouched, undo his tie at the end of the day, and bury his face in the crook of his neck, inhaling that damned pine scent, that perfect, heavenly scent that was all Jack.

How could that ever happen? Their lives, their jobs, Jack's sexuality. Everything was against Ethan.

"I don't know," he choked out, fighting back the lump in his throat. "I know what I want," he quipped, trying to smile.

"Yeah, no shit. I know what you want, too."

"Scott, please." Ethan shook his head. "I'm a mess. I don't do... this."

Finally, Scott seemed to look at him, to really see him. Ethan felt

Scott's eyes tracing his profile, roaming over his face, over the pounding vein in his temple. Could he see the sorrow that seemed to cling to him? "What is *up*, Ethan?"

"I never chase straight guys," Ethan blurted out. "I fucking hate this shit. I don't like reading signs, and trying to figure out what a guy means when he says or does something. I hate this. This fucking uncertainty. I like my life simple. I never wanted a boyfriend. I never wanted to go through any of this relationship crap." Ethan shook his head. "That shit is hard enough in the gay scene. No thanks. And trying to screw around with straight guys? Forget it. Just give me a good one-night stand with a hot gay guy."

"Until now."

He blew out, a long exhale. "Until now."

"I wondered why you never dated. You're a good guy, Ethan." Scott crossed his arms and leaned back in his seat. "So you've gone and broken both of your rules at the same time."

Ethan nodded.

Scott squinted at him. "How well do you think you really know the president? I mean, you work out with him, you've spent time with him off-the-record, you guys chat here and there. Is that really enough for you to fall for him?" Skepticism colored his words. "Enough to throw away your career?"

Ethan clenched the steering wheel again, nearly bruising the leather beneath his fingers. "No."

"Are you going to tell the president how you feel?"

"Fuck, no!" Ethan gunned the accelerator, pushing the SUV faster down the highway. "Are you crazy?"

Scott shrugged. "What are your other options?"

Ethan stayed silent.

"This whole situation is just a shit-show of emotions for you, huh?" Scott waited, watching Ethan's nod, before he spoke again. "So, what are you going to do?"

"I think the president already did enough. I told him I couldn't stay for a drink last night in his suite—"

"In *his* suite?" Scott's jaw dropped.

"Yeah. Told him I couldn't. I was his detail lead. He buttoned up, apologized for any professional misunderstanding, and then walked out on me. He's given me the cold shoulder all morning."

Scott whistled. "You blew your big gay chance there."

"Don't say that," Ethan snapped. "Don't fucking even joke about it."

"Okay, okay!" Scott held his hands up. "Look, you did the right thing. You're strung out, losing your mind, and pissed off. How much longer were you going to do this, huh? Pretending to be his friend while you really wanted more? Hiding what you guys were doing? Someone was going to find out, and you better be happy it was just me and Daniels who caught on that you guys were too close."

"Jeff knew something was up."

"Jeff?"

"Gottschalk. Chief—"

"—of staff. Shit, Ethan." Scott shook his head. "Look, just put it behind you. Move on. You can keep your job if you stop this."

Put this behind you. How many times had he scoffed at guys in the bars, wounded and hurt and depressed after the end of their relationships? He'd been snide, then, secure in his knowledge that he would *never* hurt like they were hurting.

Now he was going to have to get over his own "man who got away". He'd have to wrestle with the what-ifs and the whys.

And over a straight guy to boot.

He needed a drink. God, he needed about ten.

"Yeah," he grunted. "I know. And you're right. I don't really know him. I shouldn't be this wound up over Jack."

Scott gave him a hard look when he used the president's first name so casually. He reached across for the radio, turning it on to the satellite channel for hard rock. Bass threaded through the SUV, shaking the windows. "Forget about him," Scott shouted over the music. "Really."

Heavy metal took them the rest of the way back to DC, pounding and pulsing in the strained silence. Ethan stewed, lost in the wilderness of his aching heart. Scott was right. There was no happy ending here, no way to sweep Jack off his feet and ride into the sunset. There was no future to this fantasy, no possibility of a relationship, no morning wake-up with Jack in his arms. The only thing he could hope for was to salvage his job for the next three and half years—or seven and a half, if Jack managed to win reelection.

Maybe he could ask for a reassignment. Work a different detail. There would be questions, and it would hurt his career. There were rumors that he was being reviewed as possible Assistant Special Agent in Charge for Headquarters. But if he requested a reassignment off the presidential detail, he'd torpedo any possible promotion.

That was what he wanted, right? A good career, promotions, achievement. He hadn't cared about relationships. Why start now? What was so special about Jack?

Daniels texted when they hit DC, reporting in that everything was secure and good to go. The White House agents were already rolling with the president, and if Ethan and Scott wanted to, they could take the afternoon off.

Ethan dropped Scott off at his house in the suburbs of Maryland. Scott shook his hand, holding on for a long moment, and stared at him over the rim of his shades. "Call if you need anything," he said. "You'll get through this. You're stronger than this."

He left tire tracks on Scott's driveway when he peeled out, and he smelled burning rubber for two miles.

He took 16th Street south into the District. Ethan turned at Columba Heights and drove into Adams Morgan.

HE ATE an early dinner at one of his favorite burger joints, a local gay-run dive with burgers named "Deep Throat" and "The Money Shot." He drank beer after beer as he sat on the patio, watching the gayborhood come alive around him. These were his people. This was where he was at home. His eyes roamed over tight, tanned bodies, skinny jeans, and popped collars on sport coats. He downed another beer.

Ethan hadn't packed club wear when he packed for Camp David, but he had a long-sleeved black shirt that clung in all the right places. He changed behind his car in one of DC's ubiquitous parking garages and swapped his cargoes for his jeans—close-fitting, they hugged his ass and showed off his muscular thighs—and then headed for the bars. First up, his pregame dive.

A group of college-age kids were making noise at the bar, loud and catty. Ethan downed another beer as he idly watched them, keeping one eye on the door. Nothing but youngsters walking in tonight. Ethan paid his tab and headed out.

He ended up at his regular haunt, a bar that wanted to be a club, but wasn't quite there yet. The dancefloor in the back was small but packed, and the bar in front was always full of men watching the dance floor. A lounge patio catered to the business clientele, with TVs alternating between the news, sports, and soft-core gay porn.

The music pounded into him, shaking his bones. On the dance floor, young, barely-clothed men gyrated in time with men dressed in rumpled suits, disheveled ties, and unbuttoned shirts. Older men hung back, watching, and sometimes joining in. Ethan slid onto a seat at the bar and ordered a beer.

The bartender grinned at him. "Haven't seen you in a while, sexy."

Ethan puffed out his chest. He smiled back. "Been busy. Haven't been able to get out."

"You were missed." The bartender winked before moving on. Ethan watched him go, his eyes glued to the sway of the bartender's ass.

This was what he needed. Yes, this. Sex, raw passion, and the feel of another man. He needed this.

An hour later, and several drinks in, Ethan made eye contact with one of the young dancers. Shirtless and blond, the younger man had a bubble ass, perky nipples, and round lips that begged for a cock. Ethan smiled at the dancer, and the younger man headed his way.

He draped himself in Ethan's lap, sweaty and smelling like sex and sin. His small shorts, up close, were dark leather, so purple they were almost black, and split down the side with a fishnet inlay.

"Hi, daddy," he purred, wrapping his arms around Ethan's neck. "I'm Blaine."

Daddy? Ethan frowned but wrapped one arm around Blaine and grabbed a handful of his ass. "Hey sexy," he rumbled. "You look damn fine out there. Can I buy you a drink to cool you off?"

"Only if you heat me up again." Blaine winked at him and leaned in close. "I'll take a dirty Martini, extra, extra dirty."

Ethan ordered, and Blaine's hands found his fly. He palmed Ethan's half-hard cock through his jeans. Closing his eyes, Ethan leaned his forehead against Blaine's sweaty hair. Yes, a little bit harder. Right there. This was exactly what he needed.

Jack's face flashed through his mind and slammed into his heart. He shuddered, and then froze. In the darkness behind his eyelids, Jack was laughing, smiling, sitting in front of the fire at Camp David and asking him for his opinion. Beneath the sweat, the spunk, and the leather, Ethan suddenly smelled pine.

"What's wrong, daddy?" Blaine whispered into his ear, sucking on his lobe. "Need a pill? A popper? I can hook you up."

Ethan pulled back, frowning at Blaine. "Why are you calling me 'daddy'?" He wasn't old enough for that shit, Jesus.

Blaine's eyebrows rose as he smirked. "Honey, you're exactly what a daddy is. Now, do you want to take me into the back room and tell me what a good little boy I am?"

Ethan blinked. Blaine stared at him, his full, wet lips pursed in a cock-sucking pout. His crotch ground against Ethan's lap. Jesus. Blaine was young. Baby-faced. Maybe twenty-one. Maybe not.

"Blaine," he started, not even knowing what was going to come out of his mouth next. His hands rose to the younger man's hips. His thoughts tumbled, one after the other. "What do you think about China?"

"What the fuck?" Blaine frowned, looking down at him as if Ethan suddenly had three heads. "China? Who gives a damn about China? Are you and I going to fuck or what?"

Suddenly, it was all wrong. This wasn't what he wanted, not at all. Blaine was wrong—too young, too hard, too naked. He didn't have dimples, didn't have blond hair streaked with gray. He didn't have a warm smile, or a friendly laugh. He didn't give two shits about the world, and he didn't want to hear Ethan's thoughts on anything.

He was just a guy to fuck.

But that wasn't what he wanted. Not anymore. Realization hit him like a gong being struck, shattering the illusion he'd clung to all evening. He just needed this to get over Jack, just a little bit of sex, and he'd be cured.

What a lie.

Ethan tried to swallow down his own disgust. Shifting, he pushed Blaine down, off his lap.

Blaine looked at him like he was last week's garbage. "Thanks for the drink, old man," he snapped. "Get some Viagra." With a snap of his head, Blaine disappeared, heading back to the dance floor and draining his Martini in one long swallow. He set the empty glass on a table he passed and slid between two businessmen in sweat-drenched suits, grinding against them both.

Spinning back toward the bar, Ethan rested his head in his hands and closed his eyes. *What now, Romeo?* He suddenly felt for all of the guys he'd scorned, all of the men he'd watch hit the bars and then fail to pull anything, too wrapped up in memories and hurt and longing for the guy they'd lost. He'd been *so* sure that he'd never be in that position. *So* damned sure.

"Sorry, buddy." The bartender slid a shot of tequila across the bar for Ethan. "On the house." He leaned down, his head right next to Ethan's. "Feeling the years?"

"I'm fucking stupid." He grabbed the shot and downed it.

"Broken heart?" He waited for Ethan's nod. "Well... I get off in three hours. I can help you forget about him."

"Thanks," he grumbled, "but I think I'm going to head home."

The bartender smiled, disappointment hidden behind his easy-going grin. "Okay. The invitation is open, though. Just come on back if you'd like." He eyed Ethan. "And, how about I call you a cab?"

Ethan nodded before burying his face in his hands. Ten minutes later, the bartender tapped him on the shoulder and told him his ride was outside. Ethan threw a wad of cash on the bar top—far too much for a tip, but he didn't care—and headed outside. His brain was already aching, and the hangover hadn't set in yet. He collapsed into the backseat of the cab and grumbled his address in Foggy Bottom. The cabbie stared at him for a few seconds before setting off.

"If you need puke, you lean out car." The cabbie snapped his fingers in Ethan's face at the next light. "No puke inside!"

Ethan cursed the cabbie out under his breath. He tried to swipe his card three times before he got it right. He was a mess. He was so Goddamn stupid. He was an embarrassment.

The cabbie watched him in silence as he finally managed to pay with his credit card and stumble out of the cab. He left Ethan behind, screeching tires and burned rubber hanging in the air.

Collapsing on the steps of his building, Ethan pulled out his phone and opened a text message. His thumb hovered over the keyboard. Who the hell could he text? Scott would just tell him he had to get over this. Daniels would be busy, out with some girl. Inada was with his family, and he didn't know anything anyway. There really wasn't anyone else he was close enough with to open up to, or to drunk text way too late at night.

He should have sat down with Gottschalk instead of following at Jack's heels. Maybe none of this would have happened. Maybe he could have gotten to know Gottschalk, made a friend, instead of getting drunk and feeling like ten different kinds of an asshole.

What was done was done, though. He'd pushed Jack away. Made an ass of himself in front of Scott. Looked like an idiot to Daniels. Gotten drunk and stupid at his bar.

And at the end of the night, he was achingly alone.

EMERGENCY NATO SUMMIT
CALLED: RUSSIA INVITED

In an historic move, NATO has called for an emergency summit meeting in Prague next month to address the ongoing security threat to Europe and the world from the Islamic Caliphate, extending an invitation to Russia for the summit.

"We'd like to find a joint European-Russian solution to joint European-Russian problems," British Prime Minister Whitehall said. "We appreciate Russia's assistance and insight in these matters. Together, we can accomplish more."

Critics of the invitation accuse European leaders of appeasement, claiming that they are prematurely giving in to Russian aggression in both Europe and the Middle East. The invitation to the NATO summit, they point out, comes with no strings attached. Russia is not required to pull back from operating on its own in Syria, or to withdraw from the occupied lands it holds.

Some political observers expect any engagement with Russia to come with a price tag, with the West requiring Russia to change its belligerent ways before agreeing to any dialogue with the aggressive Russian state.

Sources within the White House affirm that while NATO is

open to engaging with Russia to explore joint solutions, NATO is ultimately responsible to NATO member nations, of which Russia is not. All options for dealing with Russia's aggression in Europe and its operations in Syria, including direct military action, remain on the table, according to the source.

CHAPTER 9

Pentagon

"YOU'RE LATE," General Madigan growled into his secured cell phone.

"*Sorry, sir.*" The voice on the other end of the line was thin and harried. The kid was stressed. Madigan had heard that tone before, in harder times in the sandbox. "*I made contact with Al-Karim.*"

"Does he understand his next targets?"

"*Yes, sir. And he says another video will be released later this week.*"

More hostages to be executed. "Good. We need to draw the Russians and the Chinese into the target zone. Spur them on. Make them react. We do that, and we'll have this done by Christmas." Madigan grinned. "It will be a great holiday."

"*Yeah.*" Muffled sounds broke over the line on the kid's side. "*I've got to go, sir. The White House is paging me. I'll be in contact.*"

"You're doing great. Excellent work."

A pause. "*Thanks.*"

The line went dead. Madigan lowered the phone, pressing the case against his chin. If the kid was following protocol, he'd have turned off that phone the instant he hung up and removed the battery. With no power source and no active ping to the cell network, his phone would be impossible to trace by anyone.

Not that Madigan had to worry about that. The National Security Advisor, John Luntz, was an enthusiastic supporter of their mission. He'd joined their cause. He'd given invaluable assistance during the mission's first days, when they were operating on prayers and secrecy. Luntz, like Madigan, was a patriot. Someone who looked ahead.

It was too bad about General Bradford, though. He wouldn't understand their mission.

There would be a purge when the time came, in the White House and the government as a whole. It wasn't personal. It was just national security. It was the future.

And when the whole world fell apart, Madigan and his people would inherit the rubble and establish a new order, a new promise of peace and stability.

Just a few remaining pieces had to be maneuvered into place.

Then they would rip the world to shreds, and none of the president's maneuvers for peace would make one bit of difference.

CHAPTER 10

Taif, Saudi Arabia

COLONEL SONG LEANED over Faisal's chair, bracing against the prince's desk. He stared at the monitors, watching Faisal work.

"Here, this phone number calls these individuals with an update. Now this number—" Faisal typed furiously, calling up a second screen. "Is a legitimate contact. When we called our partners at the American embassy in Riyadh and tipped them off about the Russians building a base in Syria, all of these numbers were called. Embassy officials, state department officers, the CIA in Langley..." Faisal scrolled through the numbers in his phone tree, a diagram of who called who in the United States government. "But, then *this number* was called." He pointed to an isolated number, all alone. "And it's the same phone number we have flagged as one that Al-Karim receives calls from."

"Al-Karim, the leader of the Islamic Caliphate's military wing in the greater Levant?" Colonel Song's eyes pierced Faisal.

"Yes. *That* Al-Karim. We know nothing of the person who called him, though. The number doesn't correspond to anything we have in our databases. It's not assigned to any government agency, and we haven't been able to trace it." More typing. "We did more digging, though. We know that this mystery phone calls the vice chairman of the Joint Chiefs. It calls the National Security Advisor. It calls Langley." He listed off five numbers that the unknown cell phone had called. "But we can't pinpoint its identity. The phone is kept off unless it's making a call. And whenever a call is placed, it's always on the move. We've tracked its location in Washington DC, Turin, and Maryland."

"Maryland." Colonel Song frowned. "Camp David is in Maryland. Do you have the coordinates of the phone call?"

"Let me pull them up." Faisal threw one of the windows from the desktop monitor to the wall monitor embedded across the back of his office. A few quick searches, and then the data file for the call intercepts opened. "Here you go."

Colonel Song nodded. "That is Camp David."

"You know that? How do you know that?" Faisal frowned, staring between Colonel Song and the data. "Camp David is the American president's secret retreat."

"It's Camp David. And it's not that secret. It's on Google." Colonel Song leaned back. "Someone close to the American president is running communications with Al-Karim."

"Is Al-Karim CIA?"

"No. We've already confirmed that."

"Could whoever it is be responsible for setting up Hu?"

"Possibly. He could still be a decoy." Colonel Song tapped one finger against his lips. "Have you kept Mr. Hu alive in the digital world?"

Faisal nodded. "He flew *Saudia* to Thailand last week. He's in Jakarta next week and then checking into the Burj Jumeriah the week after."

"Good. And the email account in his name that Al-Karim's lieutenant was emailing is still active?"

"Yes. We've been watching it. No messages from Al-Karim's men, or from the Caliphate."

Colonel Song paced in front of Faisal's desk, one finger still tapping his lips. "Hu was set up as a fall man. Someone built him a double life, one as a Caliphate supporter. A sloppy bank transaction through Saudi Arabia brought him to your attention." Colonel Song nodded to Faisal, a kind of acknowledgement. Faisal held his chin high. "You discovered this falsity. Started digging. And you have found an unknown connection between a member of the American president's administration and Al-Karim."

"Yes." Faisal fidgeted in his seat. Was he supposed to have more? Colonel Song was as mysterious as an alien. He couldn't read the emotionless spy. He was also, quite honestly, terrifying.

Adam, I wish you were here to help—

He banished the thought, almost as soon as it appeared.

A new worry rose in its place. "You said that this wasn't the Americans." He frowned. "You said, after the G-7, that you were sure it wasn't the Americans."

"This is not the Americans." Colonel Song stopped, facing Faisal. "The American government is not this... Daedalean." He shook his head. "This is something deeper. A splinter cell broken off from the American government, perhaps. A breakaway faction operating outside of sanctioned governmental policy." He hummed under his breath. "But who do they take their orders from?"

Song strode across the room, back to the list of calls made by the mystery phone, along with the dates, displayed on the wall monitor. "Each of these dates and locations corresponds to a trip made by the American president. Whoever this caller is, he is within the president's circle. Perhaps he gets his orders from the president."

"Or," Faisal said slowly, "the American president is unaware of what is happening."

"We won't know that until we know what it is they are planning." Colonel Song nodded once to Faisal. "I will return to Beijing and get my people on hacking that phone number. We will find a way to record those calls."

"How? We can barely track the phone. It is offline and unpowered when it is not in use."

Colonel Song smiled. "We have our ways." Turning on his heel, the colonel marched away from Faisal, toward the door.

He paused at the doorway. "This is excellent work, Your Highness," he said. "You have learned how to turn the Americans' tactics against themselves. Well done."

CHAPTER 11

Washington DC

Fridays at the White House were usually quiet. They were working days, catch-up days from the craziness of the rest of the week. Jack liked to stay in-house on Fridays, if possible, and connect with his team.

He also took his coffee on the second floor of the Residence, spending an extra hour upstairs catching up on briefs and reports. Jack had confided in Ethan once, months ago during a morning workout, that he liked to give his staff as much stress-free time as possible, and that meant him staying out of their way.

Friday morning, then, was the perfect time for an ambush.

Ethan paced on the first floor of the Residence, just in front of the grand staircase in the marble-covered Cross Hall. Chandeliers glittered above, and portraits taller than Ethan hung along the walls. Staid and stately visages of past American legends stared down at Ethan, judgment harsh and pointed in their painted gazes.

He could imagine Jack perfectly, sitting one floor above. He'd seen it before, when he had made up excuses to walk with Jack, escorting him side by side and chatting, laughing even, as they made their way up to the Residence. He'd linger for a few stolen moments, shame burning the soles of his feet. But he'd loved it, each and every time.

He shouldn't be here. But that was now the motto of his life. He shouldn't be here, he shouldn't be doing this, and he shouldn't be feeling what he felt. He shouldn't be in this mess.

But he was, and he had two choices. Forget everything. Run away. Hide his feelings. Bury his emotions and kill this fledgling, tender whisper of hope and longing that had sprung up within him. Or... throw caution to the wind. Engage. Face this and see what happened. Roll the dice. Go with the flow.

What if this was what he was missing? Ethan hadn't even known he *was* missing anything until the past few months, or the past week, even. Sitting on his front stoop and swiping through his phone with no one to text was a humbling moment. Six months ago, he hadn't been this pathetic. He hadn't been this empty. Or had he?

Something had woken up in his heart. Something deep inside him was yearning for Jack. For everything the man was: his quick mind, his dimpled grin, his warm heart. The man who wanted to save the world, but hated the pageantry in place for world leaders. Who had buried his wife and come back from that moment, wanting to fix what was broken, and what had taken her from him. Who sneaked away from sitting with the pretentious French president to sit with a friend and share a beer instead.

Who had offered Ethan his hand in friendship.

And Ethan had pushed him away.

He just hoped it wasn't too late.

Agent Sanders eyeballed Ethan, watching him pace. He stayed silent, though, and looked away when Ethan glared at him.

Ethan checked his watch. Zero nine thirty. Jack should be done any moment. He inhaled, held his breath, and ran his hands through his hair as he exhaled. God, what if he was too late?

Footsteps rang out, descending the stairs. Ethan whirled, wide-eyed. His throat closed.

Jack padded down the stairs, his nose buried in a file folder.

He didn't see Ethan.

Now or never. Ethan grabbed his courage with both hands. Part of him still wanted to run. Time to cross the Rubicon. "Mr. President," he called. He only grunted a little bit.

Jack paused, hesitating before his foot landed on the bottom step. Looking up, he met Ethan's gaze, but his face was impassive, completely blank. "Agent Reichenbach. Can I help you with something?"

Not the glowing reception he'd hoped for. "Yes, sir. I have a proposal for you. Something, uh, that you asked for a few days ago." He held up a manila folder. "Can I walk you to your office, sir?"

Jack stared at him. "Sure," he finally said and kept walking.

Ethan motioned for Sanders to stay back. He jogged to catch up with Jack before he made it to the door to the West Colonnade. Ethan snagged the door handle just before Jack, sliding close to his body as he pushed it open. Pine wafted into his nose, and he barely held back a soft moan.

Shifting beside Ethan, Jack slipped past him. "Thanks," he muttered, looking out over the Rose Garden.

They walked in silence for a few feet. *Get it together! You're going to blow it!*

"So what's this proposal—" Jack began, at the same time Ethan spoke. "Mr. President, I have—"

They both froze. Jack turned to Ethan, his eyebrows quirked up in a question. On their left, the Rose Garden was in glorious bloom, bursting with color and the scent of summer.

"I have something for you, Mr. President." Ethan held out the manila folder. "It took a while to get to this place. But I believe that this is right. I just ask for your consideration in this matter. It's... delicate." He clamped his lips shut.

Silence. Jack stared at him, slight frown creasing his forehead. His eyes flicked to the manila folder and, finally, he reached for it.

Down the colonnade, the door to the Oval Office opened. Jeff Gottschalk poked his head outside. "Good morning, Mr. President. Agent Reichenbach."

Ethan smiled back and waved. "Morning, Mr. Gottschalk." By the time he turned back, Jack had already flipped open the folder and was reading the single sheet inside. Swallowing, Ethan followed Jack's eyes as he read Ethan's handwritten message:

Mr. President -
    This is my personal cell phone number. I'll be fired if anyone finds out I gave this to you. But I'm sorry for what happened at Camp David, and I really wish I'd stayed and had that beer with you.

Jack closed the manila folder. He took his time meeting Ethan's gaze. When he finally did, his normally warm eyes were closed off. "I'll take this into consideration, Agent Reichenbach. Have a good day."

Ethan waited until Jack had met up with Gottschalk and disappeared into the West Wing before he let himself exhale. He tipped his head back and let the warmth of the summer sun play over his skin and the scent of the White House roses—blood-red and bleeding all over the garden—fill his nose. Anything to get rid of Jack's memory.

FRIDAY EVENING, the Caliphate seized another city in northern Iraq, further dividing the country and splitting Iraq into the no-man's-land of the Caliphate, the Kurdish region of the north, and the beleaguered capital, Baghdad. When the Caliphate moved in, they executed everyone who stood against them, or didn't immediately join their rigid rules, or who looked sideways at them. All the civilians who tried to mount a defense—the Iraqi military had long since fled—were executed, as were police, teachers, and politicians. Gruesome videos flooded the Internet, along with cries of rage and anguish from refugees scattered around the world. They cried for it to stop, taking to the streets throughout Europe in a night of furious protests. The protests turned as they wore on, and cars and garbage bins were lit on fire, and windows smashed in Paris, Berlin, and Budapest.

The White House buzzed until the wee hours of the morning, trying to figure out what to do next. Jack and his national security team buried themselves in the Situation Room, going over intelligence reports and news broadcasts. They watched the Europeans deploy riot police, and as the sun rose in Europe, smoke billowed on the morning winds.

They argued late, strategies and scenarios to combat the Caliphate batted down as those for and against bitterly argued. Harsh words flew around the room.

There weren't any pressing American interests in the region.

Russia and China were embroiled in the region now.

Let the fight stay isolated in the Middle East.

The loss of life was tragic, but ultimately, not an American problem.

By that logic, Ethan heard Jack snap, not much at all would be an American problem.

"Strange bedfellows were made from common enemies," General Madigan offered. He spoke over the arguing directors, proposing to continue their wait and see approach to the region. "Let's see what the Russians do. They have more interest in the region than we do right now."

Ethan slipped out after that. He'd only ducked into the Situation Room to check on the agents standing their posts and to deliver each a fresh cup of coffee. His eyes lingered on Jack, but Jack never looked Ethan's way.

He stayed late in Horsepower, reviewing intel reports from the field offices and the advance team's proposals for the upcoming NATO summit in Prague. He had good relations with the security services there. It would be a coordinated, high-stress travel event, but it wouldn't be difficult. Ethan signed off on the advance team's travel plans.

After walking through the White House and checking on his agents, he finally left just before midnight. The overnight shift was set, and the agents taking a break in Horsepower were playing a pickup game of basketball, playing with the battered plastic hoop suction cupped to the mirror and the office's old ball. He waved and walked out as Agent Beech laid up a basket around Agent Caldwell, to loud cheers and jeers.

Gottschalk was on his phone outside the Situation Room as Ethan walked out of Horsepower. Gottschalk waved, smiling as he pulled the phone down and away from his mouth. "Have a good weekend, Ethan."

The White House parking garage was quiet. Ethan slid into his SUV, but hesitated before starting the car. Leaning back, he let his eyes slide closed. He'd been hopeful just this morning. Maybe too hopeful. His first full weekend off-duty loomed before him.

He was going to sleep this whole mess off.

HIS PHONE BUZZING on his nightstand woke him up just before nine AM. Squinting, he grabbed it, reaching across his bed and pulling it into the pillows with him. Shirtless, Ethan rolled onto his back with a groan before pulling the phone up to his face.

A new message greeted him.

Is this Ethan?

His heart skipped a beat. He checked the area code. It wasn't DC. Ethan pulled up the Internet and searched the number. It was a Texas number. Austin. He swallowed.

[Is this POTUS?]

You really can call me by my first name. Especially if we're engaging in clandestine texts now.

Ethan exhaled hard, a smile breaking his face in two. Jack was texting him. That had to mean something.

[Sure thing, Mr. President.]

You're hopeless.

Ethan struggled for something to say. He pushed himself up, leaning back against his headboard.

[Long night? You guys were still going strong when I left at midnight.]

We called it quits just after one am.

[And you've slept, right?]
Yes, Mom.
[Just doing my duty. Can't have a POTUS go insane from lack of sleep.]
Your dedication is admirable. You should be promoted.
[Ha. I'm fired if anyone finds out about this. And a promotion would take me out of the White House. I'm happy where I am.]

There was a long pause. Ethan stared at the phone, willing another text to buzz in. His foot jiggled under the covers. God, he had to pee. But he didn't want to miss a message. Cursing, Ethan ambled out of bed and padded into the bathroom. He bit his phone between his teeth and pissed, and naturally, the phone nearly cracked his teeth when it buzzed. He spat it out, catching it one-handed as he finished.

You mentioned that before. I don't understand. Why is it a big deal if we are friends? I'm friendly with other members of my staff.

He washed his hands and headed back to bed, trying to figure out what to say.

[Your staff are all princes of politics. It's all good to be friends with them. We're just the help, sir. It's unseemly to befriend us. Beyond that, it's an agent's job to maintain objective distance with their protective detail assignment. If someone gets too close to a protectee, they might make a bad judgment call, or be prejudiced toward that protectee. There's also a power differential, and a power perception. The rules are there to protect you, sir.]

He bit his lip after he hit *send*. He'd just condemned himself and made it sound like he was all right being fast and loose with Jack's security. He typed quickly.

[Getting to know you has made me more dedicated to you, sir. And to your safety.]

Ethan waited.

That's good to hear. I have never had any security concerns. You and your men are amazing. And I'd like to think that, as adults, we know how to separate professional and personal.

That stung in all the wrong places. Wasn't that exactly what was wrong with Ethan? He shifted, heaving a sigh.

[One would hope, sir.]

What do you mean about a power perception?

Oh boy. They were going all sorts of places they shouldn't.

[You're the POTUS, sir. Technically, we're supposed to follow all of our own rules. But if a POTUS demands something different, then we usually give in. We're not proud of it, but what do you do when the POTUS demands something? So, if there is an interpersonal relationship and a president were to demand something... personal from an agent, would the agent feel obliged to give in? Would they feel like they could say no to the POTUS?]

OMG. Is that what happened here, Ethan? I was worried that I'd pushed you into something you didn't want. Did I?

Shit. Ethan typed furiously.

[NO. No, sir. I gave you my number freely. That was my choice. I have decided to carefully bend the rules here. I'm not giving in to anything from you. You're not pressuring me, sir.]

Another long pause. Ethan stared at his phone. Kept refreshing the screen when it went dark. He flopped back on the bed, resting the phone on his chest. Nothing.

Eventually, Ethan headed for his kitchen. He tossed his phone on the kitchen island and pulled out a carton of OJ and eggs. He didn't bother with a glass for the OJ as he scrambled three eggs, all the while sliding glances to his silent phone.

Halfway through breakfast, his phone buzzed.

That's quite disturbing, Ethan. I'd hate to think that anyone would do that, much less someone in this office. Has it happened before?

[Yes.]

Please know that I will never do something like that. If you even think I am demanding or asking for something that isn't allowed, or pressuring you, or anyone, for... anything. Please smack me.

[LOL. I won't smack you, sir. I'll politely lean in and ask if you're sure.]

Well, maybe you can growl a bit.

Fuck. Ethan dropped his fork. His cock twitched. Damn it. Jack wasn't flirting. He wasn't.

He stared at his phone. He had no idea what to say in response to that.

What are you up to today? You're not here, are you?

[Nope. I have the weekend off. Not doing much of anything right now. I was sleeping in...]

Ethan grinned. Time to let his hair down. If Jack could dish it, then he could take it.

Damn. I have a talent for ruining your days off. I'm sorry.

[No worries. This is better.]

Silence, again. Ethan bounced the phone in his hand. Was that too much?

This may sound strange, but would you like to come over and watch the ball game later? The Nationals are up in the series. I'm rooting for my Texas Rangers, of course, but any summer day with a game is good, right? Please, feel free to decline. You don't have to hang out at your office on your weekend. No pressure. But I have always meant it when I said I wanted to get to know you better.

Jesus. Ethan closed his eyes. As much as he wanted this to be a date, as much as he wanted to read between the lines and find all sorts of signs and signals, he couldn't do that. He couldn't project his desire on him. Jack was just looking for friendship. He'd said so earlier. He just wanted to be friends. Ethan couldn't pretend this was anything more than that.

[I would like to, sir. Sounds like fun. I'm concerned about how to go about doing that, though. Technically, I'm not supposed to be hanging out with you on my days off.]

So just leaving the door unlocked and hollering at you to come on up won't work?

[The alarms would go off if the doors were left unlocked. And I'd pass about half of my detail, all of them wondering why I was there and why I was with you.]

Sounds like that's a no?

[No. It's not a no. It's a 'let me figure this out.']

[Sir.]

You really can call me first name. Especially if we're doing secret base-ball missions now.

*by my first name

Grinning, Ethan texted back quickly.

[All right, First Name. :)]

You're hopeless. :)

I'm just going to be banging around this big empty house until the game starts. Let me know if you'd like to come over and how you'd like to conduct this secret mission. I leave all tactical matters in your hands.

[LOL. All right. I'm going to go for a run and think it through. I'll text you soon, First Name.]

I'll have the beer cold and ready for you, Hopeless.

Ethan dropped his phone on his kitchen table with a clatter. He stared at it, and then buried his face in his hands.

Now they had pet names for each other. This wasn't helping. But it felt so good, so deliciously good.

He headed for his bedroom, stripping off his boxers and kicking them toward the top of his overflowing laundry pile before grabbing his running shorts from the floor. His boxers fell down the mountain of his laundry, fluttering to the wood floors. Damn. He was down to the last few suits in his closet and had to run by the dry cleaners, or he'd be naked at work by Tuesday. Ethan stared at his closet and the last two suits hanging in place as an idea slowly formed.

ETHAN JOGGED THE NATIONAL MALL, looping from Foggy Bottom down to 2nd Street, out to the Lincoln Memorial, and then east past the reflecting pool. He sprinted up the hill to the Washington Monument and then jogged down the backside, running at a comfortable pace past the Smithsonian toward the Capitol.

Jack consumed his thoughts.

He stopped for a rest on the green across from the Capitol. His phone was pumping music into his earbuds, and as he readjusted the armband, he saw his message light blinking. He pulled his phone out, wiping sweat from his forehead.

Jack had texted him again.

Do I have to play nice with the French? Can I tell them to go get stuffed?

Ethan chuckled.

[*Yikes. What happened?*]

He shouldn't be asking. Add that to the list of "shouldn'ts".

They're being difficult over the NATO summit next month. They were all on board with wanting Russia there when we were at Camp David. Now they are blaming the invite on us. Naturally. It's not like I need more complications in our foreign policy.

[*No, you seriously don't.*]

I thought you were running?

Ethan held up his phone, snapping a quick picture of the Capitol building and pushing it over text to Jack.

Lies. You didn't just run there. You drove.

He pasted a ridiculous grin on his face and took a quick selfie. Dripping with sweat, red-faced, and bare chested. Not his greatest picture ever. He pressed *send*.

Wow. That's impressive. You're quite a beast. To be honest, I cry sometimes after you leave, when we run together. You can go forever. I might call you the Energizer Bunny.

Ethan closed his eyes and threw his head back, dropping the phone to his side as he clenched his hands. His phone case whined in his fist. Exhaling, he loosened his grip and focused on keeping his dick soft. He didn't need to pop a boner in his running shorts, and definitely not because the president had called him an Energizer Bunny.

[*Please don't let that get out. I'll never hear the end of it on the detail.*]

I won't say a word. Scout's Honor. Should I tell the stewards to expect Mr. Bunny tonight?

[*It's your funeral. :)*]

:) Hop along, Mr. Bunny.

Enough. Ethan popped his earbuds in and slid his phone back into his armband. On a whim, he turned up Pennsylvania Avenue, running north. The White House loomed before him, gleaming and serene. Would Jack be on the Truman balcony, enjoying the sun? He stopped at the fence, snapping another picture just like every other tourist. One of the gate guards noticed him and nodded. Ethan nodded back as he sent the photo to Jack.

Hey, you're early.

[Just passing by. Or hopping by, as I'm sure you'll claim.]

I waved to you from the Oval. You know, I didn't think there'd be this much work when I applied for this job. Who can I complain to about this workload?

[God?]

Ha! If only the Caliphate would take a weekend off once in a while. Or just disappear entirely.

[We could only be so lucky. Hopping on, First Name. This bunny has miles to go.]

You're disgusting.

[It's only ten miles. You can come with me sometime.]

How about you come swimming with me? Couple laps in the pool and I'll smoke you.

Ethan tucked his phone back in his armband and jogged on. He'd stand there for hours, texting back and forth, if he wasn't careful, dopey grin on his face and all. Nope, no time for that. He had to get home, get his clothes to the dry cleaners, and get dressed up in his suit again. Tonight, he was headed back into work to, ostensibly, catch up on a few things. If he just happened to swing by the Residence, and happened to end up spending a few hours with the president...

They could make this work. Whatever *this* was. They could.

ISLAMIC CALIPHATE TARGETS CHINESE RECONSTRUCTION PROJECTS IN IRAQ & EAST AFRICA

On the heels of the Islamic Caliphate's brutal slaying of two more hostages, Caliphate fighters attacked reconstruction projects in western and central Iraq, and aid projects in Somalia and Kenya. The Iraqi projects were run by the Chinese government. In Iraq, Chinese expatriate workers were executed, and the video was posted online to the Caliphate's social media accounts. In Somalia, workers managed to flee the attack, some jumping into the port waters to escape.

The Chinese response has thus far been a recommitment of personnel and materials to Iraq. Beijing promised to uphold its commitments to the embattled country, which include a two-billion-dollar aid package.

In order to safeguard their projects, the Chinese are planning to ask for a deployment of "security forces" alongside their projects. While no details have been given as to who or what these security forces are, most experts believe that they are Chinese military personnel.

China is reportedly asking for up to 100,000 security forces to be allowed into Iraq, which is just under the total number of soldiers that the United States used in their invasion of Iraq in 2003. Baghdad is expected to approve Beijing's request.

CHAPTER 12

Washington DC

JACK GROANED, throwing his head back against the couch and his hand out toward the TV. "C'mon! Dick Cheney has better aim that that!"

Next to him, Ethan snorted, almost choking on his beer. He coughed and stared at Jack.

"What?" Jack gestured to the TV again. "They're playing awful!"

Ethan shook his head and smiled wide. "You tell 'em, Mr. President."

Jack winked and took a drag from his own beer.

This was good. Better than he'd expected, actually. Ethan was just as he'd imagined: smart and fun, and even a bit playful, when he relaxed. He'd seen hints of the man beneath the agent, and he'd wanted to get to know him better for months. Befriend him.

Finally, after a few misses and a fitful start, they were actually hanging out. Drinking beers and watching a ball game together.

Sure, Ethan still looked over his shoulder at every squeak and sound behind them. He was still nervous, and Jack could understand why. They weren't supposed to be hanging out in the Residence, and they weren't supposed to be friends, according to the rules of the

Secret Service. He'd considered canceling this, texting Ethan back and telling him never mind, he didn't want to put Ethan in a position where he could get into trouble or damage his career or his professionalism. But Ethan had insisted he was doing this because he wanted to, and...

Well. He wanted to, too.

The game rolled on, and his team moved up to bat. A couple of misses, a few hits, and the bases were loaded. A new batter came up to the plate, and Jack groaned again, sinking into the couch cushions. "This guy hasn't driven anyone home since his junior prom."

Next to him, Ethan laughed, deep and rich. Jack beamed, and then he clinked his beer bottle against Ethan's when Ethan held his out for a *cheers.*

"You're something else, Mr. President."

"Jack." He took a sip of his beer. "C'mon. You can say it. Jack."

Ethan just grinned. "Mr. President."

I'M SO SORRY.

Jack's eyes darted to Jeff Gottschalk. Jeff frowned and stared down at the Residence's speakerphone, nodding along with the Senate Majority Whip, speaking over the line. Jack kept his cell phone angled toward his chest, and his thumb hovered over the keyboard.

[It's okay. I understand.]

Ethan was waiting—literally—in the walls of the Residence. Waiting in the hidden stairwell he used to sneak upstairs, just a few feet down in the East Sitting Room. He'd been on the way up to watch another game, but Jeff had come up to the Residence first, an urgent call from the Senate on hold. They'd had to take it, but he still felt shitty, leaving Ethan waiting, out of sight and hidden. Like a dirty little secret.

That's not what Ethan was. He deserved better than that.

Frustration clawed at Jack. Ethan was a good guy. This was wrong, treating him like this.

His thumb hovered over the keyboard. *Tell him to go home. Tell him this isn't right, him hanging out in the walls. Tell him you're sorry.*

But he didn't.

Instead, he tapped his foot and nodded along with Jeff, and then hurried his chief of staff out of the Residence once the call was over. He felt like an ass, but he tried to bury that, smiling wide when he saw Ethan heading down the hall.

He passed Ethan a beer. His smile faded, turning to more of a grimace. "I'm so sorry."

"No worries." Ethan raised his beer. "It's nothing. And I really do understand."

"It won't happen again. You deserve to be treated with more respect."

Ethan smiled slowly. "I appreciate that." He cleared his throat. "But we do still have to keep this secret. So I understand."

Jack nodded but glared at the burgundy wallpaper and bronze sconces. "Yeah." Sighing, he beckoned Ethan over to the couch. "All right, enough of this. We've got a game to watch."

"You going to rip the batters a new one again?" Ethan winked.

"Only if they play terribly. Their fate is entirely in their own hands!"

JACK SNIFFED THE AIR AGAIN, poking his head out of the Oval Office. Mrs. Martin, his secretary, snorted at him.

"Do you know how long it's been since I've had a good artery-clogging burger?" He took a deep breath, closing his eyes. "Oh, that smells good."

He pulled out his phone and texted Ethan. *Who got the burger? And where is it from?*

His phone buzzed. *[Doing recon now.]*

Jack smiled.

"I can get the kitchens to prepare you a burger, Mr. President."

"No." Sighing, Jack leaned back, his head on the doorjamb.

"They are awesome. But..." He sighed. "Too healthy, sometimes. The pizza isn't greasy enough. I don't feel my heart stop when I eat it."

Mrs. Martin shook her head, her lips pursed. "Just what we need. The president *trying* to give himself a heart attack."

His phone buzzed again.

[Patterson. One of Reyes's staffers. From a hole in the wall, he says.]

Smells amazing. The chefs here would never make something so unhealthy. I think it's against their contract.

[You might be right. Far too dangerous.]

But I work out all the time! You make sure of that.

[There's a legend in the Secret Service. A terrible story of the risks and responsibilities of this job. The cautionary tale of The President and the Pretzel.]

Jack laughed, his shoulders shaking. One of his predecessors, a man who had been president when Jack was in college, had choked on a pretzel, and panicked Secret Service agents administered the Heimlich until he puked. It had been on the news for ages, and a pillar of pop culture for his predecessor's entire presidency.

You would never let me suffer such a fate.

[You are correct.]

Chuckling, Jack headed back into the Oval Office. He left the door open, though, and sniffed the air one last time.

Two hours later, as the day wound down, and his staff was closing up shop for the weekend, someone knocked on his doorframe.

"What's up?" Jack looked up, his reading glasses sliding down his nose.

Ethan's head popped into the doorway. "Mr. President."

Jack grinned. "Come in." He stood, abandoning his work, and tossed his glasses on his papers.

Ethan wore a sly smile, and he kept something hidden behind him as he headed for Jack.

The smell hit Jack first. A burger and a side of fries. Greasy, salted, and still warm. He breathed deep, moaning as he exhaled. "Oh God..."

A flush stained Ethan's cheekbones as he brought out a bag from behind his back. "Special delivery, Mr. President."

"I'm nominating you for a presidential medal." Jack shucked his jacket over the back of his chair, loosened his tie, and undid his cuffs, rolling them up to his elbows as Ethan brought the bag over. He set it down on Jack's desk, scooting his papers over to clear a space, and then plopped a drink down beside the bag.

"And one chocolate milkshake."

His eyebrows shot up. "Now, that's asking for a heart attack."

"Which is why I will be watching you eat." Ethan pretended to take up post, squaring his shoulders and clasping his hands in front of him.

Jack tore the bag open. Two burgers and two fries. Perfect. He held one up for Ethan with a smile.

He seemed hesitant, but Ethan finally stepped forward, sitting in the chair beside Jack's desk and taking the burger. Jack unwrapped his and leaned back, propping his feet up on the bottom drawer of the desk. "This is heavenly." He spoke around a giant bite. "My hero."

Ethan's flush was back, and he held Jack's gaze for a long moment, longer than they'd ever had before. He seemed to be searching for something to say, but then he smiled slowly and bit down on the corner of his lip. "Just doing my job."

Jack shook his head and nudged Ethan's shoe with his own. "No. You're being an awesome friend. Thank you."

Ethan smiled again, but this time, it was tighter, and it didn't quite reach his eyes. "Mr. President," he said, nodding once.

JACK THOUGHT about Ethan off and on throughout the weekend.

He swam laps in the pool Saturday night, and as the water flowed past him, his thoughts once again turned to his friend. What did Ethan do on his days off? What kinds of hobbies did he have? He worked out, that was for sure. That muscular body of his didn't come from a diet of burgers and neglect.

Did he watch movies? Go for hikes? Ethan had been with the Secret Service for over a decade, so he'd probably already done most of the tourist attractions in DC. Jack, even though he'd lived there for years, still hadn't made his way through all the museums. If he wasn't the president, maybe he could have asked Ethan if he wanted to kill an afternoon checking one out. Grab some beers after. Maybe a game.

Did Ethan have a girlfriend? He'd admitted to being a loner over Christmas, and had sacrificed his holiday so his agents could be with their families, but he had to have someone special in his life. A good guy like that deserved to have someone love him. Hopefully he was having a great weekend with them.

Maybe he'd do something special for Ethan. Let him know how much he was appreciated. How grateful he was for his friendship, and his performance as detail lead.

Jack ate his Sunday dinner in the Residence's kitchen, munching on a salad as he stared at the walls and listened to the hum of the refrigerator. His mind spun on, thinking of what he could do.

HE SEARCHED for Ethan on Monday, eyes darting through the crowded hallways of the West Wing. Monday mornings were always busy, a rush of people and briefings and everyone cramming the happenings of the weekend into the first four hours of the day. He went from meeting to meeting, bouncing between calls and his office and the Roosevelt Room while swiping through his cell and fielding emails from congressional leadership and his staff. No texts from Ethan, though. Nothing since they'd wound down on Friday, sharing burgers and fries and jokes between the two of them.

But there. Just down the hallway. Turning the corner with two of his detail agents and talking to them softly, Ethan headed right for Jack and his team, their two groups about to pass each other.

Jack smiled as Ethan looked up, holding his gaze.

Ethan stopped talking, his mouth freezing mid-word.

Ethan's agents stared at him and then at Jack.

"Hey." Jack kept smiling as he passed by Ethan and his men. "Have a good weekend, Agent Reichenbach?"

"I did." Ethan sounded breathless. His lips quirked up, and his eyes shone. "You, Mr. President?"

"Quiet and boring. Always good for a president." He winked and threw Ethan another smile over his shoulder as he moved away. He almost spun around, keeping up the conversation, but he settled for one last glance and grin before he ducked into the Cabinet Room.

A few hours later, his phone buzzed with an incoming text from Ethan. His belly button clenched, and he smothered his grin as he dragged the phone closer while the secretary of the interior kept talking.

[Got a few more heckles for your repertoire, Mr. President. "Gotta swing that bat yourself. Batteries aren't included!" "What position do you play? Left bench?"]

His feet tapped beneath the table, his heels bouncing against the carpet.

Love them. Can't wait to use them. Coming over for the game on Thursday?

[If you'd like me to.]

Of course I want you to come.

"Mr. President, as we're preparing for the summit in Prague..."

Jack looked up, darkening his screen as he turned his attention back to his Cabinet meeting. His foot still tapped, though, and there was a zing inside him, a rush that seemed to race through his veins. His smiles came a little easier for the rest of the day.

TUESDAY, Ethan walked into Jack's private dining room off the Oval Office and stopped dead. His jaw dropped.

"A thank you for the burgers." Jack smiled and pulled out a chair, gesturing for Ethan to take a seat at the table. Prime rib, mashed potatoes, green beans, and buttery rolls filled the surface, an all-American feast. "And because I wanted to."

Ethan moved as if dazed and took a seat as Jack waited. He frowned. "Mr. President—"

"It's nothing." Jack waved away whatever protest Ethan was trying to spout. "I wanted to do this for you. A thank you for everything you've done for me. This is the least I can do."

He seemed to not know what to say after that, his lips trying to form a protest before giving up and pressing together in a tight smile. "Thank you, Mr. President," Ethan breathed. "This is... exceptional."

"So are you." Jack laid his napkin across his lap. Ethan coughed and reached for his water, taking a long gulp. "Let's chat about Prague. This is going to be a big summit. Let's get on the same page. Make sure everything goes smoothly."

He listened as Ethan outlined their security procedures, using knives and forks and even the salt shaker as props on the table. Jack wanted to learn, and he asked questions about Ethan's perspectives and his tactics, and then stole one of Ethan's props when he wasn't looking.

Ethan looked stunned, gobsmacked when Jack snagged the little salt shaker that was supposed to be his presidential SUV. He stared at Jack, his jaw hanging open, a tiny grin playing over his lips.

Jack slid it back to him, chuckling.

Eventually, Ethan pretended to stab Jack's hand with his fork when Jack made yet another grab for one of Ethan's props. Jack sat back, snorting and giggling while Ethan fought his own laughter. It was incredibly unpresidential, but it felt *good*. Like being with Ethan was permission to be himself, and he didn't have to be so stately and important all the time. He could be goofy. He could try to wheedle that smile out of Ethan. Could relax, and let the warmth he felt around Ethan flow through him, their friendship lifting him up for the rest of the day.

They finally finished lunch, and Ethan had pushed aside all of his props, a small mountain of silverware and utensils far away from Jack's reach. Sitting back, Jack tried to stall, not ready for their time together to end. He twirled his glass of iced tea, making circles on the tablecloth. "So. Do you play pool?"

ETHAN SHOOK his head and glared at Jack. He drained his beer, pointing accusingly at Jack as he swallowed. "Again?"

"Sorry." Jack wasn't sorry at all. He winked at Ethan when Ethan shook his head, glaring.

"You suckered me." Ethan pointed, wagging his finger. "You pretended this would be a fair game."

"I did nothing of the sort!" Jack pressed his hand to his own chest, his jaw dropping in feigned outrage. "All I asked was if you wanted to knock some balls around."

Blushing, Ethan rolled the pool balls across the table, where Jack was setting them up for another break. "Yeah. You said it would be fun to *practice*. Implying that you *needed* the practice."

Jack shrugged. "Maybe I meant it would be fun for *you* to practice."

"Mm-hmm." Eyes narrowed, Ethan waited until Jack stopped laughing, smothering his grin by biting his lip, before he made his break. Balls bounced around the pool table, and Ethan sank a stripe and a solid. He called for stripes.

Jack waited until Ethan had made his shot before speaking. "Did you see the news about the Caliphate targeting China in Somalia?"

"Yeah." Ethan looked up, a frown creasing his forehead. "Although, China doing anything in Somalia is interesting on its own."

Another stripe fell into the pocket.

Jack nodded. "I keep trying to guess at their motivations. There could be a hundred, but which is it?"

"China could be trying to woo more of the continent." Ethan's tongue poked out as he frowned. "Trying to get more of Africa to pivot their way?"

"Definitely. But Somalia? They'd do better pouring more money into Kenya. They already built that deep-water port for Mombasa. And bid for a massive transportation contract across Tanzania and Uganda."

"If they can bring order to Somalia, they'll be heroes in both Africa and the Middle East. The rest of the world has tried. Maybe they're taking their turn." Ethan's eyes flicked to Jack as his ball sank into the pocket.

Slowly, Jack smiled. "I thought you said you weren't any good at international relations or politics."

Ethan took a long minute to chalk his stick, not looking at Jack. "I've been reading up on things." He shrugged. "I'm trying to learn."

Something bloomed in Jack's chest, a warmth that curled his toes and made his smile go soft. "You've always been better than you gave yourself credit for. I love hearing your opinions."

Ethan flubbed his next attempt, and he scooted away as Jack lined up. He sank his first solid, but the shot was sloppy.

"I do mean that, Ethan." He looked up from the table and found Ethan's eyes burning into him as Ethan leaned against the back of the couch. "I do."

[*SHIT. I left my suit jacket up there last night.*]

Blinking, Jack rubbed his eyes and read the message again. The sun hadn't come up yet, and he was propped up on one elbow, sleeping in his undershirt and boxers, or, more accurately, stuck between sleeping and waking thanks to Ethan's text.

K

[*You've got to go get it. What if someone finds it?*]

They'll find a jacket?

[*One not yours. In the Residence.*]

Sighing, Jack flopped back, scrubbing his hand over his face. A moment later he was up, sniffing and blinking and shuffling out of his bedroom and down the hall to the game room.

He smiled, though, when he saw Ethan's jacket tossed over the couch. Grabbing it, he headed back for his bedroom.

I've secured the package.

Ethan was quiet for a while.

[Thank you.]
No prob.

Ethan looked out for him. The least he could do was look out for Ethan in return.

THREE WEEKS and over a dozen secret meetups later, Ethan was more confused than he'd been before.

Spending time with Jack was supposed to help satiate his yearning. He was throwing caution to the wind, taking a chance on building a friendship with a man who *meant* something to him, more than anyone had in Ethan's memory. He'd told himself over and over that they would stay just friends. It was all Jack could give, and it would be more than enough. He could yearn for Jack in the silence of his heart and focus on building their friendship. Their *platonic* friendship.

So why was he more fixated on Jack than ever? And why was his heart screaming at him to do something, to reach out to Jack, cup his face in both hands, and caress his lips in a tender first kiss?

He was failing massively at separating the personal from the professional.

But Ethan laid part of that blame at Jack's feet, too. If he didn't know better, he would have thought Jack was flirting with him.

It had started simply. Ethan headed back to the White House the Saturday afternoon after they first texted to catch up on work he'd already caught up on. After an hour wasting time in Horsepower, he headed out for a sweep of the grounds, checking in on his detail agents. That took him to the Residence, where he happened to run into Jack... and where he spent the rest of the afternoon and evening. A few beers and one long ballgame later, Ethan slipped out of the Residence through the secret stairwell in the East Sitting Hall, all the way to the bottom floor, and sneaked back to the West Wing via the underground tunnel. No one had seen him.

And it had been perfect. Absolutely amazing.

Well, once he got past his nerves and the fear that he was about to be caught by one of his agents. But the detail didn't go into the Residence unless they were requested, and Jack had purposely sent the stewards away. Once Ethan had let go and relaxed, he'd finally allowed himself to fully appreciate the moment, the man, and the friendship he was being offered. Hours later, his cheeks hurt from laughing at Jack's bad jokes and aggressive game calling, and he'd practically floated as he sneaked out of the Residence.

Every few days, Ethan slipped up to the Residence. At first, it was to watch sports together, but after Jack asked him if he played pool, they spent their time in the game room breaking sets together and trading off stripes and solids.

Ethan was too distracted by Jack to clean the table while Jack mopped the floor with Ethan, over and over.

And, the texting continued, even increased. As did the jokes.

Hey. Come stand watch during the next Cabinet meeting, k?

[Yes, sir. Is there a threat?]

No, but there is a game. Every time Jim says "let's hang that out on a shingle", Jeff and I are going to take a drink of water. Whoever's bladder bursts first loses.

Jim was the Ambassador to the United Nations, and he loved his colloquialisms. Ethan smothered a grin. He was watching the previous shift's brief when Jack's text came in, and laughing while the outgoing shift lead was discussing threat matrices wouldn't be good.

[Do the American people know that you're a total goof?]

Do they know that the Energizer Bunny protects me?

[This bunny has to go to work, First Name. Hopper 1, out.]

Hippity hop! :)

Or, when Ethan was certain Jack was in a meeting with the congressional leadership in the Oval Office.

What's the best thing about Switzerland?

[Good food, decent beer, and of course, the banking. Pretty sweet military too. Why do you ask?]

Well, that's all good, but you know, their flag is a big plus. :)

[Oh my God. It hurts.]

Ba dum tissh! I'll be here all week.

[How did you get elected?]

But, he sent one of his own back later that afternoon. *[Did you hear? The dictator was really upset about the neckwear he had received as a gift. What a tie rant.]*

He heard Jack's laughter through the White House walls.

He was just so *distracted* by Jack, during the day and in the evenings when they hung out.

Seldom get-togethers turned into frequent hang outs, which turned into seeing each other often... and now he was with Jack way too often to be sensible.

But he couldn't stop. He couldn't stop spending time with Jack. Jack was like a drug, and he was greedy for every moment they were together. Every evening, the beers they shared mixed with his euphoria and left him walking on air, and he always drove home replaying their conversations, remembering the curve of Jack's smile and the sound of his laughter or the light in his eyes when he'd tease Ethan.

But by the time he pulled back the covers and slipped into his bed, Ethan's thoughts would turn again, questioning what it all meant.

If he were a woman, this would obviously be flirtation. Jack would be flirting with him if he were a woman. If Jack was gay—or even bi—this would also be flirtation. He'd see the signs: lingering eye contact, and a challenge buried in the gaze. Looks darting down, undressing each other with their eyes. A different play to their conversations.

But Jack wasn't gay, and he didn't know that Ethan was gay, so this was just male friendship. Straight dude bonding. It was foreign to him, alien, and nothing in his past helped figure this out. Even his friendship with Scott and Daniels wasn't helpful. They knew he was gay, and there had never been a question of flirtation or boundaries. There wasn't anything murky there. And back in the Army, he'd mostly flipped between missions and going out, slipping off to bang guys at bars when he wanted to get away. Same with DC.

This though... It didn't mean what he desperately wished it would mean. Jack was straight.

Right?

———

JACK PINCHED the bridge of his nose and squeezed his eyes closed as he braced his elbows on the Resolute desk. The French president kept talking in fast, angry French, and his translator was struggling to keep up.

"...and he's saying that the idea is nonsense, and he was against it from the start—"

"Now that's just not damn true!" Jack interrupted the French president, growling. "You were all on board with this emergency NATO summit at Camp David, *and* you wanted to invite the Russians!"

Blistering French erupted over the line. Jack held the phone away from his ear, and his translator, holding her own handset, winced. The Joint Chiefs, sitting on Jack's couches, glared.

"He says he recommended it as a publicity ploy—"

"Oh, bullshit," Jack snarled. "Look—"

The French president snapped something and cut the line.

Jack's glare turned frigid, and he exhaled through his nose as he hung up the phone.

"All right." He took a deep breath. "General Bradford. Walk me through our fall back options for moving on the Caliphate *without* any international support."

An hour later, Jack rolled his neck, trying to fight back against the headache blooming at the base of his skull.

If only Ethan were there. He could roll his eyes and snark with Ethan, lambasting the French president and his flip-flopping.

He pulled out his phone and leaned back in his chair, keeping it below the desk. General Madigan was discussing troop movements through Turkey with the chief of staff of the Air Force, and for a moment, no one was looking at him.

Would it be too much if I issued an Executive Order mandating that we go back to "Freedom Fries" instead of French fries? Is that too far?

Ethan buzzed back, and almost as soon as he felt the phone vibrate, the tension in his shoulders started to uncurl. *[If it makes you feel better, every president has nearly had an aneurysm over the French.]*

Jack smiled. *Oh good. So it's not personal.*

"Mr. President?"

"Yes?" He sat up, keeping his phone on his thigh.

Bradford frowned. "What do you think about the possibility of using Israel's bases as a launch point for our air missions?"

Jack blew air through his pursed lips. "We've steered clear of that for decades. Never wanted to make Israel a bigger target than she already is."

"But Israel and the greater Middle East are on the same side for this one. Everyone wants to see the Caliphate go. Everyone."

"It's a possibility." Jack chewed on his upper lip. "Let's put it on the back burner for now."

The phone on his desk beeped, and his secretary's voice filled the office. *"Mr. President, the British prime minister is on the line for you."*

"Thanks, Mrs. Martin."

Jack set his cell on the desk and waited for Mrs. Martin to connect the prime minister to his desk phone. He swiped a quick message back to Ethan.

Gotta go. Brits are calling back and the generals are getting grumpy I'm texting.

His desk phone rang, and he picked it up. "Madam Prime Minister."

[Please focus on the world, First Name.]

Smiling, Jack sent a text back as the prime minster started in on the French president, her softly accented voice grumbling about the old Frenchman.

I've always been good at multi-tasking.

EVERYONE FINALLY LEFT the Oval Office after six PM.

Exhaling, Jack folded his arms across his desk and rested his forehead on his wrists. The summit was coming up fast, and everything seemed to be fraying at the edges. The French, the Russians, and the refugees in Europe, terror attacks, protests raging overseas.

Sometimes, being the president wasn't all it was cracked up to be. He'd wanted to heal the world, but the world stubbornly refused to be healed. At best, he was just trying to put Band-Aids over bullet holes and play whack-a-mole with flare-ups around the globe. It was hard to get traction when he felt like all he was doing was playing the world's largest game of Twister.

And at the end of every day, he flopped face-first into bed and did it all over again in the morning.

Another lonely night stretched in front of him. Eating alone, reading a few briefings, and then catching some TV until he fell asleep on the couch. Then he'd stumble to his bedroom, and everything would repeat itself.

But maybe it didn't have to be that way.

He pulled out his phone, opening up Ethan's text messages. Was it selfish, asking Ethan to hang out with him? Ethan spent a lot of time at the White House as it was, between working and their clandestine friendship. Some days, the promise of seeing Ethan later was the goal he trudged forward for. And their texts always made him smile, even when nothing else did.

That's what friends did for each other. What Ethan did for Jack, for sure.

He hoped he was half as good a friend to Ethan as Ethan was to him.

Did Ethan look forward to when they hung out? He swallowed, frowning as dark thoughts edged into his mind. Did Ethan see their time together as another one of his duties? Was this all... just a big show?

No. No, he couldn't think that. Not with the way Ethan had looked when he'd given Jack his cell phone number. Terrified, and hopeful, and possibly constipated, too. Wide-eyed but pushing forward.

I'm beat. I can't do this president thing any more. I need to call it a day before I get punchy and pull a Reagan.

He tapped at his desk and hovered over his phone, waiting for Ethan's response.

[Go home, First Name. You have the best commute of anyone.]

Jack grinned. He loved Ethan's nickname, his own typo turned into a playful jab. Ethan had never once bent on calling him Jack, but this was a good compromise. It felt special, at least.

Or the worst. People have a habit of finding me when I want to hide.

Ethan's text came back almost instantly. *[Playing hide and seek as the president is not advised. We tend to get a little bitchy when that happens.]*

LOL. I bet. Hey, come on up? I feel like banging some balls around and having a few drinks.

He bit his lip. Ethan could have plans. Maybe he had something else to do other than hang around at his office after he was done with a full day of work. He had a life outside the White House, unlike Jack.

[You know, I'm really glad you have a speechwriter, sir. Lemme finish up a few things here. Then I'll slip up the east stairs.]

Jack grinned. *Ha! Jokes! I'll make sure to not push a chair in front of your secret passageway. See you later!*

CHAPTER 13

White House Residence

JACK WAS ALREADY two beers in by the time Ethan headed up. He texted as he headed for his stairwell entrance, and Jack told him to come straight on up to the game room. When he arrived, Jack was taking a pull from his beer, his button-down undone and untucked over his suit pants, showing off his white undershirt. His shirtsleeves were rolled up, and Ethan had to drag his eyes away from the soft skin at his elbows and force himself not to give Jack a long, lingering once-over while Jack waved hello to him.

On the wall, the flat-screen TV blared, talking heads arguing back and forth about the upcoming summit and Russia's posturing.

"*I just think that we're setting ourselves up for a huge catastrophe by inviting the Russians,*" one of the male commentators said, speaking loudly over his female spar. "*There are no, I repeat, no, zero, zilch, requirements for the Russians to change their behaviors!*"

"*Ignoring the Russians and their aggression has done* nothing!" his counterpart argued. "*Ten years we've been ignoring Russian invasions in Eastern Europe. And not just us! Europe, too! Shouldn't we be doing more? Taking a lead in the world and stepping up, engaging the Russians?*"

"*America doesn't negotiate with terrorists or brutal regimes—*"

Ethan grabbed the remote and clicked the TV off. "C'mon. You've heard all that before. You need a break."

Jack nodded, but stayed sitting on the back edge of the sofa. "Yeah. I know. But I can't get it out of my head."

"How can I help?"

"I'm starting to feel like I'm on the edge of World War Three."

"Is it that bad?" Ethan stepped closer, unconsciously trying to comfort Jack.

Jack sighed. "The Russians are saber-rattling again, and the threat of them seizing more territory is real. They're operating on their own in Syria, maybe even helping the SPG, a hack government that's just robbing the country. Add to that the Caliphate, a stateless terror group that's murdering hundreds of people a day and destroying lives across the region. Who nukes who first? The Caliphate, if they get their hands on a nuke? Iran and Russia, taking out the Caliphate and obliterating the Middle East? And Europe…" Jack shook his head.

"Every day, there's another terror threat uncovered on the continent. The refugee resettlement zones are powder kegs with smoldering fuses. Radicals recruit disaffected youth, angry at the shaft they've gotten from life. They didn't come to Europe as terrorists, but being left in the resettlement zones for years and stuck without any future prospects hasn't made them eager to join the European community."

Ethan loomed over Jack, and if he could have, he would have stroked Jack's arms, massaged his neck, his back.

"And now the Chinese are deploying to Iraq?" Jack rubbed one hand over his face, exhaling. "Am I Chamberlain, right before World War Two? Am I just appeasing the aggressor? Am I focused too much on 'peace in our time'?" He swallowed. "I just don't know what the right choice is sometimes."

Jesus. Ethan chewed on his lip, watching Jack's shoulders slump as he took another pull from his beer. "What do you *want* to do?"

"Tell the Russians to fuck off, order troops into Syria to straighten that place out, and bomb the Caliphate into the Stone Age." Jack shook his head. "I hate seeing all the devastation, all the death and the pain, all the time. There's so much hurt over there. People are just trying to live their lives, but they're caught in the middle of this hell." Jack drained the last of his beer in a long swallow. "But where does 'wanting to save the world' fit into 'protecting American interests'?"

"I think American interests are helping the world, sir. And I think that would be a pretty balls-out maneuver, sir. I'd vote for you in a heartbeat if you did that. People are sick of the death and the horror. We've watched and waited for so long, and nothing has changed. Maybe we *should* help out. If we're the world police, as we're always accused of being, then why don't we do some good? Authoritarian regimes and thug states hold power and territory because the world does *nothing*."

"And why don't the Australians, or the Swiss, or the Chinese go ahead and deploy troops on a humanitarian mission? We're not the only ones who can save these people. But if we do nothing, no one else will. And if we do deploy, we're going to lose soldiers over there to save lives that, at the end of the day, *aren't* American." Jack looked down as his fingers picked at the label on his beer bottle. "I know what it's like to be told your soldier isn't coming home."

Fuck it. Ethan reached for Jack's shoulders, squeezing gently. "Mr. President, I believe in you. I know you're going to do the right thing. And, speaking as a former soldier, I think it's time we do something, sir. We'd lose some great people, yes. But, if it's something that's right, and something that you believe in..." He couldn't finish.

"I don't want to start the next World War. Telling the Russians to go fuck themselves won't stop a war. It will likely start one. But they haven't been interested in cooperating for years."

"I know you'll figure it out. If there's *any* president who could get us through this time, it's *you*."

Jack looked up, holding Ethan's gaze. The blue in his eyes burned, like ice turned to flame. He stared, not blinking, searching Ethan for something. Ethan stayed still, not breathing, as his thumbs stroked over Jack's shoulders.

"Thank you," Jack finally said. He smiled, soft and slow. "You don't know how much I really do value you."

Ethan kept his smile tight, trying to hide his disappointment. *You don't know how much I care about you.* "Can I distract you?" he said instead. "How about a game?" He nodded back to the pool table.

"Yes. Definitely. And no more talk about this. I want to hear something different." Jack popped up as Ethan stepped back. He set down his empty beer and grabbed his pool stick. "Pour yourself a drink and tell me stories about you."

Ethan's hands shook as he poured a glass of whiskey, neat, from the dry bar in the back of the room. This wasn't a night for beer. He needed something stronger. "Me? You don't want to hear my stories."

"Yeah I do." Jack lined up at the break and took the opening shot. Balls scattered around the table, and he sank two solids. "Solids again. Come on. Try to distract me while I shoot."

Breathe. Breathe. Ethan's hand clenched around his pool stick. His eyes trailed over Jack's back, down to his ass, and then back up to his face. Jack was concentrating on his shot, and he didn't see Ethan's wandering eyes. "I'm really not that interesting."

Crack. Another solid sunk. Jack waggled his eyebrows at Ethan as he sauntered around the pool table, lining up for his next shot. Now he was facing Ethan, making a shot that had him staring right at Ethan's crotch.

Ethan shifted, trying to hide his half-hard cock.

"You know, you've been spending a lot of time here at the White House. Either working or spending time with me." Another crack, another ball sunk. Jack moved around the table again, this time not looking at Ethan. "I don't want to monopolize your time. You said once you were a loner, but you've got to have some kind of social life. Girlfriend?" He leaned down, his tongue peeking out of his lips as he set up his next shot.

Now or never. Ethan inhaled, exhaled, and then inhaled again. He was dizzy, suddenly light-headed. Was he really about to do this?

"No girlfriend. Not that there would ever be. I'm gay, sir."

Crack. Another clean shot, and a perfect sink of the number four ball. If the revelation surprised Jack, he didn't show it. He leaned back, searching for his next shot. "Cool," he said simply. "No boyfriend, then?"

Jesus Christ. Is he or isn't he? Ethan had opened the door, and if Jack was even remotely interested in him, he should be crashing through like the Kool-Aid man. *If* Jack had been flirting. But he seemed to not care, and while part of Ethan rejoiced that Jack didn't care about his sexuality, another part screamed inside of him, desperate and frustrated and confused and yearning. "No boyfriend." He hesitated, closing his eyes as another solid sank into the pocket. "I met someone who I think I'd like to be with, though."

"Oh yeah?" This shot was harder, and Jack stretched for it. He put a spin on the cue ball, and the seven ball slipped sideways into the side pocket. "What's he like?"

"Brilliant," Ethan said quickly. His eyes burned as he stared at Jack, watching him study the table. Only the eight ball was left, and if Jack sank that, he'd have run the table without Ethan taking a single shot. Jack's head cocked to the side, his eyes narrowed as he studied the angles. "He's perfect. Brilliant, hilarious, confident. I think he can do anything." Ethan swallowed. His eyes traveled Jack's body, slowly. "He's gorgeous, too."

"Wow." Jack flashed him a quick smile, big and warm. "Seems like a catch. And you, Ethan, sound smitten." Jack called the corner pocket with the tip of his pool stick. "Where'd you guys meet? And what are you going to do? Going to ask him out?" Jack turned his head, winking at Ethan. "I suppose I can learn to share you." He turned back to the table and made his shot.

A perfect sink.

Jack stood, smirking.

Ethan smiled back. The moment crystalized in his mind, a perfect moment folded into the depths of his heart. The soft, subdued light of the lounge, the deep wood paneling, the green felt of the pool table, all contrasting with the brilliance of Jack, standing there in a slouch, one hand on his pool stick, his shirt unbuttoned and loose and his hair disheveled.

Jesus Christ, I love this man. I'm in love with him.

"C'mon, Ethan. What are you going to do?"

He was moving before he knew it, padding around the table to Jack's side. Jack watched him, a small smile on his face, his eyes open and relaxed, just waiting for Ethan's answer.

"This," Ethan breathed. He reached for Jack's face with one hand, cupping his jaw. Jack's stubble, barely grown from that morning, scraped against his palm. "*Jack...* I'm going to do this."

Leaning in, Ethan pressed his lips to Jack's. Barely brushing, he parted his lips, his tongue snaking out and slipping across Jack's full lower lip. Ethan moaned, and tried to step closer. His hand slid along Jack's jaw to the back of his neck, his fingers brushing Jack's soft hair.

Jack's hand pressed against Ethan's chest, pushing hard.

Pushing him *away*.

Ethan broke the kiss with a gasp and fell back as Jack stared at him.

Confusion rained from Jack's eyes. He stared at Ethan like Ethan was suddenly different, entirely so, from the man he had trusted only a moment before. Jack tried to speak, his lips tried to form words as Ethan's world crumbled around him.

"Shit," Ethan hissed. "Shit!"

"Ethan..." Jack dropped his pool cue. It clattered to the carpet. "I'm... *Ethan...* I'm sorry... I'm not... I'm *so* sorry..." He shook his head, blinking slowly. His open mouth wavered, seeming to search for something to say.

Trembling, Ethan threw the pool stick onto the table beside him, knocking balls every which way. Fire flooded his body, burning him alive. He was so stupid. So fucking stupid. He knew he shouldn't have done that. Fuck! What was his problem? "No. I'm sorry. I shouldn't have—" His throat closed around his words. His vision blurred. Ethan blinked fast. Damn it, he wasn't going to break down over this. He fucking wasn't.

Jack was still staring, motionless. Ethan chanced a quick glance at him.

And looked away immediately as his heart shattered again,

sucking the air from his chest. That wasn't what he wanted to see on Jack's face. Not ever.

"I gotta go," Ethan growled. "I'm sorry. I'm so fucking sorry."

He took off, racing out of the game room. He didn't even use the secret stairs. He thundered down the grand staircase, blowing past the agents standing post in the Cross Hall. He jogged down to the tunnel, and he didn't stop until he was all alone, buried underground between the Residence and the West Wing.

Collapsing against the wall, Ethan pitched forward, pressing his forehead to the cold concrete.

He was powerless to stop the tears that burned the corners of his eyes. They slipped free, hot trails of shame, of mortification. He couldn't breathe, and he gasped, trying to stop the pain in his choked throat. Roaring, Ethan slammed his fist against the cement, once, twice. *Fuck, fuck!*

Pain rocketed up his arm as his knuckles split, torn skin and blood smearing against the dirty concrete. Shuddering, Ethan sank to his knees, huddled against the wall over his bleeding hand.

Four hours later, Ethan sat at the sky bar at Dulles airport pounding vodka tonics. He had a bag stuffed with suits and cargo pants next to him and a red-eye ticket on a plane to Prague, boarding in half an hour. Maybe it was cowardice to run, but Ethan had to get away. He couldn't face Jack, not now. Not after exposing himself, revealing his love, and being dismissed.

Jack *wasn't* gay, or bi, or anything else. He *wasn't* flirting with Ethan. He *didn't* want him. It had *all* been in Ethan's head.

Exactly as he'd told himself. Exactly what he'd yelled at himself about. This was exactly—*exactly*—what everyone had told him would happen.

Ethan stared at his phone, at his text messages. Not a peep, not a word, from Jack.

He signaled for another drink, keeping his red-rimmed eyes downcast.

Get to Prague. Handle the back end of the summit. Stay away from Jack.

When he got back, he'd request a transfer. He didn't even care where. Send him to Alaska. Or to Utah. Send him anywhere. Just get him away from Jack. Get him away from his heartbreak.

Ethan ran his hand over his face, and when his drink arrived, he downed it in one long drag.

Just numb everything. Make everything go away. Make all the pain disappear.

———

CHAPTER 14

Washington DC

JACK STAYED ROOTED in the game room as Ethan fled. "Ethan, wait!" he tried to call out, but the words stuck in his throat. Frozen in place, he watched Ethan run.

Exhaling, he collapsed in half, bracing himself with his hands on his knees. He stumbled sideways, slumping against the couch. One long slide had him sitting on the carpet, leaning back as he breathed hard and fast.

Hyperventilating, that's what he was doing. He was hyperventilating. *Calm down, Jack. Breathe in and out.* He tipped his head back, trying to focus on the ceiling.

Ethan's suit jacket, tossed over the back of the couch, stole his gaze.

He reached for the black jacket, tugging it down into his lap. It was bigger than his own. Ethan was bigger, stronger, taller, more muscular. He was like a poster boy for the Army, with muscles for days and an all-American cut jaw. He could have anyone—guy or girl —he wanted.

Why the hell had he fallen for Jack?

Ethan's words played on repeat in his mind. *Brilliant. Hilarious.*

Can do anything. Gorgeous. The way Ethan had spoken... He wasn't just smitten. He was head over heels.

For *him*. Ethan was head over heels for *him*.

Jack slammed his head back against the soft couch. His hands gripped Ethan's jacket.

Slowly, he pulled it up to his nose.

Ethan's scent—soap, citrus, and a hint of sweat—teased him. His eyes drifted closed.

A moment later, Jack ripped the jacket from his face. What was he doing? Ethan was his friend. He'd become his closest friend, if Jack was honest with himself. He'd become important to him, deeply important, in a way that had surprised him.

But he wasn't attracted to Ethan. He wasn't gay. He wasn't even looking for a relationship. He never had, not since Leslie's death.

What was he going to do?

———

DAYS BEFORE NATO SUMMIT, RUSSIA TURNS AGGRESSIVE

Days before an unprecedented NATO Emergency Summit, Russia moved troops and tanks to Abkhazeti, a breakaway province of Georgia that aligns itself with the Russian Federation.

The Russians' troop movements suggest a possible invasion of Caliphate-controlled Iraq. Abkhazeti is only 1200 miles from Mosul, a critical city controlled by the Caliphate. Russia has also stated it will "aggressively defend" its interests in Iraq and the Middle East, including its deployed personnel, and will take "all necessary actions to prevent the loss of Russian life."

European leaders expressed nervousness that these latest moves indicate a possible future land grab by the belligerent Russian state.

CHAPTER 15

Prague

ETHAN WOKE at the Aria Hotel in Prague with a blinding headache.

Groaning, he rolled away from the window, burying his face in his pillow. Sunlight streamed through the glass, striking the window box of tulips and daisies, reflecting off the whitewashed castle walls surrounding Ethan's hotel room.

It was quintessentially perfect. The hotel was a renovated minor castle, steps from the more famous, and huge, Prague Castle. The walls of the Aria had been painted a blinding white while red clay tile roofs overlapped the meandering, tiered gothic walls built against the side of a hill in the center of the Little Kings Quarter. Parkland spread out around the former castle gardens, built for royalty centuries before. The Aria had a view of the Little Kings Quarter, Prague castle, the Charles river, and old town. Gothic sculptures dripped from rooftops and garden walks, pointed steeples mixed with medieval reconstructions, and cobbled streets wound through the ancient city, bringing the hustle of people and honking European cars together in the morning frenzy.

Ethan pulled his pillow tighter over his head. Beside the bed, an empty bottle of duty-free whiskey lay on its side, uncapped.

His phone buzzed, clattering on the floor. Ethan lunged, falling out of bed. Groaning, he tried to crawl to his phone. *Maybe it's Jack,* his heart whispered. Maybe, maybe.

It was Welby.

Ethan had made him leader of the advance team after moving him out of the temporary lead detail position. He hung his head for a moment, but flopped onto his back, kicking away the sheet that had tangled around his legs as he fell off the bed. "What?" he growled as he answered.

"Sir, we're ready to start POTUS's movement rehearsal."

Shit. Ethan struggled to sit up. The sunlight blinded him, and he flopped back down. "What time is it?"

"Zero nine thirty, sir. You said you wanted to start right on time."

"Yeah, yeah." Rubbing his eyes, Ethan rolled over and pushed himself up to his knees. The room swam, and he held his breath as he struggled to keep his stomach down. "Look, I'm running a bit late. Get the team started now. I'll catch up with you. I'll be down in a few minutes. Leave an agent with a car."

"Yes, sir." Welby hung up.

Exhaling, Ethan sagged back on his heels. He peeled open his eyes, wincing against the sunlight.

He glared at the phone in his hand. No texts. No texts last night, no texts when he landed, and no texts this morning. Jack was ignoring him.

Fuck! Ethan hurled his phone across the hotel room. It bounced off the wall and fell, plastic cracking as it impacted. Swallowing, Ethan fell forward, burying his forehead against the carpet.

He flexed his right hand. His knuckles were still swollen and bruised. He'd washed the dried blood off at his condo before heading for Dulles, and he could move all of his fingers. Nothing was broken. But it hurt like a bitch.

His heart hurt worse, though.

Ethan pulled himself to his feet and headed for the bathroom. Just a few more days. He'd be through with this and could request a transfer. He could get away, far away. Just a few more days.

CHAPTER 16

Washington DC

JACK BLINKED, staring at his notepad. He was doodling, trying to draw a perfect triangle. The angles weren't right, and he'd already tried a dozen times before. Voices echoed around him, but they sounded far away, as if underwater. His brain wouldn't work, wouldn't think. He blinked again.

"Sir? Mr. President?" Jeff nudged him. "Are you okay?"

Starting, Jack dropped his pen. "I'm fine," he lied. He straightened, adjusting his jacket, and stared across the table at his Cabinet. "I'm sorry, what were you saying?"

Lewis Parr, the secretary of defense, shared a long look with the secretary of homeland security. "Mr. President, you are supposed to fly to the NATO summit tomorrow afternoon, and the Russians have put troops and missiles less than a thousand miles from Prague in their occupied lands in Romania. This is a direct threat, sir. We have to respond."

"They're also moving heavy lift aircraft into the Abkhazeti region of Georgia. We think there's a chance they're going to invade Iraq while the summit is going on." Jeff leaned forward, glancing sideways at Jack. "France has been saying 'I told you so' to every news outlet that will listen. The Germans and the British are keeping quiet, sir. They're waiting for our response."

"And what is our response?" Jack stared at his Cabinet, assembled around the table.

Silence.

Ethan's face flashed behind his eyelids as he blinked. Jack inhaled deeply, keeping his eyes closed.

"We can deploy troops to our bases in Europe. We can have two divisions mobilized in twenty-four hours." Lewis leaned forward, his hands clasped on the table.

Jack's eyes opened to slits. "And turn an already tense situation into a hair-trigger Mexican standoff?"

"Mr. President, we can pull out of the NATO summit," secretary of state Elizabeth Wall said. "We don't look great, but we save face. We're not meeting a belligerent aggressor while it's actively building up troops in Europe and the Middle East."

"That will defeat the entire purpose of the summit, Elizabeth."

"Hasn't it already been defeated, sir?"

Jack grabbed his pen, drawing another triangle. *What do you want to do?* Ethan's voice rolled through him, replaying their conversation. He wanted to close his eyes and go back to that memory. *Ethan, why do you have so much faith in me?*

What was the right call? Match the Russians? Aggression for aggression? America's tried and true response to the Russians for the past hundred years?

Or, something different?

"As much as I truly want to tell the Russians to go screw themselves, we can't just keep ignoring this and hope it all goes away. That hasn't worked for decades." Jack peered around the table, looking his Cabinet in the eyes. This wouldn't be popular. "No. We will go to the summit. And, I'll meet with the Russian president. Try to defuse this mess before we're all in the middle of World War Three. We have to try the diplomatic route before we send Europe back to a World War."

"Sir—"

"I've made my decision. I want intelligence on the Russian president, and everything we have on the Russian political environment. If he's got troubles with the teachers' unions, I want to know. If his uncle hasn't paid the electric bill, I want to know. I want to know everything we've got before I leave." He glanced around the table again. "Send your concerns to Jeff. I'll review them and get back to you."

Standing, Jack flipped his padfolio closed and headed out. The rest of the Cabinet stood and silently waited for him to leave.

Had he just condemned Europe to another invasion? His fingers clenched around his padfolio.

Jeff followed him into Mrs. Martin's office. "Mr. President?"

Jack paused but didn't turn around.

"You all right, sir?" Jeff stepped close, speaking into his ear. His chest brushed Jack's arm.

Jack shivered. His eyes closed. "I'm tired, Jeff," he croaked, lying. "Just tired."

Jeff squeezed Jack's shoulder. "Take a break. You need to stay rested." He squeezed once more and then stepped away. "If you need anything, let me know."

"Thanks." Jack nodded, not looking at his chief of staff. He breezed past his secretary and into the Oval Office, shutting the door behind him.

Alone. Finally alone.

Leaning back, Jack closed his eyes as he sank to the floor. What was wrong with him? He couldn't focus. He couldn't think straight. There were a million things he should be thinking about, and none of them had anything to do with his love life. He was balanced on the precipice of a conflict that could tear the Western World apart, and yet... He was lost in his memories, replaying every moment he'd ever shared with Ethan. Their bullshitting. Watching the games. Getting surprised with burgers. Surprising Ethan in return.

Exhaling, Jack thunked his head against the back of the door. *Ethan...*

Every memory was shaded now, colored with the knowledge that Ethan wanted him. Was Ethan trying to seduce Jack?

No, he couldn't think that. The utterly devastated crush to Ethan's face when he'd pushed him away hadn't just been about a failed seduction. When he pushed Ethan away, it looked as if he'd ripped Ethan's heart out.

His mind betrayed him, bringing up a memory he wanted to forget. Instead of bringing down Ethan's jacket to give back, like he'd done every other time, he'd kept it. He didn't know why, but he had. He hung it up in his closet, tucked among his other suits so the stewards wouldn't take it away to be dry cleaned with his laundry. Why was he keeping it? Why had he smelled it again as he hung it up?

He wasn't gay. He wasn't attracted to men. Hell, he hadn't been attracted to anyone since Leslie's death. He'd been a monk, a celibate warrior-politician dedicated to public service. Women had been attracted to him before, had asked him out. He'd had no trouble turning them down. He hadn't thought twice, and it hadn't ever bothered him. Not like this.

So why was this so hurtful? Why did it feel like he'd ripped his own heart out, alongside Ethan's? Why did he have this aching, excruciating hole in his chest?

Was he angry? No, he wasn't angry at Ethan. Scared? No, that was stupid. He had nothing to be scared of. He had no reason to be afraid. One man's affection didn't scare him. Ethan was his friend. Ethan was... important. So very important.

Swallowing, Jack let his eyes slide open. He stared unseeing across his office, watching memories play in his mind. Ethan, leaning in for his kiss. The feel of his hand, warm, gentle, cupping his jaw. His dry lips caressing Jack's. The slide of Ethan's tongue.

Gasping, Jack leaned forward, his head between his knees as he tried to catch his breath. Damn it, what was wrong with him?

Knocking on the door behind him jolted through his body. "Mr. President?"

Jack scrambled to his feet, straightening his suit jacket and running his hands through his hair. "Yes?" He hoped he didn't sound as desperately nervous as he felt.

Mrs. Martin poked her head through the door. Agent Daniels was behind her. "Mr. President, time to head to the Roosevelt Room. Your next appointment is ready."

"My next appointment?" His mind was blank. He kept glancing at Daniels. *Where is Ethan?*

"You have a speech-preparation session with your team, sir." His secretary frowned at him. "Are you feeling all right, Mr. President? You look pale."

"I'm fine." Jack reached for his padfolio, still on the floor. "Thanks for asking." He tried to smile.

His smile faded as he turned to Agent Daniels. "Shall we?"

Agent Daniels nodded. His eyes lingered on Jack as he passed him by, but he remained silent.

Jack's shoulders slumped. It should be Ethan walking with him. They'd be talking, heads leaned in close. He'd ask him for his opinions on the summit, on the Russians. If there was one voice he wanted to hear, one man's advice that he wanted, it was Ethan's.

Jack hesitated at the door to the Roosevelt Room. Sorrow tugged at the base of his heart. What had happened? Why had everything gone so strange? Where would they go from here?

He wanted his friend back.

THE SPEECH-PREPARATION MEETING WENT LONG. Jack wasn't fully in the meeting, and everyone else knew it. How could they not, when they were trying to regain his attention every other question? Jack canceled the rest of his afternoon and stayed in with his speechwriters. He was going to get this done. The world's security might depend on it.

Which only made him feel like more of an asshole. They were hovering on the precipice of an all-out confrontation with Russia, and by extension, an explosion in the Middle East, and he was distracted by his own personal problems. Was distracted by a single kiss.

Damn it, why had Ethan kissed him? It wasn't like he didn't have enough to worry about. No, that wasn't fair. Ethan had kissed him because he wanted to. Because of how he felt. And, by God, how he felt. The way he'd described what he saw in Jack...

Enough. He was going around in circles.

Jack paced in the empty Roosevelt Room, ostensibly reviewing the prepared remarks the team had pulled together that afternoon. He'd already sent away two stewards asking about his dinner plans. He wasn't hungry. He'd barely managed to finish a piece of toast that morning. He kept thinking about the burgers he'd shared with Ethan. Ethan had done that, had gone and grabbed burgers for the two of them because he cared about Jack. Because he wanted to make him happy.

And he'd been very happy.

Had that been a date?

Groaning, Jack leaned against one of the conference table chairs and glared up at the ceiling. Why was this affecting him so much? One kiss, one man's attraction. In the grand scheme of things, it wasn't a big deal.

But it is. You miss Ethan. You haven't had a friend like that in years. You know it's true.

Yes, he'd been focused on his career. He'd been driven, first by Leslie's death and then by his drive to change and improve the system. Friendships in politics were tokens, people who could do favors and who could call on him in exchange. The few people he'd had in his life who were grounded, normal, and balanced had been on the periphery. His running mates. Workout buddies. But he'd never befriended them. Never sought them out, gotten to know them, spent time with them. Relied on them.

Why had he done so with Ethan? Why had Ethan become what he had: the most meaningful person in his life he'd had in years? Was it his dedication? His humanity? That open, warm heart on his sleeve... the one Jack had destroyed? The way he looked at Jack and made him feel like he really could do anything? Like he really could save the world?

"Ethan," Jack whispered. "Why me? I'm not special enough for you."

The turning doorknob made Jack jump. He stared, guilty, at the entrance, trying for smooth.

Agent Daniels raised both his eyebrows when he saw Jack. So much for smooth.

"Mr. President," Daniels began. "I'm getting off shift soon. Agent Keifer is taking over. He'll be outside if you need anything."

Jack nodded. His tongue seemed to be glued to the roof of his mouth. "Agent Daniels," he finally called out as Daniels was leaving.

Daniels turned. "Sir?"

"I... haven't seen Agent Reichenbach today. Is... is he all right?"

Secret Service agents were trained to be blank, were trained to have impeccable poker faces. But still, Jack saw Daniels blanch and his eyes tighten at the corners. Daniels shifted, his hands clasped behind his back, and raised his chin. "Agent Reichenbach took a red-eye to Prague last night, sir. He joined the advance team over there. I... thought you knew that."

Jack pressed his lips together, holding in a scream. He shook his head.

"I apologize, sir." A beat. Daniels stared at him, pinning him back with his eyes. "Is there something I can do for you, Mr. President?"

Mute, Jack shook his head again. "No," he finally said, just barely above a whisper. "No. I'll see you tomorrow on Air Force One. Goodnight."

Daniels nodded, took the hint, and left.

HIS PACING DIDN'T STOP in the Roosevelt Room. Jack finally headed for the Residence after nine PM. He avoided the third floor, and his study, and the gym, and the East Sitting Hall, all places he'd spent time with Ethan. He stared at the inside of his fridge for five minutes before shutting the doors. He wasn't hungry.

Pacing the Center Hall lasted until midnight. Russia, the summit, the Caliphate, China's deployment, Russia's deployment, and Ethan —always, always Ethan—rolled around in his brain. What should he do? What was the right course?

Jack flopped into bed after one in the morning. He tossed and turned. Stared at the ceiling. Stared at his clock.

Finally, Jack padded into the closet. There, hidden among his suits, was Ethan's jacket.

He gazed at it for a minute, warily, as if it would attack him. Swallowing, he reached out and tugged it off the hanger.

The hanger clattered to the floor, but he ignored it, pulling Ethan's jacket close to his chest, his face. Inhaling, Jack closed his eyes. Another inhale, shorter, almost a gasp, and he buried his face in Ethan's jacket.

Collapsing, Jack hugged Ethan's jacket close, suddenly screaming, angry, rage-filled screams, and then, suddenly sobbing, heaving, chest-aching, heart-wracking sobs. He smothered his face in the fabric as he lay on the closet floor, huddled in a ball. Ethan's jacket caught his tears, soaking beneath his face, and Ethan's scent lulled Jack, carrying him to sleep as his sobs slowly subsided.

HE WOKE COMING in his boxers.

Jack groaned, grinding his hips against the carpet, more than half-asleep. Wet come squished around his balls, soaking his boxers.

He bolted upright, eyes wide, and stared down at his crotch.

He backed away, trying to escape his own come, brushing at his boxers and the stain beneath him on the carpet. *No, no!*

This couldn't have happened. He couldn't have just come in his boxers like a teenager. And—*shit!* Come on the White House carpet wasn't the legacy he wanted to leave behind. Jack ripped off his shirt and rubbed at the stain, furiously trying to soak it up. The stench of sex hit him full in the face.

Jack fell back on his ass, leaning against his suit pants hanging on the bottom rung in the closet. What the hell had happened? He hadn't come in... had it been years? After Leslie, his sex drive had died. He'd masturbated a few times after a few years, and then a bit more as time went on, but he couldn't actually remember the last time he'd touched himself. What did that say about him? He was basically sexless. Practically a robot. He certainly felt like one.

His dreams, fragmented, flashed in his mind.

He'd been dreaming of Leslie, of his wife. Her smile, the way she laughed when they first met. How his heart had beat faster, every time he saw her. The first time they made love, sliding over her body, kissing his way down her neck.

He'd nuzzled warm skin, and his hands had stroked down a thigh.

A strong, hairy thigh, flexing powerfully beneath his touch.

He'd kept kissing down the warm neck, across the quivering Adam's apple, and down to a broad, hairy chest. Muscled, and heaving beneath his touch. Beneath his lips. A deep voice, breathing his name, reverent and pleading.

Ethan. He'd been dreaming about Ethan.

He flushed, suddenly burning up. Embarrassment flooded him, followed by shock. He'd been dreaming about Ethan. Flashes of memories flooded Jack: Ethan protecting him, shielding him from crowds and unseen danger. Ethan running beside him at Camp David. Ethan's smile and his laugh.

Ethan's lips, kissing him.

Jack exhaled, shaking. His dream memories grabbed him, replaying the feel of Ethan beneath his hands.

What would have happened if Ethan had turned him against the pool table and kissed him deeper?

What if he had grabbed Ethan and kissed him back?

What the hell was wrong with him? He wasn't gay. He wasn't attracted to men.

But he'd just come, dreaming about Ethan.

He was ridiculous. Jack hauled himself up, shucking his ruined undershirt over the stain. Ethan's jacket lay in a crumpled mess on the floor. He stared at it. Come had smeared on one corner. Tears stained the collar.

Jack grabbed the jacket and balled it up. He wanted to throw it away. He wanted to bury his face in it again. He wanted to rip it to pieces. He wanted to put it on and wrap Ethan around him.

Instead, he headed back to the bedroom. The clock showed four AM. He wouldn't be getting any more sleep tonight.

Suitcases lay open on the loveseat at the foot of his bed. The stewards had packed for him yesterday, but they left the personals for Jack to finish. In a few hours, he'd be heading on Marine One to Andrews Air Force Base, and then to Prague.

Jack stuffed Ethan's jacket into one of the shoe pockets in his suitcase. Even to himself, he had no explanation for doing this.

Slowly, Jack padded backward out of the bedroom, never taking his eyes off his suitcase. When he backed into the door, the knob jabbing him in his kidneys, he bolted outside, slamming it shut behind him. His heart was pounding, beating a bass rhythm that drowned everything else out, and he couldn't hear, couldn't see, could barely stand. Finally, he managed to catch his breath, slowly, in and out.

Sticky with come-soaked boxers, Jack slid down the door and buried his face in his hands.

CHAPTER 17

Prague

"KNIGHT ONE TO CASTLE KEEP. Vigilant on the move. Leaving airport and headed for Castle."

Ethan keyed the radio in the command post at the Aria Hotel. "Castle Keep to Knight One. Acknowledge movement. Route is clear and ETA is twenty-four minutes. Drawbridge will be down when you arrive."

"Roger Castle Keep. Knight One out."

Daniels's voice clicked off the radio. On screen, the presidential motorcade, a red dot on the map of Prague blown up on a wall-sized projection, moved from the airport to the Czech R7, heading south toward the city. Daniels was Jack's driver, in the presidential SUV. Scott was running as point man in Ethan's place while Ethan headed up the command post, Castle Keep, at the hotel. Knight was the code-name for the agents moving with Jack.

Vigilant was Jack.

Ethan clenched his cup so hard the paper crumpled. Black coffee spilled over the side, hitting the back of his hand. He shook it off, wiping cold coffee on his cargo pants.

His head still ached, two full days after downing that bottle of whiskey. He'd picked it up on a layover in Frankfurt, and he'd downed the entire bottle overnight between Frankfurt and Prague, and in the cab to the Aria. An eminently stupid move, but one he'd welcomed at the time. He'd just needed to not feel anything, just for a few hours.

Now, he felt nothing but pain. And not just the headache and the sore liver, either. Jack had landed in Prague, and that had ripped open the wounds on his heart, all over again.

He had no one to blame but himself.

"The president has thirty-five minutes at the hotel before he has to depart for Prague Castle." There was a reception for the heads of state in Vladislav Hall in the Czech president's castle that evening. "ETA to Prague Castle is ten minutes." Welby stood next to Ethan, waiting.

"Just enough time for President Spiers to unpack." Ethan could picture it. What would Jack's face look like when he walked into his suite? He was at the top of the castle-turned-hotel with a breath-taking view over the city. Prague Castle glittered from the balcony off his bedroom. Opulent didn't even begin to describe the space. European decadence dripped from the walls, with medieval sconces, gothic sculptures, and original Renaissance artwork. He'd swept Jack's room himself, the final inspection.

He just wished he could see Jack's smile when he saw it.

Welby peered at Ethan. "Would you like to brief the president when he arrives, sir?"

Even though Welby was the advance team lead, since Ethan had arrived, he was the ranking agent. It would make sense for him to brief Jack on the security procedures for the summit.

"No. No, you go ahead and take care of it." Ethan's stomach clenched. He didn't want to face Jack. Not now. Not ever.

Ethan watched Jack's red dot draw closer.

THIRTY-FIVE MINUTES WAS enough time for Jack's aides to haul all their luggage into the hotel and for the whirlwind hurricane that was Jack's support team to descend upon him. Rolling suitcases thundered down the hall as doors slammed, and aides and advisors congregated in the halls, sharing the Wi-Fi password and reading emails to each other. Ethan stayed in the command post, one floor below Jack's suite.

He couldn't help it. He listened in on the open mic while Welby briefed Jack.

Jack sounded exhausted, which was just another thing for Ethan to be pissed off at himself about. Undoubtedly, that was his fault. He'd heaped another problem on Jack's shoulders in the midst of an international crisis. He just needed to stay away, keep his distance, and Jack would realize he wasn't a threat. He wasn't going to harass him again. Or try to kiss him.

Assault & battery, his mind whispered. *Touching without consent.* Unwanted *touching without consent.*

Jack answered Welby's questions with one-word answers and grunts, acknowledging the security plan, their timeline, and the emergency procedures should the worst happen.

"*We depart in...*" Ethan listened in, imagining Welby checking his watch. "*Ten minutes, Mr. President. We'll knock on your door when it's time.*"

Jack grunted, and Ethan heard Welby excuse himself.

"*Agent Welby?*"

"*Yes, Mr. President?*"

Ethan pressed the headset to his ear. Jack's voice made his bones ache, but he wanted to hear just a little bit more.

"*Is Agent Reichenbach here?*"

Ethan froze.

"*Yes, sir. Would you like me to get him for you?*"

"*No!*" Jack practically snapped at Welby.

Ethan's blood turned to ice.

"*No,*" Jack continued. "*I just wanted to check. No need to bother him.*"

"Yes, sir." Welby excused himself again, and Ethan heard the door open and close before he ripped his earpiece out and leaned forward, desperately trying not to lose it entirely in front of everyone.

God, what had he done?

———

CHAPTER 18

Prague

Vladislav Hall in Prague Castle was everything a gothic medieval banquet hall should be.

Jack's wide eyes soared over the vaulted ceilings and the exposed wooden beams honeycombing the cathedral-like space. Gold-toned paint covered the stone-hewn walls. Five handcrafted bronze chandeliers hung on thick iron chains. Fading sunlight and flickering candlelight glittered in the warbled panes of the arched windows along the far wall. The windows were the oldest surviving pieces of Renaissance architecture in the world, outside of Italy.

NATO's leadership moved in the hall, soft chatter and the tinkling of crystal echoing with the sounds of delicate forks and bone china. Sausage, duck, and rabbit sizzled on tabletop spits, surrounded by artfully arranged hors d'oeuvres and stacks of embroidered linen napkins. Waiters moved among the presidents, prime ministers, and chancellors, carrying trays of wine, beer, and champagne.

"Here goes nothing," Jack murmured. On his right and his left, Agents Collard and Daniels flanked his every move. Secretary Elizabeth Wall was behind him, with her own Secret Service detail, and behind the both of them, Jeff and his team brought up the rear.

Jack's entrance was announced to the hall, and most of the heads of state applauded politely.

Noticeably silent was the Russian president, slowly eating a skewer of seared rabbit. He stared at Jack, smiling slowly.

It wasn't a friendly smile.

Jack headed right for him. "President Puchkov," he said, extending his hand. "I am so glad you were able to make it."

The Russian president, Sergey Puchkov, stared at his outstretched hand.

The sounds of chatter in the hall faded.

"Mr. President," Puchkov rumbled. Tall and lanky, the Russian president overshadowed Jack's almost-six-foot height. His long arm reached out, one cold hand clasping Jack's. "I did not think *you* would make it."

"It takes more than your troops going for a walk to keep me from attending." Jack pumped Puchkov's hand once more before letting go. "America's commitment to our NATO allies is absolute."

Puchkov grinned. He set his rabbit skewer on a passing waiter's tray and grabbed two flutes of champagne. "A toast, Mr. President." He passed one of the glasses to Jack. "To our mutual military maneuvers!" Puchkov sipped his champagne, his dark, laughing eyes watching Jack like a hawk. "You feign surprise?"

Jack blinked. He didn't take a drink. "What am I supposed to be drinking to, again?"

"Your military has also taken a bit of a walk. A division, I believe, mobilizing to your Hoenfels Training Center, yes?"

Fury unfurled within Jack, one slow tendril at a time. He hadn't ordered that. He'd explicitly ordered *not* to move those troops. Not that he could reveal that to Puchkov. "I'm sure you understand."

Puchkov chuckled under his breath. He finished his champagne. "We will have so much to discuss here, Mr. President. The world hangs in the balance, no? I am looking forward to it." A quick nod, and then the Russian president walked away.

"Mother fucker," Jack hissed. He trembled, seething, practically seeing red.

"Mr. President?" Collard was at his elbow instantly.

It should be Ethan.

"We're leaving," Jack grunted. "Let's go."

HOLLERING at the secretary of defense in the backseat of his SUV wasn't how Jack wanted his first evening in Prague to end. Lewis said he didn't know what had happened but took responsibility for the troop movement nonetheless.

"This isn't the message I wanted to send to the Russians, Lewis!" Jack shouted into the phone. "I wanted to start this summit from a spirit of cooperation!"

"I understand, Mr. President. I didn't issue these orders. But I take full responsibility for this mistake, and I will find out how this happened, sir."

"Do that. And put our European forces on lockdown. I need to cool this situation down, immediately."

"Yes, sir."

Jack sighed. "Help me, Lewis. I don't need to fight the Russians and my own people. We need to get through this together. Got it?"

"Yes, sir. I understand."

"Please let me know when you have information for me on what happened here." Jack hung up after Lewis agreed. He pitched forward, resting his phone against his forehead.

What would Ethan say? If he were in the car, could they have talked about this? Or at least texted, from the backseat to the front seat? He glanced forward, watching the silent forms of Agents Daniels and Collard. They were Ethan's teammates. His closest coworkers. His friends.

Had they known? No. Ethan had wanted to keep their friendship a secret from everyone. They couldn't know.

Did they know about Ethan's feelings for him?

Jack swiped his phone's screen and pulled up his text messages. Ethan's texts were still right on top, the last messages they had exchanged from three days ago. Was it only three days? His thumb hovered over the keyboard.

What on earth would he even say?

I'm sorry? I'm not worth your affections? I'm having wet dreams about you, and it's the first time I've come in I can't remember how long? I don't know what that means... but I can't get you out of my mind?

Jack powered down his phone's screen.

———

MOST OF THE presidential travel team was exhausted and had already turned in by the time Jack got back. He spent almost two hours with Jeff in his suite, going over the talking points and his speech for the next day, and making adjustments now that they were on the defensive. Jack kicked Jeff out when he caught his chief of staff smothering his third yawn.

He should be exhausted. He hadn't slept much the night before, but he was running on some crazed mixture of apprehension and adrenaline. Tomorrow was it. He'd face Puchkov, stop this aggression... or fail.

Jack paced, long yards back and forth across his suite. It really was a fabulous room. What would Ethan have thought of it? Would he have fiddled with the sconces? Thrown a pose with Jack, poking fun at the medieval paintings?

God, he was lonely. So achingly lonely.

Before he knew what he was doing, he grabbed his phone and dialed the Secret Service command post.

An agent he didn't recognize by voice picked up. *"CP, Agent Torres."*

"Agent Torres, can you please send Agent Reichenbach to my suite?"

"Agent Reichenbach? Uh, yes, sir, Mr. President. Right away."

"Thank you." Jack hung up the phone, dropping it into the cradle with a quiet, controlled click.

What on earth was he doing?

CHAPTER 19

Prague

ETHAN CLOSED his eyes outside Jack's hotel room door. He'd been summoned, officially summoned. Shit, it was all going to come out in the next few minutes. Censure, Jack's anger, his dismissal. He would have preferred to not have done this over an open net, but maybe that was what he deserved. He would bear his shame, and his mistakes.

He knocked twice. The door clicked open beneath his touch.

"It's open," Jack called from inside.

Inhaling deeply, Ethan steeled himself one last time before pushing into Jack's suite.

Jack stood in the center, his jacket off, shirtsleeves rolled up, tie undone, and hair disheveled. His reading glasses were perched on top of his head, slightly askew, and his hands tangled together in front of him.

He looked perfect. Ethan's heart ached.

Straightening, Ethan clasped his hands behind his back and cleared his throat. "Mr. President."

Jack opened his mouth. Closed it. His fingers twisted.

He held Ethan's gaze, his bright blue eyes staring at Ethan. One breath became two, became five.

Ethan licked his lips.

Jack started, turning away. He swayed, leaning against a side table and bracing himself with one hand.

"Mr. President?" Ethan stepped forward but hesitated. "Are you all right?"

"I need to get out of here," Jack finally said. He turned burning eyes toward Ethan. Urgent desperation shone in his gaze. "Please, Ethan. I need to get out. Just for a little bit."

He blinked. "Out where, sir?"

Jack swallowed. He threw his hand out toward the window and the Little Kings Quarter. "Just... out, maybe around the block? Grab a drink somewhere?"

"You can have a drink here, sir—"

"No, it's not the booze. I'm... I'm suffocating in here, Ethan. I need to get out. Walk around." Jack pressed his lips together. "Please. Please help me get out, just for a little bit."

Ethan closed his eyes. The suggestion was ridiculous. But did he have the power to turn Jack down, after everything?

"Did you call me because you knew I'd have to help you?" he whispered.

Jack looked away. "I—"

"I'll do it," Ethan interrupted. He didn't want to hear that answer. "I'll do it, but we do it *my* way. I'll get some agents. We'll run a dot formation. We never leave your side." Ethan fixed Jack with a hard glare. "Understand, Mr. President?"

"Yes."

"Do you have anything casual?"

Jack rummaged in his suitcase, flipping through sweat pants and shorts before pulling out a pair of jeans and pullover sweatshirt with a hood. Ethan spotted a clump of black fabric sticking out of the corner of Jack's suitcase.

"Put those on. I'll be back with a few more things to dress down in." He headed out. "I'll be back with the agents in ten minutes, Mr. President."

"Ethan—"

Ethan stopped, but didn't turn around.

"Thanks," Jack said under his breath.

He left the suite without a word, not looking back.

In the hallway, Ethan pulled up his radio, speaking into the mic clipped to the inside of his suit jacket sleeve. "I need a full detail dressed in plain clothes for close surveillance, and I need Agents Collard and Daniels dressed down in civvies and armed in the command post in five minutes."

Screw the dot formation. He'd never leave Jack unprotected. Even if Jack hated the thought, he was getting a full detail. "Vigilant is going on a walk."

CHAPTER 20

Prague

THE LITTLE KINGS Quarter boasted a bevy of bars and restaurants, most of them open to the wee hours of the morning. Ethan, Daniels, and Scott ferried Jack out of the Hotel Aria through the back entrance and then snaked him down around the walls and onto the cobbled streets. The rest of the detail was out of Jack's sight, already in place on the route ahead, in their SUVs and walking unnoticed in front of Jack.

Jack tugged the beanie Ethan had given him farther down his head. He'd traded his suit for a hoodie, and with the beanie, he looked every bit the part of a European barfly. Ethan, Daniels, and Scott rounded out the façade with their casual pants and long-sleeved sweaters.

The night was cool, cooler than in Washington, and the air was crisp. Ancient battlements and stone walls rose about them, along with castle spires and medieval towers. Prague Castle loomed, glowing at night and seemingly floating above them. Cobbled streets twisted and turned beneath their feet, ancient walkways through the timeless city.

Looking sideways, Ethan saw Jack smile and his shoulders uncoil as they headed up the street. His own heart unclenched just the slightest. If Jack needed this, he'd be there for him.

Ethan had stationed agents in every one of the bars along their route and had three teams shadowing their movements. When Jack suggested, on his whim, ducking into the third bar on the right, Ethan played along, pretending that it was an off-the-cuff decision, and that he didn't have the place already fully secured. He'd ordered his, Daniels, and Scott's mics left open. Everyone on the detail, and all of the teams shadowing them and stationed in the bars, would be able to hear every word.

"The *U Maleho Glena*?" Ethan spoke the name of the bar aloud, alerting the agents inside. "Sure, Mr. President." Ethan gave the bar a once over, counting windows and doors and exits as he headed up the steps. Jack followed between him and Daniels, with Scott bringing up the rear.

He entered first, stepping through the threshold and holding out his hand, stalling Jack as he did a quick check of the inside. Four agents sat in the bar, strategically placed, and they each met his gaze casually before looking away. More signaled that they were on the way in his earpiece. Ethan spotted another four agents set up across the street, leaning against the antique gaslight and pretending to pal around.

The bar was actually a jazz club, crowded but not overpacked. Dreadlocked musicians wailed on saxophones and drummed out a slow, swaying beat, and a voluptuous brunette wrapped in red silk belted out a tragic song. Ethan couldn't understand the words, but the sound of her voice stole into his soul, cupping the fractures of his broken heart. He wanted to stay and listen forever. He wanted to run away and never return.

Instead, Ethan led Jack to an empty space at the bar. He stood between Jack and the rest of the club as Daniels took up the other side, between Jack and the wall. Rough stone lined the club, and the dark walnut bar top gleamed. Behind the bartenders, underlit glass shelves showcased the liquor selections. Ethan eyed the bottles. This was a high-class place.

Jack leaned back and watched the jazz band, tapping his toe in time with the beat. Ethan had stolen a pair of Converse from one of the tech agents in the command post, and Jack currently sported a pair of high-top Chucks with frayed laces. It fit, in a nerdy way, and Ethan had tried hard not to smile when Jack looked at him for approval.

The bartender arrived, and Ethan ordered for Jack. He didn't think twice about it, asking for a local beer that was dark and rich, more of a lager than a pilsner, roasted and heavy and not too hoppy. He'd drunk with Jack enough to know his taste in beer.

Daniels, apparently, thought it was strange. He stared at Ethan as the bartender moved off, mouthing "what the fuck?" to him with a frown.

Ethan ignored him.

No drinks for him, or for Daniels or Scott. Or the rest of the agents on the team. They had better all be nursing water or soda.

When Jack's beer arrived, Ethan turned and leaned up against Jack's side. He passed it off wordlessly, trying to be quick, but Jack turned and beamed at him, warm and friendly. It stole Ethan's breath, and he clenched his jaw and gnashed his teeth, trying to stop a sudden sob from tearing free of his soul. The sultry brunette crooned a lingering last note, seemingly for Ethan's tortured heart alone.

He turned away from Jack and leaned against the bar.

Daniels stared at him. Ethan could feel Scott's eyes boring into his back. Fuck. He was so fucked.

"*Omluvte...*" Behind Ethan, a petite blonde was trying to reach the bar. She spoke again, in Czech, and squeezed between Jack and Ethan. "*Omluvte, prominte.*"

Frowning, Ethan tried to push her out. "Hey. Please, back away."

"Oh, excuse me," she said, switching to accented English. Jack moved aside, giving her more room at the bar.

Ethan glared at him over the woman's head. Damn it, they weren't supposed to let anyone near.

"Excuse me," she said again, smiling apologetically at Ethan and Jack. "I just need to order."

"No problem!" Jack grinned and turned with her, facing the bar. "What are you drinking?"

Oh God. No, for fuck's sake, no. Ethan's glare turned murderous, and Daniels and Scott both stood at the ready. They looked to Ethan, waiting for direction.

Ethan waited, too. Jack wasn't actually going to flirt with this woman... was he?

She giggled again. She was tipsy, just shy of being drunk. "I drink whiskey," she said, looking Jack up and down, slowly. "American whiskey."

"American whiskey?" Jack laughed.

"It's strong and cheap. Like Americans." She winked up at Jack as one hand poked him in the chest. "You are American."

"Maybe."

"You look familiar..." Now she was peering at Jack, trying to read his face.

"All right, that's enough." Ethan pushed his way between Jack and her. Jack stepped back, almost colliding into Daniels, but made room for Ethan's sudden entrance.

She stared at Ethan, wide-eyed, before her expression soured. "Excuse me," she snapped. "You are very rude."

Suddenly, Jack was back, leaning against Ethan's side and taking a pull from his bottle of beer. "Sorry, ma'am," he said, in his best cowboy twang. "This is my boyfriend, and he doesn't like to share."

All the air seemed to get sucked out of the universe. Ethan's head swam, colors blurring and blending, and dimly he registered the sound of glass dropping and breaking. The woman's shocked face morphed, turning to happy laughter, and she apologized over and over as she waited for her drink. Jack waved her off, still glued to Ethan's side. The warmth of his body turned searing, and Ethan jerked away, trying to escape.

Jack stumbled. Scott grabbed him, steadying him.

Everyone stared at Ethan.

Scott and Daniels had murder in their eyes.

Jack's gaze hurt the most. Confusion warred with fear, an anxious, deep fear buried in his fractured blue eyes.

Fear of *him*. God, fear of him.

Ethan turned his head and pulled up his sweater sleeve, speaking into the mic. "Quarterback is rotating out. I need an agent inside at the bar, *now*." Fury raged within him, roaring through his veins. He couldn't see right, couldn't hear right. There was broken glass beneath his feet—Daniels's water glass—and he kept stepping on the ice cubes. Ethan kicked the glass and the ice against the wall, shattering the last big chunks into dust.

Frowning, Jack's mouth dropped open. "What? There are others here?"

One of the agents in the corner booth stood and headed their way as another two from across the street started up the bar's steps outside.

"*Yes*," Ethan hissed, whirling to face Jack. "Do you think for *one second* that I would take any risk at all with your life?" He turned away. He couldn't look at him. Not now. Not after he'd done that, said *that*.

Ethan's replacement finally arrived. He stared at Ethan, hooded eyes trying to hide his laughter. To the other detail agents, this was a joke, a hilarious story they'd throw around the CP for how the president got rid of a drunk trying to pick him up in a Czech jazz bar.

It wasn't funny to him. "I'm rotating out." He pushed his way past Scott—who purposely rammed him with his shoulder—and headed for the exit.

"Ethan! Ethan, wait!"

Ethan heard cursing and the shuffling of barstools, and then heavy footfalls behind him. He kept going, tearing open the door and heading down to the cobbled street. The night air hit his face, and though it was cool, it did nothing to quell his blazing fury or soothe his screaming heart.

"Ethan!" Jack came thundering down the steps behind him, followed by Scott, Daniels, and the other agents, all trying to catch up.

He couldn't let Jack chase after him, unprotected and exposed like that. Cursing, Ethan spun. *"What?"*

The replacement agent's eyes went wide. No one ever spoke to the president that way.

Jack didn't blink. He stood his ground. "What happened, Ethan? What's wrong?"

"What's wrong?" Ethan tried to control his voice, tried to keep himself from shouting. He shouldn't rage at Jack, not in front of half of the entire detail. He saw Daniels pull Scott, and the replacement, back. "What you said in there..." Ethan's throat tightened as his rage melted, turning to anguish. His hands clenched, made fists over and over. *It's still an open mic. Careful what you say, asshole!*

"That was just a joke," Jack said softly. "I was just trying to get rid of her."

"Not like that!" Ethan growled through clenched teeth. Damn it, his eyes were watering. He blinked fast and looked away. He couldn't look at Jack. "It may be hilarious to you, but to me—"

"It just came out!" Jack's hand rose, reaching for Ethan, but he stopped. Pulled back. "It just slipped out. I wasn't thinking."

"It means something to *me!*" Ethan hissed. God, he was shaking. He was going to fly apart. Ethan squeezed his eyes shut. Tried to release his fists.

Jack was silent.

"It's done, Mr. President," he finally said. "You should go back inside."

"No." Jack shook his head. He looked away. "No, I'm finished. Let's go."

Ethan nodded once. "Quarterback calling it in. All agents, rendezvous at *U Maleho Glena* immediately." Agents poured out of the woodwork, teams streaming from alleys and behind buildings and streetlamps. Others walked out of bars up and down the street. Over fifty agents assembled around Jack in moments.

Jack shook his head, chuckling under his breath. It wasn't a happy chuckle.

"Take him in." Ethan nodded to the team. "Everyone, form up."

"Mr. President." The agent closest to Jack motioned forward as the rest of the agents formed a loose bubble around him.

Jack moved off, not looking at Ethan.

Ethan waited, standing in the middle of the street as Daniels and Scott slowly walked toward him.

"What in the *fuck* was that?" Scott hissed. "Goddamn it, Ethan!"

Daniels crossed his arms and shook his head. "What is going on with you two?"

God, he didn't need this shit. He already knew he'd fucked up. He already knew he'd made a mistake. He didn't need Jack rubbing his face in it, and he certainly didn't need shit shoveled on him from Daniels and Scott. Not now. Not when he just wanted to run in front of the nearest train, or rip apart the stone walls surrounding them with his bare hands.

Or collapse to the ground and just let out all of this aching, agonizing pain.

Ethan shot both of his friends a withering glower. "*Nothing* is going on between us."

"That didn't look like nothing!" Scott bellowed. He stepped forward, menacing, toward Ethan.

Ethan lashed out, grabbing Scott in a headlock and pulling him down. Scott fought back, punching Ethan in the stomach and kneeing his thigh. Grunting, Ethan pulled away, spinning out of reach, but Scott ducked down and came up with a right hook across Ethan's face.

"Stop!" Daniels shouted. "Jesus, stop that shit!"

Ethan squinted, holding one hand to his cheek. He ran his tongue over his teeth, checking to make sure they were all there and none were loose. So far so good, but his head ached and his eye was pounding. "Fuck, Scott."

"Fuck *you*, Ethan!" Scott bellowed. "What are you *doing*? You said it was fine! You said it was nothing!"

"It fucking is nothing!" Ethan roared. "He doesn't want me! He doesn't want anything to do with me!"

"He called you his boyfriend!"

"He was throwing it in my face." Ethan spat on the cobblestones, checking for blood.

Finally, Daniels looked at Ethan with something other than anger. His eyes darkened as his lips twisted. "What happened?"

He'd fucked up, that's what had happened. He'd fallen in love with the wrong man and, like a delusion, expected something to come from that. What a dumb fuck he'd been.

"A mistake."

CHAPTER 21

Prague

DAMN IT!

Jack hurled his borrowed beanie across his suite. Dark wool puffed against the white brick wall, falling to the plush carpet. Through his window, Prague Castle glittered, golden light dancing over the gothic city. Prague had been called the most beautiful city in the world by dozens and dozens of world leaders. It was like a dream, a slice of heaven come to life, or a sliver of imagined perfection. In the sunlight, the city had an almost wavering quality, as if suspended in time, a half-breath away from vanishing in between blinks. *Timeless*, people said. *Romantic.*

Slumping, Jack buried his face in his palms, and his fingers slid through his messy hair. He tugged on his blond strands, groaning through clenched teeth as he sat on the edge of his bed.

Prague was devastating. Prague was heartbreaking.

Bitterness sat in his stomach, heavy and rancid. Burning shame sat in his chest, spreading through his lungs until it hurt to breathe.

Why had he made that stupid joke?

Everything had been going... well, not perfectly, but better than it had been the day before, when he hadn't seen a hint of Ethan. Hadn't heard his voice, or seen his smile. Granted, Ethan didn't usually smile when they were traveling, or when he was commanding the Secret Service outside of the White House. But, he'd always tried to cajole a little grin out of Ethan, before—

Before.

Before their kiss, and his fumbling shock, and—

And his *rejection.*

There really was no other way to put it. He'd *rejected* Ethan, *physically* pushed him away. And after Ethan had bared his soul, had confessed to falling so deeply for the man who had captured his heart. The way he *spoke* about who he'd fallen for...

Before Ethan had kissed him, he'd thought, in the back of his mind, that that guy was one seriously lucky man. Whoever it was Ethan had fallen for. Because he was going to get all of Ethan's heart, and all of the incredibleness that was Ethan, and—

Exhaling, Jack pushed the heels of his palms against his eyelids. What had he done tonight? Exactly what Ethan had warned him about? Exactly what other presidents had tried to do? Abuse their powers? Push on a friendship that had gone a little too personal? Get what he wanted? Going out for a beer at a jazz bar in Prague while the world held its breath?

For a moment, in that dark bar with the mournful singer and the wailing saxophone, he'd felt almost normal again. Like he wasn't the president. Like he wasn't surrounded by bodyguards, but was standing next to his best friend. Just the two of them having a good time together.

Or... could it have been a date? If it had just been him and Ethan, and the rest of the agents—whom he hadn't even *known* were there— weren't there, what could the night have been? Would Ethan have looked at him like he had over the pool table? Would he have had that same tangled, fearful hope in his eyes?

Would he have tried to kiss him again?

His thoughts had gone around and around at the bar, like a hamster determined to break its wheel, and the only thing that had kept him grounded was the feel of Ethan's warm body against his side.

And then the woman had interrupted.

Half of a beer, the unrestrained feeling of freedom, Ethan at his side—his heart had been beating wild, drumming through his whole body like he was two seconds from flying apart, and for that moment, he'd thought he could do anything. Be anything. Or anyone. But when she'd started to flirt, it left a bad taste in his mouth, like it was all wrong, like he was already someone else's. He'd felt that for years after Leslie had died, but eventually that had faded.

Ethan interrupting the woman had lined up the stars for him, made him see the obvious constellations.

She was pissed, of course, at being shoved aside by someone who she didn't know was a Secret Service agent just doing his job. Ethan, at his most intense, could be formidable, and his scowl had made even Jack take a step back from him on the campaign trail once or twice. Never, ever had he felt safer than when he was beside Ethan. Nothing could break through that grizzly bear, and he pitied the person who tried.

But the woman at the bar didn't deserve to be shoved off, not for doing nothing wrong, and so he'd leaned into Ethan, rested his head on his broad shoulder, and said what he had said:

"I'm sorry, ma'am. But this is my boyfriend, and he doesn't like to share."

God, *everything* had come apart. *Again.* Ethan's fury had been palpable. The entire bar had thrummed with it, nearly everyone turning toward them as if Ethan was a black hole, sucking the world and everything in it toward his rage. Jack had stumbled, off balance, and had tried to go to Ethan, but Agent Collard's hands on his arms had stilled him. In moments, Ethan was gone, growling and scowling and shaking.

"It meant something to me," Ethan had hissed, when he'd tried to apologize.

"'It just slipped out'." Snorting, Jack shook his head and ran one hand down his face. "What the hell were you thinking?" Berating himself out loud was more real than berating himself in the silence of his mind. "I'm sure that made him feel special, Jack. Great job."

Why had he said it? And what had he been thinking, leaning into Ethan like he'd done?

It's been on your mind. You dreamed about it. Last night. You remember.

Slowly, Jack breathed out. He swallowed and pressed his hands together in front of his face.

Yes. Yes, I did dream about it. About him. About him... and me.

You liked it. You dreamed about it again on the flight over.

He squeezed shut his eyes. *Could I...*

You dreamed about it.

Jack pushed to his feet and paced, slow strides across his bedroom suite to the doors and back to the edge of his bed. He was arguing with himself, and he didn't know if he was winning. Or what was at stake, even, if he won.

Yes, he'd dreamed about Ethan. About... being with him. Memories of making love to his wife had morphed into dreams of seducing Ethan. Of caressing his body. Exploring his strength, his masculinity. Kissing him, over and over, like the kiss he'd ruined by that pool table. His dreams had blurred at the edges, a murky quality to their lower bodies. His hands had mapped every inch of Dream Ethan's broad chest, had kissed up and down his neck, sucked on his lower lip until it was kiss-swollen and ruby red, but... anything further had faded into some kind of fog. Unknown territory. Untouched, in more ways than one.

Shifting, Jack sighed, closing his eyes as he stopped in the center of his hotel room and tipped his head back. Now he was hard. His body *wanted*, parts of him that hadn't been given any attention for years suddenly clamoring for every moment of his time. Every spare thought in his mind.

His eyes opened and fell on his suitcase.

Dreams were dreams. It wasn't like he had conscious control over them. They could just be the firings of his body responding to touch again, to stimulation, to another human being's affection.

Maybe it was time to see if these were *just* dreams. If he could map out those blurry areas, and try—truly—to map out where his heart and his body and his mind were trying to take him.

Five steps took him to his suitcase. His mind went deliberately blank as he dug around, rummaging at the bottom for a clump of black fabric he'd shoved inside, deep down and balled-up.

Ethan's suit jacket uncurled in his hand as he tugged it out, crumpled and wrinkled, and stained on one bottom pocket.

He didn't look too closely at what that stain was.

Jack headed for his bed. He laid Ethan's jacket on the mattress and never took his eyes off it, methodically stripping out of his own clothes and leaving them in a heap.

Naked and trembling, Jack slid into Ethan's jacket. The sleeves were too long and the shoulders too broad, and he felt like a kid playing dress up, but Ethan's scent—*his scent!*—surrounded Jack, burrowing down to his bones and into his blood.

He crawled into his bed, just in the jacket like some kind of fetishist, and lay back. He let his mind go, wandering over his memories of Ethan—from the bar earlier, from the night by the pool table, from every one of the times they'd stolen away together. He remembered his dreams, and dove into those as he closed his eyes and tipped his head back.

He took charge this time, in his mind. He laid Ethan back, slid his hand down his chest... and *down,* farther, into those gray areas. Let himself explore, taking his time, doing to Ethan, in his mind, what he was doing to his own body.

Jack's hands moved everywhere, over his flushed skin, shaking as he panted, as he trembled, and sweat slicked over his body. Ethan's scent rose, like it was actually Ethan there with him, and Jack kept his eyes closed, screwed shut so tightly. He didn't want to break the spell. Didn't want to open his eyes and realize Ethan *wasn't* actually there. Not when he was making love to Ethan in his fantasy, and he was more turned on than he could ever remember being before, ever.

After, he had a good freak out, minutes of panicked breathing as he frantically tried to wipe away the evidence of what he'd done.

Ethan's jacket was ruined. Beyond ruined. And he was stained—branded, it felt like—with searing shame. What had he done? Thinking about his friend like that...

But wasn't that the point? Wasn't he trying to... figure it all out?

He already liked Ethan. Ethan was his best friend. Months spent at each other's sides and their shared jokes, and the time they stole away together, had solidified that for him. Ethan was a gem, a rare man of truly astounding character. Ethan made his days better, brighter, just by being in them.

His head—and even his heart—already knew what they wanted. Ethan's absence was like a physical ache, a bruise on his soul. He *missed* Ethan. Badly.

It wasn't fair to pretend that nothing had happened between them. To pretend that Ethan's feelings were trivialities that they could ignore. He'd wanted to celebrate when he heard Ethan had fallen head over heels for someone. There was no way he could ever dismiss that. He could never—*would* never—ask Ethan to pretend that his heartache could so easily be pushed aside and suggest they carry on as if nothing had ever happened.

He couldn't ignore what had happened. And he didn't want to keep going like this, missing Ethan like a festering wound.

Was he actually, *truly*, thinking of...

Fifteen years was a very long time. Long enough to decide that he was going to be a widower for the rest of his life. He'd made his peace with that years ago.

But Ethan had walked into his life—bold, brawny Ethan—and he wasn't going to pretend that their friendship wasn't already bordering on the edge of something he wasn't ready to name just yet. He knew himself enough, at least, to know that he fell with his heart first. Had that happened here? And he didn't even know?

Could he *actually* start a relationship? With *Ethan*? While he was the *president*?

The past hour had proven that he, in fact, could... at least physically.

But fifteen years of solitude and no small measure of fear held him back. Stilled him on the bed, and kept him frozen as he trembled, wrapped up in Ethan's jacket. What should he do? What was the right choice? Where did he—they—go from here?

Eventually, he got Ethan's jacket back into his suitcase. He perched on the sofa across from the bed, staring at the indent in the mattress, dressed in a pair of faded boxers and an undershirt.

One thing was for certain. Ethan was *never* getting his jacket back.

RUSSIA: ANY US MILITARY MOBILIZATION IN EUROPE WILL BE "AN ACT OF WAR."

Russian President Sergey Puchkov this morning announced that any American troop mobilization within Europe would be considered an act of war.

President Puchkov spoke before traveling to Prague, where he is to meet with the president of the United States in order to discuss the security situation in Europe and the continued threat of the Islamic Caliphate.

The United States has yet to respond to the Russian president's statement.

CHAPTER 22

Prague

ETHAN CHANGED the ice in his baggie and poked at his swollen eye in his hotel room mirror. Scott hadn't spoken to him on the walk back, instead jogging ahead and leaving Ethan with Daniels. Daniels didn't say much, but he didn't berate Ethan either.

His phone buzzed.

Ethan squinted at the lit display. It was after two in the morning. Was Scott wanting to shout at him again? Didn't he know Ethan already hated himself for what he'd done?

He grabbed the phone and plopped back on the bed, resting the ice bag on his swollen eye. It would be purple tomorrow. He swiped the screen on.

It was a text from Jack.

Please rejoin the detail tomorrow. The Russians want to meet early. They say they have something for us. I need you with me. I need you there. Please, Ethan. And then, after the summit, can we talk?

Goddamn it! Ethan clenched the phone in his hands until the cracked plastic strained, creaking in his grasp. Gritting his teeth, Ethan hurled the phone across the room as his chest collapsed and his heart exploded, and his sobs pulled him over until he buried his face in the pillows, roaring out his pain.

———

THE NEXT MORNING, Ethan held open the door to the presidential SUV for Jack at exactly zero seven fifteen. "Mr. President."

He hid his swollen black eye behind his sunglasses. They didn't stop him from seeing Jack's tightly wound, nervous expression as he came off the elevator in the hotel lobby, or how that changed, morphing to surprised relief mixed with pain as he saw Ethan. Still, Jack didn't say anything to Ethan as he approached, or answer his car-side greeting.

Gottschalk slid in after Jack, nodding once to Ethan. Secretary Elizabeth Wall followed behind, scrolling through her phone. Ethan shut the three inside and then ducked into the front passenger seat.

Daniels was driving. Scott had stared at him, silently, when he told him he was taking back his position as point man on the detail that morning and moving Scott to the CP.

Scott hadn't actually said anything to him at all since the night before.

It was a ten minute drive to Prague Castle. The Russians had asked for an early morning meeting with Jack, prior to the start of the summit.

Ethan listened to Jack, Gottschalk, and Secretary Wall going over their last-minute prep while stealing glances in the rearview mirror at Jack.

"What do we think it is that they have to offer us?" Jack's glasses were perched on the tip of his nose as he bounced looks between Gottschalk and Wall.

"Unknown, sir." Gottschalk leaned forward. "They wouldn't say over the phone. They said that President Puchkov would only speak to you, and only face-to-face."

Jack sighed. "I don't like this. I don't trust Puchkov, and I don't see why they'd be in a giving mood after what happened yesterday. You saw what they put in the papers. They're threatening war."

Ethan frowned.

"Sir, the troop deployment to Germany has been halted. They should have picked up on the downgrading of our forces overnight." Wall flipped through papers in her padfolio.

"While I have him alone, this is a perfect opportunity to bring up all the other problems we have with the Russians." Jack sent a sour look to Gottschalk. "In for a penny, in for a pound. We cannot let them continue to operate on their own in Syria."

"Or make another land grab in Europe." Gottschalk held Jack's glare, not flinching.

"Georgia is also calling us about the Russian mobilization in Abkhazeti," Secretary Wall said. "We can't let that go unanswered."

"What has Baghdad said about the Russian threat of invasion?"

"It's... difficult to get anyone in Baghdad on the phones these days," Wall demurred.

"All right. All right." Jack nodded to himself. He glanced up at the mirror, meeting Ethan's gaze. "I'm going to see what Puchkov has. I'll be demanding that he pull out of Abkhazeti, withdraw from the occupied lands in Europe, and agree to international collaboration in regards to Syria." He exhaled. "Think he'll laugh me out of the room?"

Gottschalk and Secretary Wall shared an uneasy look.

Daniels slowed at Prague Castle's dignitary entrance. "Knight One to Castle Keep," Ethan said into the mic. "Vigilant has arrived at Chessboard." He listened to Welby's acknowledgement as he slid out of the SUV and held open the door for Jack and his team.

Jack buttoned his suit next to Ethan as Gottschalk and Wall moved away.

"Did you hear all that?" Jack asked under his breath.

"Yes."

"Thoughts?" Jack smoothed his hands down the front of his jacket.

Ethan turned toward Jack. Despite everything, he still believed in

Jack, to the depths of his soul. The pain he felt was of his own making, not Jack's. "You can do this. I know that you can, Jack." Ethan inhaled quickly. "There is nothing that you can't do."

Jack's eyes slid closed. "You think too highly of me," he whispered. He opened his eyes. Met Ethan's gaze through Ethan's shades. "I'm glad you're here."

"I'm with you all the way, sir," Ethan whispered back. After a moment, he cleared his throat. "Ready to head inside, Mr. President?"

"Yes, Agent Reichenbach. Lead the way."

PRESIDENT PUCHKOV SAT ALONE DRINKING coffee at a breakfast table when Jack walked in. Moments before, Jack had traded a long look with Ethan before shutting the door and leaving himself and Puchkov together.

"I'll be right out here," Ethan had whispered.

"I'm glad," Jack had whispered back.

Now, it was just him and Puchkov.

"Join me, Mr. President!" Puchkov gestured to the single chair across the small round table. "The Czech coffee is good here. Russian export. It can start diesel engine." He poured Jack a full cup of deep black coffee and then slid the saucer across the table. "We have much to discuss."

Puchkov brought one hand down on a plain manila folder tucked next to his coffee cup.

"You must be a morning person." Jack sat across from Puchkov and inhaled the coffee. "This does smell delicious."

"Russian. I promise you. You'll never have better coffee, ever. Your American stuff..." Puchkov dismissed Jack's notion of coffee with a wave of his hand. "Come. Take a sip. Tell me what you think."

Jack smiled, saluted Puchkov with the bone china coffee cup, and took a swallow. The coffee was hot, thick, and deep roasted. It had body, and legs, and it sat heavy on his tongue, like melted chocolate, before sliding down his throat.

It was the best coffee he'd ever tasted.

"You are right, Mr. President," Jack said with a smile. "This is delicious."

"Ah. You know, the coffee is not the only thing I am right about." Puchkov held Jack's stare as the temperature in the room plunged.

Jack sat back in his chair, all traces of his smile gone. Of course, Puchkov had games. "And what is that?"

"I am right that you want to see what is in this folder." Puchkov's fingers tapped on the folder, one after the other.

Jack said nothing for a long moment. "You wanted me here, but you've done nothing but threaten me, Europe, and the Middle East for months. I'm not playing games with you, Puchkov."

"Fine. Here." Puchkov pushed the folder across, a sour look on his face. "I am not trying to play games with you, Mr. President."

"Your announcement about our troop movements being an act of war sure sounds like games."

"Bah." Puchkov waved Jack away and sat back. "You know how it is. Posture, for the media."

Jack took the folder but held Puchkov's stare. The Russian president had beady eyes and a thin nose straining off his narrow face. Deep furrows were etched into his cheeks, a lifetime's worth of hardship and few smiles. Not that there would have been many smiles in the KGB or the FSB, where Puchkov had earned his experience.

"Go on." Puchkov crossed his legs.

He flipped open the folder.

A photo stared back at him. He blinked.

Al-Karim's right hand man, his lieutenant, Talib Al-Syria, stared up at Jack from the photo. His eyes were desperate, searching for something, and a Russian military officer held him back in a bruising bear hold. Jack supposed if he was locked in a Russian embrace, he'd look the same. Talib was soaking wet, and bruises covered his chest and neck. Blood ran down his temple. His lip was split, and there was a fresh burn stretched across his right shoulder.

"You know this man, yes?"

Jack glared at Puchkov over the folder's edge. "Everyone knows

Talib Al-Syria. He's gone to ground. No one has been able to get any intelligence on his movements, not for years. When was this taken?"

Puchkov checked his watch. "About three hours ago." He waited for Jack's response.

Silence.

"We caught Mr. Talib up on the Iraq-Iran border." Puchkov waved Jack's sudden frown away. "Yes, we are already in Iraq. We moved into Iraq when we moved into Syria, but you were all so concerned about Syria that you paid no attention to what we were doing over the Black Sea." A smarmy smile, his hands outspread. "You are so concerned about something that has already been happening, Mr. President."

"What do you want from me?"

"Ah. It is actually what *you* want from *me*." Puchkov leaned forward, elbows on the table. "We have Talib. We caught him smuggling a dirty bomb across the border from Iran to Iraq."

"*What?*" Jack bolted upright, nearly upending his coffee.

Again, Puchkov dismissed Jack's concern. "Meh, you know the Caliphate has been wanting a nuclear bomb. Why are you so surprised?"

World War III seemed more and more imminent. Jack tried to control his breathing, tried to get a grip. Ethan's voice played in his mind. *You can do this. I believe in you.* Swallowing, Jack tried to bury his blooming shame. *Ethan, you think too much of me.*

"As Iran's ally, should I assume that you knew of their nuclear capabilities?"

"We know of certain factions within Iran. We know of their capabilities," Puchkov corrected. "And they, being friendly allies, tipped us off on the Caliphate's acquisition."

Apparently, talking to Puchkov was how he talked to the Iranians nowadays.

"You know the Iranians hate the Caliphate. Shi'ite, Sunni..." Puchkov shrugged, downplaying centuries of religious conflict with a roll of his shoulders. "We took Talib before he made contact with Al-Karim."

"Why not wait and get Al-Karim at the same time?"

"You Americans! We have Talib, one of the most wanted men on the planet, and you complain we did not gift wrap him for you!" Puchkov's hands slammed onto the table. He leaned in close, no longer joking, suddenly serious. "We did not wait, Mr. President, because like you, we do not want to see a nuclear weapon destroy the Middle East. There was a chance he would detonate before meeting Al-Karim. We did not see that as an acceptable risk."

Jack studied the Russian president. Was any of this true?

Could he take the chance that it was not?

"I would have made the same call," he finally said. "You have my thanks."

"Bah." Puchkov pushed away from the table and crossed his arms. He was always moving, never still. "I do not want your thanks. I want to trade."

And here it is. Jack leaned back. "Trade what?"

"Talib."

"For?"

"You will close your military bases in Kazakhstan. And Uzbekistan."

Jack shook his head. "Out of the question. We fly reconnaissance flights over Iran from those bases. We cannot close them."

"I *know* you fly reconnaissance flights from there," Puchkov groaned. "And the Iranians *know* you fly reconnaissance flights from Kazakhstan. Everyone *knows* you fly those missions, Mr. President. Your bases are not as effective as you believe. Did you know about Talib, for example?"

Jack stayed silent.

"Here is what I propose. You close your bases in Kazakhstan. We, in the spirit of international cooperation and community, and all of that—" Puchkov rolled his wrist, paying lip service to the fundamentals of international law and goodwill. "—will welcome you into our northern Iraq bases. You may launch your missions from there. We will share our Iraqi intelligence with you, and allow you to fly through northern Iraqi airspace from your bases in Turkey."

"Does Baghdad know you're already in their country?"

"Baghdad does not know anything that happens outside of Baghdad. The entire country is the wild, wild west." Puchkov rapped on the tabletop. "I will make this better for you. We will cease our independent operations in Syria. I have wanted to for a while, but this gives me good cover. Russia will bring a motion to the United Nations, requesting a joint military operation. We will take the lead, naturally, but it will all be on the up and up." Puchkov spoke American idioms easily, though his Russian accent was thick and heavy, cutting on the words.

"That's good," Jack mused. He leaned forward as well, watching Puchkov. "But it's not enough. You didn't just invade Iraq, and you didn't just launch military operations in Syria without any kind of international oversight or cooperation. You also invaded sovereign nations in Europe. You seized countries, democratic countries. This we cannot sit by and ignore."

"*I* did not do this. My predecessor did."

Jack stayed quiet.

"You ignored it for ten years, yes?"

"*I* did not ignore it. And *I* am the president now."

Puchkov leaned back, smirking. "I do like you, Mr. President. You have *muda*." He pointed to his crotch. "Balls."

Jack raised one eyebrow.

"I will agree to this, and to this only: I will hold elections in the disputed territories before the end of the year. In these elections, I will ask the people to vote on a referendum. Do they remain a part of great Russia, or do they cut all ties and go back to being weak and alone?"

It was almost too easy. Jack peered at Puchkov. The Russian president was jiggling his foot and tapping his fingers on the tabletop.

"What do you say, Mr. President? Do we have a deal?"

"Draw down your forces in Abkhazeti, too."

"They were just for show." Puchkov grinned. "We will coordinate with you, of course, on deployments to northern Iraq. You will want to put your Special Forces in-country, yes?"

Jack didn't answer. "Why do you want the bases out of Kazakhstan and Uzbekistan? Why is this so important to you?"

Puchkov's smile disappeared from his face. His easygoing façade, his gamesmanship, disappeared. "Because it is." His lips twisted as he bounced his foot, up and down, over and over. He sighed. "Mr. President, we have a chance, right now, to change the world. We can try to work together for once, yes? America and Russia? We have something you want. I want something from you. We can help each other. Maybe even help the world, yes?" Puchkov frowned. "Now, do we have a deal, Mr. President? Shall we deliver Mr. Talib to your embassy in Moscow?"

"What is your timetable?"

"We cease operations in Syria immediately. We propose a UN resolution before the end of the year. We announce the referendums... mmm, next month. They will be held in December." Puchkov's eyes bored into Jack. "Your bases will close within twelve months."

"Eighteen."

"Twelve months, Mr. President. Or no deal."

Twelve months. The military could break the bases down by then. There weren't regular long-haul flights in and out of Afghanistan anymore, not since the withdrawal years ago. What would they lose?

What would the Russians gain?

Was this the right course? How many lives would be saved? Russia would rejoin the world community in helping to find a solution for Syria and the Caliphate, instead of adding to the problem. Europe would see a lifting of the Iron Veil that had started to fall. They would get Talib and any intelligence that Talib might have. Maybe even Al-Karim.

How many lives had the Russians already saved by stopping Talib?

Puchkov was right. It was an opportunity to change their course. America and Russia, working together. It had been almost a hundred years since that had last happened, and they'd changed the world then.

Could they do so again?

I believe in you. I know you can do this.

Exhaling, Jack held the image of Ethan in his mind as he closed his eyes. *I hope this works, Ethan. I'm trusting your trust in me.*

"Twelve months. But you provide food aid to the refugee resettlement zones in Europe."

Puchkov rolled his eyes, but he nodded, waving his hands in the air. "Yes," he drawled, "we will feed the precious refugees."

Standing, Jack held out his hand. Puchkov rose as well, grasping his palm and pumping his arm, once.

"My people will deliver Talib to your embassy at six PM today, in Moscow." He nodded. "We will be in touch, Mr. President."

Without another word, Puchkov strode away, disappearing out of the room through the back entrance leading out to the castle's gardens. His security detail waited, swooping down around Puchkov the moment he was outside.

Jack collapsed to his chair. Had he just made a mistake? Or saved the world?

Behind Jack, the door clicked open. Ethan slipped into the room, checking everything, his head on a swivel.

"Mr. President? Puchkov and his entourage just left the castle." Ethan's footsteps faded into the plush Oriental carpet. "Are you all right?"

Looking up, Jack saw Ethan's black eye for the first time. "Ethan! What happened?" He reached for Ethan's face.

Ethan intercepted his hand gently and guided his arm back down. "Don't," he whispered. "Please."

Jack nodded, even though his chest was collapsing and his throat was clenched tight. Ever since that kiss, nothing had been the same. How could he right this? How could he fix this?

"I need to get with my team," Jack croaked. "Stay near. I want to hear your thoughts." Jack stood but paused. "If that's all right?"

Ethan looked away. "You know I'm with you all the way."

Why did it feel like all the way was just about to end?

RUSSIA DEPARTS NATO SUMMIT
BEFORE IT BEGINS

Russian President Sergey Puchkov left the emergency NATO Summit in Prague this morning before it began. This abrupt departure came on the heels of a one-on-one meeting between President Puchkov and President Spiers in the early morning at Prague Castle.

"Russian troops will immediately suspend military operations in Syria until sustainable international partnerships can be created. Russia has always believed in the full cooperation of nations," Puchkov said. "Russia wants all nations to know that they have the backing of the international community, led by Russia. To that end, we will introduce a resolution in the United Nations to build a coalition of nations that will address Syria and the Middle East's ongoing security concerns, including the Islamic Caliphate."

CHAPTER 23

Prague

THE REST of the summit passed in a blur.

Ethan stayed with Jack as he debriefed with Gottschalk and Secretary Wall, dissecting his exchange with Puchkov. Gottschalk and Wall were on the phones after that, calling Washington, and Moscow, and everyone in between.

There was space, in the middle of all of that, for Ethan to lean in and whisper in Jack's ear, "You did the right thing."

When Jack swayed back, leaning into him, Ethan didn't know what to do. He pressed his hand to the small of Jack's back, steadying him, and then stepped away. Jack shivered beneath his touch, and Ethan pulled away as if burned.

Russia's announcement changed the tone and tenor of the meetings. Suddenly, leaders were arguing over troop deployments and what they could contribute to a peacekeeping force, and what they needed to keep at home, securing their homelands. In the afternoon, they finally got to discussing shared intelligence across Europe and increased alert systems for the prevention of future attacks.

Instead of dinner, there was a cocktail reception, and a host of

NGOs were invited. Dignitaries and leaders from aid organizations, reconstruction contractors, and humanitarian missions joined the politicians over hors d'oeuvres.

Penelope de Mendoza turned more than one head when she walked into the hall. She wasn't wearing anything special. As the president of Borderless Doctors, she had publicly committed to not reveling in appearance and circumstance. She wore a simple sheath dress and a shawl woven in Nepal, and her long brunette hair hung loose in cascading waves.

The French president was on her in a heartbeat, hooking his arm through hers and guiding her around the room.

Ethan shadowed Jack during the reception, standing just behind his shoulder. When the French president finally wound his way toward Jack, with Penelope on his arm, Ethan's stomach fell to the floor.

"Mr. President." Penelope curtsied as Jack took her hand in his. It was a delicate gesture, almost royal.

Jack smiled wide. Ethan looked away.

"Ms. Mendoza. I've heard so much about you. Your organization's aid work around the world is unparalleled." Jack held out his arm. "Might I steal you for a moment?"

Penelope gladly traded the aging French president for Jack, slipping onto his arm. Though she was gorgeous and moved like a princess, she had a sharp mind, and within minutes, she and Jack had their heads together, speaking about the Syrian situation and the needs on the ground.

Ethan wanted to vomit, standing behind the two of them.

He'd gotten the message, thank you, and he didn't need this reminder. Yes, Jack was straight. No, Jack didn't want him. But did he need to be there when Jack found someone he did want?

His mood soured throughout the night, even after Penelope bade a gracious farewell to Jack and moved on, talking to the British prime minister for another hour while the two women drank wine by the Renaissance windows. He was quiet during the drive back to the airport, and he parked himself in the below-deck bunk area when everyone boarded Air Force One.

No one bothered him. No one tried to talk to him. Not even Daniels. Especially not Scott.

When his phone buzzed just before take-off, Ethan didn't want to answer. He lay on the bunk, trying to forget about his life, trying to figure out how to word his transfer request to Director Stahl. He'd be lucky if he could still transfer after this trip. He might as well just resign.

His phone buzzed again, rattling against his chest.

He swiped the screen on.

Jack.

Can we talk?

Ethan. Please. I'm begging you. I don't want to leave things like this. Please. Come to my office on AF1? We have ten hours on this flight. Let's use them.

He didn't want to do this. He didn't want to face Jack, or have to face himself and what he'd done. He'd broken the rules, violated the regulations, and obliterated any and all boundaries between him and Jack. He had no one to blame for his heartache but himself.

[I'm on my way.]

Time to get this over with. He'd listen to Jack fumble through an explanation of how he was flattered, but straight, and Ethan had to get over his feelings and move on. He'd nod and agree and then escape, and when they landed, he wouldn't ever see Jack again.

He could only hope.

Ethan trudged up the stairs back to the main cabin. A steward passed him in the hall, carrying a tray of waters for the press pool in the rear. In the front of the plane, Jack's private office doors loomed large, leading to the president's suite onboard the plane. Beyond the office, Jack had a bedroom and a bathroom, and even a shower. Down the hall was the conference room where Gottschalk liked to spread out on long flights.

More than once, Ethan had covered Gottschalk with a blanket

and turned out the lights in the conference room after he'd passed out.

He knocked twice, hard. Jack called out, "Come in."

He slipped inside. Shut the door behind him.

Jack stood slowly behind his desk. "Thank you," he whispered. "I'm glad you came."

Ethan let his eyes roam over Jack. He'd allow himself that. It was the last time, after all. Jack had shed his jacket and his button-down, and he was just in his untucked undershirt and his suit pants. He'd kicked off his shoes beside the desk.

"I'm sorry," Ethan started. "I'm sorry for what I did. I shouldn't have... I shouldn't have kissed you. I shouldn't have fallen for you. I shouldn't have given you my cell number, and I shouldn't have spent any time with you at all. Everything that happened is because of my poor judgment, and all of it is my fault." He swallowed. "I'm very sorry, Mr. President."

Sighing, Jack slumped. His shoulders sagged, and his fingers rubbed against one another, over and over. "It's not all your fault, Ethan. Don't take all the blame."

Ethan looked away. If he could, he'd leap from this plane. Land anywhere else, anywhere in the world.

"I didn't know—I didn't think—" Jack stopped, stuttering, and exhaled. "Looking back, it seems so clear. But I didn't know at the time what was happening."

"Sir, you don't need to do this." He spoke through clenched teeth. "I'm going to request a transfer as soon as we land. We don't need to discuss this anymore. And you don't need to worry about any inappropriate behavior from me." Ethan paused. "Any *further* inappropriate behavior."

Jack's head shot up. His eyes were blown wide, shock lining the edges of his gaze as his face blanched. His lips thinned as he pressed them together. Ethan watched his Adam's apple rise and fall in a long, slow swallow.

The moment stretched long, silence straining the air between them. The sound of the jet engines thrummed through the office, vibrating the floor beneath Ethan's feet. It sounded like static filling his brain, like the electric smear that had taken over his mind, white-washing his world in a chorus of "should-have"s and "if-only"s.

He should leave. He should excuse himself from the office, but Ethan stayed where he was. Jack seemed to be working up to something. He licked his lips and looked away. Looked down. Leaned forward, bracing his hands against the desk. Exhaled.

Finally, Jack met Ethan's gaze.

His naked terror speared Ethan, and his breath hitched.

"I don't want you to leave," Jack breathed. His voice was rough, catching on what sounded like fear stuck in his chest. "I want you to stay."

"I can't." Ethan hated the way his voice cracked, fracturing on his heartbreak. "I can't. Not like this."

Jack's eyes widened as he drew a ragged breath. But his gaze was strong as he stared at Ethan. "Then let's figure out how to make this work."

Ethan's heart skipped a beat. He opened his mouth, but no words came out.

Straightening, Jack held his head high, and even though fear still poured off him, Ethan watched him gather his strength. "When I fell for my wife," Jack began, his voice shaking, "I was consumed with thoughts of her. I wondered what she was doing every moment. I couldn't wait to see her again. The sound of her voice raised my spirits. Her smile made my day. I wanted to spend every minute I could with her." Jack blinked fast and cleared his throat. He looked down, staring at his desk for a long moment. "The more I got to know her, the more I fell for her. I knew what was happening, and I fell for her with my eyes wide open. I welcomed it."

When Jack looked up, all of the air in Ethan's lungs burst from him in one quick gasp. Longing had replaced Jack's fear, fathoms deep, and mixed with hope and sorrow. "When I am around you, I feel like it was when I fell in love with her. Like... I'm falling for someone again."

Ethan couldn't breathe. His palms itched, and his bones were on fire, burning him from the inside. "You're straight."

"All my life." Jack licked his lips. "The past fifteen years I've actually been celibate. I thought that sex and romance and love were gone from my life. I didn't want to even consider anything after Leslie's death."

Not again. He didn't want to be the asshole who reminded Jack of his dead wife again. "Please, sir. *Stop.* We don't need to—"

"Listen to me, Ethan, damn it." Exhaling, Jack ran his hands through his wild hair. The ends stuck up, crazy. "I met and married my wife, and I loved her with all my heart. At thirty, I shelved my sex life and pushed away anyone who wanted anything romantic from me." He hesitated. "And at forty-five, my best friend kissed me, and I can't get that kiss out of my mind."

Suddenly, Jack was on a roll. He started to pace in the cramped space behind the desk, pushing the chair away. "Today, when Penelope Mendoza was with me, all I could think of was how much I wanted that to be *you*. I wanted you leaning in close to me, Ethan. I wanted to be solving the world's problems with *you*. And before, I wanted to be exploring Prague with you at my side. I want you in my life. I want to see you every day. I want to hear your voice. I want to spend my free time with you and steal away just to hear your laugh." He stopped, staring at Ethan. "I blurted out that joke in the bar because the thought of you and me together has been in my mind since you kissed me."

"Stop. Please. *Stop.*" Ethan shook his head, trying to erase Jack's words. "You don't know what you're saying—"

"Something is happening here. I don't know what it is. I wouldn't have ever known... I wouldn't have ever even considered this if you hadn't kissed me. You were my friend, my best friend now, and I probably would have kept up a long-term friendship with you, never realizing what—" He inhaled sharply. "—what this could be," he finished, his voice soft.

"You're just isolated. Lonely. This is just the isolation of the presidency talking. If you had *any* other options, you wouldn't be saying this." Ethan turned away.

"Damn it!" Jack's hand slammed down on his desk, slapping the surface and cracking the air in the office. "I can't sleep because I keep coming all over myself in my dreams! Dreams about *you*!"

Whirling, Ethan's jaw clenched as he stared at Jack.

"I don't know what's happening to me!" Jack hissed. "I don't know what it means that I feel this way about you! I *can't* get you out of my mind! I want to be with you *all* the time! It feels like I'm falling for someone all over again. Falling for *you*." Jack shook as he exhaled. "Everything I think I know about myself is in flux." He looked into Ethan's eyes. "What do I do? I can ignore this, and I can let you transfer away. We both can bury this, and I can go back to my loveless life. I can let you go."

Ethan couldn't take this. His heart was going to explode, or he was going to vomit or spontaneously combust. Fire and ice raged inside of him, scorching his soul. His head ached, and his teeth ground together. He was going to crack a tooth, he just knew it.

"Or I can face this. Let myself keep falling for you. Accept that I..." Jack bit his lip. "That I can fall for a *man*. Despite everything I've ever known."

"You can fall for..." Ethan shook his head, trying to clear the screaming from his mind. This wasn't happening. He was dreaming, and he was going to wake up sobbing again. "What are you trying to say? That you want a gay experiment? Because I can't do that. I can't be your gay test, Jack. I care too much about you."

"No." Jack slid around the side of his desk, stopping across from Ethan, only feet away, but it seemed like miles. Or farther. "I never thought that I would feel this way for a man. But I *do*. I want *you*, Ethan. And now I have to figure out what to do about that." His chest heaved. "I want to figure out how to make this work. I want to try, Ethan. Because..." A pause, and Ethan felt his heart burst. "Because when you truly fall for someone, you have to be willing to try anything to make that work. I don't know the future. I don't know if it will work between us. But, I am asking you... Can we give it a shot?"

"You are the president…"

"Only for the next three and half years. I'm not the office. You know that better than anyone."

"You're worth more than one term."

Jack smiled, wistful. "You think so highly of me. I don't know what I did to earn your respect. But, Ethan, the way you look at me." His eyes shifted. Heat smoldered in his gaze. "It makes me feel alive."

Ethan closed his eyes, trying to breathe. The world was spinning too fast. Ethan was really asleep, probably moaning in his bunk below decks, and he'd wake any minute. *Please, wake up. Wake up! I don't want to hear this anymore. I don't want to hear my dreams come true only for them to end!*

"You're straight," Ethan breathed. "You'll decide this isn't for you. You like the idea, but you won't like the reality."

"I jerked off thinking about you last night," Jack blurted out. "After we got back from the bar. I came… harder than I have in over a decade. And," he quirked his head to the side. "Did you forget the wet dreams I've been having? I haven't had one in, God, years. They started with women, but now… It's all you. Your body. Us, together. All I can think about is you."

Hissing, Ethan's eyes ran over Jack's body, drinking him in. The thought of Jack, touching himself and thinking of Ethan, blazed through him. "You really want this? A man?"

"I really want *you*." Jack swallowed. His hands clasped the desk behind him. His knuckles were white. "Can we go slowly?" His voice finally shook. "I want to say I'm brave, but… I am nervous. I do want you, though. I want to try this. With *you*."

"What does slow mean? I want to be absolutely clear."

"I'm not ready to have sex with you yet, but I want to kiss you again." Jack's chin lifted. "Is that clear?"

God, Ethan was going to die. His eyes squeezed shut, and he prayed, harder than he'd ever prayed before, to wake up that moment. Or to stay asleep forever. For this moment to never, ever end.

When his heart kept beating and the world kept spinning, refusing to fade away into a dreamscape, Ethan opened his eyes.

Jack was waiting for him.

The choice was his. How had it come to this? He'd screwed everything up. That didn't lead to happy endings. He wasn't supposed to end up with who he wanted most in the world, not after everything he'd done. But, God, Jack was standing there, waiting for him.

He had to choose. Did he step forward and take this chance? Reach for Jack and hope that it would work out? Figure out how to love a straight man negotiating brand new territory?

What did he want?

He wanted Jack like he wanted oxygen. Like he wanted his heart to keep beating. He wanted, so *deeply*, so *badly*, but that want ignored the realities of the world. They would have to hide. They'd have to hide *everything* from *everybody*. It was wrong to be with Jack on so many levels. He'd lose it all if they were discovered.

So would Jack. The risk he was taking... It wasn't just his sexuality he was playing with. If word of this got out...

Ethan squeezed his eyes shut. How could he do this, knowing the risks? Knowing what Jack could lose if it all went wrong?

How could he turn away from Jack offering him his heart? He wasn't strong enough to make that sacrifice, no matter how much of a hero he wanted to be. He was just a man, a man compromised by love.

He had to choose, and the weight of the decision almost crushed his soul. Go to Jack. Find their love. Find some way they could love each other, despite everything. Live with secrets and lies until they could be free. Share his life with the best man he'd ever met, ever, in the world.

Or turn away. Break Jack's heart, like Ethan's heart had shattered. Risk nothing. Leave the world to go on turning, without the risk of it falling to pieces when this all came out, and when everything came crashing down. Jack would survive, and he'd continue on. Didn't the world need him as president? How much would it hurt when this leaked out, and when Jack was destroyed by his willingness to give love a second chance?

It was the choice of a lifetime, and more than just two hearts hung in the balance.

To love or to wither. To cherish or to destroy. Their world, together, or the world at large.

Ethan opened his eyes.

Jack was waiting, still.

He wasn't strong enough for this. Wasn't strong enough to deny his heart and choose to save the world instead.

He was just a man. A man who yearned. A man who loved.

"I'm with you all the way, Jack," Ethan breathed. "As long as you'll have me."

Slowly, Jack smiled, though it wavered on the edges. "I will hold you to that."

They stood, staring at each other, as the moment stretched. Tension poured in, replacing the warmth of their words.

Ethan blinked. What now? What did he do? How was he supposed to navigate a relationship, and one with the *president*, no less? There were a thousand things they needed to discuss, but he just wanted to drop to his knees at Jack's feet and push the world away.

Jack cleared his throat. "You took the initiative last time. It's only fair that I..."

Before Ethan knew what was happening, Jack strode forward, his eyes locked on Ethan's and filled with determination. Frozen, Ethan watched as Jack's hand rose, cupping his jaw in a tender, gentle hold.

Jack's thumb stroked over Ethan's cheek. "You held my face," he breathed. "No one has ever done that." Leaning forward, Jack's lips brushed Ethan's.

His lips were dry, slightly chapped from the recirculated air on Air Force One. He tasted like coffee and cream, and the stubble above his lip scraped over Ethan's skin. Jack's hand snaked around Ethan's neck, tugging him closer.

Ethan made a noise, something between a moan and a whimper

that he'd have been mortified to hear any other time. He was shaking, trembling, and his soul was on fire. Finally, something other than pain touched his heart. Relief flooded through him, overwhelming him entirely, and Ethan gasped into their kiss.

Stepping forward, Ethan's arms wound around Jack, one arm around his waist and the other tangling in his hair, cupping the back of his head. His tongue slipped out, teasing at Jack's lips, and then, a moment later, touched Jack's tentative tongue in return. Groaning, Ethan pulled Jack closer as his knees went weak and his heart surged, filling his body with the sudden rush of his love for Jack. God, he was already in love with Jack, had already fallen in love.

Ethan pulled back, holding Jack purposely at arm's length. Jack gasped, wrenched away from Ethan's arms and his kiss, and he stared at Ethan with blown-wide eyes and swollen lips.

He shook his head. "I went too fast the first time. I scared you. I'm not doing that again. Not ever." Ethan breathed out, trying to calm his racing heart. "You said slow."

"I also said that I want you." Jack's voice was too low, pitched in an octave Ethan had never heard.

It went straight to his cock, via his heart.

"I said that I wanted you, and that I can't get you out of my mind." Jack pulled Ethan's hands off his shoulders, escaping his restraint. He looked into Ethan's eyes. "Kiss me like you really want to. That's what I want, right now."

Ethan crashed into Jack like a man bedeviled, wrapping him up in his arms and caressing his skin. His hands roamed over Jack's back, over his shoulders, until one hand tangled in his hair again, the other snaking beneath Jack's shirt at the small of his back. Ethan's lips nuzzled Jack's, suckling and nibbling, and then their tongues were dueling, caressing and stroking back and forth. He backed Jack up until Jack hit the front of his desk, his ass bumping into the edge.

Jack scooted up onto his desktop without breaking the kiss. His hands dragged Ethan closer, pressing their bodies together from chest to thighs.

Ethan's hard cock pressed against Jack's.

Shuddering, Jack hissed, and his hands grabbed Ethan's suit jacket, tangling in the lapels. "Ethan," Jack breathed. His hips rocked forward.

Ethan jerked, his cock rock-hard, and then he pulled back, breaking their kiss. His lips clung to Jack's, his teeth tugging on Jack's lower lip. Exhaling, Ethan pressed their foreheads together as his hands cupped Jack's cheeks.

He stepped back again, pulling his thrusting hips away from Jack's.

"You said slow." Ethan's thumbs stroked Jack's cheekbones.

Jack nodded, panting, and licked his lips. "I did," he breathed. "I did." Jack's hands rose, grasping Ethan's wrists, and his thumbs stroked over Ethan's bounding pulse point in return. His eyes slitted open. Ethan could barely see any blue around the edges of his blown-wide pupils.

"Are you okay?" Ethan dropped a kiss to the tip of Jack's nose. "Too much?" His hands were shaking against Jack's skin.

"Just enough." Jack smiled, slow and easy, and the warm happiness falling from his gaze melted Ethan's spine. He grinned back.

The moment broke when Jack yawned, his face twisting and contorting as his eyes widened and his jaw cracked.

Chuckling, Ethan kissed the top of Jack's head. "When did you last sleep?"

"I haven't been sleeping well," Jack moaned, pressing his face into Ethan's neck. "Between the summit, the Russians, and dreams about you..."

"I'm sorry." Ethan wrapped Jack up in his arms, rubbing up and down his back.

"Mmm. Not your fault." Jack yawned again. He pulled back, his smile still there, but sleepy. "Come with me."

Ethan stepped back, giving Jack room to hop down from the desk. His skin went hot as he chastised himself for pushing Jack against his desk and humping him on the heels of his request to go slow. He couldn't think with his cock, not now.

Jack led Ethan to his private cabin. A queen bed lay untouched, and Jack's suitcase sat on a luggage valet next to a leather armchair. In the back of the room, a sliding door led into Jack's private bathroom. Ethan hovered in the doorway as Jack sat on the edge of the bed.

"We have ten hours until we reach Washington. I know we have a lot to talk about. We've got to figure out how this—" He waved his hand between them both. "—will work. Are you busy on the flight?"

Ethan shook his head. "No. I was hiding in the bunks down below."

"No more hiding." Jack shifted on the bed, patting the space next to him. "I'm pretty tired, but we can talk for a while?"

It was all kinds of dangerous to slide into bed with Jack, but Ethan swore to himself that he'd behave. He shucked his suit jacket, tossing it over the leather armchair, and rolled up his shirtsleeves. Jack scooted back, sitting up against the headrest.

"We're going to have to be so careful about this, right?" Jack reached for Ethan's hand as Ethan crawled up beside him.

Ethan leaned back, wrapping one arm around Jack's shoulders and tangled their fingers together with his other hand. "More than careful," he sighed. "This has to stay secret. No one can know. Not a soul. The fallout if anyone finds out…"

"You'll lose your job."

Nodding, Ethan squeezed Jack's hand. "I'm more worried about you. Your presidency would be ruined. A secret gay love affair?"

"I don't care about the press or the public." Jack shook his head. "Who I want to be with is my own choice."

His words felt like a fire had started in Ethan's chest. Hope was growing in him, despite his gnawing fears. Turning, Ethan pressed a kiss to Jack's temple. "It would still be devastating. I want to spare you that."

"So we stay in hiding." Jack rested his head on Ethan's shoulder. "We go back to what we were doing before. Seeing each other in secret. But now we're… together."

Ethan nodded. His hand stroked the back of Jack's head. Silken blond strands slipped through his fingers.

"We'll have to figure out how you can stay the night." Jack squeezed his fingers as he spoke.

It was almost too much. Ethan's head swam, and the sudden fear that he truly was dreaming crashed through him again. He held his breath, desperate to not wake up this time, until the terror subsided. "We go slow," he murmured, pressing another kiss to Jack's temple. "We'll figure it out. There's no rush."

"I want you to be happy," Jack whispered. "I don't want you to settle for anything less than you deserve."

Ethan turned, smiling at Jack in his arms, his head pillowed on Ethan's shoulder. "You already make me happy," Ethan breathed. He smiled, letting Jack see the fullness of his emotions, the depth of his feelings finally pushed into his gaze. "Happier than I've ever been, Jack. You don't know what you mean to me." His eyes searched Jack's. He saw a joy that mirrored his own, shining bright. "I will do anything it takes," he whispered. "Anything. For you."

Jack tried to stifle a yawn. Ethan laughed.

"I'm starting to fall asleep." Jack smiled and raised his hand, cupping Ethan's cheek. "Stay? Let's ignore the world for ten hours. I want to stay at your side."

"You know I'm with you all the way." How had everything turned out so perfect? He was supposed to lose it all. He wasn't supposed to have his dreams come true.

Ethan leaned forward, capturing Jack's lips again. Jack smiled into his kiss, and Ethan grinned back, his heart skipping a beat. "Get some sleep, Mr. President."

"*Jack.*"

Ethan's smile grew. "Jack," he breathed. *My Jack.*

Jack's eyes slid closed, and then he was asleep, softly snoring in Ethan's arms. Ethan traced his face with his eyes, mapping the lines, the curve of his cheeks, and the strength of his jaw. God, he was gorgeous. So stunningly beautiful, and he only seemed to get more handsome every day. Was that Ethan, falling deeper into love?

Was this wise? No, probably not. Definitely not. There was too much at stake if they were discovered.

But there was too much to lose if they didn't try. A lifetime of happiness, joy in each other's arms.

Love.

Could Jack truly love him? Could Jack, an otherwise straight man, truly fall in love with him, a gay man? And desire him, even? If their kiss was anything to go by, then maybe it could work. Jack had been hard when Ethan had pushed him up against the desk. Hard because of *him*.

Jack was the single bravest man Ethan knew. To take a chance on love, when that love seemed so far outside of his reality, of the contours of his world. Could Ethan have done the same thing? Probably not. He probably wouldn't have decided to take a chance on a relationship with a woman, if the situation had been reversed.

Whatever it was that they created, however they figured this out between them, one thing was certain.

It was worth it.

ETHAN INTENDED TO STAY AWAKE. He wanted to think this through, figure out a plan for how to cover his tracks. Try to figure out what to say to Daniels. Try to fix his friendship with Scott.

None of that happened. He fell asleep holding on to Jack, their heads pillowed together on the bed, and the next thing he knew, hard knocks pounded on the door to Jack's cabin.

"Mr. President?" One of the Air Force One stewards called through the door. "Mr. President, we're landing momentarily."

"Shit!" Ethan scrambled, helping Jack up as they both blinked sleep from their eyes. "Goddamn it!"

"It's all right." Jack grabbed Ethan's arm, steadying him. "It's all right. I'll see you back at the White House."

Ethan waited until he heard the steward leave. He pressed a quick kiss to Jack's cheek and ducked out to the office, where he rolled down his sleeves before slipping out to the main hallway. Flight attendants passed him by, carrying the last of the flight's refuse to the forward staging area. Ethan crossed to starboard and headed forward, toward the Secret Service cabin on the main deck. Inside, agents were buckling in for landing.

Ethan slipped in and sat in the empty seat next to Daniels. He buckled his belt and rubbed his face.

"Where have you been?" Scott grunted, not looking at Ethan.

"Busy."

"Where's your jacket?"

Fuck. Ethan closed his eyes and ignored Scott. He'd left his jacket draped over the chair in Jack's cabin.

They landed smoothly, and then it was the mass movement of people disembarking from Air Force One. Jack was first, followed by the agents on duty. Ethan hung back with Scott, Daniels, and the others coming off their rotations in Prague, and waited for the new shift to get the presidential limo ready. They'd ride back in the chaser SUVs.

Ethan clambered down the gangway after the press had taken photos and Jack had answered their short questions, and then slid into the back of his limo. Ethan held his smile in, even though his heart sang as he watched Jack. The sun was setting as they landed, and the warmth of the summer sunset seeped into his soul. He smiled up at the sky instead of at Jack, laughing under his breath.

Scott nudged Ethan and grunted toward one of the SUVs at the back of the line. "Ride with me."

"Agent Reichenbach!" Jack's voice broke through the noise of the crowd, sailing over everyone.

Ethan and Scott both turned.

Jack jogged toward them, holding Ethan's jacket and wearing a wide smile. "Here you go, Ethan." When Jack passed the jacket into Ethan's hand, his hand brushed Ethan's, and his face lit up.

Ethan couldn't hold his own grin back. "Thank you, Mr. President."

Jack jogged back to his limo. Ethan turned around and came face-to-face with Scott's murderous glower.

They climbed into the last SUV, Scott in the driver's seat. The door slammed behind Scott hard enough to shake the truck on its wheels.

Scott waited before starting the engine. They watched Jack's limo pull out, silence straining their friendship.

"Are you being fucking stupid?" Scott finally growled. "I mean, are you being so *fucking* stupid that I *don't* even want to know?"

Friends for years, even before joining the Secret Service. They'd been in the same unit in the Army, different ranks, but sharing missions and beers and injuries. Scott had been the first Ethan had come out to. They moved up the ranks of the Secret Service together, countless details and advance trips and campaign stops shared between them. They had no secrets from each other.

"Yeah," Ethan grunted. "I'm being fucking stupid." He swallowed, thinking of Jack sleeping in his arms. "But it's worth it."

"Worth your *job*? Worth his *presidency*? Worth *everything*?" Scott braked hard at the light, slamming down on the turn signal.

"I think so. *We* think so."

"Jesus..." Scott shook his head, his face a stone mask. He gunned the accelerator, merging onto the highway at the end of the motor-cade. "What do you need from me?"

"Scott, you shouldn't get involved. This is my choice. Our choice."

"I'm already fucking involved," Scott snapped. "I already know about it, even though I don't fucking want to." He almost snarled. "And you're my Goddamn friend. If there's someone on this planet who you actually feel this way about, actually want to fall for, despite it being the stupidest fucking decision you've ever made, well—" Scott shook his head, sighing.

Ethan gripped Scott's shoulder. "Thanks." His voice was tight. "Maybe... sometime you could cover for me?"

Silence. "I'll think about it." Ethan nodded and sat back. It was more than he deserved, having Scott's grumpy acceptance. After a moment, Scott spoke again. "Are you happy? Really?"

"Yes." Ethan spoke instantly. "God, yes."

"Looked pretty fucked up in Prague. And taking the president out for a drink? Jesus, Ethan. I mean, that was out there."

"We had to figure some things out. We finally talked." Ethan shrugged. "And he needed to get out. That was a hard summit. The Russians have been playing games with him, and they surprised him with a high-value intel target this morning. The target was supposed to be delivered to our embassy today."

"Talib Al-Syria?"

"How'd you know?"

Scott shrugged. "He's the second most-wanted target. If it was Al-Karim, it would be all over the news." He gripped the wheel, kneading the leather. Ahead, the motorcade passed through the White House gates and pulled up to the Residence. "Look, you're wrapped up in some pretty crazy, insane, fucking dangerous stupid shit now, all right? You've got to be careful. Watch your six, man."

Ethan stared hard at Scott. Was that fear hidden behind the steel of his voice? "I'll be careful."

"You let me know if you need anything. Understand? Fucking anything." Like always, Scott was gruff and short when he was stressed.

"Yeah. I got it." Ethan finally smiled at his friend as they parked. "Really. Thanks."

"Don't fucking thank me," Scott growled. "I should be reporting you."

Through the window, Ethan watched Jack climb out of the limo and head up the White House steps. Jack turned, searching the motorcade, and he flashed Ethan a quick smile when he spotted him toward the back.

Then Gottschalk was at his side, and the vice president met him at the pavilion, and the business of being president descended around Jack once again.

Five minutes later, as Ethan was walking down to Horsepower with his duffel on his shoulder, his phone vibrated.

Want to come up?

It was close to eight PM, and the hours of sleep they'd managed to grab on the flight were barely making a dent in Ethan's exhaustion. He was dog-tired, his black eye still ached, and he hadn't eaten a real meal since before he'd kissed Jack beside the pool table. But, the promise of more time at Jack's side was a siren's song, and he was helpless against the lure.

[Leave the east stairwell unlocked. :)]

For you. Always.

CHAPTER 24

Saudi Arabia

FAISAL ANSWERED his cell phone on the third ring, even though there was no ID to the caller.

"*As-salamu alaykum*." He picked at his robes as he sat back in his limo.

"*Faisal*." Colonel Song's voice broke the ease of Faisal's afternoon.

"Colonel. Has something happened?"

"*The Russians delivered Talib Al-Syria to the American embassy in Moscow this evening.*"

"What?" Faisal bolted upright. "How did they find him?"

"*Unknown. But our mystery caller placed a call to General Madigan, vice chairman of the Joint Chiefs, this evening. We were able to record it. Listen.*"

Faisal pressed his cellphone to his ear. Colonel Song started the playback.

The first voice spoke, deep and heavy, and growling through his anger. "*What the hell happened? How did the damn Russians get their hands on Talib?*"

The second man, the mystery caller, answered. He was younger, and he was angry. His voice was almost a growl. *"We don't know, sir. They caught him with the nuclear package from Iran."*

"Goddamn it."

"The Russians offered him in trade to the president, sir. They're delivering him to the Moscow embassy tonight."

"This cannot happen. Talib cannot be taken into US custody. Our mission will be blown."

"Don't worry, sir. I'm taking care of it. Talib won't make it to the embassy alive."

"You'd better be damn sure."

"I am."

General Madigan spoke again. *"The news from the summit is even worse than I expected. We're losing ground here. This isn't where we wanted to be. We're supposed to building toward war with Russia. Not working on peace deals and negotiating."*

"No, sir."

A heavy sigh.

Faisal pressed the phone against his skull, trying to hear more, as if he could divine the identity of the speaker all on his own.

"We're going to need to change tactics. We need to move to plan B. We need to shake things up even more." Madigan paused. *"We need a sacrificial lamb. The stakes have to be higher."*

The mystery caller hesitated before he spoke. It was a first for the man, and Faisal held his breath. Was that meaningful? *"Yes, sir,"* the younger man finally said. Was his voice different? Did he sound hesitant?

"Make sure Talib is dead. Bring me your ideas for initiating plan B." Madigan grunted, and then the call was over.

Colonel Song came back on the line. *"Do you recognize the second man's voice?"*

Faisal shook his head. "No. I don't. You don't have his voice print on file somewhere that you can cross reference?" He said it almost as a joke, but Colonel Song's silence made him pause.

"We're searching for his identity," Colonel Song finally said. *"Talib was delivered to the American embassy yesterday."*

"Alive?"

"*Dead. He'd been dead for hours.*"

Faisal muttered a soft prayer beneath his breath. "He would have been able to reveal so much."

"*Mr. Hu is no longer needed. You may end his online afterlife.*"

"What do we do about their 'plan B'?" Faisal stared out the window of his limo, watching northern Saudi Arabia sail by. Plan B could mean anything.

"*We wait.*" Colonel Song's voice was hard. "*And we find this mystery man.*"

"Do we alert someone in the American government? This general and his partner are dangerous." Faisal swallowed. He knew who he wanted to call. He knew who he *needed* to call. But, he wasn't answering when Faisal reached out, not anymore. Would he even listen to this? Or would he continue to ignore Faisal?

Faisal's heart ached, empty and burned, withering in the Saudi sun like a Bedouin without an oasis. He was atomizing without his smile—

"*We don't know who they are working for or against. If we reveal what we know to the wrong people, we could lose everything. We're a half step ahead right now. This mystery caller is the key. We must know more.*"

Adam would never be connected to something like this. We can trust— Faisal shut down his own thoughts, swallowing hard.

No. He'd left Faisal. And he wasn't coming back.

They were on their own.

———

BREAKING NEWS - NUCLEAR BOMB BLAST IN KENYA

A nuclear detonation occurred in downtown Nairobi at eight forty-two AM, local time, on Wednesday, September 13th. Initial reports claim that a twelve-block radius in Nairobi has been reduced to a crater. The mushroom cloud hovered over the city for five minutes, long after a 600-foot-wide fireball incinerated everything around the blast radius.

The blast happened without warning, stunning an international community that had enjoyed an autumn of relative calm. Two months after the emergency NATO summit, international cooperation against the Caliphate had been steadily improving, with Russia and the United States partnering against the Caliphate in Syria and Iraq.

The Islamic Caliphate has claimed responsibility for the nuclear explosion.

CHAPTER 25

Washington DC

THE CALL CAME in the middle of the night, one of the nights Ethan had stayed at the White House with Jack.

The Navy steward on duty overnight knocked on Jack's bedroom door before poking his head inside. "Mr. President?"

Ethan woke instantly. He froze, keeping his eyes closed, but loosened his hold around Jack's waist.

Jack came awake slower. He rolled toward Ethan before sitting up and blinking at the light streaming in from the cracked door. Naked, with his hair sticking up every which way, swollen lips, and a kiss-bruise on his collarbone, Jack looked debauched.

"What's going on?" Jack grunted.

"Mr. President." The steward stayed at the door. There was no way he didn't notice Ethan in the bed, but he also didn't acknowledge the oddity of finding a man curled around the president. The stewards, like the Secret Service, were trained not to comment. "There's been a nuclear attack in Nairobi. The National Security Watch has a live feed in the Situation Room."

Jack bolted upright, flinging back the covers, and slid out of bed. He was naked, and he fished for his discarded boxers thrown carelessly to the floor. "Wake everyone," he said, sniffing sleepily. "Get everyone to the Situation Room. And what time is it?"

"Two AM, sir." The steward nodded and shut the door.

Ethan was moving before the door latched, jumping out of bed, grabbing his own boxers and suit pants, and pulling them on quickly. Jack tossed his undershirt at the back of his head as he whirled, searching. They both slipped into their button-downs in silence, still trying to wake up.

THE PAST TWO MONTHS, since coming back from the summit, had been amazing. Terrifying, at times, and with more than a few close calls. But as far as Ethan was concerned, each day had been better than the last. He was living in a dream, a fantasy come to life. And it was perfect.

They were figuring it all out, slowly. Figuring out how to be together.

Ethan had fantasized and daydreamed about being with Jack so many times before they'd gotten together. He'd nurtured hot and heavy fantasies about grabbing Jack and holding him tight or bending him over his desk in the Oval Office, or sweeping him off his feet and seeing Jack melt in his arms, delirious with desire and wanting everything Ethan could give him.

Reality was different.

Jack was a human being, with desires and fantasies of his own, and his own preferences, and negotiating the spaces between them, and exploring their burgeoning relationship, was an ongoing process.

In the past, Ethan had been the pursuer, chasing his partners at bars and clubs and whenever he'd picked up a man out and about in the world. He'd been the aggressor, seducing his partners in a whirlwind of passion. This was different, and Ethan initially held back from a hot and heavy pursuit of Jack. *Slow*, he'd told himself. *Let Jack lead.*

Jack had taken control, driving the pace of their relationship.

Jack had also started to pursue Ethan, chasing the chaser, and Ethan found himself in the odd position of being seduced, even dated, for the first time in forever.

It was so *entirely* different from anything he'd fantasized about, and anything he'd expected, but now that they were there, and now that they were building their reality, Ethan *loved* every moment of it. He loved the slowness, the deliberate surety of their relationship. How he was being pursued—seduced—by the man who already owned his heart.

The slow burn, the discovery of each other, the anticipation rising like lightning between them, sizzled against Ethan's soul.

And, for a man who hadn't had sex in a decade and a half, Jack seemed quite happy leading Ethan down the road of his personal sexual revolution.

The first night, they were both too tired and too relieved to do anything more than lie in bed and kiss a bit before falling asleep in each other's arms. Ethan slipped out before dawn, avoiding the stewards, and drove to his condo for a quick shower and change before heading back.

After that, Ethan could barely stay away, and Jack invited him up to the Residence every evening.

Watching baseball together turned into Ethan lying with his head in Jack's lap, Jack's fingers stroking through his hair. Then, unbuttoning his shirt and slipping it off his shoulders. By the bottom of the seventh, Ethan was lying shirtless and panting, and he was sure that Jack could feel the pounding of his heart as Jack stroked Ethan's bare chest, fingers tugging on Ethan's chest hair.

Ethan gave Jack a massage that night, straddling him and digging into his muscles with long, deep strokes, from the small of his back to his neck. Warm skin melted beneath his touch as he worked out knots Jack had ignored for over a decade. Beneath him, Jack shifted from a coiled tension—nervous apprehension at having a man touch him so intimately for the first time?—to groaning with contentment and relaxation, and arching into Ethan's touch. Jack was a melted pile of warm smiles and open-mouthed kisses at the end, and he nuzzled Ethan's cheek with his nose, cuddling close, as he fell asleep.

A few nights later, Jack changed the rules of their pool game. For every ball sunk, the other player had to take off a piece of clothing. Jack told Ethan the new rules with a wink and a smile before breaking and running the table. Ethan ended up in just his boxers and a blush.

"If you run the table, do I at least get a kiss?" Ethan had asked.

Jack turned serious. "You never need a reason to kiss me. Or a game."

Ethan had kissed him then, drawing him into his arms and holding him close. Jack slowly turned him, pressing Ethan against the pool table, and the kiss stretched long. Ethan finally pushed him back with an apologetic look down at the tent of his boxers.

"Your turn to break." Jack had stepped back and set up the balls as Ethan collected himself.

Ethan was too fired up and too distracted to run the table, but he got Jack down to his bare chest, though still in his dress pants, before he flubbed the next shot. Jack scratched next, and then it was back and forth, ball for ball, until they were both in boxers and chasing the eight ball.

"There's a joke in here about sinking balls in holes, right?" Jack said as Ethan lined up for his shot.

Groaning, Ethan thunked his forehead down on the table, dropping his pool stick on the felt. "You are a complete tease."

Ethan couldn't stay the night after that. He couldn't lie next to Jack and not *ache*, desperately wanting to press his body close to Jack's. He had to do this right, though, and he left after a long, sultry kiss, one that almost had him coming in his pants and had Jack's eyes blown black with desire.

Later, when he got home, Jack texted him.

Should I tell you that I jerked off to that kiss? And that I thought of you, standing there in just your boxers? And remembered the feel of your chest beneath my hands? Your strength, your muscles... Your body...

[Yes. God yes, you should tell me that.]

Do you think of me?
[Every single moment.]
I miss you. Come back?
[Not if we want to go slow.]
:) You're too good to me.
[This matters to me. I don't want to hurt you. Or scare you. I want this to work so badly.]
It is working, Ethan. It is so working.

He couldn't text after that, and he was caught between choking up, falling in love, and needing to come. He'd ended up in his bed in a mess, jerking off and trying not to cry and hoping, desperately, for this to keep going.

They still worked out together in the mornings, but instead of Ethan slipping off to shower in the Secret Service locker room, he smuggled his suits in his gym bag and showered after Jack in his bathroom. They downed breakfast shakes together, too, in Jack's private kitchen in the Residence. Jack chopped fruit and vegetables as Ethan measured out protein powder and soy milk. It was simple and domestic, and they spent most of the time joking around.

Jack sent Ethan's world spinning higher one morning after their workouts, doing nothing more than being himself. Jack was slicing strawberries, and he sent Ethan a sly, surreptitious glance before motioning to the protein powder on the counter.

"Can you grab that?"

Ethan did as asked, leaning in, and Jack flicked strawberry juice at Ethan's workout shirt, and then swiped his juicy hand across Ethan's chest.

Shocked, Ethan stepped back, staring at Jack.

"Oops." Jack grinned. "Guess you'll have to take that off now. Don't want it to stain."

"I don't care about stains." Ethan tried—and failed—to smother his own smile.

Jack pushed out his bottom lip.

Slowly, Ethan peeled his sweaty gym shirt over his head and

dropped it on the floor. The cool air of the kitchen had his nipples going hard as beads of sweat evaporated off his skin.

Jack's eyes darkened. He dropped the fruit, moving to Ethan, who stood motionless with his back to the sink. Jack traced Ethan's ribs before flattening across his abs.

Ethan shuddered, but stayed still. His knuckles went white where he gripped the counter. Panting breaths escaped his lips as his body trembled.

Jack moved carefully, his eyes tracing the path of his hands, as if mesmerized by Ethan's chest. His fingers spread across Ethan's skin, sliding up through his chest hair before hitting a nipple. Ethan grunted and closed his eyes.

They flew open again when Jack licked his nipple.

"Jack..." His knees buckled.

Jack's hands continued to roam, squeezing his pecs, pinching his nipples, and tracing the lines of his ribs. Jack grabbed Ethan's waist as he leaned close, nuzzling his cheek before he pressed a lingering kiss to Ethan's open mouth.

Ethan thought he was going to break the counter. He finally let go and cradled Jack's face, even though he was practically trembling apart.

As they kissed, Jack's erection slid against Ethan's, hot, heavy, and hard. Ethan whimpered and broke away.

Jack pressed a kiss to his temple. "The more I fall for you, the more attracted I am to you," Jack whispered. "I can't get enough of you, Ethan."

Ethan had jerked off furiously in Jack's shower later that morning, almost blacking out when he came.

They made out a few nights later, stretched on the couch and slowly peeling off layers. For the first time, they let their bodies rock and roll together, their hard cocks—encased in boxers and suit pants —slide against one another. It was kisses and bare chests and heavy petting, and hickeys left on collarbones, and nipples being sucked, but they kept their pants on. Jack's eyes smoldered when Ethan rolled him over and kissed his belly, or when he held Jack's thigh as he rocked his cock against Jack's.

But Jack's eyes burned, brilliant and heated, when Ethan was on his back and Jack was between his legs, his hands roaming over Ethan's body, or gripping Ethan's knees and spreading them wide, or kissing Ethan with open eyes as he thrust against him.

Ethan filed that away and let Jack roll him over. Let Jack be on top.

A playful text from Jack upped the tension one Thursday afternoon. Ethan was meeting with the team leads of the detail, reviewing procedures and problems and answering questions.

So you're considered a bear, right?

The text had flashed across his screen, and his phone had been out on the table in the Mess, where he was chatting with the other agents. He palmed his phone and slid it into his pocket, coughing. One of the agents who had caught the message, but didn't understand the caller ID, smothered his grin.

Later, Ethan texted back.

[Where did you learn that?]

I've been doing some research online. You are a bear, right? I'm using that correctly?

[OMG. Are you searching gay sex terms on the White House network?]

No, I'm searching for men having sex with men on the White House network. I found bears, and they look kind of like you. I like it.

[Jesus Christ. You're watching porn?]

It was my lunch break. I was doing research, but then I thought... why not just watch the real deal?

[...]

[First, gay porn isn't quite the real deal. There are a few more steps they gloss over. And second... Goddamn, the thought of you watching that... or doing research.]

:) You're way hotter than the guys online. Don't worry.

[You know you can ask me anything. I want you to be comfortable.]

And I want to know what I'm doing with you. Want to make you happy.

[You do. :) And yes, I can be considered a bear. A muscle bear specifi-cally. I'm glad you like bears.]

There's one bear I really like. More than all the others. He's the sexiest.

[... He's about to ruin his pants.]

Maybe we can take care of that later.

They jerked off in front of each other that night, kneeling on Jack's bed with their boxers pulled down and kissing slowly, in time with their strokes. Jack's hand rested on Ethan's chest, and Ethan squeezed Jack's hips, but he held back from dragging him close.

It was the first time Jack had seen Ethan's naked body. His heart leapt to his throat, grinding through ten different kinds of anxiety as they watched each other, let their eyes linger on naked cocks and stroking hands. He had kept his cock covered around Jack, always keeping his boxers on or a towel around his waist after showering and while getting ready.

There was a big difference between being shirtless and petting and being confronted with an actual cock, hard and aching for touch.

Jack had been more than courteous about his space, giving him privacy in the giant bathroom made for two while Ethan dressed.

Jack changed the rules on that, too, the next week.

Ethan had just finished brushing his teeth when Jack walked into the bathroom. Jack was already dressed, dark suit pants impeccably pressed, white dress shirt starched and crisp, and a red tie knotted perfectly at his neck. He leaned back against the bathroom counter, arms crossed, and watched Ethan.

Nervousness stole through Ethan, and he kept stealing glances Jack's way. "See something you like?"

Jack nodded. He stepped forward and reached for Ethan's towel.

Ethan stayed still. He watched Jack, but Jack's eyes were on his own hands, slowly tugging open Ethan's towel. Jack let it drop to the floor without a word.

And then, Ethan was fully naked in front of Jack. The warm air of the bathroom, still humid, tickled the backs of his thighs, but it was Jack's eyes roaming over his body that seared his soul. Long, lingering looks traveled up Ethan's legs and over his chest before dropping down to his groin.

He couldn't help it. Ethan's cock hardened, filling and rising as Jack watched him.

Jack bit his lip and grinned. His burning eyes finally met Ethan's.

"Can I touch you?" Jack's voice was too low, and rumbled over his words.

"*Please*," Ethan breathed. His brain caught up to his need. "But only if you're sure," he said quickly. *Please be sure!*

"I am." Jack moved close, his eyes locked on Ethan's cock. He reached for Ethan, his hand trembling. "What do I do?" Jack whispered. His fingers ghosted over Ethan's shaft. Brushed the tip of his cock.

"Anything," Ethan moaned. He shuddered, and barely held back from grabbing Jack's shoulders to stay upright. "It's like touching yourself. Just do what you like."

Jack grasped his cock in a firm fist, one thumb stroking over his cockhead, and started moving, stroking, building a slow rhythm. Ethan moaned again. He shuddered as Jack kept stroking him, pumping him up and down.

Jack's gaze seemed torn between Ethan's hard cock sliding through his fist and Ethan's face, twisting and gasping as he panted.

"Faster."

Jack squeezed as he sped up, and Ethan bucked, grabbed Jack's shoulders, and exploded. He came all over Jack's hand, spurting come in rivulets that ran between Jack's fingers and soaked his palm.

Jack stared at him, his jaw hanging open, and then at his come-drenched hand.

"Are you okay?" Ethan gasped. *God, please, don't let this be the end. Don't let this be the moment he decides he can't take it.*

Jack grabbed him, his clean hand wrapping around Ethan's neck and pulling him close for a wet, openmouthed kiss. Tongues dueling, Jack moaned as he reached for his own belt.

Ethan batted his hands away and backed him up until he hit the bathroom counter. "Jack," he grunted, in between sucking Jack's bottom lip into his mouth and licking his tongue. "You sure?"

"Yes! Touch me! Ethan, please!"

He had Jack's pants undone in a moment, and then Jack's hard cock was out, glistening with precome. He should have just jerked him off, like Jack had done, but Ethan had been dreaming of this moment for *months*.

He dropped to his knees and nuzzled Jack's cock. The scent, the hot muskiness of Jack, hit him full blast, and he felt his own cock stirring again between his legs.

Jack let out a breathy, moan-filled scream as Ethan swallowed him deep. Jack's hands fumbled behind him, knocking down toothpaste and deodorant and searching for something to grab onto before he reached for Ethan. His come-wet thumb stroked over Ethan's cheek, over the hollow of his sucking.

When Jack blew, deep in Ethan's throat, Ethan reached between his own legs and stroked himself off again, grunting and whining and swallowing Jack's come. He came for the second time on the bathroom floor, a puddle appearing between his knees. His over-sensitive cock tried to retreat, and he leaned his forehead against Jack's thigh.

Boneless, Jack sank to his knees, his perfect pants ruined, shirt disheveled, tie stretched and loosened.

"I'm sorry," Ethan grunted. His voice was rough. Cock-roughened. "I shouldn't have done that."

"Shut up," Jack breathed, "and kiss me."

Jack groaned into their kiss, almost falling into Ethan, and Ethan's arms wound around him, holding tight. It was perfect, absolutely perfect.

Jack surprised Ethan with a hand job in the kitchen after their morning workout the next week, and Ethan barely had time to set down his protein shake before Jack was down his pants, his hand wrapped around his cock. Jack kissed him, sucking on his lip as he jerked him fast, and Ethan spread his feet, grabbed Jack's shoulders, and prepared to come.

"Mr. President, we got word from the Hill that—" Gottschalk stopped dead in the kitchen doorway, his mouth hanging open.

Jack whirled as Ethan tore away, ducking down and nearly falling to the floor.

"Jeff!" Jack's eyes were wide, panicked. "Jesus, Jeff!"

"I'll, uh... I'll wait outside." Stunned, Gottschalk disappeared in a daze, his jaw still unhinged.

Later, Gottschalk came back into the kitchen, but this time, Ethan was sitting at the small dining table and Jack was standing far away from him, across the kitchen. Gottschalk stared at them both. "I didn't see anything," he said. "As far as I'm concerned, there was nothing to see." He grinned, self-deprecating. "Though, I will knock when I see a closed door from now on."

"Thank you, Jeff." Gratitude poured from Jack's voice. "This is new. And special."

"And secret." Gottschalk nodded. "You have nothing to fear from me."

Gottschalk sent Ethan a quick smile as he slipped out of the kitchen, after he'd briefed Jack on the status of legislation they were watching. It had just left committee in the middle of the night and was headed for a controversial floor vote.

They weren't keeping their relationship as secret as they'd originally planned. Besides Gottschalk, the stewards *had* to know. Ethan spent more nights at the White House than he did at his condo. Suits of his hung next to Jack's, and he had a toothbrush, deodorant, and a razor in Jack's bathroom. They tried to sneak around in the early morning, pretending that Ethan hadn't just woken up in Jack's bed, but there was only so much they could do.

"I'm not the first president to have a secret love affair," Jack had said.

"With a man?" Ethan stole a carrot from Jack's dinner plate.

"Some historians say Lincoln had male lovers." Jack swatted the back of Ethan's hand with his fork. "We will be fine."

If they were being lazy in the Residence, Ethan made up for it with the Secret Service. He slipped in and out of the Residence using secret passages and the underground tunnel, and Scott covered for him with made-up reasons whenever an agent caught him wandering around after hours. After Ethan had spent seven days straight at the White House, Scott started moving his SUV so no one would notice that he hadn't ever left.

At night, they'd read briefing papers spread out on Jack's bed, discussing the day and planning for the next. They would laugh and steal glances at the other when they thought they wouldn't be caught, and reach for one another for a handhold, or a long, lazy kiss. When the lights went out, Ethan pulled Jack close, burying his face in the back of Jack's neck. They started in boxers and undershirts, and then it was just boxers and bare chests, and warm skin against warm skin.

They'd woken up slowly the past Sunday in each other's arms, hard erections straining their boxers as they rolled together, slow thrusts building as their kisses grew. Ethan gathered Jack close, stroking his cheeks as they kissed, and then he rolled over, bringing Jack on top. Just a little bit more, and then maybe they'd roll apart and jerk off in front of each other.

Jack's knees pushed at Ethan's thighs, spreading them wider as his arms wound around Ethan's head and neck. He pulled back, breathless. "Lose the boxers?" Jack whispered.

Ethan froze. "If you're—"

"I'm sure." Jack grinned down at Ethan, cutting him off.

Jack sat back and slid his boxers down his legs. His cock jerked free, rock-hard. Ethan lifted his hips and shucked his own pair, throwing them to the side carelessly.

Jack clambered back into Ethan's arms, and between Ethan's legs. Their thighs brushed, and then their cocks, and then they were naked together, rocking against each other, body to body, for the first time.

Ethan's heart lodged in his throat, frantic and terrified and hopeful. Everything else they'd done could be excused, but being naked cock to naked cock and writhing in the arms of another man, sweaty and needy and wanting, was a pivotal moment.

They rocked together, Jack on top and surging against Ethan.

Ethan kissed him and never let go, sharing breaths between nibbles and sucks on Jack's lower lip. His legs wrapped around Jack's waist, urging him on, trying to draw him closer.

Jack was everywhere, all around him, his arms around Ethan's neck, his thighs pushing against the backs of Ethan's legs, his cock driving into Ethan's. Ethan wasn't used to this, to be being surrounded and enveloped by another man, but Jack was taking control, wrapping Ethan up in his arms and kissing him breathless. Ethan wasn't usually the one being made love to, but he realized, as Jack breathed a kiss against his cheek and buried his face in Ethan's neck, that that was *exactly* what was happening.

Jack came with a gasp, moaning against Ethan's neck. The heat of his come, scorching on Ethan's cock, triggered his own orgasm. Ethan grabbed Jack's hips and pulled him down, rutted up into the slick, wet heat, and exploded.

Pulling back, Jack beamed down at Ethan, breathless and laughing. "We just…"

"Yeah." Ethan smoothed strands of Jack's hair, sweaty against his skin, off his forehead. "Yeah. We did." He licked his lips. Grinned. "Okay?"

"Great." Jack smiled as he leaned down, kissing Ethan slowly.

ONLY TWO DAYS LATER, they were jolted awake in the middle of the night with the news from Nairobi.

The news was too big, suddenly, to bother with hiding. Once they were dressed, Jack motioned for Ethan to come with him. He jogged with Jack down the main staircase, ignoring his agents' looks of surprise as they breezed by their posts in the Cross Hall.

"What on earth happened?" Jack's heels rang out on the marble, fast and clipped. "Where did this come from?"

Ethan scrolled through his phone, reading headlines as quick as they came in. "The Caliphate has claimed responsibility."

"Is this because of our negotiations with the Russians? Payback for the UN mission we're putting together for Syria?"

"It's got to be." Ethan tugged open the door to the West Wing for Jack. "There isn't a reason given yet. News reports are just saying that they claimed responsibility, but they're not reporting a manifesto or anything." They jogged through the empty West Wing, bypassing the night cleaning crew as they ran for the staircase leading down to the ground floor.

Jack stopped before the last step. "Ethan... I want you in there with me."

"You know I can't." Ethan shook his head, pocketing his phone. "I'm not supposed to know any of this. I'm not supposed to be talking with you about anything."

"Or be my boyfriend, but you are."

He couldn't help it. Ethan smiled and looked down, trying to hide his flush. "Boyfriend, huh?"

"Yeah." Jack pushed on Ethan's shoulder, a tiny grin on his lips. "You a commitment-phobe?"

Now was not the time for that conversation. "Go save the world, Jack." He looked up and down the stairs before leaning in for a quick kiss. "I can't be by your side right now. But I am with you all the way."

Jack cupped his cheek, smiled, and then jogged down the last step and around the corner, into the Situation Room.

Later, after Ethan had checked on the agents posted around the West Wing for the night shift and reassigned two agents to stand post inside the Situation Room, seated at the back, he made four cups of coffee from the White House Mess and stacked them in his hands. Ethan slipped into the Situation Room and passed out two cups to his detail agents.

He took the third to Jack, meeting his gaze briefly as Jack bounced rapid-fire questions off his national security team and the Joint Chiefs. Everyone was sleepy, but they had the wide-eyed look of adrenaline-fueled fright running through their veins. There hadn't been a nuclear strike since World War II.

The fourth cup he kept, nursing it as he lingered in the background, trying to stay out of sight. Intelligence flashed on screens around the room. A Navy commander onboard a ship stationed in the Red Sea reported details of their ongoing reconnaissance flights over Nairobi. News was streaming in from all over East Africa— Kampala, Dar es Salaam, and Addis Ababa. The secure feed to the US embassy in Nairobi was down, and Secretary of State Wall couldn't confirm whether it had been hit or not.

The deputy director of the CIA barged in an hour late, trailed by the National Security Advisor, John Luntz. "Mr. President," Gary Luss, CIA Deputy Director, said, dropping a pile of file folders and a stack of messy papers on the edge of the conference table. He had a cell phone jammed between his ear and his shoulder. "I have contact with the CIA station chief from Nairobi. Bill Dix."

Luss threw the cell phone back to the NSA watch officers, who transferred the call to the speakerphone embedded in the center of the table. Jack leaned forward, taking over the call. "Bill, are you with us? This is President Spiers."

"Mr. President!" On the phone, Bill coughed hard. *"I'm here. Don't know how long the battery will last on this sat phone, but I'm here."*

"Where are you? Are you safe?"

"The bomb went off somewhere south of us, toward downtown. The mushroom cloud covered our area, but that's dissipated. Everyone in the embassy made it into the shelters. We've got a lot of wounded. Lots of burns and cuts. All the windows blew, and the heat was incredible. People got hurt in the evacuation to the shelter. The ambassador is pretty banged up."

"We're already working on an evacuation plan for everyone there. We've got the *Truman* headed to the Med right now, and the *Arleigh Burke* is in the Red Sea. We'll get you guys out of there and get you treated ASAP." Jack nodded to the Joint Chiefs. Already, attachés were scrambling, working two cell phones each and typing furiously on secured laptops.

"Thank you, Mr. President. That will be very welcome news for everyone here."

"Do you have any information about the ground situation, Bill?"

"Yes, sir." Bill cleared his throat again. *"The bomb leveled a crater*

half a mile wide. We could see it from the embassy. About a mile outside of that, everyone in the area was burned up bad. Buildings blew out, and everything is on fire. There's mass panic in the streets. We haven't heard from the government. Military vehicles have been driving through the capital, and we've heard a lot of gunfire."

"Is there any indication that this could have been a prelude to a larger attack? Any evidence of foreign fighters moving in?"

"I don't have that intelligence, sir. I'm sorry." Bill coughed again, sounding like he was about to hack up a lung.

"Bill, you're just fine. Thank you for making contact. Sit tight, keep the phone near you, and we'll call you with our rescue plan shortly." Jack waved to the chief of naval operations and then pointed to the phone. Nodding, Admiral McDonald stood and jogged back to the watch officers to take over the phone call. The speakerphone went dead.

The meeting rolled on, and slowly, more information and intelligence flowed in. Ethan hung in the background, catching Jack's eye every so often. By dawn, the room was exhausted, buzzing from caffeine and running on fumes. They had a plan, though, to evacuate the embassy and any American personnel in-country, and a deployment schedule for reconnaissance flights over the impact zone. Intelligence assets were being contacted, searching for any clues or insights into the attack, and into what was happening in the broader terror world.

And, Jack demanded that the United States spearhead a relief operation, beginning that day. A combined task force of military personnel and aid organizations was being assembled, along with decontamination equipment, food, shelter, and medical assistance.

"I want to address the nation at eight AM." Jack rubbed his eyes and pinched his nose. His jaw cracked as he yawned wide.

Gottschalk, standing next to Ethan and fielding emails on three different phones, nodded and stepped forward. "I'll get Pete on it." Pete Reyes was Jack's press secretary. "He's already working on some early drafts. I'll get with him. We'll have something for you by seven thirty."

Jack nodded. "Everyone else, report back in with updated intelligence as you receive it. I want comprehensive briefs on the hour. I also want to talk to the Russians, the Ugandans, the Tanzanians, and anyone you can get on the line in Kenya. And the British."

And with that, Jack stood, thanked everyone for coming in, and headed out. Ethan fell in beside him, as did Gottschalk. The two detail agents trailed behind as they headed up the stairs for the Oval Office.

"You should get some rest, Mr. President," Gottschalk said.

"I'm fine."

"Mr. President." Ethan glanced sideways at Jack. "At least try to lie down for a little bit."

"Did you get any sleep last night, sir?" Gottschalk shot Ethan a quick, dry look, hiding a smirk.

"Yes," Jack said, at the same time Ethan said, "Not much, no."

Jack glared at Ethan. "This is conspiracy."

"Collusion," Gottschalk corrected. "And it's for your benefit. Try to lie down in your office, sir. You don't want to look like a ghost when you address the nation." Gottschalk tried, and failed, to smother another grin. "I'll try to keep Agent Reichenbach out of your hair."

They stopped outside the door to the Oval Office. Sighing, Jack turned to both men, fixing each with a glare. The effect would have been greater if there weren't dark circles beneath his eyes, belying his exhaustion. "I want to see one of you in here at seven fifteen. Not a minute later."

Gottschalk and Ethan nodded, and after Jack disappeared into the Oval Office, they shared small, tired grins before heading their separate ways.

US LEADS WORLD IN PROVIDING MASSIVE AID AND RELIEF TO NUCLEAR-STRICKEN NAIROBI & ANNOUNCES JOINT AIR STRIKES AGAINST ISLAMIC CALIPHATE

The United States has assembled the largest aid response ever for nuclear-stricken Nairobi. Over twenty nations have committed significant resources to the African nation, and Russia has emerged as a strong partner to the US in President Spiers' humanitarian efforts.

Sources in the White House say that President Puchkov and President Spiers have spent many hours on the phone together, a sign of strengthening relations between the two countries.

The United States and Russia have also planned joint military operations against the Caliphate in response to the attack on Nairobi and are cooperating with sharing intelligence in the region.

CHAPTER 26

Washington DC

"HEY SCOTT, YOU GOT A MINUTE?" Daniels hovered behind Scott on the White House terrace above the West Wing, waiting while Scott finished a call on his cell phone.

Scott whirled around, eyes wide. "Jesus, Daniels. You startled me." He slid the phone into his pocket. "What do you need?"

"I was called into headquarters this morning."

Scott's eyebrows shot straight up. "HQ? Why? And all by yourself?"

Daniels nodded. "Yeah. They wanted to ask me about Ethan." Daniels licked his lips. "About Ethan and the president."

"Shit." Scott pulled Daniels away from the walkway, until they were tucked around back and hidden from view. "What kind of questions? And who was asking?"

"Man, it was the director!" Daniels exhaled, shifting across his feet as he shoved his hands in his suit pants. "They called me straight up to Director Stahl's office, and then he was talking to me one-on-one. Asking me questions about how much time Ethan was spending with the president. About whether I had seen anything unprofessional or in violation of regulations. And was there anything going on between the two of them."

"Jesus. What did you say?"

"I said I hadn't seen anything. And that, as far as I knew, there wasn't anything going on. But, Scott. Shit, man. Should we tell 'em?"

Scott sighed and leaned back against the wall beneath the awning. "I'll take care of it."

Daniels nodded. "Thanks. And, lemme know if they need anything."

CHAPTER 27

Washington DC

ONE WEEK after the nuclear blast, aid organizations and the US military flooded into Nairobi. Refugee camps had been built north of the capital, out of the range of the radiation and the winds, and away from the devastation, the disease, and the decay in the rubble. Thousands upon thousands had died. Thousands had been incinerated in the initial blast, and the shock wave crashed through Nairobi's shantytowns and business districts cramped together in the capital. Burned and rotting bodies lay in the streets next to twisted concrete and melted steel.

In medical tents, hundreds of people sweated and vomited through radiation sickness. Twenty died each hour.

The survivors huddled together, living in refugee tents and shelters set up by the bevy of aid organizations and militaries that had flooded in. Borderless Doctors managed five mobile hospitals around Nairobi. The African Union mobilized troops from Tanzania, Uganda, Nigeria, and South Africa. American soldiers patrolled the streets side by side with their African partners.

Random soccer matches broke out amongst the soldiers and teenagers trailing behind the patrols.

Through the fear, people were surviving.

Questions still lingered. "Why" hung in the air, unanswered. The Caliphate had been noticeably—suspiciously—quiet, and even its operations inside of Syria and Iraq had dwindled.

The Assembly of the African Union, a conference of all the heads of state of the member nations , called for an emergency meeting in Addis Ababa, capital of Ethiopia. President Amameka, the president of the assembly, invited Jack, along with other world leaders, to join the assembly.

Jack thought it was a great idea. He enthusiastically agreed to attend and to do everything that he could to help with Nairobi's reconstruction.

Ethan hated everything about the proposed trip.

From a security standpoint, it was a nightmare. A disaster waiting to happen. Jack wanted to fly into a region beset by nuclear terrorism, only weeks after the blast. Radiation levels had dissipated, and Nairobi was functioning better than many had expected under martial law, but it was still an absolutely ridiculous idea.

Ethan was overruled, though, by nearly everyone. Gottschalk thought it was a good move, and Reyes, Jack's press secretary, thought it would be phenomenal press. Jack thought it was the right thing to do. The Joint Chiefs assured Jack that they could keep him safe on the way there and back. The CIA assured him that, as far as they could tell, the situation on the ground was safe, and that the assembly would be well protected.

They all turned to Ethan, then, as head of the presidential detail, and asked if he and his men were up to protecting Jack overseas in Addis Ababa.

Ethan knew a lost battle when he saw one. He agreed to draw up security plans for the trip.

Long, sleepless nights followed, and his and Jack's first real fight. Ethan asked him—almost begged him—to reconsider and to call the trip off. Jack accused Ethan of wanting to keep him in the gilded cage of the White House. Ethan roared back, shouting that it wasn't *just* Jack's life in his hands; it was the love of his life as well.

Jack retreated to the Oval Office, leaving Ethan in the Residence to cool off.

Frantic tension tore at Ethan's insides. He did want to keep Jack in a cage. It was safe in a cage. The White House was a cocoon, a secure, controlled place where he could ensure Jack's safety. Flying around the United States was stressful enough, and flying to overseas European summits was almost soul-suckingly exhausting.

But taking Jack to East Africa? To Ethiopia? On the heels of this nuclear attack?

It would show the world Jack's commitment to people everywhere. Following Prague, and his pact with Russian President Puchkov to jointly combat the Islamic Caliphate, Jack had somehow taken on the image of being a champion of the world. He'd seen Jack's bemusement at the appellation. If it helped the world in any way, Jack had said, then he'd embrace it.

Jack could do a lot of good. As president, he already had made a huge impact. Working with the Russians for the first time in decades, and combating the Caliphate together. Ensuring elections within the Russian-held European territories. Committing more troops and more shared intelligence to European allies and thwarting terror attacks. Launching the largest aid mission in history for Nairobi, and saving thousands and thousands of lives. He was building peace one day at a time, despite everything stacked against him.

But Jack couldn't do *any* good for *anyone* if he was dead.

Ethan slumped on Jack's bed—their bed, for the past two months —and sagged forward, holding his head in his hands.

That was it. That was the root of it.

He was petrified of losing Jack.

Dying was the ultimate loss, and death was something neither Jack nor Ethan were strangers to. Ethan had lost soldiers and friends in the wars. Jack had lost his wife.

But the thought of Jack dying sent Ethan into a near apoplectic rage, and he'd loosed that on Jack, shouting at him and screaming about the stupid trip to Ethiopia.

It was all just a mask, a convenient cover for the gnawing, aching, soul-splitting fear that he was going to lose Jack somehow, someway.

Jack eventually walked in on Ethan struggling to hold it all together, lost in the twisted tunnels of his anxiety. Ethan had dropped to the floor, his back to their bed, and he was clinging to the carpet as he clenched his jaw hard enough to crack a tooth. His eyes gleamed, wet panic desperately being held back through sheer force of will alone.

Knees popping, Jack sat on the carpet in front of Ethan, sighing as he folded himself down. Ethan couldn't look at him at first, but when he did, the first of his tears trailed down his cheeks. "I'm terrified of losing you," Ethan mumbled. "It's my biggest fear. My worst fear."

Jack pulled Ethan into his lap, tugging on his shoulders until he pulled him off-kilter. Ethan fell into Jack's hold, his face buried in Jack's shirt as his arms wound around Jack's waist, and sobbed. Jack held him through every tear, stroking his back and rubbing his neck.

Ethan's sobs weren't pretty. They were hard, aching, and pulled from his fearful heart. Snot soaked Jack's shirt. Ethan's head throbbed, and he clung to Jack like a drowning sailor clung to a piece of flotsam.

"I'm with you all the way," Jack whispered in Ethan's ear. "You won't lose me."

"I'm in charge of your *life*," Ethan groaned. "It's in my hands." *Now* he understood the rules, finally, in a visceral, real way. He was paralyzed, nearly incompetent with fear.

"Don't put this all on yourself. You're not an island." Jack stroked the back of Ethan's neck as Ethan pressed his forehead to Jack's shoulder and sighed. "I rely on a whole team of smart people. You are often my smartest person."

Ethan snuffled.

"But right now, you're not seeing everything. Open your eyes, Ethan. See the whole field. You've got help. Pull in Agent Collard and Agent Daniels. They're your friends. They can help you set this up." Jack pressed a kiss to Ethan's hair. "And you have me. Ethan, you have me."

Ethan's hand found Jack's, and he threaded their fingers together. "What I said, when I shouted at you…"

"Shhh." Jack kissed him again. Stroked his arm. "You don't need to say anything."

But Ethan *wanted* to say it. He wanted to tell Jack over and over that he loved him, that he was frighteningly incomplete without Jack. That Jack was the love of his life, and that he knew it like he knew he needed to breathe.

Maybe it was better not to say it if Jack couldn't say the same. Ethan could stay in his sheltered dreamland, and if there was one thing he'd learned about himself, it was that he craved his fantasy dreamland.

"WE'VE WORKED with our partners overseas to spread out the arrival of each head of state."

Ethan, dressed in black cargo pants tucked into combat boots and a Secret Service t-shirt, gestured to the flat screen behind him in the main conference room on Air Force One. It was the final run-through, the last briefing before Jack and the entire team landed in Ethiopia. Jack sat at the head of the conference table, smiling at Ethan. Gottschalk and Reyes flanked him on either side. Secretary Elizabeth Wall, CIA Director Lawrence Irwin, and National Security Advisor John Luntz also sat at the table, watching.

Scott and Daniels sat at the end of the table nearest Ethan. Scott had helped Ethan draw up the security plans for the trip, and Daniels had grounded both Ethan and Scott when they barked and shouted at each other over the details.

Welby leaned against the wall in the back. Welby had taken Inada's spot in their four-man detail after Inada requested more time with his family.

Ethan continued on with his presentation. "Mr. President, you are the first head of state to arrive. The British prime minister is due four hours after we touch down, and President Puchkov four hours after that. Like in all foreign trips, local law enforcement is taking the lead in civil security and protection. The Ethiopian Federal Police will secure the route from Addis Ababa's Bole International Airport to the prime minister's palace. Travel time is fifteen minutes proceeding north-northwest on Airport Road toward downtown Addis Ababa." Ethan moved through the slides as Jack continued to smile at him.

"We will also be deploying two USSS counterassault teams." The counterassault teams were the Secret Service's version of a SWAT team. When activated, five men shadowed the president's every move, on foot, by vehicle, or by air. "CAT Team One will follow the president's SUV in their own vehicle. CAT Team Two will be airborne, monitoring the ground from a chopper flying above the motorcade. They will call out any bogeys and engage any bandits on the roadways as allowed." Counterassault teams each carried a sniper in addition to specialists dedicated to close quarters combat. The rules of engagement, though, were always a damper in foreign lands.

"The Ethiopian Federal Police will have plainclothes officers walking the streets. Agents from the advance party will be standing sentry alongside the Ethiopian National Defense Forces on the route. As soon as we land, Agent Welby will be boarding a chopper at the airport and personally coordinating our operations with the chief of the Ethiopian Federal Police.

"Secretary Wall, Director Irwin, Mr. Luntz, Mr. Gottschalk, and Mr. Reyes will ride in the third and fourth SUVs, along with a dedicated detail team for each vehicle." His eyes met Jack's. "Myself, Agent Collard, and Agent Daniels will be providing close detail protection for President Spiers. We will ride in the SUV with you, Mr. President. Two up front. One in the back beside you." Ethan nodded to Jack. There were no questions about who would be in the backseat next to Jack. "And we won't leave your side."

Silence hung in the air after Ethan's final words.

Jack smiled. "I am confident that I will be more than safe. Excellent work, Agent Reichenbach."

"We will confirm our egress plan and provide a final run-through once we're on the ground. We expect to be in country for thirty-eight hours. We'll convene an egress debrief on the ground in the prime minister's palace." Ethan powered down his slides.

Scott nodded to him, a tiny smile curving his lips. Daniels toed his boot, his own version of a high five.

"Thank you, Agent Reichenbach. I'll touch base with you after this meeting." Jack was still smiling, but it didn't reach his eyes.

Time for Ethan and his team to go. As he'd said to Jack before, he wasn't the president's advisor, and even though Jack said he wanted him to be in all of the meetings at his side, it just couldn't happen.

Instead, Ethan gathered his laptop and his fellow agents and slipped out of the conference room.

ETHAN'S PHONE BUZZED MIDFLIGHT. One of the perks of Air Force One —dedicated cellular service. Scott and Daniels were playing cards, and Welby was passed out and snoring when Ethan stood and headed out of the Secret Service compartment.

"Have fun," Scott called. "Don't wear yourself out before we land." Ethan flipped Scott off as Daniels snorted into his cards.

Jack was waiting for him in his private cabin, barefoot and in just his pants and undershirt. "Hey gorgeous," he said, grinning. "That was a great presentation. You've done a great job."

"I'm still worried. I'll be worried until we get you safely back onboard Air Force One and we're flying home."

"I will be perfectly safe. I trust you. I trust your men. I trust your plan." Jack reached for Ethan, drawing him close, even though Ethan was frustrated and sullen. "When do we refuel?"

"We land in Frankfurt in four hours. We're wheels-down for thirty minutes, and then it's ten hours to Addis Ababa."

"I told everyone that I was getting some sleep and I wasn't to be disturbed." Jack ran his hands over Ethan's shoulders and down his bulging biceps. "Did you shrink this shirt before you squeezed into it? It's like it's painted on." Jack's hands continued to roam, crossing over Ethan's chest and down his flat stomach.

Chuckling, Ethan tried to push away the anxiety gnashing at his back teeth. "You like?"

Jack nodded, and then he tugged Ethan's shirt out of his pants. "I think I'll like it better on my floor."

Ethan laughed and let Jack pull his shirt up, but Jack tangled Ethan's arms and pulled the fabric tight, covering Ethan's eyes with his shirt halfway off his head and his arms bent back. Slowly, Jack captured Ethan's mouth, stroking his tongue across Ethan's lower lip.

"Ethan," Jack breathed. "Let me take care of you."

Mute, Ethan nodded, and he let Jack lead him to the bed.

CHAPTER 28

Addis Ababa, Ethiopia

WHATEVER ETHAN HAD EXPECTED when coming to Addis Ababa, this wasn't it.

He'd expected a third world hellhole, a dusty, barren, trash-filled landscape of despair and degradation, like all the third-world shit-holes he'd deployed to in the Army. He'd expected dangerous glances and angry, hateful faces. He'd been on guard for the worst.

He didn't expect a glittering airport, steel and glass shining bright in the sunlight and gleaming with brilliant white paint. White tile inside the airport had been polished to a high sheen, and the stores ringing the concourse could have been in any European airport. Prada, Louis Vuitton, Chanel. The entire concourse had been shut down for Jack's arrival, and they were the only ones walking through, heels clicking against the tile.

An attaché met them in the concourse and escorted Agent Welby away, back to the helo landing pad. "We'll meet Commissioner Maleke at a secure location."

Welby and Ethan shared a quick nod—Ethan right by Jack's side —and then Welby was off.

General Zabanya greeted Jack at the airport's entrance with a warm smile and a huge handshake.

The advance team already had Jack's SUVs lined up at the curb. Ethan held open the door for Jack before sliding in after him.

Jack gripped his hand once they were inside. Ethan pressed a kiss to Jack's knuckles as he laced their fingers together.

Scott and Daniels pretended not to notice.

Two helicopters rose behind the airport and flew over the motorcade. One veered north, heading toward downtown Addis Ababa. Welby, being taken to meet the police commissioner. The second flew lower and slower, following the motorcade.

They set off, moving in a long line away from the airport and heading toward downtown Addis Ababa. The capital loomed ahead, glittering skyscrapers and modern buildings set against the Ethiopian highlands. The Ethiopian Federal Police led the motorcade, police cars wailing their two-note sirens and motorcycle cops mixing with horse-mounted police sergeants. All normal traffic had been pushed to the side of the road. People hung out of minibuses watching the motorcade and tuk tuks jawed for space on the cramped, dusty shoulders, trying to push on. Along the road to the capital, one-story shacks, made of corrugated steel and claptin roofs, were subdivided into stall shops, selling everything from tires and decrepit motor parts to wilted fruits and vegetables.

Behind the presidential motorcade, General Zabanya rode in his own vehicle.

"Two kilometers down," Daniels said from the front seat, calling out the distance of the route. "One kilometer to Bulbula River and Cape Verde Street."

Ethan's thumb stroked over the back of Jack's hand.

AGENT WELBY HOPPED from the helicopter on the landing pad behind a three-story colonial that looked like it had been transported from the American colonies in the 1700s to Ethiopia. Red brick chimneys rose from the slanted roof, and colonnades lined the front and back of the staunch building. Black shutters framed every window, offsetting the light brick exterior.

"Where are we?" Welby shouted over the chopper wash to the attaché guiding him into the building.

"Come. The commissioner is waiting."

They jogged together up the grand staircase inside, footsteps ringing with loud echoes. Something gnawed at the base of Welby's brain, tickling down his spine. Where was everyone?

The attaché urged him along, waving Welby down the third-floor corridor. All of the windows were open, and Welby could see the motorcade driving north on Airport Road. They were approaching Bulbula River, the first landmark.

Welby's gaze slid back to the attaché. His uniform was unkempt, almost sloppy.

Almost like it didn't quite fit him.

"Hey. Where are we? Where is everyone else?"

"They are waiting for us."

"Hey. *Asshole*. Where the *fuck* are we?"

The attaché glared. "Somalian embassy. We took it over. This way. Quickly." The attaché pushed open a door at the end of the hallway, entering a room overlooking the road and the approaching motorcade.

Welby's hand dropped to his gun, holstered on his hip. He stepped through the doorway.

In the center of the room, Commissioner Maleke stood waiting in his dress uniform, wearing every one of his medals. He was sweating, fat drops rolling down his skin and staining the high collar of the thick wool. He looked up as the door opened and stared at Welby.

Welby tightened his grip on his sidearm.

"I am sorry," Commissioner Maleke said. "They have my family."

Before Welby could draw his weapon, bullets shot past him, slamming into the commissioner. Behind Welby, three masked jihadist fighters sprang forward, ducking out from their hiding spots tucked into an alcove along the wall. The commissioner fell to his knees, bleeding out.

Welby flipped the switch on his radio. Three jihadis, all armed with assault rifles, stood against him in a closed space.

He wouldn't live through this, but he could damn well warn the president. "Break! Break!" he shouted. "Code—"

From behind, one of the jihadis leaped on Welby's back, ripping his earpiece out of his ear and pulling on the throat mic until it choked him. Gasping, Welby tried to peel the jihadi's hands off his mic cord.

He didn't see the knife rise and fall into his shoulder, or rise again and slide across the exposed skin of his neck.

Welby hit the floor next to the commissioner.

ETHAN JERKED as Welby's broken transmission shot through the radio net. Daniels unholstered his weapon as Scott gripped the steering wheel.

"What's happen—" Jack started.

He didn't get to finish.

Across the street, the tip of an RPG poked out the back window of a minibus.

"RPG!" Ethan hollered. "Go! Go!"

The RPG launched with a roar and its distinctive whistle-whine as it shot through the air. Ethan heard glass shattering as the blow-back blasted out the windows of the minibus. "Go!" he shouted again, his whole body tensing, waiting for the impact. His hand squeezed down on Jack's, tight enough to bruise.

Instead of slamming into the side of their SUV, the rocket sailed over their heads, heading straight for CAT Team Two's chopper.

"Safety!" Ethan shouted into the radio, the codename for CAT Team Two. "Incoming! Evasive action, now!"

The chopper pilot cursed and spun, veering over the street in tight, cramped quarters, but the RPG clipped the rear rotor, chewing up the tail section of the helo. *"Break, break,"* the pilot called out over the radio. *"Safety has been hit. Safety has been hit."*

They spun in the air, struggling to maintain altitude, and Ethan saw members of the CAT team clinging to the cargo net and the handholds in the Black Hawk's open bay. *"Safety is going down. Brace for impact."*

There wasn't anything they could do from the ground. Jack's mouth fell open as the helo sputtered and spun, heading for the dusty highway behind them. Daniels twisted in his seat, staring wide-eyed.

Goddamn it. Ethan's heart pounded, a staccato rhythm beating against his ribs. He kept holding on to Jack's hand, hard enough to hurt. Fuck, it was all coming apart, in the space of twenty-three seconds, on a dusty road in Addis Ababa.

They had a backup plan for this. If shit hit the fan, like he'd been fucking promised that it wouldn't, then emergency procedures called for the motorcade to divert to the British embassy, three miles away to the northeast. The American embassy was five miles away, and straight through Addis Ababa's downtown.

Scott jerked a hard right on Cape Verde Street, tires sliding and spinning in the dirt, brakes squealing, as the helo crashed behind them. Metal screamed, crunching and cracking as the rotors whomped into the ground, fracturing on impact. They sped away, the engine roaring, but Ethan, Jack, and Daniels spun in their seats, watching the chopper come apart in the middle of Airport Road.

Radio static blared, a fuzzy, warbling whine. Daniels cursed and ripped his earpiece out.

Turning back around, Ethan shoved his head between the two front seats, watching the road they'd diverted onto. Scott gunned the SUV's engine, screaming them away from the crash site.

Embassies ran on either side of the street, a *who's who* of countries that hated America. Chad, Congo, Burkina Faso, Palestine, and Somalia, all in a row, all overlooking the roadway.

The *deserted* roadway.

Gone were the onlookers, the passersby, and the civilians watching the motorcade. Fear spiked within Ethan as his adrenaline pumped, flooding his body. Damn it, this was exactly what he had been afraid of. Tension coiled tight around his spine. His muscles clenched, ready for action. God help the man who tried to take Jack from him. His thumb stroked down the back of Jack's hand. Ethan knew, suddenly, that he would be killing people that day. The choice settled within him, heavy, but necessary.

He reached behind the backseat and grabbed an M-4 from the gun locker in the cargo area.

Jack watched him, wide-eyed but silent.

In an instant, dozens of masked fighters waving assault rifles poured from the side streets, flooding onto Airport Road and Cape Verde Street. Some rolled minibuses into their path, lit on fire and belching black smoke. Others fired their weapons wildly, spraying the sky with bullets. Once deserted, the roadway was suddenly choked with fighters, with masked men wielding death, intent on murder.

"Where the fuck did this come from?" Daniels shouted. "CIA said there was no intel for this!"

Ahead, five masked fighters lined up in the middle of the street, pointing their rifles at the president's SUV.

"We've got bandits!" Scott's voice held a touch of panic beneath his hard steel.

"Run them down!" Ethan bellowed.

When the bullets started flying, Jack flinched, cringing back from the windshield. Bulletproof, the glass spider-webbed with each impact, but didn't shatter.

"Faster!" Ethan shouted. "Run them off the road! Get past them before you can't see out of this damn window!"

Scott grit his teeth and gunned the accelerator.

Ahead, a fresh patch of concrete caught the afternoon sunlight.

"Oh fuck," Ethan breathed. He had a moment to grab Jack and

push him back, holding him in his seat as he threw his shoulder into Jack's before Scott drove over the freshly poured concrete.

An IED buried just that morning exploded as they passed, launching the SUV into the air. The entire car blew off the ground, thrown through the air carelessly, flying like a toy. Tumbling and twisting, the SUV squealed and bounced when it landed, rolling over and over until it finally settled upside down in a long, sliding skid across the road.

Ethan's head slammed against the rear passenger window, and he blinked fast, trying to still the cascading waves of dizziness and triple vision that blurred his sight. Glass exploded, the windows shattering as the SUV crunched and crumbled on every side. Sparks erupted, a shower of sparks enveloping them as the roof skidded down the road. Daniels shouted, low and through gritted teeth, and Scott repeated the same words over and over. "Oh fuck, oh fuck, oh fuck!"

When they finally stopped, Ethan unbuckled his seatbelt and fell face-first to the roof of the SUV. He groaned as his world faded in and out, blacking out before fading back in. Burning rubber seared his nose. Smoke filled his eyes. The grit of the road rubbed against his skin and crunched between his teeth. Glass shards dug into his knees, his palms. His radio screamed. The CAT team following the president's SUV was taking fire and had been separated from Vigilant and Quarterback... The general's vehicle going up in flames after a rocket blast.... Armed jihadis rushing the streets.

Bullets flew, slamming into the reinforced steel of the ruined SUV.

He rolled on his belly and looked out of the shattered windows. Feet ran toward them, coming from every direction.

Ethan flipped on his back and looked up at Jack. His heart stopped.

Jack wasn't moving. Blood dripped from his scalp, running down his temple.

"Hey, Jack." Ethan reached for his cheek. Cupped his face and his neck. Felt for a pulse as he held his breath.

God, there it was. Fast and thready, but there it was. Exhaling hard, Ethan fought for control. "Jack. Jack, wake up. C'mon, Jack, we've got to get out of here!"

In the front seat, Daniels groaned and unlocked his seatbelt. He fell forward, landing on his hands and knees on the destroyed windshield. "The fuck?" he moaned.

"Get Scott moving," Ethan barked. "And get a perimeter set up! They're fucking coming for us!" He turned back to Jack as Daniels reached for Scott, just beginning to move and groan.

"Jack..." Ethan breathed. "Don't do this to me..."

Finally, Jack blinked. He coughed, and his eyes tried to focus on Ethan's face. "What happened?"

"We're under attack," Ethan said. He reached for Jack's seat belt. "We have to go. There's more of them coming for us. We're cut off from the rest of the team. We've got to move on foot." Ethan wrapped his arm around Jack's shoulders and clicked the seat belt release. "We've got to go, Jack."

Nodding, Jack collapsed against Ethan. He winced and shook his head, seeming to try to clear it.

"Are you with me, Jack?"

"All the way." Jack squeezed Ethan's hand. "Let's go."

Ethan shimmied out of the SUV on his belly, his hands cutting open on the shattered glass spread out on the street. Daniels and Scott kneeled at the front and back of the SUV, popping off rounds from their M-4s at the crowd of jihadis surging their way.

"We've got to move!" Scott shouted. Blood streamed from his nose. Bullets zinged toward their crumpled SUV from all angles, from shooters high in the buildings and down low on the streets. "We're in a kill box!"

He helped Jack slide out of the SUV, tugging on Jack's bulletproof vest through his shirt to drag him the last few feet.

"What's our situation?"

"CAT Two is down," Daniels called. "CAT One is stuck between their crash site and us. The general's car exploded, cutting off the main route back to the airport. Gunshots fired in all the overwatch buildings along the route."

Fuck. Their entire security cordon had been compromised. They were on their own. The details assigned to the other SUVs would be getting their protectees back to safety by any means possible. Their priority was the people in their SUVs. Not the president. Not right now.

Which way to go? Make a move toward the crash site and hope to regroup with the CAT teams? Or head for the British embassy, three miles away by foot?

Ethan leaned up against the back of the overturned SUV and fired at the incoming jihadis. The riotous crowd had dispersed, hiding behind flaming minibuses and taking cover from their gunfire. They'd be back, though.

Bullets zinged past his head. Return fire.

The way back to Airport Road was jammed with fighters and wreckage. Burning minibuses and piles of flaming tires blockaded the route. They couldn't head that way.

He looked down Cape Verde Street. More fighters, and more minibuses. Some were on fire. Others sat silently in the middle of the road. Waiting.

Fuck. It had to be a trap.

But they couldn't stay put, not with bullets slamming into the SUV next to their heads.

Ethan covered Jack with his body and shouted, "We have to make a run for it! We have to head for the British embassy. It's three miles northeast up this road. It looks like they've got traps, so we run low, we run fast, and we stick to the center of the street. Scott, you take point. Daniels, you and I run with Jack. I'll watch the rear. Daniels, you keep your head on a swivel and check left and right. Heads up, call out anything you see. Trash, a pile of debris, anything that could cover a bomb." He exhaled.

Jack's face was tight, his eyes pinched and filled with pain. Blood dripped from his forehead, catching on his eyelashes. "Understood."

Ethan quickly spat the plan into his radio as he fired down the road, trying to scatter the jihadis from their path. "All right, on three, we break. Scott, you take the lead. Daniels, take Jack. I'm right behind." Ethan swallowed and held Jack's gaze for a moment that seemed to stretch for forever as bullets whizzed through the air.

"Ready?"

Scott and Daniels shouted back, ready to go.

"One... two... three!"

Scott leaped from behind the SUV, firing bursts of shots as he moved, concentrated on the fighters hiding behind the minibus across from the downed SUV. Daniels followed a moment later, dragging Jack behind him and shooting at another flaming minibus. Inhaling quickly, Ethan jumped out, popping shots off at fighters who were edging out from behind their hideouts.

They ran fast, tearing down the center of the road and shooting at anything that moved. Daniels grasped Jack's shirt in one fist and balanced his M-4 in front of him one-handed. Ethan trailed Jack's footsteps, shadowing his every move as he popped shots at the fighters chasing behind.

A zinging bullet slammed into Daniels outstretched arm. Blood sprayed, flying through the air and staining Jack's shirt as Daniels went down, tripping at the impact.

"Fuck!" he shouted, reaching for his arm.

"Go! Go!" Ethan urged Jack forward, up against Scott, and he grabbed Daniels by the back of his bulletproof vest and dragged him down the road. "Daniels, talk to me!"

"Fucking hell!" Daniels roared. His hand covered the bullet hole, blood oozing through his fingers. "I don't think the artery was hit!"

Their radios crackled to life. *"Quarterback, be advised. Reinforcements en route from the British embassy. Helo inbound."*

Thank God. The cavalry was coming. They wouldn't have to run the whole way, if they could just survive this damn street.

More shots rang out in front of Scott's feet. He jumped back, spun, and fired on a fighter leaning out of a broken second-story window in the Chad embassy. "We've got to get off the street!"

Ethan looked left and right. A minibus was just ahead of Scott, seemingly inviting. Ethan's stomach sank.

Scott grabbed Jack and headed for the minibus as more shots

rang out. It was a soldier's move: seek cover and concealment, and regroup as you run. But Ethan had a bad feeling about the minibuses, a sinking, frantic, sickening feeling. "No!" he hollered. "Scott, Goddamn it!"

Jack and Scott ran closer, drawing near the minibus. Ethan grabbed Daniels, dragging his friend to the side of the road. He dropped Daniels into a shallow drainage ditch in front of the embassy. "Cover the rear." Ethan shoved his M-4 back in Daniels's hands. Bloody, Daniels took the weapon and aimed up the road, where a crowd of jihadis were advancing slowly, chanting and firing into the air.

"Fuck..." Ethan hissed as Scott hustled Jack against the side of the minibus. Swallowing, he leaped out of the ditch, ready to run to Jack's side. He couldn't leave him out there. He couldn't leave him exposed to a trap. In his mind, he saw the minibus exploding, saw Jack disappear in a fireball. He couldn't breathe as the images grabbed him, strangled him. *No!*

In the back of the minibus, a jihadi popped up, an RPG in his hand. Scott spun, and he shot through the windows, shattering glass and hitting him in the chest. The fighter lunged out through the window, trying to grab Scott. Scott swung down with the butt of his rifle, smashing the stock into the fighter's skull, and then pulled his body through the window. He fired three rounds into the fighter's chest as he lay on the ground.

The jihadi didn't move.

Jack huddled near the back of the minibus, blood-spattered, frozen.

Ethan met his gaze.

"Ethan..." Daniels called. "Something's fucking happening!" Behind them, the swarm of fighters in the road had crammed together, standing in a tight bunch, away from the sides of the street and behind the nearest flaming minibus.

Ethan whirled, his weapon up. He saw the crowd of fighters. Standing, watching.

Waiting.

He spun again. Saw Jack leaning against the minibus, next to Scott. On either side of the street, two- and three-story embassy buildings of brick and glass and columns rose over the street. Other than the fighter in the minibus, dead at Scott's feet, there were no other people around them.

Memories hit him, dredged up from countless missions where he thought he'd never get out alive. *Building Contained IED warning signs. Be on the lookout for unexplained empty zones. Large buildings that can be turned into shrapnel. People avoiding a building or area.*

"No!" Ethan roared. He took off, running toward Jack.

A volcanic eruption bloomed on either side of the street, sound and fury and a blinding blast that blew Ethan off his feet. He hit the ground hard, skidding and rolling, and lost his weapon. All around, buildings blew apart, bricks and glass and metal flying every which way. Walls crumpled and collapsed. Fire exploded, flashing as bombs hidden in the embassy buildings ignited. Piles of weapons stacked near the bombs lit off, and rockets singed through the air, haphazard and without direction. Fiery hail rained down on the street, debris and detritus falling to the ground. A ragged metal minibus hood blasted over Ethan's head, slicing into the ground and standing straight up, embedded in the concrete. The ruins of the embassies hitting the street sounded like pounding rain on the ground, all around Ethan.

His teeth shook as the ground kept shaking, booms rocking the air all around. He thought he heard his radio, but the sound was too far away, echoing and tinny. Blaring roared in his ears, a ringing that felt like he was inside the booming echo of the Liberty Bell.

"Quarterback! Report! Quarterback, what is your status! Do you have Vigilant?"

Another voice crackled through the radio, heavily accented. *"Foxhound 23 on station in one mike."* The British. They were only a minute out.

Jack. Where was Jack? Ethan pulled himself to his hands and knees, struggling. He couldn't breathe, and his leg wouldn't move. He tried to crawl, but his knee gave way. He fell to his face, lying in the dust and smoking debris of the road. *Goddamn it! He had to get to Jack!*

Through the smoke, Ethan could just make out the silhouette of the minibus Scott and Jack had been next to. He wiped his eyes, struggling to focus through his double vision.

Two bodies lay on the ground, completely still.

"No!" Ethan bellowed. He tried to drag himself forward, pulling with his arms. "No!"

One head lifted, and Ethan saw Jack's soot-covered face look his way. The whites of his eyes gleamed through the smoky haze.

Ethan froze, gasping. A sob ripped through him.

Scott looked his way next, motioning for Ethan to crawl their way. He saw their lips move, but his ears were still ringing, and he couldn't make out the words. He could finally see, though, that they were sheltering under the minibus. Scott must have rolled them under when the first blast went off.

Behind the minibus, Ethan spotted three helos hover over the street, beating away smoke from the explosion and raging fires. Gunfire erupted from the sides of the choppers, raining down at the fighters as soldiers fast roped to the ground.

Hands grabbed Ethan's legs.

He rolled and came face-to-face with a group of jihadis.

Ethan tried to kick, but only one leg moved. There were so many fighters, suddenly swarming him, grabbing his legs and grabbing his arms. He thrashed, but they held fast. The helos fired on the jihadis, but Ethan spotted a fighter kneeling beside him with an RPG on his shoulder and another six fighters all lined up with assault rifles, firing back at the British.

He fought, thrashing and punching as much as he could. The jihadis kicked him in the stomach and the ribs, and he felt the impact even through his bulletproof vest. One fighter started punching him and didn't stop, and his head smacked against the concrete, bouncing hard. Blood filled his mouth. Coughing, Ethan spat into his attacker's face, spewing blood and black dirt.

The jihadi pushed the barrel of his rifle against Ethan's forehead, digging the metal tip into his skin. The grit of the road dug into the back of his skull. Ethan gasped, struggling for air. Jack's face swam in his mind: smiling, laughing, loving. He cried out, his eyes going wide as he wished, for one last time, to see Jack. In his last moment, it was all he wanted. Just to see the love of his life.

The jihadi slammed his rifle hard into Ethan's head.

Ethan's world went dark.

CHAPTER 29

Addis Ababa, Ethiopia

BENEATH THE SHATTERED MINIBUS, Jack shrieked, pounding on the concrete and thrashing against the British soldier who was tugging him out by his legs. "Go get him!" Jack hollered. "Jesus Christ, go get Ethan!"

The British soldier ignored him. He grabbed Jack by his bullet-proof vest and hauled him up to his feet. "I've got the package!" the soldier shouted.

A second team of soldiers dug Daniels out of the drainage ditch, flinging away flat pieces of metal that had trapped and covered him. Collard helped them, hauling Daniels out and helping to carry the unconscious agent back to the chopper. On the ground, five British soldiers fired on the crowd, trying to keep them at bay.

The crowd fired back. One jihadi aimed an RPG at the chopper coming in for a landing.

"We've got to go! Now!" The British soldiers rallied back, retreating and shooting as they moved for the chopper.

Jack struggled against the soldier holding him tight. "Fuck you!" he screamed. "We're *not* leaving without Ethan!"

Collard turned dark eyes to Jack. "We can't get him!" he roared over the chopper's rotor wash. "They've got him!"

"We are *not* leaving him behind!"

Collard hopped into the chopper, pulling Daniels with him. "The job is to get *you* to safety, Mr. President! *That's* the mission! Not saving Ethan!" Collard grabbed Jack and hauled him in as well, with the Brits' help. "He would put you on this chopper and leave himself behind!"

"Fuck you!" Furious, Jack struggled against Collard, trying to leap from the helo. Collard grabbed him and held him in an iron grasp. The Brits piled in, still firing. One soldier downed the man with the RPG, but another fighter picked it up.

"Go! Go!" The leader of the British team shouted to the pilots. "Go now!"

"No!" Jack bellowed as they lifted off. He kicked against Collard, but one of the British soldiers jumped on his legs, holding him still. "Get off me!"

Beneath the chopper, the fighters hefted Ethan's unconscious body in the air, holding him aloft in a sickening parody of body surfing. Gunshots fired after the British helicopter, chasing their retreat through the smoke and the devastation.

PRESIDENT SPIERS ATTACKED IN ADDIS ABABA. SEVEN AMERICANS INJURED, ONE MISSING

The president came under heavy attack in Addis Ababa, Ethiopia today while en route to the Assembly of the African Union in Nairobi. The president was forced from his motorcade by a high-intensity IED.

The United States Secret Service provided protection for him until the nearby British embassy was able to rescue the president and his detail.

Other Secret Service agents came under fire in a separate attack on the Secret Service helicopter providing aerial security and on the agents manning posts along the motorcade's route. Ethiopia's General Zabanya was also killed.

Seven Secret Service agents were wounded in the attack: three in a helicopter crash, three during a street battle while trying to evacuate the president and other officials back to the airport, and one critically after being stabbed in the neck.

One agent remains missing, reportedly captured by jihadist fighters.

CHAPTER 30

Addis Ababa, Ethiopia

THE BRITS FERRIED JACK, Collard, and Daniels all the way across Addis Ababa to the American embassy.

The American embassy was on lockdown, and Marines scrambled as the British arrived, guiding them in to the landing pads in the courtyard. The ambassador and the embassy medical staff waited along with the Marine lieutenant colonel in charge of embassy security.

When Jack jumped out of the helo, blood-and-soot-covered, his suit torn, and his face messy with dirt and tear tracks, everyone paused. The ambassador's mouth dropped open.

Jack stormed up to the Marine officer. "Colonel, we have a man missing out there. I need your men to go out and retrieve him."

Collard helped Daniels onto the waiting stretcher before following Jack.

The colonel stared at Jack, hesitating. "Sir... we don't have the authority to do that—"

"I'm giving you the authority!" Jack roared. Ethan was out there, in the hands of whomever had attacked them. They had to get him back, and get him back now. He'd accept nothing else. "Go and get our man!"

Swallowing, the colonel's eyes tightened. "Sir, my orders are to put you on a chopper and get you out to the *Arleigh Burke* in the Red Sea, right away. You've been attacked, sir, and we need to preserve the United States government and get you to safety."

Collard shifted behind Jack, pressing against his side. "Colonel," he said, "I believe you have a unit of special operators here. Assigned as backup from Djibouti for the president's visit?"

The colonel nodded, once.

Collard tugged on Jack's arm, drawing him to the side. "Mr. President," he said, speaking softly. "You need to get out of here."

"I am *not leaving* without Ethan." How could Collard leave Ethan behind? His friend? Ethan had talked about Agent Scott Collard before, had shared stories of their friendship. Collard was supposed to be Ethan's *best* friend, like a brother to him. Jack didn't know the man well, but he knew Ethan liked him, knew Ethan trusted him. And now?

How could Collard have done that? How could he have left Ethan there? Jack wanted to tear into the man, shake him until he admitted he was wrong. Until Ethan was back at their side, safe and smiling again.

"Mr. President," Collard insisted. "Ethan would want you to get all the way to safety."

"Don't you *dare* tell me what Ethan would want! You don't have that right!"

Collard's eyes flashed. "Ethan *ordered* me to do anything and everything to save your life," he growled. "Even leave him behind if I had to make that call. I didn't think I *ever* would, but I just *did*. I just left my best friend behind, Mr. President, because he sacrificed himself for you. Because he *loves* you."

Silence. Jack grit his teeth together until he saw spots dance in front of his eyes.

"You have to get to safety. Everyone else is already inbound to the *Arleigh Burke*. You'll meet up with Secretary Wall, Director Irwin, NSA

Luntz, and your chief of staff. Work with them to figure out what went wrong." Collard looked away, clearing his throat. "But listen to me, Mr. President," he growled again. "I'm staying here. I'm going back out there. And I won't come back without Ethan."

This isn't happening. This isn't fucking happening. Jack exhaled as his head swam, colors and sounds bleeding together. He heaved a shaking gasp.

"Bring him back to me," he finally whispered. His voice trembled. "*Please.*"

Collard nodded. "Go, Mr. President. For Ethan."

He nodded, blinking back tears. Together they walked back to the Marine colonel. "Colonel," Jack grunted, wiping his nose. "Gather your operators together. Agent Collard has a mission for them. And take me to the *Arleigh Burke*."

THE EMBASSY DOCTOR insisted on checking him over before he clambered into the helicopter. Aside from cuts and bruises, he was fine. Daniels was loaded up afterward, bandaged in a sling and holding his own bag of IV fluids. Jack managed a smile for the young agent and clipped the IV bag to the main cargo rail of the helo for him. In minutes, Daniels was asleep.

Three other Marines sat in the chopper with them, silent and staring over the city. Addis Ababa faded away, replaced by the scrub highlands of Ethiopia and the barren, dry cliffs abutting the Horn of Africa. The helo skirted Somalia, heading instead for the waters over the Red Sea before turning southeast.

Jack stared at the water, not seeing a thing. How had this happened? What had happened? They were on their way to the capital and everything had been fine. The CIA had repeatedly assured him and Ethan that there weren't any active threats. There weren't any indications of movement into the country by foreign fighters. Ethiopia was stable, they said. It wouldn't happen there.

Well, it *had* happened. They'd come under attack in a big way.

And Ethan...

Jack's throat closed. He shuddered, exhaling quickly, and squeezed his eyes shut. His blood ran cold as his heart pounded out a terrible rhythm, a demanding bassline echoing in his skull. *You left him! You left him! Go back! Go back! You'll never see him again!*

Looking down, Jack tried to smother the rising sob building in his chest. He closed his eyes, but the image of Ethan, flat on the ground with a jihadi slamming the barrel of his rifle into his forehead, was burned into the back of his eyelids. He didn't want to see that, not ever. He'd never close his eyes again.

The pounding within his head and his heart boomed, deafening him.

No. This isn't the end. It isn't. Collard was going back out there. He was going to bring Ethan back. He was going to bring Ethan *home.*

There was so much he hadn't said to Ethan, so much he still needed to say. So much they still needed to do. This was too new, too special, to end. It couldn't end here, not in a backstreet battle in Addis Ababa. This wasn't the end.

Jack clung to that hope, to that prayer, with everything in his soul.

JEFF WAITED on the *Arleigh Burke's* flight deck with a grim, sullen look. He'd ditched his suit jacket, but soot and blood still stained his normally crisp white dress shirt.

Jack helped Daniels out of the helo and onto the Navy stretcher waiting on the flight deck before jogging to Gottschalk. "What's the situation? And where is Director Irwin?"

"He's in medical. Shrapnel in the leg."

"When he's out, I'm going to rip that leg off myself. Where the fuck did this come from?"

"Unknown, sir." Gottschalk swallowed. He licked his lips. "Sir, there's been a development. The commander has set us up in the Ward Room. There's something you need to see."

JACK WALKED into the silent Ward Room and stopped dead.

On the far vidscreen, Ethan's face—beaten, bloody, and disfigured with a broken nose and two black eyes—stared out from the monitor.

The *Arleigh Burke's* commanding officer stood, as did Secretary Wall and his National Security Advisor, Luntz. Both looked rattled. Elizabeth's hair was in disarray, and dirt stained both of their cheeks.

"What the hell is this?" Jack growled. His blood boiled, burning his veins.

"This was broadcast just minutes ago, Mr. President." The *Arleigh Burke's* commanding officer, Commander Conrad, stepped forward. "My intel guys picked it up." He hesitated. "It's not pretty, sir. Are you sure you want to see it?"

"Yes." Jack's hands balled into fists. Gottschalk stepped close, bracketing Jack from behind. His shoulder leaned into Jack, silent support.

Commander Conrad signaled for the video to play.

Onscreen, Ethan jerked, pulled back by the hair by an unseen person. Someone threw him down, and then silhouetted men started tearing into him, kicking and punching his prone body. Ethan slowly curled up, shielding himself, but his breaths were wet and labored.

"Americans!" a heavily accented voice shouted. "We have one of your Secret Service Special Agents! He is in our custody! He will be sacrificed to pay for the crimes of the American government! As Allah wills it, the great Satan will be destroyed!" One of the fighters drew a long knife from a sheath on his belt.

"No!" Jack shouted. He grasped the conference table's edge. "No!"

The video went dark.

"What happened?" Jack whirled on Commander Conrad. "Did they— Is he—" *No, no, no!*

"We don't know. There's no demand on this video. Usually in a hostage situation, we see a demand. Here..." Conrad exhaled. "We're not sure if they plan on executing him publicly, or if there will be demands coming."

Jack's mind whirled. He tried to breathe, drawing in short gasps that only made him dizzier. *Focus, focus!* He dropped his head, hanging it between his shoulders, and rubbed his temples. Blood flaked onto his fingers. *What would you do if this wasn't Ethan? Go through the steps. Go through the process.*

"Can your people trace the signal? Do they know where this came from?"

"We're working on that now, sir. We can have a team on location in thirty minutes after we zero in."

Fuck the usual process. This is Ethan! Jack shook his head. "No. No, get on the line and call the embassy in Addis Ababa. Agent Collard is taking a team out. Get them the information. He can move faster."

"Sir, a ground team moving out of the American embassy—"

Jack cut Commander Conrad off with a snarl. "I don't want to hear it, Commander! I don't want to hear anything other than that we've rescued our missing man! So get the information to the embassy! Now!"

Conrad nodded. "Yes, sir." He slipped out of the Ward Room as Jack started to pace.

CHAPTER 31

Ethiopian Highlands

GROANING, Ethan curled into a ball. He tried to count his injuries based on the waves of pain rolling through his body. Bruised ribs, possibly cracked. His knee was flaring. His shoulder was out of joint. His stomach ached. Maybe internal bleeding. And his nose was definitely broken.

Spit landed on the side of his face. "American pig!" a jihadi shouted. Drool dripped down his cheek. Another jihadi laughed.

Someone grabbed Ethan's hair, yanking his head back. Overhead, a single bulb illuminated the dank room. Stone walls and a dirt floor contained Ethan and the group of fighters. He tried to count them, but he lost count somewhere between seven and ten.

A long blade glinted in the bulb's light. Stained with rust and blood, the blade had seen a lot of action. A lot of death. Ethan shuddered, trying to back away from it.

"I will cut your head off like a dog," the jihadi hissed.

"Wait!"

Across the room, a heavy metal door slid open, creaking on ungreased slides and old hinges. An older fighter with his face uncovered and clothed in mismatched fatigues walked in, flanked by two more fighters. Bodyguards, if Ethan read them right.

The newcomer strode to Ethan and stood over him. His face was dark, blocked from the light. Ethan squinted. He winced when the newcomer's boot dug into his dislocated shoulder, pushing him back until he was flat on the ground.

"So," he crooned, mocking laughter in his voice. "You are the American president's lover."

Shocked gasps rang out around the room, followed by chuffs of laughter and short, bitten-off curses in Arabic. Ethan caught the slang for "butt-fucker" in the mix of fast Arabic.

"He'll never negotiate," Ethan managed to grunt. "I'm worthless to you."

A wicked smile made Ethan's guts squirm. "Your death," the man said, chuckling, "will devastate your president." Slowly, he knelt.

Ethan wished he had the strength to move, to fight back, to reach out and grab his neck and strangle this man until his eyes turned blue and his tongue hung out of his mouth.

"I will enjoy your death. I will savor it, and cherish it, and know that I have hurt your president where others could not."

As the man stood, Ethan finally saw his face.

Al-Karim.

CHAPTER 32

COMMANDER CONRAD WASN'T ALONE when he returned to the Ward Room. Director Irwin trailed behind him, limping, with a thick bandage wrapped around his thigh.

Jack stared Irwin down, like he'd stare down rotten food or yesterday's garbage.

"Mr. President," Conrad said, interrupting Jack's seething rage. "We got the video's location and transmitted it to the embassy and to the Pentagon. They will be providing drone footage of Agent Collard and the Marines' movements from a launch out of our base in Djibouti. Also, General Madigan has assumed personal command of this mission. He will be coordinating operations from the Pentagon Situation Room and has launched support helicopters from Djibouti for your team."

Exhaling, Jack leaned back in his chair at the conference table. *This will work. They'll bring Ethan home. They will.*

At Jack's side, Gottschalk shifted, scooting closer. Jack smiled at him, though it was thin and lined with fear.

SCOTT MOVED with the Marine Corps Special Operations team leader,

Lieutenant Adam Cooper, as they advanced on the partially hidden bunker buried in the Ethiopian hills eighty klicks southeast of Addis Ababa. Arid tracks of land lay open to the sky, windswept and barren, with only a scattered tree here and there to break the desolation. Tumbled rocks sat in piles, and the bunker entrance almost looked like another mound of boulders and scrub Ethiopian highland.

But a signal from Ethan's jihadi kidnappers had come from these grid points.

Scott gripped his weapon tighter and shuffled behind Lieutenant Cooper.

One sentry sat outside the bunker, eating a fig. He'd left his weapon propped up against the bunker's stone entrance.

A single shot from Lieutenant Cooper's rifle ended the sentry's life. He flopped to the ground, a hole in his head.

They moved quickly, lining up on either side of the bunker's entrance. A dark tunnel disappeared underground. They couldn't hear anything, but if anyone had heard their gunshot, they'd be welcoming more fighters to the party any moment.

No one burst from the tunnel entrance. Everything was silent.

Quick hand signals from Lieutenant Cooper distributed the team. Cooper took the lead, Scott at his shoulder, as they started down the tunnel. Once inside, the men folded NVGs down from their helmets and over their eyes. The tunnel ahead changed, morphing into a tumble of green and white shapes, harsh angled and barren.

The tunnel branched, forking left and right. Cooper set three men at the entrance to the left fork and led the rest of the team down the right, silently.

Laughter bounced down the stone halls.

Cooper gave the signal to freeze, a fist held in the air.

Ahead, a door squeaked on old hinges, gone rusty from disuse and dried out from the arid desert.

Two jihadis turned the corner ahead of Cooper. They didn't see the blacked-out Marines in the dark tunnel.

Cooper and Scott waited until they were close, then reached out and grabbed both men, palms tight over their mouths. The jihadis flailed, but Cooper and Scott pulled them in, wrapping them up in a sleeper hold. They squeezed and then jerked, and the men fell to the ground after a loud crack, dead.

Cooper motioned the team forward.

They came to a sliding metal door, rusted out and warped. Cooper lined up his men behind him, ready to breach. Scott stood opposite, his rifle raised and ready.

On three, they threw the door open, jerking it down the rails and pouring into the room. Cooper's men cleared the corners, firing at masked fighters and jihadis stunned motionless by the surprise attack.

A tarp stretched from corner to corner. Ethan kneeled in the center beneath a bare bulb, his head pulled back by his hair and his throat exposed. Masked fighters stood behind him, all wielding assault rifles.

One held a machete.

Cooper and Scott each put three bullets in the machete-wielder's chest, dropping him to the ground. The rest of the team opened fire, taking down the fighters surging forward. Ten jihadis in all jostled elbows in the room, shouting and trying to fire back on the surprise Marines, but only three got off any shots before Cooper and the team took them all down.

"Clear!" Cooper finally said, his voice ringing through the dark room. Overhead, the dirty lightbulb swung wildly back and forth, painting the room in dusty light and deep shadows.

Cooper's men echoed his words, calling *all clear* in their corners.

"Ethan?" Scott ran to Ethan, crumpled on the tarp and not moving. "Ethan, damn it, answer me." He sniffed as he crouched down next to his friend. The room stank, a combination of third-world sweat and piss, and something deeper. Something that hit the back of his tongue and made him gag. Something that tasted like fear.

"Ethan?" Carefully, Scott rolled him over, cradling his head. Ethan's t-shirt was ruined, bloodstained and torn to shreds. His body was a mess of bruises, and dried blood coated his face.

Ethan stared up at Scott through slitted eyes. He blinked, and then rolled his head away and grimaced.

Relief flooded through Scott. "He's alive!" For now, at least. Grunting, Scott hefted Ethan over his shoulder, carrying him on his back. Ethan whimpered as Scott moved.

Cooper was already on the radio. "Ballroom, this is Black Knight 6. We are go for extract."

All the way from the halls of the Pentagon, General Madigan's crotchety voice broke over the radio. "*Outstanding. Two helos inbound from station in three mikes.*"

Cooper rounded up his men, sent them out of the room, and then ordered the other team to clear and blow the second tunnel.

Moments later, booms echoed through the bunker, and dust fell from the ceiling. Grenades going off from the other team.

Scott hitched Ethan higher on his shoulders and followed behind Cooper, heading for the bunker's exit.

Two black dots on the horizon drew close as they filed out of the bunker. Scott could just make out the faint whirring of rotors.

"Ballroom, Black Knight 6. Be advised, orange smoke is friendly." Cooper popped a canister of orange smoke from his pack and threw it in front of the bunker, signaling to the chopper pilots.

"*Ballroom acknowledges,*" Madigan said.

Then there was a smear, an electric whine and a screech that had everyone reaching for their earpieces and ripping them out, cursing. Cooper jammed his back in and reset his radio. "Ballroom, come in. Ballroom, come in."

ONBOARD THE CHOPPERS, General Madigan spoke directly to the pilots on a secure line from the Pentagon. "*Those sons of bitches took out our entire team. I want you to light up that bunker, and any human being you see on the ground. Don't you dare leave until that bunker is gone and every living soul in that AO is dead. The 'hajis have stolen one of our own smoke grenades. Don't be fooled by the smoke.*"

"Yes, sir."

The pilots zeroed in on the men standing outside the bunker.

JACK WATCHED from the perspective of the drone hovering above the battlespace. He saw black silhouettes crawling out of the bunker.

"Are those our men?" His eyes flicked to Commander Conrad, looking for information.

Conrad frowned and turned to Director Irwin and NSA Luntz. "I'm not sure. The vantage here is pretty high up. I can't get detail."

General Madigan's voice broke through over the speakerphone on the conference table. *"Mr. President, we're having communication difficulties with our team right now. We're not sure who those men on the ground are. There were reports of shots fired and some grenades before everything went dark. Those could be fighters waiting to attack our choppers. But our helo pilots will vector in close."*

Jack nodded, even though Madigan couldn't see him. He clasped his hands in front of his face and rested his forehead on his knuckles. *Please, Ethan, please come home to me. Please.*

"BALLROOM, COME IN. BALLROOM, COME IN." Cooper frowned and cycled through the radio again.

"Sir..." One of Cooper's men rose from his kneel. His nametape read *COLEMAN*. "Those helos aren't slowing down."

Cooper looked up. "They're coming in to attack!" he shouted. He grabbed his radio, trying to broadcast on a shortwave frequency to reach the pilots directly. "Chopper pilots, this is ground team! We are friendly! Do not attack! Orange smoke is friendly!"

Bullets roared out of the helo's gun batteries, chewing up the hard-packed earth in front of the team. Cursing, Scott dove sideways, rolling with Ethan away from the path of the bullets. One of Cooper's men screamed.

"Jesus!" Cooper scrambled in the dirt, waving at the helo pilots, though they stayed out of visual range. "We're on your fucking side!"

The second chopper joined the first, spitting out bullets and striking a second member of the team.

"Get back in the bunker!" Cooper hollered. "Move, now, now!"

Scott grabbed Ethan, threw him over his shoulder again, and then tore off toward the bunker's entrance. Bullets chased his feet, bounced off stones and clipped the pack on his back. He dove for the darkened entrance, landing in a heap on top of two of Cooper's teammates.

"Move, move!" Cooper shouted, running into the tunnel after the remnants of his team made it inside. "Go deeper!"

Above, the mechanical whir of the helos loading their rockets chilled Scott's blood. He grabbed Ethan under the arms and dragged his friend, until one of Cooper's men hefted Ethan's ankles and they ran down the dark tunnel together.

"Go, go!" Cooper shouted. "Deeper! If they fire their rockets, this whole bunker could—"

His words were cut off by the roaring tunnel's collapse. The sounds of exploding stone mixed with the rage of flames from the rocket's impact, overpowering everyone's screams.

"No!" Jack leaped from his seat as the bunker exploded in a blinding flash of light, whiting out the monitor. "What happened? Where is our team?"

"*Mr. President,*" Madigan said gruffly. "*Our chopper pilots reported that the men on the ground were jihadist fighters impersonating our men. They took fire and had to respond.*"

Jack's eyes darted around the room. Panic rose like a tidal wave in his chest, breaking on the fractures of his heart. "No," he whispered. "Where is our team? Agent Collard? Agent Reichenb—" He couldn't say Ethan's name. His voice choked off as his throat closed, and he fell forward, barely catching himself on the edge of the table. *"Where is our team?"*

"Mr. President..." Madigan's voice faded away. Commander Conrad looked down. *"Our team was eliminated. They're gone, sir."*

Jack shook his head, over and over, and he backed away from the table. His breaths came too fast as he stared at the screen, at the destroyed bunker burning and lying in rubble. They were supposed to rescue Ethan, bring him back to Jack. He was supposed to meet Ethan on the flight deck, wounded but alive, and then he'd kiss him in front of everyone. He didn't care, not anymore, about secrecy or hiding or keeping their love a secret. He loved Ethan, and he wanted the world to know it, and damn the consequences.

But Ethan wasn't coming home.

He wasn't flying back to Jack, and Jack wouldn't ever be able to tell him that he loved him.

Roaring, Jack flung his chair sideways. It rolled fast, slamming into the *Arleigh Burke's* bulkhead. His heart, so recently made whole again, cracked, revealing his tender love for Ethan hidden deep within. Why hadn't he *said* something? Why hadn't he told Ethan?

He'd never get the chance.

The world spun, and he stumbled backward. Strong hands grabbed him, steadying his waist and keeping him on his feet, and then arms wrapped around him from behind. "Jack," a voice in his ear mumbled. "Jack."

The hands spun Jack around, and he came face-to-face with Jeff. There was a sheen to Jeff's eyes, wet and weary, and he wrapped Jack up in his arms and drew him close. "Jack," Jeff whispered again, sighing.

Jack let it all out, falling into Jeff's arms as his sobs tore through him. He grabbed his chief of staff, wrapping him up in a furious grapple. He shuddered, trembling as his worst fears, fears he'd ignored and pushed away, fears he'd said weren't ever going to happen, crashed in on every side.

How could this happen to a man twice? He'd buried his wife, and now he had to bury his lover, a man he'd come, almost inexplicably, to love. He'd taken a chance, and he'd found a love that couldn't be named, that couldn't be contained, and that had redefined his life in ways he had only just begun to discover.

And now, it was all gone. All of the love. All of the happiness he'd found. All of the joy he'd discovered in Ethan's arms.

Jack slumped against the bulkhead, still holding on to Jeff, and slid to the deck. Jeff went with him, never letting go. The others slipped out of the Ward Room, giving him privacy, but Jack couldn't care less about privacy. His sobs bruised his throat and ground through his chest. Snot and tears soaked Jeff's shirt.

He didn't want to open his eyes. He didn't want to stop crying. He didn't want to acknowledge that this was real, and he'd have to move forward from this moment. No, not yet. He couldn't let go yet.

GENERAL MADIGAN SPOKE DIRECTLY to the chopper pilots again. *"You boys did great work. Did you confirm the jihadis' identities?"*

"No, sir. By the time we got in ID range, the bodies outside the bunker were burned up. No positive ID."

"No worries, boys. You did great. Come on back to Djibouti."

Madigan clicked the radio off and picked up his phone.

CHAPTER 33

Ethiopian Highlands

"EVERYONE OKAY?" Cooper's voice, choked with dust, broke through the gloom of the collapsed tunnel. "Sound off!"

Scott coughed, trying to breathe. Something was on top of him, crushing his ribs. He shoved in the darkness, and someone grunted. *Jesus, Ethan.* "Ethan? You still with us?"

Groaning answered him, and a wheeze.

"L-T, we've got to move." Scott shifted, crouching over Ethan. "He's hurt bad."

"We can't move yet." Cooper spoke through the darkness. "We're penned in here. We've got to dig out. And I can't raise anyone on the radio."

"Forget the radio." Scott threw his mic and earpiece across the crumbled tunnel. "We were targeted by those helos. Someone sent them to take us out."

Cooper's silence hung in the darkness.

"We need a new plan," Scott snapped. "We need to know what's going on."

PRESIDENT TO ADDRESS NATION
& WORLD FROM USS TRUMAN

The president is set to make a major address following the attack on him and his motorcade in Addis Ababa, Ethiopia, from the carrier deck of the USS Truman, stationed in the Mediterranean Sea. Since the attack, the administration has come under bitter criticism, with many in Washington saying that the president should never have made the trip in the first place.

Unrelated to the attacks in Ethiopia, two helicopters from the Camp Lemonier, the US Naval Expeditionary base in Djibouti, crashed while on a training mission on the border of Ethiopia and Djibouti. Both crews are confirmed dead.

CHAPTER 34

USS Truman

"MY FELLOW AMERICANS..." Jack licked his lips, the familiar words of the opening to the presidential address falling from his lips. Across the flight deck of the USS *Truman*, sailors stood at attention, and a press team filmed his every word. He wasn't standing at a podium, though. He was just himself. Just Jack.

A sob almost took him by surprise. "Just Jack" had been what Ethan used to tell him he adored. Not the president. Just Jack.

Clearing his throat, Jack pushed on. The ship didn't have a teleprompter, so he was winging this one. It didn't matter. It all came from the heart, from the place where Ethan lived inside him.

All of this is for you.

"My fellow Americans and citizens of the world," Jack continued. His voice caught on the words, and he cleared his throat again. "Today, there was an attack on the presidential motorcade on the way to the Assembly of the African Union leaders' to address the situation in Nairobi. Ethiopia lost their Federal Police commissioner and their general of the National Defense Forces. We join them today in mourning.

"Americans also grieve today, and no one more than myself."

Jack's voice wavered. He inhaled quickly. Held his breath. "Today, America lost true heroes. Men who gave their all. Today, Special Agents Scott Collard and Ethan Reichenbach gave their lives in order to save my own." Jack looked right, off the flight deck, and into the horizon. He blinked fast, not caring about the news camera. "Also lost were a United States Marine Corps Special Operations team. To these men, and to their families, I owe you my life and my gratitude.

"But gratitude cannot bring back these men." Jack bit his lip, forcing his tears back. "Gratitude cannot save lives going forward. Gratitude is a cold comfort to those left behind."

He thought he could do this, but standing there, trying to pretend that he wasn't one of those left behind, one of those lost and mourning and clinging to empty words, was slicing the remnants of his soul in pieces. *Ethan... I do this for you.* He kept repeating his words, imagining Ethan's smile as he stared at the rivets in the deck and gathered his strength again.

"Today, I come to you with a promise of action. I come to you with a vow. I will not allow another American, or any human being, to be taken from this earth because of terror, fear, and oppression. I will stand up to those who sow terror and who fight against freedom. I will no longer let excuses stand in the way of doing what is right. Today, I call on my fellow world leaders to join me in taking a direct stand against the Caliphate. We will not sit by in the world while nuclear bombs are detonated in cities, and the best of our people are ripped from our lives. These acts are acts of war made by desperate terrorists bent on destroying people's lives."

Jack looked directly into the camera. "I am, today, promising that America will respond. We are coming for you. We are coming to free those whom you have enslaved. Rescue those whom you have harmed. Restore what you have destroyed. We are coming on the ground, over the sea, and from the skies. We will eliminate you, and any enemy of the human race who allies with you, from the face of the earth.

"President Puchkov, leaders from NATO, I call on you to join me in this promise. Together, let's commit to securing the world for all people in every land. Allies, I call on your continued support and your friendship, and thank you for your continued backing thus far."

Looking up, Jack closed his eyes as he stared at the stars. Somewhere, Ethan's soul was in a better place, a place free of the horrors that had gripped the final moments of his life. An old quote came back to him, drifting up from his memories. *"What if the stars above are simply holes in the sky where our loved ones look down on us from above?"*

He had two stars now. The pain from Leslie had faded, and what was left was a scar on his heart. He'd thought that scar meant the end, but Ethan had shown him a brand-new life, a new side of himself, and he'd felt more alive than he'd ever remembered being. What was next, after Ethan?

It was too new to consider. For now, he'd fill his life with this purpose. With destroying those who took Ethan from him. With ridding the world of monsters and men who wielded evil and malice as weapons.

Love had been ripped from his life. Let vengeance take its place.

CHAPTER 35

Ethiopian Highlands

IT TOOK hours to pull themselves free of the rubble in the tunnel.

Scott worked with Cooper's team, but one man sat with Ethan at all times. They rotated through, counting Ethan's shallow breaths and checking his pulse every fifteen minutes. The team doc did what he could, pumping a bag of fluids into Ethan and palpating his injuries. He set Ethan's dislocated shoulder while Ethan was unconscious, and Ethan didn't stir as his bone popped back into place. Scott frowned at that.

When they neared the tunnel entrance, Cooper slowed his men down and quieted everyone. They listened for ten minutes, straining their ears for sounds of helicopters, or soldiers on the ground, or anything that spelled danger.

After their own helos had fired on them, what did danger actually mean? Who could they trust?

What had happened?

Finally, the team pushed through the broken stone and the collapsed dirt of the bunker entrance and escaped to the arid desolation of the Ethiopian highlands. Night had fallen, and in the hills, the darkness seemed palpably thick, an almost visceral smothering that covered the team. Discovering the burned bodies of two of their teammates didn't help.

"What now, L-T?" A junior Marine, Park, chewed on his lip.

Cooper glared into the idle distance. He seemed to be a study in stillness, a portrait of calm, but Scott spotted his surging pulse just above his collar.

"We need to get this man to a hospital," Doc said, crouching next to Ethan. "He's not doing well."

"There's a village ten klicks to the west. We passed it when we came in." Cooper drew a quick map in the dust, shining his red-tinted flashlight on the ground. "You two, hike in, find a vehicle, and get back here. Get all the fuel you can."

The two men he pointed to, Coleman and Ruiz, nodded and took off, jogging into the night.

"When they get back, we head north. We make for Massawa in Eritrea. There's a port there, and lots of smugglers. We take a boat over to Jazan, in south Saudi Arabia."

"Saudi Arabia?" Doc spun in the dirt, staring at Lieutenant Cooper like he'd grown a second head. "Why not head for our base in Djibouti?"

"Those chopper pilots came from our base, and they fired on us. Heading back isn't the right move. Not now."

"But Saudi?" Scott joined in, questioning Cooper. "How does that help Ethan?"

"We drive all night, and we'll be across the Red Sea by morning. I have a contact in Saudi. Someone I've used before. He'll help us." Cooper's eyes flashed. "Are you done questioning my orders?"

Doc raised his hands and turned back to Ethan silently. Scott nodded, and he stretched out on the dry dirt, lying against his pack next to Ethan and listening to his wet, shallow breaths. Doc hummed as he worked on Ethan, checking his whole body before checking him again.

Above, the stars sprayed out across the sky, brighter than Scott had ever seen. The whole arm of the Milky Way was glowing, almost as if the galaxy were falling to the ground. He thought he could see from horizon to horizon, and every star in between, gleaming and glittering in the sky. It was beautiful, more beautiful than any sky before.

Cooper's dark silhouette pacing against the spray of stars and Ethan's labored, short breaths took away the majesty of the night. Scott squeezed his eyes shut and tried to block it all out.

COOPER'S MEN came back with a beater truck. The top of the cab had been sawed off and the interior was open to the sky. Scott and Doc piled in the back with Ethan and the others while Cooper rode up front, packed in with Wright and a younger Marine named Fitz. It was cramped in the truck bed, and Scott rode with Ethan's head in his lap and his arms around his friend's shoulders. His hand rested on Ethan's chest, and he counted the fast rise and fall of his shallow breaths.

They drove through the night, cutting through dry washes and traveling across arid landscapes. Desolate, lonely winds blew around the truck, whipping through their clothes and under their helmets. Mountain goats grazed in fields they blazed through, scattering into the night with angry bleats and the rumble of rusted cowbells. They didn't stay to see if there was a shepherd nearby.

The truck petered out of gas after they blew across the Eritrean border, but with fifty klicks still to go. Dawn's first light crept over the horizon, fingers of peach and aubergine staining the night sky like spilled watercolors. Scott hefted Ethan onto his back again, wincing at the load. Ethan wasn't a small man and carrying him so many times—and leaping, running, and throwing him when they'd had to escape back into the bunker—had done a number to his back and shoulders. Still, he carried on.

They stayed to the backroads and the mountains of Eritrea until they neared the coast. In the brush, they stripped their uniform insignia, ripping it off their blacked-out uniforms and burning everything. They moved on in plain combat fatigues, boots, their packs, and helmets. They looked like any ragged group of mercenaries plying their trade in the wilds of East Africa, weapons and all.

Ethan slung across Scott's back may have raised an eyebrow anywhere else, but in Eritrea, no one cared.

They made it to the port in Massawa after the sun had fully risen above the horizon. Roosters crowed in the dusty streets, strutting after chickens and dogs, all scrabbling for scraps of food in the filth-strewn gutters. Massawa seemed like the dumping ground time forgot, a mashup of decrepit buildings and rotten structures from every era. Medieval Muslim palaces shared weeds and dust with clapboard shacks and rusted corrugated tin roofs. Minarets crowded alongside pirated satellite dishes, and bare, rusted rebar stuck straight out of squat mud-brick buildings, a builder's ambitions for a second story thwarted sometime in the last two hundred years.

They moved down the main street, choking on dust and passing bored Eritreans watching them with dead eyes. No one lifted a finger as they moved through town. No one bothered to stand from their stoops. Women and men slouched against ramshackle tin shacks as they tried to sell rotten vegetables, and shirtless children ran in the street kicking a deflated soccer ball, wearing sandals made from used car tires.

The port was nothing more than a crumbling section of concrete and a line of pylons stretching along the wharf. In the fifties, it might have been new. A sunken yacht was still moored at the pier, some Gulf elite's toy that went down and was never retrieved. Simple wooden dhows were tied up together, handmade fishing nets folded with care and homemade fishing poles lined up in the bottom of each boat.

Cooper found someone who spoke Arabic, and then they were led to a single-mast dhow with a sail that was more patches than original canvas. Doc gave Cooper a dubious stare before helping Scott and Ethan into the boat.

The crossing was windy, and waves splashed over the side of the dhow and soaked the men. Scott tried to shield Ethan as best he could, but the salt water splashed over his face, and Ethan sputtered, coughing, but didn't wake. That, more than anything else, worried Scott, and he kicked at Doc until the Marine stopped clinging to the side of the dhow and came to their side.

Doc was a sickly shade of green, but he checked Ethan over. After, he shook his head and leaned against Scott, shouting over the wind and the waves that there wasn't anything he could do, not right now. Ethan's injuries were internal, and unless they found a hospital and figured out what was going on, they'd never know what to do. He slapped Scott on the back, though, and offered up some grim Marine humor. "He's stayed alive this far," Doc shouted. "He's got that going for him!"

The port at Jazan, Saudi Arabia, was worse than Massawa. Fifty yards out from the fishing pier, the rusted hulk of an oil tanker run aground lay on its side, half in the water and half exposed to the air. Sullen faces stared out from a rotten hole in the hull, children sitting on rocks poking through the iron belly of the tanker. Fishing lines stretched from their poles, but the baskets beside them were empty.

The dhow dropped Cooper and the team off at the end of the fishing pier, a slanted pile of wooden boards that bobbed in the waves. Boulders ringed the edge of the wharf, and fishing boats were tied to ragged wooden stakes pushed in between the rocks.

Cooper paid for the trip with MREs gathered from the men, his flares, and a canteen of water.

Then they stood on the barren wharf in Jazan, Saudi Arabia, gazing up and down empty streets and listening to the silent morning. Not a soul seemed to stir.

"Now I need a phone." Cooper squinted behind his shades. Ahead there was a gas station, maybe two hundred yards off. Scott shifted Ethan's body, hiking him high on his back. He'd moved to the fireman's carry, and though his shoulders were getting a break, his lower back was spasming.

One of Cooper's men pulled out his cell from his back pocket and handed it to Cooper.

"No. Keep your cell phones off. We're still on radio silence."

Cooper jerked his head toward the gas station. The advertisement for petrol was 0.48 Saudi riyals. "Move out to the gas station."

With a sigh, Scott hiked after the Marines, gritting his teeth. Ethan started mumbling, groaning with each of Scott's steps. "Hang in there, big guy."

"Jack..." Ethan moaned. "Jack..."

"Not yet, buddy." He rolled his shoulder, trying to stop the burning in his back. "Just me."

Doc hung back with Scott, walking with him and Ethan instead of ahead with the Marines.

When they arrived at the gas station, Cooper was already on the phone, speaking fast Arabic and wearing a heavy frown.

Faisal ordered his men to make the two-hour flight from Riyadh to Jazan in half the time. They screamed out of Riyadh's airport ahead of a long line of commercial planes, citing royal business and playing the privilege card.

In the air, Faisal pulled out his cell phone and dialed the number Colonel Song had left him. The phone didn't ring, but still, Colonel Song answered after only a few moments of dead silence.

"How can I help you, Your Highness?"

"Colonel." Faisal picked at his robes and crossed his legs. He uncrossed them a moment later. "Colonel, I have some surprise guests coming for a visit."

Silence.

"Guests I think you'll be very interested in." He hesitated. "I think you should come visit as well."

"Who are these guests?" Colonel Song's voice dripped with heavy scorn and serious suspicion.

Faisal swallowed. "American ghosts from Ethiopia."

CHAPTER 36

Aviano Air Base

FROM THE USS TRUMAN, Jack flew to Aviano Air Base in northern Italy. The Air Force base doctor wanted to check him over again, but Jack refused, asking instead for a room in the Bachelor Officer Quarters where he could take a shower and lie down while the base prepped Air Force One for his flight back to the States.

After Ethiopia, and after Jack had been evacuated out of country by the Marines, Air Force One took off with the rest of the presidential motorcade that had escaped back to the airport. CAT Team Two had fought their way out of the downed chopper and rescued Welby, bleeding out in the abandoned Somalian embassy. Welby clung to life all the way back to Air Force One, and the president's physician saved his life on the conference room table. The Ethiopian Federal Police fought the jihadis until the fighters dispersed and ran for the highlands.

Jack was alone—finally—in the BOQ room they'd found for him. The rest of the studio apartments had been emptied, the occupants told to go be busy elsewhere while the president rested for a few hours. He tried to feel bad about that, but it was difficult to feel anything at all.

The world seemed to not exist, or to only half exist, like seeing through the curved edge of a glass, or flipped around in a mirror. Since that moment in the Ward Room on the *Arleigh Burke*, when he'd lost everything, the world and everything in it had seemed to be nothing more than a series of scenes cut from a movie and assembled the wrong way. Actions in isolation. People spoke to him, but he couldn't make out their words. Everything was hazy, garbled. It was all he could do to draw in breath after breath.

Aching loneliness clutched at his soul, but he pushed that away. No, there was no time for loneliness. He had work to do. He had to exterminate Ethan's killers.

President Puchkov had phoned, and the call had been routed to Jack's cell from Washington. For the first time, the Russian president sounded something other than flippant and arrogant, and his deep brogue had lingered on the heavy consonants as he gave Jack his condolences. "I will raise toast to your fallen men tonight," he growled. "And count on Russia to help you bring vengeance for this attack."

Jack slumped forward, leaning against the bathroom counter in the studio apartment, and tried to clear his mind. He kept his eyes down, not looking at his reflection.

"Ethan..." he whispered, "what do you think I should do? These people deserve to die. They murder indiscriminately. They destroy lives. They've destroyed countries. We should be doing more to help all the thousands—millions—who've suffered at their hands. And, they took you from me. If I act now, am I saving lives?" Jack bit his lip. "But this will cost, Ethan. Am I taking someone's loved one away? Will someone feel just like this one day because of my choice? Will I be the one to break people's hearts and take the loves of their lives away from them? If I prevent future deaths, but give lives to do so, what is gained?" He sighed. "Am I looking ahead at stopping another genocide... or walking into another Vietnam?"

He looked up, finally meeting his own eyes. He was haggard, and the lines on his face seemed etched deeper into his skin overnight. He'd always been lean—a swimmer's build, they'd said—but in one day, he'd become gaunt. Hollows filled his cheeks, sallow and pale, and his hair seemed to be more gray than blond. "What do I do, Ethan?" he breathed. "I need your wisdom. I need your advice."

Silence. If he'd hoped that the mirror would shimmer and Ethan's reflection would smile back at him, or that he'd hear Ethan's voice speaking from on high, then he was out of luck. Ethan was gone, and he'd never hear his voice again.

Jack pushed away from the counter and headed for the shower. There was a generic bottle of shampoo and a half-used bar of soap in the dish. Jack stripped, piling his clothes on the toilet before peeling off the bandages on his forearms and his cheek. Raw gashes and bloody scrapes just scabbing over clung to the gauze. Several reopened, oozing fresh blood over his skin.

He turned the water up as high as it would go, almost scalding. Steam poured from behind the glass enclosure. He stepped in, hissing as the water hit his skin.

He stayed under the spray, letting it hit his chest and pound against his body. The beating rained down on his heart, until the pain on his skin matched the ache in his heart. Jack pressed his forehead against the shower wall as his sobs rose again.

So stupid. He was so stupid. He should never have come on this trip. He should have bombed the bastards to the Stone Age his first day in office. He should have done a thousand different things. If he had, maybe Ethan would still be with him.

Slowly, Jack sank to his knees in the shower. His hands dragged down the shower wall, and red-tinted water swirled in the drain. Tears mixed with the steaming water flowing down his cheeks, and the sound of the shower washed out his choking, gasping cries.

When the water went cold, Jack grabbed the bar of soap and scrubbed at his skin, over and over, until he was pink and raw.

JACK SAT at his desk on Air Force One, staring into the middle distance. Two months ago, Ethan had pressed him against his desk and kissed him. He'd grabbed Ethan back, drawing him close, and that had been the start of them. The memories played in his mind, a never-ending stream of moments and kisses and dreams, all lost.

Knocking at his door made Jack blink. He held his breath. "Come in."

Agent Daniels, dressed down in jeans, a sweatshirt, and wearing a sling, entered. He held a black duffel in one hand.

His eyes were red-ringed and puffy, and he didn't meet Jack's gaze.

"Agent Daniels." Jack stood and came around his desk. He gestured for Daniels to sit on his office couch and then collapsed next to him. "How are you?"

Daniels shrugged. His eyes pinched as he pressed his lips together. "Doc says the bullet wound is good. Through and through. No issues."

Jack stayed silent.

"I..." Daniels stopped. Started again. "I don't remember the street battle. They say I was knocked out during the IED." He closed his eyes. "I can't believe they're gone," he whispered.

Jack looked away.

"M'sorry," Daniels grunted. He wiped at a tear that had slipped loose and sniffed. "I know it's hard for you. I, uhh..." He hesitated and then reached for the duffel he'd dropped on the couch. "I thought you'd want this. It's Ethan's bag. It's not much, but he left some dirty laundry and his cell phone behind." Daniels shrugged as he passed the bag to Jack.

Slowly, Jack unzipped the flap and pulled out Ethan's balled-up button-down. He'd changed on the flight into his tactical clothes, ditching his suit. Jack brought the collar to his nose. It still smelled like Ethan. The smell grabbed him, squeezing his heart. He closed his eyes.

Eventually, he pulled back. "You knew."

Daniels nodded. "I saw it happen. I mean, I saw you guys fall for each other. Ethan was crazy about you. Willing to break every rule in the book, even the ones he thought were gospel." Daniels snorted, a tiny smile on his lips. It faded. "I didn't think you were gay, though. Sir."

Jack shook his head. "I'm not."

Daniels frowned.

"I don't consider myself gay. Being with Ethan wasn't some kind of realization of who I was deep inside. It wasn't a... yearning of my hidden gay man." Jack frowned and rubbed Ethan's shirt between his fingers. He hadn't spoken of this to anyone, not even Ethan. They'd carefully avoided any talk at all about Jack's sexuality, and what it all meant. "It was just me falling in love," Jack finally said. "And figuring out how to make that work with Ethan."

"I'm not sure I could be with a dude. No matter how I felt about him."

Jack smiled. "When you love someone, really love them, you'll do anything. Figure anything out. Because having them in your life is worth more to you than living without them. That's how I felt about Ethan." He chuckled, looking down, and fought back against his heart's sudden hysteria. God, it had been *perfect* with Ethan. Absolutely perfect. "The fact that the sex was actually pretty amazing was a nice bonus."

He would never have that again.

Memories were cascading through his mind again, like a film reel spinning out of control. He stood. "Thank you for bringing this to me. Please let me know if you need anything, Agent Daniels."

When Daniels looked up at him, Jack finally saw all of the loneliness, the heartache, and the guilt Daniels was burying, shoveled so deep within him that he hoped no one would ever see it. Daniels blinked, and the moment was gone, his anguish replaced by a bland, flat glaze to his eyes. He stood, nodded once, and headed to the door.

"Levi..." Jack fumbled. He didn't know what to say. He knew what Daniels was feeling. God, he knew what he was feeling, but what could he do? He didn't have anything else to give. Not after this. "Levi, don't be a stranger," he finally said.

Daniels didn't say a word as he ducked out of Jack's office.

Director Irwin waited outside. Jack caught his gaze through the doorway.

Irwin looked down, staring at the carpet.

Good, Jack thought. Vicious wrath tore through him, hatred and bitter wrath singeing his veins. His blood leaped, like raging hounds chasing down prey. *I should stake you out on a road in Syria and let them have their way with you. Let you feel what I felt.* But Irwin wouldn't ever feel the true depths of Jack's horror, or his agony, or have his heart broken as perfectly and surely as Jack's had been. He'd never watch the love of his life lie in a street with a gun to his head, and then wait, with bated breath, for his rescue, only to watch the entire mission explode in a firestorm of bitter regret and shattered lives.

Wordlessly, Jack motioned for Irwin to enter. He stood in the center of the room, his arms folded, legs spread, and waited while Irwin took a seat.

The couch where Ethan and I made out once, flying on a quick trip to New York City for a benefit banquet— Jack shut down his memories, and the image of Ethan lying back, breathless and debauched and grinning as he reached for Jack for one more kiss.

"Director Irwin," Jack began. His voice was cold fury and nuclear fusion, power contained and waiting to explode. "I hold you singularly responsible for the events in Ethiopia."

"Sir—"

"Shut your mouth!" Jack bellowed. "You don't get to talk! The time for talking was *before* this trip! *Before*, when you should have done your job and informed us all of the situation on the ground!"

"Sir! There was no evidence of foreign fighters in Ethiopia! There was no report of jihadist activity!" Irwin turned pained eyes up to Jack. "My people assured me that this would be a responsible risk."

"A responsible risk?" Jack held himself back from lashing out. "Two of my agents are *dead*, and an entire Marine team! I was almost killed!"

"Mr. President..." Irwin looked down again, his shoulders sagging. "I don't know how this happened."

"Well, we're going to find out. I expect your resignation before we land in Washington. And you will appear before the Senate to answer for your egregious failures of intelligence. Congress will get to the bottom of this, and if they feel it is warranted, they will begin an investigation." Jack paused. "I would rather air drop you to Syria and leave you to take your chances, but I suppose watching you rot in prison will bring some level of satisfaction."

Director Irwin stayed silent. He blinked and then closed his eyes. "You'll have my resignation in an hour, Mr. President."

"Get out," Jack growled. "I don't want to ever see your face again."

CHAPTER 37

Taif, Saudi Arabia

SUNLIGHT STREAMED THROUGH AN OPEN WINDOW. White gauze curtains fluttered in a light breeze, and Stargazers and Tiger lilies swayed in a crystal vase just beneath the open window, set on a mirrored table inlaid with gold etchings and glittering mosaics made from rubies, emeralds, and sapphires.

Ethan blinked, holding his eyes closed before opening them again. He turned his head—slowly; he wasn't sure it would stay on his neck, what with the pounding behind his eyes and at the base of his skull—and more of the ornate room came into view. A wide, palatial space, with marble floors and columns leading to an open balcony. There was a crystal chandelier overhead, and a Turkish rug that would have cost more than most houses in America spread across the floor.

He lay on a wide bed, covered in sticky sheets. Sweating, he pulled them back, kicking them off slowly. His feet tangled, and Ethan struggled through the dullness of his foggy mind. He recognized the touch of sedatives in his system, and he took a deep breath as his head swam. When the dizziness passed, he tried again, and then he was free of the tangled sheets.

Someone had changed his clothes. He was wearing white cotton pants and nothing else. His bare feet twitched. Thick wrappings bound his chest and ribs. Gingerly, he poked himself, and tried to breathe deeply. No stabbing pain. Bruised ribs, maybe? His knee was wrapped as well, and he winced when he tried to flex it. Bandages were scattered across his arms, and more scrapes and bloody scabs lay uncovered as well. His stomach had a gauze pad taped to it, and a small circle of blood in the center. He peeled that back. Saw stitches in his abdomen.

Where was he? How had he gotten here? He'd been on a tarp in the darkness, listening to gutter Arabic decry him as an American whore and the man-lover of the president, and a pig to boot, while staring at the rusted blade hoisted high by the filthy jihadist who had spat in his face. He'd been checking out, mentally disappearing and turning off the lights. He hadn't wanted to be there when the knife fell.

Most of all, he didn't want Jack's last sight of him to be one of horrible savagery. The president was briefed on every execution video terrorists put out. He had never thought that he'd end up as the star of one.

Then, shouts. Banging. Bullets. He'd already been half-delirious by that time, beaten and bruised and bleeding inside, and he'd collapsed as soon as the hand griping his hair had let go. His head hit the tarp-covered dirt, and he was out.

And now, he was reclining in a palace, Middle Eastern by the look of it, and recovering from his wounds. Someone had performed surgery on him. Who had rescued him? If it was the US military, why wasn't he back in the States, or on a military base somewhere? This was no military base.

Ethan pushed to his feet, standing unsteadily next to the bed. He held his hands out, searching for balance, and waited. After a moment, he took a step, and then another. Slowly, Ethan padded away from the bed, crossed the room, and pulled open the door.

He'd expected it to be locked. It wasn't.

An open hallway greeted him, lined by more columns. Voices

floated his way, the words seemingly in English. He stumbled forward.

The hallway dead-ended in another round room, open and breezy and just as ornate. Rugs covered the marble floor, and delicate couches shared space with round floor cushions and piles of satin and brocade pillows. The windows were open, more gauze curtains fluttering, and vases of roses sat on stands every six feet. A flat-screen TV hung on one wall, and before the TV, Ethan saw a team of men—Americans, by the look of them—relaxing and cleaning their weapons while they watched a news broadcast.

"What the hell is going on?" Ethan leaned against the doorframe, sagging as exhaustion hit him hard.

"Ethan!" From the corner, over by a fridge recessed into the wall, Ethan saw Scott whirl around, wide-eyed. He dropped a diet soda and took off, jogging across the room to Ethan's side. He slipped Ethan's arm over his shoulder and guided him to the nearest couch, bitching at the man on it to move his ass.

"What's going on?" Ethan lay back as he sat down, trying to catch his breath. "What happened?"

"We rescued you." Scott gestured to the rest of the team. "Lieutenant Adam Cooper and his Marines flew over from Djibouti. We traced a signal the jihadis who grabbed you left behind to the bunker they were holding you in. We stormed it, got you out." Scott stopped talking. He scowled.

There was more. Ethan could tell. The sudden silence, the way the rest of the Marines were all watching him carefully. "Where are we? If you rescued me, why aren't we at a hospital?"

"We're at the summer palace of one of my intelligence contacts, Faisal. He's a prince in the royal family, but somewhat of a black sheep. He runs the Saudi Intelligence Directorate. I've connected with him on Gulf intelligence before." Lieutenant Cooper stood, setting down his weapon. His eyes were dark, with deep bags hanging beneath them. Something hung in his gaze, something that looked like pain.

"Why are we here?" Ethan still couldn't figure it out. Why were they in some Saudi prince's palace instead of at a US base?

Dread grasped him, choking the breath from his lungs. "Oh God. Is Jack..." He turned to Scott. He'd seen Jack be pulled out by the Brits, but what if something had happened on the helo?

"The president is safe. He's back in DC." Scott looked down.

"Hey!" Doc shouted from the pillow he was leaning on and clicked off the mute button on the remote. "It's starting! Guys, c'mere!"

"What's starting?" Ethan struggled to sit up. On the TV, coffins lay in a long line, draped with American flags. Jack stood at the front of the group, his eyes screwed shut as his lips twisted.

"Our funerals," Cooper said. "We're dead."

Ethan stared at Scott. His mouth fell open, but no words came out. "How", "why", and "who" danced in his mind, questions he couldn't find the voice to say.

"It was our own government," Scott breathed. "Our own government killed us."

CHAPTER 38

Washington DC

THERE WAS SOMETHING ABOUT A BUGLE, something about the curves of brass and the shallow bell that, when played, sounded like a soul was breaking.

Lonely notes from "Taps" slid down his bones, catching in his joints alongside the shards of his broken heart. Pristine grass crunched beneath his feet, and above, a cloudless sky stretched over Washington, more perfectly blue than he'd ever seen. In the curve of the bugle's bell, Jack caught his reflection, glinting in the sunlight.

A man alone. A man with no one. A man with a twice-broken heart, and eyes exhausted of tears.

His eyelids slid closed. Another tear slipped down his cheek, like a knife slicing over his skin. His breaths came fast, shuddering inhales between lips gone chapped and frayed. Blinking, he didn't wipe his tears away.

His heart still hammered, pounding in time with the clap and bang of the gun salute over Ethan's casket. He'd tried to hide his flinch, the fracture of his soul as the gunfire cracked.

Bang. Memories of a dusty side street. Bullets whizzing through the air as he ran behind Scott, frantically looking behind him for

Ethan. Tasting sand and grit and blood, and meeting Ethan's panicked gaze, just before—

Bang. The world exploding, white noise and screaming and buildings falling down. Losing Ethan in the dust and then seeing him again, trying to crawl for Jack. Gritting his teeth, bleeding, his fingers sliding in the dirt, fire and rage burning in his eyes, just before—

Bang. Ethan swaying on a tarp in the darkness beneath a single bulb, a machete to his throat, on the vidscreen in the Ward Room. Watching the rescue mission from a drone's perspective, hoping one of those dark dots would be his lover. And then—

Inhale. Exhale. Another tear slid down Jack's cheek.

Soldiers surrounded Ethan's flag-draped casket, standing at attention. Soft orders, from their sergeant, and then they lifted the flag as one, holding it taut before folding it in half. Snapped it flat again. White-gloved hands started folding at the stripes, carving perfect triangles into the fabric, each twist and turn a slam into Jack's stomach.

Wasn't one flag enough? Wasn't one broken heart enough for one lifetime? How did this happen to a man twice? How could he accept this, Ethan's flag folded off his casket, when he'd only just realized how deeply he could fall in love with him?

The stars wrapped twice around the triangle-folded flag, as if they were wrapping up Ethan's life, holding his memories and his soul in the crisp canvas. If he shook the flag out, would Ethan tumble free? He wanted to try. Wanted to grab the flag and scream, fall to his knees and bellow, sob into the rough fabric and wail, beg for a second chance at a second chance.

He squeezed his eyes closed as the sergeant tucked something into the folds of the flag and called for his team to come to attention.

Hands rose slowly, saluting, as the sergeant made his way over to Jack. Precise steps. Deliberate movements. A hard face, a mask of stone-cold discipline.

He stopped in front of Jack. Met his gaze.

Everything in Jack wanted to scream. To collapse to the grass. To fall against this sergeant, this man of stone and steel, and let himself weep. He didn't want to be strong. Not for this. Not when he had to reach out and take Ethan's flag.

The sergeant waited for him.

Lips shaking, like Jack was speaking silent words he'd never get to say to Ethan, his hands finally opened, lying flat to accept the flag. His fingers trembled.

The weight of Ethan's flag hit his soul, a thousand times heavier than the simple folds of canvas could be. This man, this man he loved, could not be reduced to what Jack had left. His smile was brighter than those stars. And even though Jack was a patriot—was the president, for God's sake—he'd rather have Ethan alive than the stripes he held.

Something warm hit his palm, from within the folds of the flag. He searched for it, and his fingers found the brass casing of a blank round fired during Ethan's gun salute.

Everything always ended in war, in combat. Was that the lesson of his life? Of his generation? Those who lived by the sword, died by the sword, and he was fated to fall in love with two warriors who gave their all.

Around Jack, people fell away. Secret Service agents who had come to mourn their detail lead, and who weren't on duty protecting Jack. Staff from the White House who knew Ethan, had served with him. Everyone who had come to pay their respects to Ethan, and to the others. Agent Collard's wife and daughter were a huddled mass of tears and black dresses down the line at his casket. Ethan's funeral had been the last in a too-long string, an endless day of agony and mourning.

He was left alone at Ethan's casket, his detail staying back as if they knew to leave him with Ethan one last time.

How many moments had they stolen alone? Slipped away from the others for a quick conversation, a brush of their hands, a smile hidden behind corners and closed doors? How many times had other agents faded away, and it had just been him and Ethan for minutes they could snag in between the hustle and bustle of the West Wing?

This was their last moment. The last time he'd be by Ethan's side.

Ethan wasn't in the casket, but Jack's heart was, and all of his hopes and dreams for the both of them.

Jack held his shaking hand over the polished wood and clutched Ethan's folded flag against his chest.

"I should have told you that I had fallen in love with you," he whispered. "I should have said it every chance I could. You should have known."

Slowly, his hand fell, fingers brushing the sun-warmed wood. His throat clenched, and he forced back a sob that kicked out his knees and tore the air from his lungs. He only stayed on his feet by leaning against Ethan's casket, almost all his weight pressed in the center of his palm.

"I wanted this to last..." Eyes slipping closed, Jack fought against the tears building in the corners of his eyes again. "I wanted to make a life with you. And—" Gasping, his tears broke free, rivers cascading down his cheeks. "I was okay going public about us, too. When it wouldn't hurt your career. When we could... be together."

And then he couldn't hold it back any longer, and the sobs crashed through him, waves breaking on the shards of his shattered heart. He couldn't breathe, and he heaved, everything in him desperately trying to keep it together. His bones creaked, holding up the weight of his sorrows as he strode away from Ethan, blindly aiming for his detail through the blur of his tears. The press was probably catching all of it, all of his anguish, every fallen tear, but he couldn't care about that.

Two agents bracketed him, hands guiding him at his elbows and steering him quickly to the motorcade. "This way, sir," one of the agents muttered. "We've got you."

He couldn't place the voice. He'd been at Ethan's side for so long, he barely knew anyone else on his detail.

They poured him into the backseat of the SUV and shut the door, leaving him encased in stillness and silence. The privacy screen separating him from the front of the SUV was up, and he could pretend, at least a little bit, that it was Ethan who was going to climb into the front, and he'd send Jack a text message, and they'd flirt and joke during the entire drive, just like before.

But no. Ethan was gone and all he had left was his flag.

He clutched Ethan's flag to his chest again, wrapping both arms around it like he could hold Ethan. Outside the tinted glass, Ethan's casket sat in the open, alone in the sunlight, and part of him wanted to leap from the SUV, run back to Ethan, lay his cheek against the warm oak and never leave his side. Why was he leaving? Why was he driving away? Ethan was there, he was *right there*—

The motorcade started rolling forward. He craned his neck, trying to hold on to Ethan for as long as he could.

And then, Ethan was gone.

He thunked his head against the glass and let the tears rain down, soaking his suit jacket. Once was enough. One lost love was more than enough for one life. He'd buried his wife, and now buried Ethan, and he wasn't strong enough to get through this. What had he done before, after Leslie's funeral? The memories were faded, washed out with gray, a part of his life he'd left behind. He finally dragged them back, remembering. He'd collapsed into his parents' love, letting them help him find his feet. He'd been younger, barely thirty, and he could afford to lean on others to get through those moments.

Who did the president lean on when he wanted to fall apart? For months it had been Ethan, but Ethan was gone and he was all alone.

"Why?" he breathed, his voice a fragile, brittle thing. "Why did you do this to me? Twice?"

He sniffed, wiping his nose and smearing snot on his suit jacket. "He didn't deserve this. He should have had a long, beautiful life. Should have had everything he wanted." His chin wavered again, and he fought to breathe. "This is all my fault..." Something in him killed the ones he loved. Some cosmic calculus that made his kisses lures for death. Would Ethan be alive if they hadn't gotten together? Would that have saved him, like a butterfly's wings flapping in Brazil?

He should have listened to Ethan about Ethiopia. About the dangers. Should have done *everything* differently. But he'd chosen to go, and Ethan had paid the price.

And he would live with knowing that what he'd done—the choices he'd made—had sent Ethan to his grave.

"I wish it had been me and not you," he whispered. "I don't want to face what's next. Not without you."

Ahead, the White House loomed large, and the motorcade rolled through the gates, driving up to the South Entrance. Agents waited on the steps, their faces drawn and weary.

Jeff waited for him, too.

If there was anyone who knew what he was truly going through, it would be Jeff. He'd *known*. He'd seen them together, accidentally walking in on him trying to seduce Ethan.

When his world had shattered, Jeff had been there, holding him up and catching his sobs. He'd known, Leslie, too. He'd been a part of Jack's life for his two biggest losses.

Everyone moved slowly, like they were caught in a haggard malaise. The agents opening the limo's door averted their eyes, not looking when he tried to scrub away his tears before he climbed out. Jeff saw, though, and he grimaced, walking down the steps to meet him halfway.

"Mr. President."

Inhale. Exhale. Inhale again. He was the president. He had to keep going, if for no other reason than because Ethan would want him to. And he could do something about the bastards who had ripped Ethan away from him. He would hunt them down and wipe them from the face of the planet.

No one will ever feel this way again. He swore it, in the hollows of his soul. *No one else will feel like this. No one else will lose the one they love. The love of their life.*

Swallowing, Jack nodded to Jeff. Jeff's eyes were on Ethan's flag.

He still had it in his arms. He wasn't ready to let go.

"I bought you a case for his flag," Jeff said softly. "It's in the Residence."

He tried to smile, but the tears rose again, and all he could do was shake his head, sniff and fight against his watering eyes. "Jeff—"

Jeff shook his head. Rested his hand on Jack's shoulder and

steered him up the steps, into the White House. "I'm here for you, Mr. President. We'll get through this."

Slow, deep breaths grounded him, and the click of their heels on the marble floor in the foyer.

But, he stopped. Looked around at the White House that surrounded him.

The colors weren't as bright, the lighting was dim. The pomp and circumstance had frayed edges. Chipped paint and scuff marks caught his eye.

He was now in a post-Ethan White House, and the light, and the wonder, had gone out of his world.

PRESIDENT SPIERS ATTENDS FUNERALS FOR AGENTS AND MARINE SPECIAL OPERATIONS TEAM LOST IN ETHIOPIA

President Spiers attended the funerals of the two Secret Service agents and the Marine Corps Special Operations team lost in Ethiopia. All were laid to rest at Arlington National Cemetery.

The president was noticeably emotional during the service. He openly wept as Agent Reichenbach's name and service record were read aloud. Agent Reichenbach had been the lead agent assigned to the presidential protective detail, and reports from the White House indicate the two had a close working relationship.

Agent Reichenbach did not have a family member present at the funeral. His folded flag was presented to President Spiers, who held it to his chest as he fought back tears. Later, the president rested his hand on Agent Reichenbach's casket, standing at his side for over a minute.

The president's actions come amid swirls of rumors that there was more between him and his openly gay lead detail Secret Service agent than what has been confirmed by the White House. Rumors from unnamed sources report that the two spent extensive time off-duty together, and that Agent Reichenbach was regularly seen in the Residence socializing with the president. Some have even accused the president and Agent Reichenbach of having a gay love affair. Reportedly, Agent Reichenbach spent the night in the Residence "more than once".

CHAPTER 39

Washington DC

JACK SLAMMED his hand down on his desk. "No! Damn it, I don't care! I'm not going to drag Ethan's name through the mud by answering these rumors! It's predatory journalism!"

Pete Reyes, Jack's press secretary, stood quietly in front of Jack's desk. Jeff frowned.

"Sir, these news reports are only gaining strength. People on the Hill are starting to ask if there should be an investigation," Jeff said carefully.

"An investigation? Into what? My personal life isn't anyone's business."

"But Ethan violating the Secret Service's regulations and putting your life in danger *is* Congress's business." Jeff sighed. "I'm not saying that's what happened," he said quickly, seeming to try to push off Jack's almost-explosion of rage. "But I am saying that's what it appears to be, based on the reports in the media."

"Fuck," Jack hissed. He threw down his pen and leaned back in his chair. His hands threaded through his hair and then gripped the back of his head. "What do you both recommend? To end this," he growled.

Pete and Jeff shared a long look. It was Jeff who finally spoke. "We recommend you address these reports."

"You want me to talk about these rumors—"

"But they're not rumors, sir," Jeff interrupted. "They're *not* rumors. You and Ethan *were* intimately involved."

Silence.

"And if there's an investigation, and if people have to testify, that will all come out under sworn statements. Do you want it to go that far? Or do you want to get ahead of the disclosure and manage it your way?"

Jack's eyes slid closed. He exhaled. "I want to jump off a cliff," he finally said.

Jeff and Pete stared at him.

"I'll think about it," he said softly. "I don't want to do this. I don't want to talk about Ethan, not without his permission. He's a private guy. He wouldn't want this."

"Well, sir, Ethan isn't here. We are. We have to figure this out and keep you in office."

"I don't really care about this office anymore, Jeff." He didn't much care about anything. Not anymore. "Where are we with Congress authorizing our deployments into Syria?"

"They're dragging their feet, sir. We've got bipartisan support for the bill, but not enough. Holdouts on the right say that it's too expensive, and we can't afford another ten-year quagmire in the Middle East. The left says that we have no business interfering in Syria, and we'll just mess things up more."

Jack cursed. No matter what, no matter how much he tried to do the right thing, no matter that America's European allies and the Russians were all working together for the first time in almost a century, there was always someone working against him. All he wanted was to eliminate these monsters, and to do it for Ethan's memory. After that... Jack didn't particularly care where he went, or what he did.

"Make it happen, Jeff. I'll... figure out what to say about Ethan."

Jeff and Pete nodded. They headed for the door.

"Jeff?" Jack stared out the window. In the Rose Garden, the leaves were changing colors, swirling from the trees and painting the lawn in the colors of autumn. Fall had embraced Washington. A chill was in the air, and it was the right time to start a fire and cozy up in bed with Ethan.

Except—

"Sir?" Jeff pressed when Jack was silent.

"Have you seen Agent Daniels?" Jack turned back to Jeff, ignoring the flutter of autumn leaves on the White House lawn. "I haven't seen him since Aviano."

Jeff shook his head. "No, sir. I heard from Agent Inada that Daniels hasn't shown up for his shifts."

Inada had taken over the presidential detail, wide-eyed and shell-shocked at the loss of his friends.

"Please find him," Jack said softly. "I want to talk with Levi Daniels."

CHAPTER 40

Taif, Saudi Arabia

ETHAN SPARRED WTIH SCOTT, moving through a practiced round of punches and kicks across Faisal's palatial sunroom. The couches had all been pushed to one wall, the cushions piled on top, and the Marines called out points and heckled Ethan good-naturedly. Cooper perched on the arm of one of the couches, watching with a tight smile. His gaze was still hollowed, his eyes dark and weary.

Calling a break, Ethan backed off, dripping with sweat, and reached for a bottle of water. He was building up his strength, and after a final checkup from Faisal's doctor, he'd been given the go-ahead to start working out again. His knee still twinged, but he wrapped it every day. His ribs ached, but he pushed through the pain.

"You're doing better, Ethan." Cooper clapped him on the shoulder. "Looking good."

Ethan nodded, chugging his water. He wiped his mouth with the back of his hand. "When is Faisal landing?"

Faisal, the mysterious royal benefactor sheltering them in his palace, wasn't on the grounds when Ethan woke up. He'd had to leave, Cooper had said, looking sideways. He'd be back later.

"He should have already landed." Cooper frowned, and his hands made fists at his side. He trembled, just faintly. "Want to go a round with me?"

Ethan shook his head. Walking away, he ignored Cooper's long stare and Scott's sullen silence. Scott had struggled to hold his gaze for days.

Ethan just wasn't up for jokes, or for games, or for playing basketball in the prince's courtyard or horsing around in the pool. This wasn't a vacation. Someone in the government had tried to kill them, and if there was someone trying to kill them, then how safe was Jack? More than anything, Ethan wanted to hop on the next flight and head back to DC, grab Jack, and get him to safety.

But where was safety? Who could they trust? General Madigan had been leading the rescue mission for Ethan personally. Was he responsible for the cover up of their deaths? If not, then who?

And how had Al-Karim known that Ethan was Jack's lover? How had that information traveled from the walls of the White House and the clenched lips of the Navy stewards to the ears of the most wanted terrorist in the world? Who knew—*truly knew*—about the two of them? Ethan's stomach knotted as he counted.

Someone had fed information to Al-Karim about Ethan and about Jack. Someone had set them up in Ethiopia. And someone had wanted Ethan to stay dead.

Watching Jack at his funeral had nearly ripped his heart out. Jack's tears had gutted him, and when Jack had accepted his folded flag, he'd looked so lost, so achingly alone, and so heartbroken that it took everything in Ethan to not race to his side that day, and damn his injuries. Only Scott holding him back, and Cooper explaining the depths of their pile of shit, kept him in the palace.

Each day that passed tore his heart to shreds. Each hour that ticked by, he wanted to scream. Jack was alone. Jack thought he was dead. Jack was in danger, and he wasn't by his side.

And he *missed* Jack. He missed his voice, his laughter, his touch. He missed burrowing close to him at night and waking with his warm body in his arms. He missed the light in his eyes and the touch of his lips. He missed everything about Jack with an ache that surpassed anything broken in his body.

He had to get back. He'd do anything to get back to Jack's side.

"STOP." Faisal reached for his driver, resting his hand on his shoulder. His summer palace loomed ahead, rising in the hills over Taif.

He wasn't ready to go back. Not yet. He couldn't face Adam Cooper again. Not after...

Anguish slammed into him with the backbreaking blow of a sledgehammer.

One spring day, months ago when the honey bloom was building over Taif, and the roses were approaching their peak, and Europe's perfumeries were descending to harvest the rose oil that came only from Taif's mountainside, Adam's eyes had skittered away from his, and his chapped lips had fumbled through a torrent of words. Apologies. Excuses. And a goodbye.

Watching Adam walk away from their relationship had been like exhaling and not knowing if another breath would come. Like a shivering last note held on a violin string, quivering into an echo of stillness. It hadn't felt real. After everything. After what they'd risked. How deeply they'd loved, for two years. And then, Adam had just up and walked away. It hadn't made sense.

It still didn't make sense.

He'd been a ghost all spring, and into summer. Second guessing himself over everything. Had Adam left because of this or that? What part of himself had driven his love away? What had he done? How had he not been enough? His confidence, once strong with Adam's bolstering smile, folded in on itself like a crumpled love letter.

He wasn't at his best when Colonel Song first approached him. They were trying to unravel what could be the greatest threat against the Kingdom and against the world that he'd ever seen. Someone was trying to take America out. Take down her president. Nuclear weapons were in play. The devastation to the world order, to international stability and normality, should America fall, would be worse than almost anything else.

He'd desperately wanted Adam at his side. They would have been handling this together, if Colonel Song had called just months earlier. And, even though Colonel Song had said they couldn't trust anyone—not a single soul—in America, *in shaa Allah*, he could always trust Adam.

But Adam didn't want him.

Yallah, Nairobi. The nuclear attack. The world on edge, shaking with fear. He'd watched it all come apart from Riyadh, standing beside his uncle. Uncle Abdul, Crown Prince of Saudi Arabia, had seemed to age ten years in the space of the news broadcast, and his knuckles had gone white where he clasped the back of a chair in the king's palace as they watched the television reports of the attack on the American president.

President Spiers had lived. The rescue team—*Marines*—and two Secret Service agents did not, the news said. Marines.

What were the chances? Like a scab, he'd picked over the worry until it had bled out into every corner of his soul. Adam had transferred away the day after he'd broken their relationship off. He wasn't in the Middle East any longer, but there were rumors that he was in North Africa. Across the Red Sea. Possibly in Djibouti.

The Marines had been from Camp Lemonnier. From Djibouti.

A scratchy cell phone connection to an ancient, desert-rotted pay phone in Jazan had answered his questions, breathless relief making him collapse to the floor. Adam's voice hadn't ever been that fast, or that frantic-sounding, and Faisal had promised sixteen times to get to Adam, to help him, from when he had picked himself off the floor and started running for his car and driver.

Water, food, rest, and a surgeon later, Adam's team was snoring in the sun room of his summer palace, the wounded Secret Service agent was resting in one of his spare bedrooms, his friend sleeping on the floor beside his bed, and—

And Adam had come up to his bedroom, trembling. He stank like the desert and the sea, like sweat and oil and salt, and the tang of black powder lingered on his skin, mixing with wet copper and smeared blood.

It took nothing to guide him to the bath. Strip him down, and set him in the tub. Or follow him in, holding on to the soap and a cloth like they would uphold his good intentions in perpetuity.

Adam kissed him before Faisal had washed his hair. They kissed until the water ran cold, and then abandoned the tub, and the swirls of dirt and blood and sweat in the water. Adam was still filthy, less than half washed, but Faisal hadn't cared. He pushed Adam to the bed, and Adam pulled him on top.

Adam was exhausted, and after the first time, he'd passed out with his face shoved against Faisal's neck, arms wrapped so tightly around him. That should have been it, but every time Faisal stirred, Adam woke, and he reached for Faisal again. By the time the sun rose, they were working on their fourth time, Faisal sliding into Adam's body again, gritting their teeth and kissing through the bite and the sting, but refusing to stop.

How happy he'd been then, watching the sunlight on Adam's cheeks. How certain he'd been that it would all work out. That their love would be enough.

Adam left his bed without a word. He was back to his sullen silence, his distance. Back to goodbye, and refusing to give Faisal any answers.

How wrong Faisal had been.

What else was he wrong about?

PRINCE FAISAL ARRIVED at the palace in a black limo early that afternoon. His royal security team escorted the young prince as Ethan watched from the upstairs window of the bedroom that had become his.

Faisal wasn't alone. An Asian man followed behind in a separate limo, wearing a plain suit and dark glasses. He looked up and found Ethan's gaze before heading inside.

Ethan met Faisal and the unknown visitor in the room the Marines had taken over as their own. On the patio, the Marines stopped their basketball game and jogged inside, leaning against the curtained doorway, sweating buckets and wiping their faces with the hems of their t-shirts.

Cooper embraced Faisal stiffly, looking like he was going through the motions of Middle Eastern formality and looking away as he placed two kisses on Faisal's cheeks. Faisal kept his eyes closed, his face a mask of stone throughout the exchange.

Ethan's eyes narrowed. He stayed in the back, his arms crossed in the shadows of the hallway.

Across the room, Scott's gaze bored into Ethan, but he ignored his friend's stare.

The Asian man in the suit surveyed the group. He ignored everyone else, but smiled when his eyes landed on Ethan. "Agent Reichenbach," he said. "It is a pleasure to meet you. I recognize your face from the American media. I'm sure your president will be delighted to learn that you are, indeed, alive."

Ethan's hackles rose. "Who are you and why are you here?"

Cooper stared at Faisal, waiting for an answer.

"I am Colonel Song of the Central Military Commission in the People's Republic of China. Prince Faisal and I are partners." He smiled again.

"Faisal..." Cooper stepped back. Betrayal washed over his features.

Dread pooled in Ethan's belly. He wanted nothing to do with the Central Military Commission in China.

Cooper continued. "We're not interested in Chinese involvement. This is way, way outside our agreement."

Faisal turned apologetic brown eyes to Cooper. "Adam, he is already involved. The colonel has been involved in this situation for longer than you know. He knows—"

"Did you set this up?" Ethan roared. "Are you responsible for this?" He stalked forward, glaring. All around the sunroom, Cooper's men were spreading out, some reaching casually for their weapons, others getting ready for a brawl.

"Agent Reichenbach, calm down," Colonel Song said. "I am not responsible for your attack."

"Why are you here?" Ethan bellowed. "Why are any of us here?" His rage bubbled over, boiling inside of him. He wanted to rip apart the world and get back to Jack's side, and instead, he was stuck in a prince's palace and getting talked down to by a Chinese colonel. Enough of this. He was done. "What the fuck is going on?"

"Ethan..." Scott's voice, a warning and a plea, rang out across the room.

"Hey, calm down, Agent Reichenbach." Cooper put himself between Faisal and Ethan. "This man saved your life."

"I don't care!" Ethan shouted. "All I care about is figuring out what the *fuck* is going on and then getting back to Washington!"

"General Madigan ordered your deaths."

Colonel Song's voice shattered the rising tension crackling in the room. Ethan's clawing anxiety scratched up his spine and settled in the marrow of his bones. "What?"

Even Cooper looked stunned, staring openmouthed at Colonel Song.

The colonel pulled his phone from his pocket. It was a flashy, clear-glass device, and he pressed a series of illuminated Chinese characters before holding the phone out horizontally.

General Madigan's voice rose from the phone's speaker.

"The pilots have killed the Marines and buried the president's lover. He's not coming out alive. It would have been better if those ragheads had cut off his head quickly, before the president sent a rescue mission. But the damn president acted too fast, and we had to scramble. Everything is back on track. But listen. Those chopper pilots can't make it back to base. You understand?"

Colonel Song clicked the recording off.

Silence. Silence so thick the sound of the curtains twitching in the wind scraped over Ethan's eardrums. Silence so deep he heard the heavy thump of his heartbeat speeding up. Heard the shifting of sand over sand in the prince's courtyard.

"Two helicopters went down on a training mission on the border of Ethiopia and Djibouti the same day the bunker blew during your rescue mission, according to news reports." Colonel Song pocketed his phone.

"Who was he talking to?" Cooper finally breathed.

Faisal spoke before Colonel Song. "We don't know for certain. We can't get a match on vocal recognition, and his identity has been scrubbed from the databases that we've hacked. But, we know two things about him. Whoever he is, he's close to your president. These calls have been made from the same location as the president. Washington DC. Camp David. Turin. Prague. Ethiopia. He's in the president's inner circle. Or he's a Secret Service agent."

Colonel Song's eyes slid sideways, catching Ethan. "We also know the man that the general has been talking to has been his right hand for years. They work closely together, and they have for a long time."

"How do you know?" Ethan's stomach puckered.

"It's obvious in how they speak to one another. This man is General Madigan's right hand. We believe that General Madigan and this mystery man are affiliated with Black Fox."

Cooper shot Ethan a dark look, long and lean. Ethan searched for Scott, but couldn't find him.

Black Fox was the disavowed military unit run out of the Department of Defense's Joint Special Operations Command. They'd been responsible for some of the largest victories in the past thirty years, and some of the largest and greatest defeats and embarrassments. Parts of America's darkest history were embroiled in Black Fox. If the American government wanted to overthrow a democracy or install a dictatorship, Black Fox was the unit to turn to. Officially, they'd been disbanded.

They'd officially been disbanded six times.

Ethan had seen enough inside the White House to know that they were very much still an active presence. Insidious, Black Fox had routinely scattered, burrowing into other organizations, propping up their members in new agencies, though their loyalties were always to each other and to the unit.

And, General Porter Madigan, then Major Madigan, had led the unit.

"That would explain how his identity has been scrubbed." Cooper crossed his arms, growling. "Those guys don't exist. Not just in an abstract way. They truly don't exist. Any identity they do have is a pure cover. A smokescreen. All lies."

Jesus. Dizziness stole over Ethan. He swallowed, trying to find his center. Black Fox, General Madigan. His brain hurt. "Why is Black Fox trying to kill us? What did we ever do?"

Colonel Song smirked. "They weren't trying to killing you. You just got in the way." He tapped his phone's screen. On the wall, the TV hummed on, and Chinese characters popped up, rooting through the TV's operating system. Faisal's mouth opened, but with one look at Colonel Song, he closed it.

Three windows flashed on screen: one showing a list of phone calls, dated and time-stamped, one showing a map of the Near East, and Chinese and Russian troop movements into Iraq, and one showing the dead body of Talib Al-Syria, his mangled corpse photographed in black and white.

"In the past four months, both the Russians and my own country have moved massive numbers of ground troops into Syria and Iraq. They're trying to stabilize reconstruction projects and protect their investments. Russia has committed to supporting the destruction of the Caliphate and the corrupt Syrian regime, thanks to the diplomatic efforts of President Spiers, but we aren't sure what their price for that cooperation is yet."

Colonel Song blew up the window highlighting the call logs and pulled out six calls to one international number.

"We would normally applaud this kind of international cooperation. But it is built and based around a lie. The enemy the world has united to fight is not who it appears to be." Colonel Song gestured to the call logs. "These six calls were placed from General Madigan's mystery accomplice to Al-Karim. Immediately after these calls, Al-Karim executed a major military operation. He blew up the Chinese reconstruction projects. He executed hostages. He sent fighters to Europe on terror missions. He dispatched weapons to refugees in the resettlement zones." Colonel Song stared at Ethan. "We believe that Al-Karim has been taking orders from this mystery man, and further still, from General Madigan himself."

Doc whistled from where he leaned against Faisal's couch. "The US government is running Al-Karim?"

Cooper's jaw clenched so hard Ethan heard his teeth grind.

"Not the US government." Ethan shook his head. "Whoever this guy is, and General Madigan. Black Fox." All of them together, working against everything Jack stood for.

"Do you remember when China took control of Taiwan for the province's protection, after the Caliphate attacked Taipei?" Colonel Song scrolled through the call logs, going back in time. He pulled up another window, this one showing an email account and a series of messages pinging back and forth.

"How could we forget?" Ethan's memories surfaced, Jack cast in the half light of a subdued fire in Camp David and asking him what he thought about China. He shook his head and felt his skin break where his nails dug into his arms.

"The Caliphate gained access to Taiwan through this man." On the screen, a picture of a middle-aged Chinese man, sullen and boring looking, spun in a circle. "HU" was stamped beneath the headshot. "Mr. Hu was an international businessman. His travels took him from Lebanon to Dubai, Indonesia to Iraq and then back to Taiwan. He had legitimate reasons for being in countries where the Caliphate operated, and legitimate reasons for moving massive amounts of money between bank accounts. That's why Black Fox used him as a false flag."

Cooper stopped breathing, and Ethan watched his pulse skyrocket.

"Black Fox ran money and information through accounts set up in Mr. Hu's name. A mistake in his transactions brought him to

Faisal's attention. Faisal, doing his due diligence, brought Mr. Hu in, where he, sadly, did not survive questioning."

A chill tap-danced down Ethan's spine.

Cooper's eyes flashed to Faisal. "You *knew* about this?"

"I learned it in late spring. After—" Faisal pressed his lips together, a tight line.

"These fake accounts were used by General Madigan and Black Fox to communicate directly with Talib Al-Syria." Colonel Song brought up email after email between Hu's fake email account and Talib, each discussing the then-imminent invasion of Taiwan. "Black Fox manipulated and ordered the Caliphate's attack on Taiwan."

Jack had known something was off about the Caliphate's attack on Taiwan. He'd known it back at Camp David, and he'd known it when the Chinese had asked him for a meeting. "You tried to bring this to the president, didn't you?"

"Back in late spring. Yes. He wouldn't see us."

Ethan shook his head. "How could he have suspected something like this?"

Colonel Song ignored Ethan. "When the Russians captured Talib Al-Syria, just prior to Prague, General Madigan made another call to his mystery man. He ordered Talib to be killed before being dropped off at the US embassy in Moscow. When Talib was delivered, he was dead and in a body bag."

Jack had been furious. Ethan remembered that day. It had been early on in their relationship, when everything was new and he didn't know if one moment would last, or lead to another moment for the two of them.

Scott appeared at Ethan's elbow, breathing hard. Sweat rolled down his forehead.

"Capturing Talib, and the American president's tentative partnership with the Russians brokered in Prague, put a damper on General Madigan's plans. Your president is making deals with Russia, negotiating peace, and saving Europe. He plans to save the Middle East, and for the first time, he's got international cooperation." Colonel Song smiled, but it was cold. "That, unfortunately, doesn't fit with Black

Fox's plans to upend the world. Madigan told his man that they would need to resort to a 'plan B', and that they needed 'a sacrifice'."

"Nairobi..." Cooper breathed. Behind him, his men cursed, and Doc flopped onto the couch, shaking his head.

"Nairobi was just the first step. Maybe just a practice round," Faisal said carefully. "A test."

"What do you mean? Test for what?" Ethan tried to step forward, but Scott's hand on his shoulder held him back. He glared at his friend, but froze when he saw Scott's bone-white skin and the panic in his eyes.

"We've been intercepting the mystery man's calls since Prague." Colonel Song called up a new window with four sound files queued to play. "We cannot identify Madigan's right hand man. But perhaps you can."

"Ethan!" Scott hissed. "Jesus, Ethan—"

The start of the player cut off whatever Scott was about to say. In the file, Al-Karim answered first.

"As-salamu alaykum."

"Karim. Is he dead yet?

"Not yet. We made the first video."

"There's not supposed to be *a first video. There's supposed to be one video. Your men fucked up. The Americans are coming for him."*

"He will be dead before then."

"He'd better be. We don't want to clean up your mess again."

"He will be."

"Oh. And Karim."

"Yes?"

"He and the president are lovers."

The phone clicked off.

Ethan couldn't breathe. The world spun, everything upending as everyone's eyes burned into him. He fought for words, fought to think, as the world crashed around him and betrayal stabbed him through the back.

The next sound file automatically started. The same voice, this time starting the call.

"*Do you have the package?*"

"*Yes, sir. It's secure and ready for transport to the White House. And the base has been eliminated.*"

"*Good. Are your men in position?*"

"*Yes, sir. We're ready for the invite.*"

"*And Al-Karim?*"

"*He made it out of Ethiopia. He's in the hole.*"

A pause. "*You're ready for this? The end of the mission?*"

"*Yes, sir.*" No hesitation.

"*Good. I'll see you soon.*"

The phone clicked off.

"Ethan..." Scott breathed, anguish tearing his voice in two. "God, Ethan..."

It all made sense. One man who had traveled with Jack, always at his side. Who had his trust. Who had Ethan's trust, and his friendship. Who knew about them.

Who could betray them so perfectly, so entirely.

"It's Jeff," Ethan whispered.

CHAPTER 41

Washington DC

JEFF GOTTSCHALK HEADED for the Oval Office, his eyes fixed forward, unblinking. This mission had been harder than his others. Longer, too. He'd been undercover for three years, ever since General Madigan had reintroduced him to then-Senator Spiers and recommended him as an excellent advisor.

"Get close to him," Madigan had ordered. "More info to follow."

Three years later, and they were finally executing their plan. The final moment would come, soon.

It was everything Black Fox had ever wanted. Had ever worked for. This was their Rachmaninoff's Third, their Mona Lisa. The pinnacle of their success.

Jeff paused, his hand on the door handle of the Oval Office, before heading inside. He inhaled, drawing his identity tighter around him. He was Jeff Gottschalk. He was Jack's friend and closest advisor. He was his support network during Jack's time of grief.

He was a stone cold killer who didn't blink an eye at ordering Ethan to his death, and who urged Al-Karim to slice his neck faster. He'd befriended Ethan, approaching him when he was alone and vulnerable, and then reinforced that he was someone trustworthy. Someone they could rely on.

He was going to destroy Jack, like he'd destroyed Ethan. He would be the one to put the bullet in Jack. A bonus for his three years undercover.

And when it was all over, he would be standing on top. He'd be where Ethan had been, next to the most powerful man on the planet.

Jeff pushed open the door to the Oval Office. "Mr. President."

Jack was at the desk, his head in his hands. Dark shadows hung beneath his eyes. He hadn't been sleeping much since Ethiopia. Nightmares, the stewards said, sadness in their gazes as they answered Jeff's questions.

"Sir, the daily press brief is beginning at one o'clock. If you'd like to make your comments there, we should head down now."

Slowly, Jack nodded. "Am I doing the right thing?"

"I believe so, sir. You're defining this situation. Getting ahead of the press. It's gotten more intense since the funeral."

Jack sighed and closed his eyes, standing slowly. "Let's go."

Walking with Jack to the briefing room was like leading a funeral dirge. Resignation clung to Jack, as did mourning, and an aching, soul-sucking loneliness that had settled on his shoulders after Ethiopia.

"Jeff," Jack asked in the hallway. "Have you found Levi Daniels?"

Jeff's teeth ground together. The one agent he hadn't been able to eliminate. He'd done a good job of shaming the man, though, and destroying his sense of self-worth. Maybe Daniels had blown his brains out by now. If not, he should ask General Madigan if he wanted Daniels to be taken out. It would be an easy kill.

"No, sir," he said. "Do you want me to check his apartment?"

Jack shook his head. "No. Thank you, Jeff." They stopped outside the briefing room. Jeff could hear the rabid shouts of the reporters, each straining to be called on for questions.

Jack squared his shoulders. "Wish me luck."

"Break a leg."

JACK WAVED off the rise of the press pool and the flash of cameras. "Please, sit down. I have a quick statement I want to make. I'll answer a few questions afterward."

He swallowed. Stared out at the sea of reporters. Cameras hovered in the background. Microphones angled his way. Pens scribbled on notepads. Tablet screens winked on.

What was he doing? *Ethan, what am I doing? Is this right?*

"I want to address the rumors circulating about a relationship between myself and Special Agent Reichenbach of the Secret Service."

He could hear the expectant hush that fell over the room, the intake of breath and the scratch of pencil lead against paper. On his right, Pete stared at him, his eyes boring into the side of his head like lasers burning his skin.

Pete wanted him to deny it. "You need to do a Clinton," he'd said. "You need to deny that anything meaningful took place. That it was just a slip of your attention. A meaningless indiscretion. Play it down. You can survive if you do."

Ethan, I am so sorry.

"Special Agent Ethan Reichenbach and I *were* involved in a close, personal, intimate, and loving relationship. He was much, much more than a Secret Service agent. He was my lover, and he was my partner." Jack cleared his throat and looked down at the podium. He had no notes, not for this. It was all coming from the space where his heart used to be.

Looking back up, he continued. "This was not something that I expected or anticipated would happen. Our relationship developed slowly, but deliberately." He swallowed, and his voice dropped to a growl. "I want to make one thing perfectly clear. Agent Reichenbach's work was consistently above reproach. He drafted an impeccable security plan for the Ethiopia trip. It was his plan, in fact, that ensured that I survived the assault on the motorcade. An assault that... took Ethan from me." Finally, his voice wavered, and Jack closed his eyes against the mass of lights and cameras and reporters. He inhaled, shaking, and the whir and click of cameras caught every single moment of his anguish.

He opened his eyes. "The blame for the attack in Ethiopia lies not with Agent Reichenbach, but with myself. I take full responsibility for the decision to travel, and for the quality of the intelligence that we were presented with. The buck stops on my desk." Jack pressed his lips together. The cameras clicked again, flashes strobing. "I have had two great loves in my life. My wife, Captain Leslie Spiers, and my best friend and lover, Special Agent Ethan Reichenbach. Please understand that this is a time of mourning for me." Jack folded his hands on the podium. "I'll take questions now."

The pressroom exploded. Reporters shot to their feet, arms waving in the air as they shouted over each other, each vying to be heard. Pete tried to corral the crowd, bellowing for calm and for order.

Slowly, Jack closed his eyes as dread sank through him. *Ethan, I am so sorry.*

TEN MINUTES LATER, Jack escaped the pressroom, leaving the braying reporters behind, each scrabbling for another question. All around, Jack saw his aides and his advisors already scrolling through their phones and reading the breaking news headlines.

Some winced. Others cringed.

"That could have gone better," Jeff said, falling into step next to Jack.

"I wasn't going to lie. Ethan deserves better than that."

Jeff's silence loudly broadcast his disapproval. "I think Ethan would disagree," Jeff finally said. "He'd want what is best for you."

"What's next?" Jack changed the topic and cleared his throat. He was done talking about this. He was just done.

"President Puchkov is scheduled to call in ten minutes to discuss joint military operations."

"Russians and Americans working together." Jack tried to smile. "I suppose I accomplished something in office."

Jeff shot him a tight-lipped nod as Jack disappeared into the Oval Office.

He collapsed in his desk chair, throwing his head back. That had been awful. God-awful, worse than he'd even imagined. They'd questioned him about the details—when he said intimate, did he mean that they were involved sexually? And about whether he'd known that the Secret Service prohibited relationships with protectees. And why had he deceived the American public on his homosexuality? How long had he been gay? Was his marriage real, or had that just been a cover?

"Ethan," he whispered to the empty, silent office. "I miss you every single moment."

On the corner of the desk, Mrs. Martin had dropped a folded piece of paper. Jack grabbed it. Inside, she'd scrawled down Levi Daniels's cell phone number.

Daniels still hadn't shown up for his shifts. Jack had asked Inada what he was going to do about that. Inada had just swallowed and shrugged. What could anyone do that was right when an agent was shattered and grieving and lost?

Jack pulled out his phone and punched in the numbers. Daniels's phone didn't even ring, just rolled straight to voicemail. His voice, from happier days, boomed out of the phone's speaker. *"This is Levi Daniels, and I'm not available right now. Leave a message after the beep, and I'll holler back at you as soon as I can. Kick it!"*

Smiling, Jack waited through the beep. "Hi, Agent Daniels, this is Jack. Jack Spiers." He sighed. "You know who I am," he said ruefully. "Look, I heard you're... taking some time off. Would you please meet me for lunch? I... want to chat with you. Nothing official, nothing heavy. I just..." Jack sighed. "Look, we've both lost people we love. We can drop all the bullshit around each other, right? We're both hurting, and life sucks right now. Let's let it suck together for an hour."

He clicked off the call, dropped his cell on the desk, and then buried his face in his hands.

Twenty minutes later, Jack still lay there, his head on his arms. The ticking of the clock on his shelves mocked him, marking the march of time. Outside, autumn wind whooshed through the trees, rattling heavy branches and fluttering leaves of ochre and amber, wine and goldenrod. The roses had withered, shedding their blooms across the lawns, turning to mold and rot before the gardeners had a chance to sweep them away. In the distance, car horns honked and tires squealed, the ever-present hustle and life of the city.

Jack barely lifted his head as he pressed the speed dial button on his office phone for Jeff.

"Sir?" Jeff answered within the first ring.

"Puchkov didn't call."

Calls between world leaders weren't simple affairs. They involved a team of schedulers, the security services of each country, and two secretaries to the world's most powerful men. Puchkov didn't just dial Jack's direct line. His secretary would make the call, which was routed through a constantly recorded secured line, and then passed over to Jack's secretary, who queued it up for him. If everything worked perfectly, the two leaders met on the line at the same time.

But no call ever failed.

Jeff's heavy sigh scratched over the phone. *"Probably because of the press conference."*

Bile rose in the back of Jack's throat. "I'm calling him," he growled. He hung up on Jeff and sat back, dragging the phone across the desk until he was hovering over it. He punched the extension for his secretary and told her to get Puchkov on the line while he waited.

Long, long minutes passed. The clock ticked on.

"Ethan..." he whispered, "I was starting to think of 'after the Oval Office.' After all of this. What would we do? Where would we go? Would you stay in the Secret Service? Would I take a board position somewhere in DC? Or in Texas? Would you come with me to Texas, if I left?" He closed his eyes and rested the silent phone against his forehead. "I wanted to take you on a real trip. Not a presidential trip where you were out of your mind with work. But a real vacation. Paris, maybe. Or Rome." He smiled. "Or maybe something more adventurous. You seem like the type. Australia? New Zealand? We could have fun there."

The phone clicked in his ear. Mrs. Martin spoke. *"President Puchkov in two minutes, Mr. President."*

He squeezed his eyes closed. What was happening to him? He was talking to ghosts? Speaking out loud to the memory of his dead lover? He hadn't lost it this badly when Leslie had died. What was this? The start of his descent into madness? Was he finally losing it? Was losing the second love of his life the limit of mental stability?

Jack banged his forehead against the phone handset. "Ethan..."

"Mr. President?" Puchkov's rough accent grated in his ear. *"I am not your dead boyfriend."*

Clearing his throat, Jack straightened in his chair. Embarrassment burned through him. "President Puchkov. I apologize. My mind was wandering."

"I can imagine. I saw your press conference, President Pidor."

Jack frowned. He didn't know that Russian word.

"We were supposed to chat ten minutes ago, Mr. President. I'd like to discuss our deployment plans in the Middle East. Try to coordinate our forces—"

Puchkov interrupted Jack. In his mind, he saw Puchkov waving him off, arrogantly waving him to silence. *"No, no, President* Pidor. *I think, instead, that Russia will do our own part in the Middle East. That is to say, we don't need you. Russia will act, and Russia will act decisively and with strength. It's what Russia is best at."* A pause. *"We do not need a* pidor *president's help. You will not be in office long, anyway. Your country is in shock today. How long until they vote you out, hmm?"*

"Puchkov," Jack growled. "Is this about—" His throat clenched. He couldn't say it. "After everything we've accomplished together—"

"You are a sinking ship. The world needs more than another failed American president. I thought you would be different. Good-bye, President Pidor."

Puchkov ended the call.

Jack stared at his phone. He dropped the headset into the cradle and pulled his laptop close. A quick Internet search for the unknown

Russian word brought him to the definition. *Pidor: derogative Russian slang for a homosexual: butt-fucker, cocksucker, shit-pusher, faggot, pederast.*

Hot shame burned his blood. The world seemed to expand and then contract, focusing down on the words on the screen until there was nothing else. He heard nothing and everything, the sound of silence suddenly oppressive, suddenly screaming at him. His mind threw up every insult he'd ever heard, every curse and degradation thrown in gay men's faces, now directed squarely at himself.

He closed his eyes.

A moment later, Jack roared, hurling the phone from his desk. It shattered against the wall, the plastic cracking and splintering, and the cord tangled beneath a bronze bust of Abraham Lincoln.

KURDISH MILITARY BASE DESTROYED; LOCALS CLAIM DJINN RESPONSIBLE FOR GRUESOME DEATHS

In a scene straight out of a science fiction movie, locals crept up the hillside outside Sulaymaniyah, in the Kurdistan provinces of Northern Iraq, and found a base utterly decimated. Blood was everywhere. On the walls, hanging from the ceiling. Soaking the desert sand. "It was the djinn," a local said, refusing to go near the devastated base. "The demons came and ate the soldiers."

CHAPTER 42

Taif, Saudi Arabia

ETHAN LEANED against the wall in the darkened hallway, his breaths finally slowing. Across from him, Scott hunched over, his hands on his knees, watching him with wary eyes.

"I'm okay," Ethan grunted. "I'm okay."

He wasn't okay. He wasn't remotely okay.

Rage had consumed him, burning away his conscious mind. He'd leaped, snarling at the colonel, but Cooper shoved him off. Colonel Song wasn't his target, though. He was just a messenger.

His target was Jeff Gottschalk. But Gottschalk was in Washington DC, 6000 miles away, and right beside Jack.

He'd gone insane. He'd torn apart one of Faisal's couches, ripping cushions in two before kicking out the back and then tearing the sides off the frame with his bare hands. He'd ripped his stitches. Doc shouted about the blood spilling from his abdomen, and Scott tackled him from behind. They wrestled on the ground like animals, Ethan bellowing with uncontrolled rage. Jack was in danger. He was right beside a traitor, a murderer, and there was nothing—*nothing*—Ethan could do. Not at that moment.

The impotence, the frustrated need to act, and the impossibility of saving his lover, destroyed him.

Scott finally put him in a sleeper hold, lying on his back with Ethan wrapped up in his arms and legs. His arm squeezed around Ethan's neck as Cooper and his men shouted and tried to help. Scott's voice, choking on furious tears, had finally cut through Ethan's killing frenzy. "Jesus Christ, Ethan, don't make me do this!"

He stopped fighting, relaxed in Scott's grip. Scott let go, and Ethan rolled to his hands and knees, coughing up blood onto the marble floor. Doc shit a brick at that, but the blood was just from where he'd bit his lip. Cooper helped Scott up, glaring at Ethan.

Ethan sat on the ruined cushions of the couch, stuffing spilling out everywhere, while Doc kicked aside wooden debris from the frame and knelt in front of him. Doc stitched his stomach back up, all while calling him an idiot and an asshole.

He wasn't gentle with his needle. Ethan didn't care. He welcomed the pain.

Faisal and Colonel Song had ducked out when the worst of Ethan's temper took over. They came back as Ethan was pulling his bloody shirt over his head. Fury licked at Ethan's heart, and he asked for a moment before they continued.

Scott followed him down the hallway.

"Jesus Christ," Scott breathed. "Fuck, Ethan."

"He's with *Jack*, Scott. He's right next to him. Fuck, Jack could already be dead!"

"We don't know what their final plan is. We don't know what this package is, and we don't know what the invite is. It's got to be big, though. Black Fox doesn't do small."

Ethan's teeth ground together. "Not helping."

"We've got to listen to the rest of what the colonel has to say. Then we can figure out what to do." Scott sighed, shaking his head. "Fuck... I put it all together while he was explaining everything. He knew about you two. And—" Scott straightened, his eyes bulging. "And he must have been the one to leak it to Director Stahl."

"Director Stahl?" Stahl was their director at the Secret Service, in charge of the entire agency.

"Yeah. Daniels was called into his office just before the trip. The director was asking all about you and the president. Daniels thought he was sniffing after proof of you breaking the regs."

Ethan swallowed hard. Well, it wasn't like he didn't know that he was breaking the rules and violating regulations, and that the book would be thrown at him when it all came crashing down. But none of that mattered now. Only saving Jack.

"I wanna hear the rest."

They headed back to Faisal and Colonel Song. Cooper kicked at the couch debris, a twisted scowl on his face. Faisal watched Cooper, his face blank. Doc had collapsed onto one of the torn cushions, plucking at the stuffing. The rest of the team stood in a half circle, some watching Ethan warily, others scowling at the colonel.

"What's this about a package? And an invite?"

Colonel Song turned back to the television, calling up a new window and pushing more documents from his phone to the screen.

Two news articles described a devastated base in Kurdistan. One, a western magazine specializing in strange stories, wrote 300 words about the devastation, comparing the base's slaughter to a demonic attack. Much attention was paid to the level of bloodshed and the lack of bodies.

The second article wasn't actually an article. It was an internal memo from the Peshmerga, Kurdistan's military force, describing the brutality found at the deserted, devastated base. The same amount of blood. The same sense of terror left behind. But no talk of djinn or demons. Instead, the officers of the Peshmerga asked what military force had come into their base and murdered their people, and what they had done with the bodies. Given the proximity of the base to Iran, the officer cautiously pointed their fingers toward the Islamic Republic.

"You think Black Fox destroyed a Kurdish military base? Why?" Cooper shook his head. His eyes slid sideways to Faisal.

"Because of this."

A final article exploded onto the screen, this time from the *Washington Times* in DC. *"President to Host Kurdish Peshmerga Unit in White House at Ceremony Honoring American Allies."*

"Oh shit," Scott breathed.

"They're going in the soldiers' places." Ethan's heart pounded so hard, he knew it was going to explode. "They're going to infiltrate the White House. Attack the president."

Faisal cleared his throat. "We don't believe that's all they're doing."

"You said Nairobi was just a test." Cooper's tone softened as he spoke to Faisal. The two men had a clear history together. "What do you mean?"

Faisal adjusted the long robes falling over his arms, plucking at them. "Official reports say that the bomb blast in Nairobi was a five kiloton nuclear warhead... recovered from abandoned Cold War stockpiles."

Cooper nodded.

"The source of those weapons is not... entirely accurate," Faisal said carefully. "There was a robbery at one of Saudi Arabia's military bases."

"But Saudi doesn't have nuclear weapons," Scott protested. "You don't have any reactors or any refineries."

"But we have money. And money buys anything, especially nuclear warheads that aim at Iran. Bought from abandoned Cold War stockpiles."

Cooper didn't seem surprised by this revelation. "Someone stole your nukes?"

"Someone stole a three kiloton bomb, a five kiloton bomb, and a ten kiloton bomb. We tracked the signal from their control panels into Iran. Then we lost their trails. We were searching for the warheads when the detonation occurred in Nairobi."

"And you didn't tell anyone?" Cooper's dark eyes bored into Faisal.

Faisal stared right back. "Who could I have told who would have listened?"

"So Nairobi was one of them," Ethan interrupted. His mind whirred, trying to sort through the plots and machinations. "And another one is the package Jeff Gottschalk asks about in the call." And that package, like the fake Kurds, was heading to Washington and the White House. Heading for Jack. "The third?"

Faisal looked sideways at Colonel Song. The colonel took over, crossing the room until he was standing in front of Ethan and looking him square in the eyes. "Black Fox has maneuvered all of America's enemies into the Middle East. China and Russia both have significant numbers of troops on the ground. The Caliphate is locked in the battle. Where would you detonate a nuclear warhead if you wanted to take out all of your enemies in one blow?"

"Right in the middle of the bunch," Ethan breathed. "Inside Iraq."

Colonel Song nodded.

"But why?" Scott snapped. "Why is anyone crazy enough to do this? A nuke in the Middle East? And a nuke in the White House? Why kill Americans? Why kill the president?"

Ethan saw the brutal logic to it. He saw the clean lines and the harsh decisions, the reasons for murdering so many people. It was a means to an end, an end that Madigan and Gottschalk were working toward. He understood, in a primal, bloodthirsty way, why they were doing this. "Because if you want to control the world, you first hurt everyone. Make sure they're terrified. Rip away their reality." He turned to Scott. "How better to do that than to slay the president in the White House? Obliterate the most protected place on earth?"

Scott paled.

"And then, you destroy your enemies. And you're on top of the world." Ethan swallowed back the bile rising in his throat, almost choking him. "And the people will love you for it."

Fear hung in the room, like a damp towel trying to smother a fire. Cooper kicked at the broken armrest of the couch, sending it sailing into the courtyard. His men cursed.

"What's our plan to stop this?" Ethan's thoughts swirled around Jack, circling around memories of his smile, his laugh. Gottschalk was *right there*, right next to Jack.

"Black Fox doesn't work alone." Colonel Song drew up a list of cell phone numbers, each one connected by a black line to the mystery caller's. To Jeff Gottschalk's phone. "These are other people that Black Fox has been calling. All in Washington. We know some of these people. Others aren't on our radar."

Ethan peered down the list. He knew most of the numbers. As detail lead, he'd known of everyone in the administration. He saw General Madigan's number. The deputy director of the CIA. The National Security Advisor. Other numbers he didn't know, junior officers and aides within organizations.

And one number he knew *very* well.

THEY SPENT the rest of the afternoon and half of the night working out a plan.

"Are we really doing this?" Doc asked. "We're working with the Saudis and the Chinese to... what? Infiltrate America? Attack the White House?"

"We're stopping an attack on the White House, and on the president," Ethan corrected.

"But it's the working with the *Chinese* and the *Saudis* that I'm stuck on." Doc shook his head. "Isn't this treason? That's what this is called, right? Working with an enemy of the state? Against the state?"

"Enough. We are not the enemies of the state here." Cooper shot Doc a long look, and Doc threw up his hands and headed out to the courtyard, and the rest of Cooper's team.

Afterward, Cooper, Scott, and Ethan collapsed in the sunroom, leaning on pillows and destroyed couch cushions, chugging bottles of water. Faisal had long since disappeared, retiring to his bedroom with a stiff good night and a long look at Cooper. Colonel Song sat in the corner, typing away on his tablet as holograms hovered in front of his face.

"Get some rest." Colonel Song shut down his tablet and stood. He hadn't once raised his voice, or yawned, or looked anything more than mildly intrigued by their sometimes-raucous and argumentative battle planning. "We will fly you to Riyadh in three hours."

"I hope I never see you again," Ethan called out to Colonel Song's retreating back. It was the best thanks he could offer.

Colonel Song glanced back over his shoulder. A grin turned up the corners of his mouth. "We will see, Agent Reichenbach."

THEY FLEW to Riyadh and then waited in the prince's plane, hunkered down while Faisal's sleek jet maneuvered into the same hangar as a commercial *Saudia* air transport. Money passed between hands, and the hangar was deserted for ten minutes. They moved over to the commercial transport, settling into the cargo hold between crates and boxes and stacks of misshapen cargo strapped to the frame of the transport.

An hour later, they were in the skies, smuggling themselves into America like blacklisted terrorists. The transport was bringing material to the Saudi embassy in Washington, and they made the thirteen-hour flight direct to Dulles mostly in silence. Doc started a game of poker with the team, poking at Coleman until the big sergeant shoved him, and egging Wright and Park on. Cooper slept, his legs propped up on a cargo crate and a beanie over his eyes.

Ethan and Scott sat together, silent.

"This is insane," Scott finally said. "Do you think we can really stop this?"

"I don't care if I survive." Ethan rolled his neck, trying to crack the stiffness from his joints. "It's Jack I'm worried about."

Scott shook his head. "You're disgustingly in love with the man."

Ethan snorted. Who would have ever thought that he would fall so head over heels for anyone? "I will tear the world apart for him," he said, sobering as he looked up. His eyes burned into his friend, and he saw their dark shine, an almost crazed sheen, reflected in Scott's sunglasses. "I will tear apart the planet. Cross continents, oceans..." He shook his head. "Nothing will keep me from him. And nothing will stop me from protecting him. I'll die for him. In a heartbeat."

Whistling low, Scott leaned back. "And I thought I loved my wife when I took her to Bermuda for her fortieth birthday. She's going to kick my ass when I get back. And I can't wait for it. I can't wait for her to scream at me. But the point is, I want to be there for it. I want to come back and live through this. To be back with her."

Ethan looked away.

"Ethan, the point is *not* to die for him. Okay?"

Scott bent low, forcing Ethan to look at him.

After a long moment, Ethan nodded.

"Good. 'Cause I'm sure he wants you back alive. No one wants to bury their lover, and no one wants to have to bury their lover twice."

CHAPTER 43

Washington DC

WHEN THEY LANDED AT DULLES, the same setup happened—money changed hands, and the hangar the freighter parked in was deserted. They clambered out of the cargo hold, stretching aching joints and sore backs.

"There should be a car waiting for us outside." Ethan took the lead, shouldering his backpack and turning for the side entrance.

Instead, the main doors to the hangar buzzed and started to retract, folding upward and letting in the early morning Washington sunlight.

Ethan and the team froze.

Standing outside the hangar was Director Irwin.

"Hello boys," the director called. He gave a simple wave before shoving his hands into the pockets of his flannel coat. "Heard you needed a ride?"

"I'M the director of the CIA." Director Irwin chuckled at the team's wide eyes and dropped jaws as he climbed into the driver's seat of his SUV. In loose jeans, a long-sleeved button-down, and his flannel coat, he looked more like a country farmer than a director. "Well, I was." He frowned as they pulled away from the hangar.

The team huddled behind the black-tinted windows and downed coffee from two thermoses Irwin had packed. An empty box of donuts, demolished in minutes, lay on the floorboards.

"I've built up a number of contacts over the years. Like, the head of *Saudia's* freight transport." Irwin met Ethan's gaze in the rearview mirror. "It's important to know what's flying into the country, don't you think?"

Ethan nodded. DC flashed outside the SUV's window as they drove, and in the distance, the Washington Monument glinted in dawn's light. "You said you *were* the director of the CIA?"

"President Spiers canned me after Ethiopia. Said the failure of intelligence was on me." The click of the turning indicator seemed overly loud in the suddenly-silent vehicle. "He was beyond furious. Now..." His eyes sought Ethan's in the mirror again. "I know why."

Ethan swallowed. He'd watched Jack's broadcast in Riyadh. Doc had pulled it up on a tablet Faisal had loaned the team. They'd all crowded around, watching the news on Al Jazeera and listening to the blistering commentary from the international pundits.

Everyone had tried their best not to stare at Ethan, looking down and away and sideways and up at the paneling above. He still felt their burning looks later. They already knew about him and Jack, of course. They'd heard Gottschalk's call to Al-Karim. They saw Ethan's raw fury and his desperation to save Jack. But still, having the president announce to the world that they were lovers—that Jack *loved* him—was something no one knew how to deal with.

He didn't know how to deal with it either. He'd shoved it away, for now. He had to.

Hearing the absolute agony in Jack's voice made everything worse. He was alive, and Jack thought he was dead. Would Jack forgive him for this deception?

Ethan shook his head. *Enough.* "Director, we know why there was no intelligence on Ethiopia. Your deputy, Gary Luss, is working with General Madigan. He scrubbed the intel and set up the Ethiopian operation. Probably worked with Black Fox to get the jihadis in-country."

Irwin frowned, deep lines creasing his old face. Gray hair had replaced his dark mop long ago. He kept it cut in the DC conservative style, though, fluffy and combed over to one side.

They inched through Washington's morning traffic as Ethan filled Irwin in on the pieces of the plot that had come together in Faisal's palace. His temper surged as he relayed Gottschalk's duplicity, and the betrayal stretching from Jack's chief of staff to the vice chairman of the Joint Chiefs, the National Security Advisor, and the deputy director of the CIA.

While Ethan spoke, Irwin seemed to age a decade, collapsing in on himself as his shoulders sagged and drooped. His lips pursed, and he stared out over DC's panorama as they crossed the Roosevelt Memorial Bridge. Arlington stretched behind them, rows and rows of marble headstones glinting over the hills. The Lincoln Memorial rose ahead and the Washington Monument beyond, with the domed roof of the Capitol barely visible in the background.

"I can't fault this Colonel Song and Prince Faisal for their intelligence work," Irwin finally sighed. "They've connected the dots on this one. And tracked down one of our most notorious units."

Black Fox. Ethan shoved his anger down. Now wasn't the time for rage.

"There have been rumors of certain politicians and agencies in Washington wanting to push for a stronger American position in the world. People running their mouths at cocktail receptions and poker games, mostly. They've said they want America to take control. Be the superpower everyone criticizes us for." Irwin shook his head. "Rumors have an awful habit of being true, though."

"What do you know about this Kurdish visit?" Ethan leaned forward, his head between the driver and passenger seats. Scott sat up front, his face less recognizable if anyone looked in closely. After

Jack's revelation of their relationship, Ethan's face had been splashed all over the media, all around the world. There was too much risk of him being recognized now that he was a notorious celebrity, the president's illicit lover. And a dead notorious celebrity at that. He had to stay hidden.

"I know it's happening today. The president is supposed to greet them this afternoon after the delegation has a morning at the Pentagon. At least, that's what the daily brief said." Even though Irwin was no longer director, he still had the right to receive a copy of the daily brief each morning.

Ethan's knuckles cracked as he clenched his hands into fists. *Today.* They were planning on killing Jack—and so many in Washington—*today.* If he'd been one day too late. If he hadn't recovered fast enough. Nightmares tore through his mind until he exhaled and forced them to the background. He was here. They would stop this. He would save Jack.

"At this point, I don't know who to trust," Irwin said. "Black Fox gets its claws in deep when it runs an op. It's gotten as far as the White House. Who else is in on the mission?"

"This is supposed to be its final operation before it inherits the world. This is its coup." Ethan shook his head. "We can't trust anyone. And with a nuke in play, if we tip off the wrong people, Black Fox could detonate before we ever have a chance to try to stop them. We've got to play this close."

Irwin frowned, but stayed silent.

Finally, they made their way through the sluggish traffic. Irwin veered right at the Virginia and New Hampshire traffic circle, barely avoiding a collision with a texting cabbie. They merged onto New Hampshire, driving past messy crowds of students ambling on the sidewalks and jaywalking across the redbrick streets. The tires bounced and rattled against the bumpy bricks, and their speed slowed to a crawl.

"I have a safe house at George Washington University," Irwin said, turning right on H street and then left on 23rd. Students laughed and waved to one another, bypassing the car in a sea of hoodies, scarves, and knee-high boots. Autumn had arrived in Washington.

They pulled up into a low pile of fallen leaves blown to the gutters by passing traffic, right outside one of the university's residence halls.

They got a few hairy-eyed looks as they headed inside, mostly from students briefly glancing up from their phones before looking away. One student shouted at them, calling the team a pack of 'ROTC-Nazis' before laughing and skateboarding away.

Irwin slid a keycard over the door with a smile. "Every liberal college campus has a conspiracy about the CIA spying on them. They never expect to actually find us there, though."

The safe house was the entire top floor of the building. Cooper and his men dropped their packs and secured the dorms, going room by room and noting the views from each. It wasn't a scenic tour. Cooper's men called out angles and directions, vantages for a sniper's perch.

The main dorm was a four-bedroom suite. Irwin pushed open the closets in each of the bedrooms, grinning.

"Time for your disguises, gentlemen."

Thirty minutes later, Cooper's men were decked out in the finest hipster college fashion. Skinny jeans nearly burst at the seams on some of the men's meaty thighs. Others chose the rugged look, slouching khakis with flannel overshirts and beanies tugged on their heads. Scruff they had grown since Ethiopia helped hide their faces and lend credence to their disguises. Doc, rail thin, chose skinny black jeggings and a flannel button-down. He wore a sagging beanie and shaved his face, and when he put on a pair of thick-rimmed black glasses, he looked every bit the university hipster. Cooper chose a mismatched ensemble of board shorts and a GWU hoodie.

Ethan and Scott watched, bemused, as Doc argued with Sergeant Coleman about touching up his hipster look with a bit of eyeliner. The two went back and forth, arguing like a team of punching robots, until Cooper threw a pile of discarded clothes at both of their faces.

Then it was time for Ethan and Scott's disguises.

A quick 9-1-1 call had the campus police responding to the dorm to investigate a suspected break-in. Cooper's men took up position, out of sight.

Scott answered the door when the officers arrived, welcoming them in. They looked around the sterile dorm, frowning.

"I'm really sorry about this," Scott said, just before Cooper's men fired tranquilizer darts into the two officers' necks with weapons gifted from Irwin.

They stripped the men and tied them up, then left them in the bathroom.

Scott's pants were too short, and Ethan's shirt was too tight, but they made it work.

They held the final mission brief around the dorm room's kitchen island. Cooper and his hipster team still stood like the Marines they were, mountainous men with imposing figures. They tried to slouch, tried to relax, but only Doc was able to pull off the laid-back groove and nonchalant, fuck-off attitude of a college student.

"Cooper, you and your team will join the White House tour at noon." Ethan moved the saltshaker across the kitchen island, signifying Cooper's team, to the napkin folded in the shape of the White House. "Scott and I will be in the patrol car listening to the radio. When the call goes out for an emergency at the White House, all DC units are supposed to respond. We'll be right around the block, and in uniform, we'll be welcomed inside."

"The Secret Service armory is inside Horsepower," Scott said, taking over. He sketched a quick layout of the West Wing and the White House basement on a napkin in black marker. "I'll get you down there where we can suit up." It was the weakest part of their plan, but they didn't know how else to get weapons inside the White House. The Secret Service was actually very good at its job, and they weren't trying to attack the agents on duty. Not even the secret tunnels would help Ethan this time.

"Black Fox," Ethan said, sketching out a diagram of the Oval Office and the president's private study, "will be in Kurdish Peshmerga uniforms, escorted around the White House by General Madigan, who will most likely have Jeff Gottschalk with him."

Irwin pulled up a photo of Jeff Gottschalk on his phone and slid it onto the counter.

"We don't know who else will be with them. Maybe the National Security Advisor. Maybe the deputy director of the CIA. If they've got all hands on deck, then we're in for a big fight. The visiting Peshmerga force is said to be ten strong."

One of Cooper's men whistled.

"Someone will have a bag. Or a box. Or a suitcase. That will be the nuke. We need to secure it immediately. Before anything else."

"They're not planning on offing themselves when they set off the nuke. What's their escape plan? How do they plan on detonating?" Cooper scowled, looking like he hated everything about their slipshod plan.

"We don't know all the details," Ethan admitted. "Which is why we need to stop this now. Before they have the chance to drop the nuke somewhere. We know its destination is the White House." He hesitated. "For everyone on this team, that's the main mission. Securing the nuke."

Cooper arched his eyebrows. "And your mission?"

"I will secure the president."

THERE WAS one last thing Ethan wanted to do before setting up in an alley in the stolen DC police patrol car with Scott.

He fought Director Irwin and Scott over it.

"It's too big a risk!" Scott shouted, after Cooper's team had filed out of the dorm room and were on their way to the White House. "Why risk the trace?"

Irwin frowned. "Any electronic communications to the White House should be considered breached already."

"I know." Ethan's nostrils flared as he exhaled. "But I need to send him a message. Something only he would understand. I want him to be on guard today. Prepare him, at least somehow, for what's about to happen."

"I don't like it," Scott growled. "Way too big a risk."

"We'll do it from the university library. There are thousands of students here. Even if they did do a trace, they wouldn't be able to find us in time."

Director Irwin and Scott glared at him.

CHAPTER 44

Washington DC

JACK FLIPPED through a briefing about the Peshmerga troops he was supposed to meet after lunch. A cold cup of coffee sat at his elbow, and his laptop was propped open on the desktop.

His laptop screen blinked.

Jack frowned. He turned away from the brief.

A window opened in his email program. A new message draft. The cursor blinked in the message space.

Jack stopped breathing.

First Name, I'm with you all the way appeared, letter by letter, inside the message.

The screen went dark.

Jack jumped up and grabbed his laptop. He pushed back the screen, slammed his hands down on the keyboard.

Nothing.

"Ethan?" he asked, caught between terror and hope. Was he really talking to a laptop? "Ethan, was that you?" His eyes rose, his gaze circling the Oval Office. "Ethan?"

His laptop rebooted, powering back on. The cheerful login screen splashed a picture of him and Ethan taking a selfie on the couch together in the Residence, laughing at their own ridiculousness. After his announcement, hiding their relationship seemed stupid. He'd added a picture of Ethan to the table behind him, the first and only personal picture he had displayed in the Oval Office.

Jack pounded his keyboard, typing in his password. The laptop blinked and then brought up his main screen.

There were no emails. No message drafts. Nothing at all to prove what he'd seen.

Slumping, Jack collapsed in his desk chair. His chest tightened, a caught sob that lived in the dead spaces of his heart struggling to break free. Was he losing it? Or was Ethan, somehow, contacting him? From beyond the grave?

He closed his eyes.

And then opened them. He stared at his laptop until Mrs. Martin knocked on the door ten minutes later and told him his lunch guest had arrived.

COOPER'S MEN tried to slouch their way through the White House tour. They watched the students on campus and on the Metro, trying to copy their attitudes. Mostly, they felt like idiots.

But they got on the tour, and they wandered from the Green Room to the Blue Room, trailing after the tour guide and listening to the history of the White House architecture.

Cooper kept eyes on his team and scoped out the White House in turn. When they entered, they'd caught a glimpse of Peshmerga uniforms disappearing around the corner, and had heard the booming, scratchy voice of General Madigan welcoming them to the White House.

Minutes later, while looking down the walkway to the West Wing, Cooper spotted Jeff Gottschalk talking to the Deputy Director of the CIA, Gary Luss, outside the Cabinet Room next to the Rose Garden. He tapped his nose three times as he turned back to his team.

They nodded, and then busied themselves with looking normal

as they perused the White House tour guide pamphlet and moved on to the State Dining Room.

JACK WELCOMED Daniels into the Oval Office with a sad smile. "Levi," he said. He bypassed the handshake and gripped Daniels's uninjured shoulder, an almost-hug.

Daniels wasn't in a suit. He was in jeans and a polo, tucked in, but it was the most casual Jack had ever seen him. He still wore a sling, holding his left arm immobile across his chest.

His eyes, when they met the president, were dull and lifeless, devoid of any spark or light within. He looked away quickly. "Mr. President," Daniels mumbled. "You asked me to come?"

"I wanted to see how you were." Jack slowly walked to the couches, and Daniels trailed behind. Stewards bustled in, setting plates of sandwiches and fresh baked chips on the coffee table, along with a pitcher of iced tea and two glasses. They disappeared, and Jack invited Daniels to sit. "I'm doing terrible," Jack admitted, sighing as he collapsed to the couch.

Nodding, Daniels sat across from Jack. "I can't sleep," he said softly. "I keep asking myself... what else could I have done? If I wasn't hit..." He trailed off and looked down. "I try not to remember, actually. I don't want to think about it." He swallowed. "If I remember it, then I... then I'm feeling it, and it's too real." He was on a roll, speaking fast as his eyes bulged wide. "And I can't get away from the dust and the smoke and the fire and, *God*, Ethan's last shout—" Daniels covered his mouth with one hand.

"Levi..." He didn't know what to say. "I'm sorry."

Daniels looked down, and he took a few minutes to collect himself. "I saw your press conference," he finally said. He smiled, just barely. "Ethan would have hated it."

Jack chuffed. "Yeah. He's not one for the spotlight."

"But he would have been damn proud. *Damn* proud to hear you say what you said. Be called your lover." Daniels finally laughed, a brief chuckle. "Man, when Ethan fell for you, I thought DC was gonna cry. He was *the* bachelor. He didn't have time for love." Daniels's humor dried up as quickly as it came. "When he fell for you, I knew it was something real. Something serious. Scared the hell out of me, 'cause we got some pretty big rules against it, but..." Daniels smiled. "I wanted you two to have a happy ending."

Jack closed his eyes. "So did I."

Jᴇꜰꜰ ʜᴜʀʀɪᴇᴅ down the main hall in the West Wing, heading for the Residence. General Madigan was putting on a show, touring the 'Peshmergas' around.

Madigan spoke to the Peshmerga major, leaning in close. The major was tall, with a bushy black mustache and scruffy hair poking out from around his beret, but underneath that, he was David, one of Jeff's closest friends. They'd been recruited into Black Fox together, when their mission and purpose in the Middle East had seemed to wither and die and the whole point of their lives had blown away, like sand skittering across the desert. Sitting on a crate in the desert and watching bodies burn, Jeff had wondered what point there was to going on. What did any of it matter?

Black Fox mattered.

Madigan had brought him to Black Fox and remade Jeff, delivering him to the innermost reaches of his soul, where he discovered that he was capable of *anything*. Absolutely anything.

It's what made Black Fox members so excellent at what they did.

"General." Jeff spoke softly. "We may have a problem."

David glanced at him and then turned away, pretending to be awed by the chandelier. He stayed close, close enough to hear Jeff and Madigan's conversation.

"Problem?" Madigan's eyes narrowed.

"I saw the commander of that Marine team on the White House tour. The one you said you took care of. Lieutenant Cooper."

"Impossible. He's dead in Ethiopia."

"We *believe* he's dead. But I'm confident in what I saw, sir."

"Alert the Secret Service. Tell them he's a suspicious person. They'll put him in a holding tank and they'll never get a chance to talk to him before we strike."

"If he's *here*, General, then who else survived? And how did he get from Ethiopia to the White House?" Jeff stepped closer. "If Reichenbach is alive, he could be here, too. And, if they're here, and if they're staying quiet, then they might know something." He shared a quick look with David. "They're a threat, sir. We have to eliminate them. We cannot let this fail."

Madigan sighed. He looked to David, who nodded fractionally.

"Everyone is in place?"

Jeff nodded.

"Give the signal."

CHAPTER 45

Washington DC

ETHAN AND SCOTT had parked behind a convenience store, and they sweated in their stolen uniforms and argued about Jack as they waited.

Then the radio in the police cruiser crackled to life. *"Shots fired at the White House. Shots fired at the White House. All DC metro emergency response units, respond and render aid."*

Scott slammed the cruiser into gear and tore out of the parking lot, taking the sedan over the curb and swerving across two lanes of traffic. Car horns wailed and tires screeched. Burning rubber filled the air. Ethan toggled the sirens on, and the red and blue scream blared over the city's streets.

"Do these people slow down when they hear the siren?" Scott slammed his palm on the steering wheel and the horn. "Go, go!"

They joined ten other police cars at the gates to the White House, all parked with their lights on and directing civilians away. Ethan leaped out of the car and ran for the North Entrance before Scott even hit the brakes.

"Ethan! Damn it!" Scott chased after him, ignoring the shouts from the police officers they left behind.

SECRET SERVICE AGENTS were down across the North Entrance, some bleeding out, others unconscious, a few moaning. Shots echoed through the White House. Bloodcurdling screams bounced off the marble floors before slicing through Ethan's ears.

The shots—and the screams—headed toward the West Wing.

Ethan tore off again, but Scott's hand on his elbow jerked him to a halt. "Wait for the team!" Scott shouted.

"Fuck you!" Ethan tried to shake him off.

"We work together! Don't go running off half-cocked! You'll get yourself killed!"

Cooper and his team burst around the corner, running from the East Wing. Evacuation alarms blared behind them, and more screams.

"Doc, see what you can do for these men!" Ethan gestured for Cooper and the others to follow. "Let's go, now! Now!"

IN HORSEPOWER, they found eight agents, all shot. Bullets fired at close range to the forehead for the first few, and then clusters of shots to the chest for those who'd tried to fight back. Some clung to life, and they reached for Ethan when they saw him burst in.

Scott ran to their side, ripping off his stolen uniform and using it to staunch wounds. Two of Cooper's men followed, dropping down to their knees and helping the agents cling to life.

Raw fury poured into the spaces of Ethan's soul. These were *his* agents. These were *his* people. He was hovering on the barest knife-edge of control, and the rage stoking his soul crescendoed, a surging maelstrom.

Cameras had been knocked out, taken offline. All he saw were black screens. Radios were chaos, bullets and screams rising over everything. He tried to transmit, but nothing went through.

But audio was still working in the West Wing. Ethan listened to the zing of bullets and the slap of feet racing to the Oval Office, boots pounding against carpet amid guttural curses and grunts.

The agent beneath Scott's hands pulled him down, whispering a name in his ear, the name of the man who had shot them. Blanching, Scott whirled on his knees and stared at Ethan, his jaw dropping.

Ethan already knew. He'd known as soon as he saw the last number back in Faisal's palace. He'd known, then, that even his own Secret Service was compromised. Black Fox had penetrated into his detail. Into his men.

Cooper passed out weapons, grabbing M-4s from the lockers around the room. He tossed bulletproof vests out next, and the men not saving lives strapped in and were ready to go in ten seconds.

They split up, Ethan heading for the rear staircase.

"MR. PRESIDENT!"

Inada rushed into the Oval Office, two agents flanking him, guns drawn. Secret Service Director Stahl, in the White House for the Peshmergas' visit, raced after Inada. He stopped at the door and waved at Deputy Director Luss and the National Security Advisor, Luntz. "Hurry up!" he shouted. Bullets snapped and echoed behind the men. Plaster smashed and exploded, sending puffs of dust into the air. "Get in here!"

Luss and Luntz barreled past Stahl, rushing into the Oval Office. Inada barked for them to get behind him and his men. Jack was already behind them all, pushed down and covered by the two agents.

Daniels stood off to one side, his eyes blown wide. Inada spared him a single glance. Daniels wasn't currently an agent. He'd been placed on administrative leave. He wasn't even allowed to be armed.

"Do we head for the bunker?" Jack asked.

"We can't. The shooters are between us and the bunker's entrance." Inada gripped his pistol, holding it steady as he aimed at the door. "We hold here."

Director Stahl drew his weapon.

"Sir." Inada nodded to his side, inviting the director to join them in the last line of defense for the president. It was the pinnacle of an agent's purpose—protecting the president's life. It was the worst day of an agent's life, but it was what they lived and breathed for. What they would die for.

Stahl may be the director, but he was an agent first, and he would line up and take aim against the shooters.

Director Stahl raised his weapon and aimed for Inada.

Three quick shots took out Inada and his two agents, slamming into their chests at close range. Daniels shouted and lunged, leaping over the couch and trying to jump Director Stahl. Stahl fired, hitting Daniels twice in the shoulder.

Daniels went down, lying motionless on the carpet.

JACK STARED at Director Stahl as the bottom fell out of his world. He stood slowly, his mouth falling open.

Stahl turned his weapon on Jack. "On your knees, Mr. President."

His gaze darted from Stahl to Luss to Luntz. Luss and Luntz had joined Stahl, standing on either side of him. There was a different feel to the Oval Office, a different tension gripping the air. Darkness lay in the men's eyes, hatred burning into Jack. "What are you doing?"

"On your knees!" Stahl barked. "Now! Hands on your head!"

He dropped slowly, raising his hands and lacing his fingers.

The Oval Office door opened.

Jeff Gottschalk walked in, carrying his Army backpack. Behind him were the Peshmergas.

The Peshmergas started to strip, ripping off disguises made of mustaches and wigs and berets and unbuttoning their military jackets. Beneath, they wore dark suits and crisp white shirts.

They looked, suddenly, like Secret Service agents.

"Our men are holding back the rest of the Secret Service in the

East Wing," Jeff said, nodding to Director Stahl. "They're also holding back Lieutenant Cooper and his team. He *is* here."

Director Stahl cursed. "We just need to get this over with."

"Jeff?" Jack couldn't think. Couldn't understand what was happening.

Jeff smirked.

Jack's mind blurred, the whip shot change in his reality untethering everything he knew to be true. The world slowed, and the men moving around him—stripping off old disguises, changing into new disguises, holding him hostage on his knees with a gun to his head—moved sluggishly before his eyes. Voices penetrated his mind from afar, distorted and distant. His hearing warbled, their voices dropping and stretching before snapping back like a rubber band.

"Bring the nuke here."

Jeff and the leader of the Peshmergas—no longer the leader of the Peshmergas, but a tanned American, clean cut in a dark suit and with a buzzed haircut, formerly cleverly concealed under a wig—hauled Jeff's backpack to Jack. Something heavy hit the carpet when they dropped it, a thud that shook the floor beneath Jack's knees.

"Grab his hands," the former Peshmerga grunted.

Jeff wrenched Jack's hands down from his head and threaded his arms through the backpack's straps. When he was done, the backpack hung off Jack's shoulders and down the front of his chest, the bulk hanging over his heart and abdomen. He slumped forward, the heavy weight pulling him down.

Jeff unzipped the main bag.

A tactical nuclear warhead, Russian-made, rested within. The control panel had been removed, and in its place, a cheap cell phone was wired to the ignition switch.

The former Peshmerga leader shared a quick smile with Jeff. "Had to make it look like this was the Caliphate. Well, the Caliphate impersonating the Peshmerga." He dug out a cell phone from his pocket and snapped a quick picture of Jack on his knees, the nuke hanging from his chest. "Evidence," he said, winking. "You're about to be famous, Mr. President. A sacrifice for the world. A martyr. You'll be remembered forever."

The past few weeks played through Jack's mind on a terrible fast-forward, suddenly lit from a new angle. Betrayal, ice-cold, slammed into his heart. Nairobi, the failure of intelligence in Ethiopia. So much death. Ethan.

But why? Why murder so many?

"What is this? A *coup?* You think you can just take over?" Jack spat in Jeff's face.

Jeff ignored him, wiping away the spit from his cheek.

"You murdered Ethan!" Jack roared. He started to stand. Damn the nuke around his neck, but he was going to tear Jeff's arms from his body.

The former Peshmerga leader slammed his fist into Jack's face, punching him back to the ground. Jack fell to his knees, blood weeping from his nose. Broken, by the crunch of bones and watering of his eyes. Jack spat blood as his former chief of staff smirked down at him, again. Smug superiority leached from Jeff. He stood in a cascade of smugness, a rush of vindictive pride that choked Jack and made him want to gag. Or hurl. All over Jeff and his nuke.

Ethan, I'll see you soon. I'm coming to your side. Jack sat back on his heels. If this was the end, then at least he'd see Ethan again.

DOWN THE DARKENED hallway leading to Jack's study and his private dining room, Ethan huddled against the wall in the shadows and peered through the open door to the Oval Office. Inada and two other agents were on the ground. Closest to Jack, Daniels was also on the ground, blood pooling beneath his chest. Ten men in suits stood at the windows, watching the security shutdown of the White House perimeter.

By procedure, the entire White House would have been shut down at the first alarm. The Secret Service would have been in charge of securing the president and the grounds while DC police held the perimeter until the Army arrived from Fort Belvoir. If the Secret Service was incapacitated, then the Army would breach the White House.

But with Director Stahl as one of the conspirators, the outside world had no idea what was truly happening in the Oval Office. On the dead radio, Madigan's agents were firing on Secret Service agents loyal to the president, battling in the East Wing. It was a diversion, a distraction and a way to keep as many as possible away from the Oval Office.

Ethan counted the men in the room again. Ten Black Fox soldiers. Director Stahl, Director Luss, and Director Luntz. And Jeff Gottschalk.

And Jack.

Jack kneeled on the ground, blood streaming from his nose, his eyes bloodshot and red-rimmed. He trembled, slumping with a backpack strapped to his chest and his hands laced behind his head. There was a darkness to his eyes that Ethan recognized. He was ready to die.

Ethan's heart stuttered. He forced himself to drag in a breath as he checked his pistol. He had fifteen bullets in his clip. Fourteen targets.

He couldn't miss.

Ethan swept the room again. His gaze landed on Daniels.

Daniels's open eyes stared back at him. Tears streamed down Daniels's cheeks, and a tiny smile curled his lips. From where Daniels was on the floor, he had an angled view down the hallway, something the other men didn't have.

Ethan blinked. Daniels blinked back. Then he mouthed out the ten-code for all good.

Nodding once, Ethan held Daniels's stare. He looked to Jack, then back to Daniels.

Daniels blinked, long and slow, once. *Good to go.*

Ethan tapped three fingers against his chest. Then two. Then one.

He burst into the Oval Office, bellowing at the top of his lungs. Shock and awe should work in his favor. He was a dead man, after all, bursting out of the darkness in a hail of bullets. He fired as Daniels lunged, springing from the floor and tackling Jack to the carpet. Gottschalk stumbled, knocked on his ass as Daniels collided with Jack and covered him with his body.

Bullets flew, slamming into the Black Fox soldiers.

Ethan didn't go for the chest. He aimed for the head.

Madigan's men fell around the office, blood misting through the air and spattering the carpet and walls. Shouts rang out, mixing with the crack of the bullets. Wild curses flew amid Black Fox's death screams. Ethan shot and ran, moving behind the couch for cover as he aimed for Director Luss and NSA Luntz.

Director Stahl fired on Ethan, and the bullet tore into Jack's couch. Stuffing exploded, threads snapping. A throw pillow shattered, puffing feathers wildly into the air. Another shot breezed by Ethan's cheek, a caress of hot air and scorched lead.

Ethan fired back, hitting Stahl in the neck. He went down gurgling, choking as he reached for his throat.

Two more in sight. Luntz covered behind the Resolute desk and Luss behind the couch opposite. Ethan dropped down, looking beneath the couch for Luss's feet. He lined his shot up and then fired through both couches.

Luss dropped to the ground. A stain of red spread out across the carpet.

Inada rolled, staggering to his feet and grabbing his pistol. He was pale, grunting and coughing, and he hissed with every step, but Inada joined Ethan as he stalked across the office, heading for the desk. Inada fired over the desktop, keeping Luntz pinned down.

Inada covered while Ethan dropped to the ground, landing on his right shoulder, and fired on Luntz's hiding spot. He missed first, and wood splintered, shattering off the side of the desk. Cursing, he fired again as Luntz lunged.

Luntz slumped forward with a bullet to the back of his brain.

"Enough!" Gottschalk jumped up from where he'd crouched opposite Ethan on the side of the Resolute desk. He jerked Jack in front of him and pressed the barrel of his pistol to Jack's temple. His backpack swayed as Gottschalk held Jack, the nuke slipping sideways.

Gottschalk kept his head and his body squarely behind Jack's, using him as a full-body human shield.

Daniels groaned on the ground, a third bullet in his shoulder. Gottschalk kicked him in the face. Daniels stopped moving.

Gottschalk's eyes burned, fury slamming into Ethan like a physical blow. He breathed hard, and his gaze darted around the blood-soaked Oval Office, taking in the bodies of his dead friends. "You'll fucking pay for this, Ethan," Gottschalk hissed. "You were supposed to stay dead. You were supposed to have your head fucking cut off and your headless body viewed online ten million times."

Next to Ethan, Inada wheezed. Broken ribs, Ethan guessed, by the sound. Inada must have been wearing his bulletproof vest. He was in a world of hurt, though. Still, Inada stood next to Ethan, his weapon trained on Gottschalk.

Ethan's eyes met Jack's.

Jack was the one thing Ethan truly wanted.

He'd had his duties, his obligations, his career. He'd mapped out his life, a series of assignments and missions and responsibilities that had led him through the years. He'd been happy, living a simple, uncomplicated life.

Jack had changed *everything.*

Jack was the only thing he'd ever yearned for, had ever wholly, soul-deep, wanted. Every piece of his heart and of his life had grown, completely full with his love for Jack.

He hadn't known, not at all, what he'd been missing, before Jack.

Oh, but he knew now. Gazing into Jack's eyes, he saw Jack's own love bursting free, and his joy, his relief. Ethan had fought back from the dead for Jack, and Jack was right there, waiting for him. Loving him.

But Jeff Gottschalk had his gun to Jack's head.

He should have been there to stop this. He should have seen this coming. He should have ripped Gottschalk's face off the moment he met him. He should have done more to protect Jack, the love of his life.

If Ethan hadn't known the limitless love he was capable of, he likewise didn't know the capacity for hatred his soul held. His heart had twisted so many times in the past few days, the need for furious vengeance and his clenching anxiety tearing him to pieces.

Ethan's wrath coiled tight around a deadly thirst. He would kill Gottschalk for this, for what he'd done.

He had one bullet left.

"Jack," Ethan called out. "I love you."

He fired.

Ethan's bullet slammed into Jack's shoulder, tearing through skin and muscle before passing through Jack and driving into Gottschalk's body, straight into his heart. The bullet had already started to fracture apart in Jack's body, and it shattered further inside Gottschalk's chest. Fragments shredded his aorta, sliced open his heart, and pierced his lungs.

Staggering backward, Gottschalk gasped, reached for his chest, and fell to his knees. He pitched sideways, coughing as blood poured from his lips.

He was dead before he hit the floor, face-first.

Ethan ran to Jack, catching him as he stumbled forward.

Jack cursed, reaching for his bloody shoulder, breathing fast. "You shot me!"

"I'm sorry, I had to." Ethan ripped his stolen police uniform shirt off and balled it up, shoving it against Jack's bullet wound. "It hurts, but you will be alright. It's just muscle there, you're going to be—"

"Easy!" Jack tried to push Ethan away. "This is a nuke—"

"I know." Ethan slowly peeled the backpack off Jack's shoulders, around the bloody shirt, and set it to the side. Jack hissed, wincing, but helped slide his arms free. Ethan kept one hand on Jack's wound, holding pressure.

The backpack slumped to the ground, heavy. The Army could deal with the nuke. His focus was Jack.

Jack stared up at him. "Ethan?" He blinked. "That email— Are you really here? Is this really happening? Or am I already dead?"

"I'm here, Jack," Ethan breathed. His hand rose, bloody, but he cupped Jack's face and stroked his cheekbone. "I will tear through the whole world to get to your side. Always." He smiled. "I'm with you all the way."

Jack grabbed him behind his neck, pulling him down and kissing him deeply. He moaned, desperation tinged with panic, and then Ethan's arms were full of Jack, Jack crashing against him. Jack clutched his face, and warm lips nuzzled his own, endless kisses that kept going and going.

Behind them, Inada cradled Daniels's head in his lap and tried to staunch the flow of blood from his bullet wounds, all while shouting on the phone and trying to get his agents up on the radio.

Pounding feet echoed down the hallway, boots running full speed.

When Cooper and his men burst into the Oval Office, they found Ethan and Jack locked in an embrace, arms wrapped around each other, kissing like it was the end of the world as they kneeled in the middle of the blood-drenched and devastated Oval Office.

"BACK FROM THE DEAD" HERO SAVES PRESIDENT FROM ATTEMPTED COUP & ROGUE MILITARY UNIT BEHIND MIDDLE EAST TERRORISM

In an unbelievable turn of events, Special Agent Ethan Reichenbach, lover of President Jack Spiers, seemed to return from the dead to save the day when the White House and President Spiers were attacked by the rogue black ops military unit, Black Fox.

Agent Reichenbach and his Secret Service partner were presumed dead after being attacked by US forces on orders from General Madigan, Black Fox's leader. Escaping the attack, Agents Reichenbach and Collard and a contingent of Marines made their way to an allied safe house.

Sources inside the White House say that the men then uncovered intelligence implicating Black Fox in an ongoing plot to destabilize the Middle East, as well as stir animosity between Russia and the United States.

For the length of Spiers's presidency, Black Fox had been actively working against the president's efforts around the world. Its ultimate goal was the murder of President Spiers and the takeover of the US government. Had Black Fox managed to detonate its stolen tactical nuclear warhead, the majority of Washington DC, including the White House, Congress, and most of the leadership in the administration, would have been killed. Experts agree that martial law would have been declared, paving the way for Madigan and Black Fox to assume control of the government.

Black Fox also intended to attack the Middle East, which would have resulted in the deaths of millions, including the deployed Russian, Chinese, and UN peacekeeping forces in Syria and Iraq.

The president has ordered a top-level investigation into Black Fox and into the directors and departments compromised by the rogue unit.

CHAPTER 46

Washington DC

ETHAN WALKED out of the White House a hero.

He helped Jack, supporting him as he walked, and Jack helped to support him in turn. Jack refused a stretcher, insisting instead that Daniels, Inada, and every other wounded agent be seen first.

Cooper's men had arrived moments before the Army stormed the White House. It had been a tense few moments—Cooper and his team looked like out of place college hipsters, armed to the teeth, and they took offense to being ordered to the ground and zip-tied. Scott managed to clear the confusion, and he snipped off the team's restraints as Doc bitched a blue streak.

As Ethan helped Jack down the White House steps, the eyes of the world were on them, watching from every television camera and newsfeed. Medics swarmed, helping Jack to sit on a gurney as they slapped a bandage over his bullet wound. Jack threaded their hands together, and while one of the paramedics prepped Jack's vein for an IV line, Ethan leaned in and pressed his lips to Jack's exhausted smile. They were blood-covered and filthy, but they were alive.

That image was plastered on every newspaper and news website within the hour.

Jack spent the night in the hospital. Ethan was given a quick evaluation at Jack's bedside by one of the doctors, who then promptly admitted him as well. He'd undone nearly everything Faisal's careful doctor had mended, and bones and bruises had to be seen to again, and stitches resewn. Ethan slipped out of his hospital room and sneaked into Jack's, and they spent the night together curled up in Jack's hospital bed, hands twined together and Jack's head tucked against Ethan's neck and over his heart.

THE ARMY PITCHED a hellacious fit when they discovered the stolen tactical nuclear warhead. The entire White House was quarantined, and bomb techs were called in for the nuke's transfer to a secure facility.

Within an hour of the thwarted attack, FBI agents, briefed by Scott and Irwin, stormed General Madigan's office and home, as well as the homes and offices of other named perpetrators of Black Fox. Luss, Luntz, and Stahl were dead, as was Gottschalk and his team of fake Peshmergas. Members of the Secret Service who had worked for Stahl were either dead or arrested.

But Madigan managed to slip away. He disappeared, vanishing from Washington. In his house, FBI agents found a pile of counterfeit cash, passports in fake names, and airline tickets to major cities in the world. Interpol went on high alert, but Madigan went to ground, disappearing into the ether.

JACK ADDRESSED the nation the next morning from the steps of the hospital. He had a black eye, a bandage on his broken nose, and his arm was in a sling, but he stood tall and proud.

He revealed almost everything. Black Fox, its plot, its intentions, and how it'd worked against his entire presidency. Its support for Al-Karim, and his rise through the Mideast. Black Fox's attack on

Nairobi, and again in Ethiopia. The attempted assassination of Ethan and the Marines. The attempted coup, his almost-murder, and the plan to devastate the Middle East. He promised a new dawn of transparency and an investigation and eradication of Black Fox. He swore to expose them and banish them from the face of the earth.

"Anyone who murders in darkness is an enemy of freedom everywhere," Jack said, his voice ringing loud and clear. "Standing together, our world can confront evil men who wield wicked plans. I thank every partner around the world that helped save this day, and save so many, many lives. I swear, on my presidency, to work toward making this world a better, safer world. Starting today."

He left out Faisal. And Colonel Song.

Still, his popularity soared.

JACK NAMED Director Irwin his new chief of staff. The administration —and Jack personally—moved into Blair House across the street while an army of engineers descended on the White House for repairs and cleaning.

Irwin's first task was to oversee the investigation into Black Fox and the corruption of the officials who had joined the attempted coup.

EVERY NIGHT, Jack visited Ethan at the hospital, staying until well after midnight before he headed back to Blair House. The media camped outside the hospital, filming Jack's arrival and departure.

On the fifth day, Ethan slipped out of the back of the hospital and hopped into a blackened SUV.

Jack took the afternoon off, and they disappeared up to Blair House's residence, arms wrapped around each other's waist.

At the end of the week, the administration was allowed into the White House, and Jack moved back in to the Residence.

Jack had already revealed his and Ethan's relationship to the world. Ethan's return from the grave, and his new status as an American hero, only added to the media frenzy surrounding the two of them. There was no reason to hide, not with everything out in the open, so they just didn't.

Ethan came with Jack to the Residence on Friday, and he didn't pretend to leave.

THE NEW DIRECTOR of the Secret Service, Kate Triplett, put Ethan, Scott, Inada, and Daniels on leave. Scott took his wife and his daughter to Hawaii for three weeks, burying himself in the sun and the sand. Daniels came to the White House for dinners and drinks for a straight week, and he and Jack moaned together about their gunshot wounds and their slings. Light and laughter had returned to Daniels's eyes, and one evening, when it was just Ethan and Daniels walking together in the Rose Garden, waiting for Jack to finish in the Oval Office, Daniels blurted out his anxious relief at Ethan's return.

"I thought I'd put a bullet in my head," Daniels said. "I mean, I couldn't think of any other way out. I was just so... so guilt-ridden, man. To be the only one who lived..." He trailed off, looking away, one hand in his pants pocket. The trees were bare, stripped of their leaves as autumn rolled on, edging close to winter. "When I saw you down that hallway, I thought you were an angel bringing me to God." He kicked at the grass. "But having you back, really back, is way better than that."

Ethan dragged Daniels into a bear hug, and he only let go when Daniels pretended to complain about his shoulder.

IRWIN TOOK Jack and Ethan to the FBI's morgue one night, after hours. The directors of the FBI and Homeland Security met them, and they viewed the fourteen metal slabs that held the bodies of

Black Fox's agents and conspirators. Directors Stahl and Luss, National Security Advisor Luntz, the ten soldiers posing as Peshmergas, and Jeff Gottschalk.

Jack stared down at Jeff's body and his stiff, frozen face for a long, long time.

"We don't know who these men actually are." The director of the FBI slouched against the wall, his arms folded. A cigarette hung from his lips, bobbing as he spoke. He nodded to Jeff's body and the ten soldiers. "Their identities are all fake. Their fingerprints don't match anything in the system. Every record we had on any of them has been deleted. Wiped from everything."

"Madigan is still out there." Ethan shared a dark look with Irwin.

"And he still has a long reach."

ON TUESDAY, Ethan was called in to Secret Service Headquarters and Director Triplett's office. He'd known this was coming, but he still wanted to put it off. Ignore reality a bit longer. Enjoy the freedom of being with Jack without having to hide or swallow a mountain of guilt.

But he couldn't avoid the consequences forever. He kissed Jack in the morning and headed out, taking one of the Secret Service SUVs on the nine-minute drive to H Street.

Director Triplett sighed at him when he sat down in her office.

"You're a big problem, Ethan," she said. "A huge, huge problem."

Ethan stayed quiet.

"On the one hand, you've violated every rule we have regarding personal relationships with protectees. I mean, you didn't even leave one behind. Not *one*. Nothing I could cling to, maybe pin some hope on. And you broke the rules with the *president*." Triplett raised her eyebrows at him. "And on the other hand, you're a national hero. You came back from the dead, saved the president, Washington DC, the Middle East, and kissed the man on the White House lawn. It's the stuff movies are made of."

He couldn't stop the smile that broke across his face.

Triplett wasn't amused. "You'd better enjoy it, Ethan. 'Cause the White House has said they don't want any special treatment for you. They're hands-off on this one. Your boyfriend isn't pulling rank to save you. Your destiny is in my hands."

"Yes, ma'am." He and Jack had spent hours discussing the Secret Service and what would happen next. Ethan couldn't see another career for himself, not right now. He didn't want to leave Jack's side, and he was a good agent. A damn good agent. He liked his job. But what would happen would happen, and he didn't want Jack to interfere in the agency's operations. That had bad news written all over it.

"Look, Ethan, I don't actually want to punish you. What you did was stupidly brave and utterly ridiculous. But I have to be fair." She exhaled.

Ethan readied himself for her next words. He'd never been fired before, but he closed his eyes and waited for the words.

"You're being transferred."

His eyes flew open.

"To the field office in Des Moines, Iowa. Report to the Special Agent in Charge in one week."

ETHAN HADN'T EXPECTED A TRANSFER. Neither had Jack.

"So we travel on the weekends." Jack shrugged as Ethan sliced a chicken breast in the Residence's kitchen. "We can fly to each other. It's only for another three years. Maybe less, if they let you transfer back."

"You're up for a long-distance relationship?" Ethan carefully didn't look at Jack. "I mean, it's not like either of us has a stress-free job. Or even a hint of normality. Do you want to add long-distance on top of everything else?"

Jack tugged Ethan away from the kitchen island by his belt buckle. Ethan held his hands wide, keeping chicken juice away from Jack. The sling, and Jack's still-healing shoulder, brushed Ethan's chest. "There is nothing that could keep me from you," Jack breathed. "Nothing. I don't care where in the world you are. I want to be with you."

Ethan kissed him slowly with his hands spread, beaming.

"Let's book your flights back to DC before you leave for Des Moines," Jack said, clearing his throat when they pulled apart. "We'll make this work. I promise."

JACK HONORED AGENTS DANIELS, Collard, Inada and Welby with the Presidential Medal of Freedom. The four agents beamed, glowing with pride, and Ethan led the crowd in a standing ovation that lasted a solid five minutes.

That afternoon, President Puchkov phoned out of the blue. Ethan was in the Oval Office, reading files from Irwin's investigation as Jack worked at the desk, reviewing intelligence briefs.

Jack put the call on speaker. *"President* Pidor!" Puchkov crowed. *"How are you doing?"*

"President Puchkov, you don't get to call me a faggot in Russian." Jack sighed and squeezed his eyes closed. "You need to show me some respect, or I'm hanging up the phone and you can take your proposed UN resolution and shove it up your ass."

Silence. Then, Puchkov roared with laughter, deep belly laughs that bounced off the walls of the Oval Office. *"Oh, Mr. President. I like you. You have* muda. *Balls. And! You like balls! Ha!"* Puchkov laughed at his own joke, though less raucously. *"We can be friends. Yes, we can be friends, Mr. President."*

Another sigh. Ethan shared a long-suffering look with Jack. "President Puchkov," Jack said, shaking his head. "How many people have told you you're a seriously deranged man?"

"Oh, forty or fifty. KGB doctors used to tell me all the time. Mostly after big hits to the head." Puchkov laughed again, and this time, Jack chuckled too.

"What do you want, Mr. President?"

"I want to invite you and your boyfriend to Russia, Mr. President. I want to feed you the finest food you will ever taste. Russian food. The best. And more of that coffee you like."

Jack looked at Ethan. It was the best apology they'd ever get, and the best thank-you as well. Eighty thousand Russian troops had been saved from nuclear devastation in Iraq alone.

"That's very kind of you. But what will this cost me?"

"Cost?" Puchkov scoffed. *"Cost nothing, Mr. President! Of course, we would welcome your support of our UN resolution..."*

"Yeah, yeah." Ethan watched Jack grin, despite himself. "Well, as much as I would love to enjoy the finest Russian cuisine I've ever had, I really must insist that we feed the refugees, too."

A heavy sigh flooded the line. *"Yes, Mr. President, we will feed the refugees."* Only Puchkov could sound so entirely put out and inconvenienced with so few words. *"We already have promised—and delivered—aid packages to the resettlement zones."*

"And I'm not sure it's a good idea for me to be visiting a country with such a poor record of human rights as they pertain to homosexuals."

Ethan smiled at Jack and leaned up against the desk.

"Well." Puchkov almost sounded like he was grinning. *"If there was heavy pressure—heavy pressure—from America, it is possible Russia could... reconsider some of her positions."* He could practically see Puchkov waving his hand in the air.

"Consider this heavy pressure," Jack deadpanned. "It's only polite. We are trying to be allies, are we not?"

"We are indeed, Mr. President! Keep your eye on the newspapers. You never know what will happen. And come to Russia. Bring Mr. Reichenbach."

Jack raised his eyebrows to Ethan, offering him the chance to speak. Ethan shook his head and waved Jack off.

"We look forward to it."

"Do svidaniya!"

Ethan leaned across the desk and pressed a kiss to Jack's bemused smile.

CHAPTER 47

Washington DC

JACK SEEMED DISTRACTED AND ANTSY, and he kept staring at Ethan when they were watching the football game. After the fifth time, Ethan clicked off the TV and turned to Jack.

"What's wrong?"

"Nothing."

Jack was always a terrible liar. Ethan raised his eyebrows.

Slowly, Jack reached for Ethan's hand. He laced their fingers together and kissed his knuckles.

Worry pitted Ethan's stomach. "Are you having second thoughts about us? About the distance?"

"God, no!" Jack frowned. "No, no second thoughts. Not about you." He shook his head, but he still wouldn't meet Ethan's eyes.

Ethan forced his gaze, ducking his head until his eyes met Jack's. "What's going on?"

"I have no idea how to ask this."

"You've never had a problem being blunt before."

"All right." Jack took a deep breath. His cheeks flushed. "I want to make love to you. But I'm not sure that's something you're interested in."

"We already make love." Every night, every morning, they rolled together, slow undulating and hard rocking and hot breaths and deep kisses. They came pressed tightly together, the come sticking to their bellies. Ethan frowned. "And I love it."

"I mean... more." Jack fumbled for words. "I mean... anal sex," he finally blurted out. He looked away, scrunching up his face. "Sorry, that's—"

"Don't apologize." Ethan tugged on Jack's hand until Jack turned toward him again. "Why do you think I wouldn't be interested?"

Jack exhaled, a whoosh of hot air as he gestured to Ethan, his eyes wide and his arm waving in his sling. "You're... I mean, you don't seem like the type to want... that."

Suddenly, Ethan understood. Heat flooded his body, rising to his cheeks. He'd known Jack liked being on top before when they were making out, and Jack would roll Ethan to his back and take charge more often than not. But taking their love to the next step hadn't actually crossed his mind. It had been one of those things he'd dumped in a dark box and shoved far away, thinking that would be put on hold, possibly indefinitely now that he was with Jack. Jack, a straight man learning the ways of loving another man.

But learning he was. And *wanting*. Wanting something from Ethan that he hadn't given in decades. He'd been in high school the last time he bottomed, and the rush of youth and the search for his identity had conspired to create a hasty, poorly-planned escapade. It wasn't awful, wasn't cringe-worthy, but it hadn't been good either.

This was *Jack*, though. The man who meant everything to Ethan, absolutely everything.

He stroked Jack's fingers. "What makes you think I wouldn't want that?"

Jack's mouth opened and closed, and then opened again. "You're... well, *you*." A blush stained Jack's cheeks and turned his neck crimson. "When I was 'researching', I saw a lot of twinkies as bottoms, but when I searched for bear bottoms, there were far less. It seemed... rarer. More... exclusive?" Jack threw his head back against the couch. "Please, stop me now. I'm ridiculous, and I'm stereotyping, aren't I?"

Well, there was no arguing that. Ethan nodded. Jack was stereotyping and pigeonholing, but at least he was aware. Still, the thought of Jack searching out gay porn online made Ethan's balls squirm. His cock twitched. "They're called twinks," he gently corrected.

"See, I can't even say it right," Jack groaned. "I am trying to learn everything," he said after a moment, much quieter. "It's a whole new culture for me."

"You're doing fine." Ethan reached out, caressing Jack's temple with his thumb. "More than fine. I never thought we'd get this far. I hoped, but I tried to rein in my dreams."

"What can I say? I fell in love with you."

"So, watching bears get bottomed did it for you, huh?" He winked and tried to lighten Jack's mood.

Jack's eyes burned into him. "The thought of making love to *you* does it for me." His voice dropped, almost a growl.

Jesus. Ethan swallowed. Jack wanted him. And not just for heavy petting or for a roll in the mattress, but he wanted his ass. He wanted to be inside Ethan, buried deeply inside him. He'd thought about it— probably jacked off to it, maybe even came to the fantasy of making love to him.

Inside Jack's heated eyes, a fragile nervousness lay exposed. *I want it to be good for you,* Jack had said before, more than once. The tender heart of a man who wanted to please his lover. His beloved.

Did he want Jack to take him? Make love to him?

"I haven't bottomed in years. Decades."

Jack nodded, valiantly trying not to look disappointed.

"*But,* I want you to make love to me."

Jack froze, his eyes widening. "Really?"

"Really." Leaning forward, Ethan captured Jack's lips. Jack surged forward, climbing into Ethan's lap without breaking the kiss. Jack rested his forehead on Ethan's, and his cock strained against the zipper of his suit pants.

"Not tonight," Ethan cautioned.

"That's fine." Jack smiled and kissed Ethan's nose. "There's something else I want to do first."

Jack slithered down Ethan's legs until he was kneeling on the ground between his knees. He reached for Ethan's fly, grinning, and pulled out his cock.

Jack licked him, from root to tip—slowly—and never took his eyes off Ethan's.

Ethan grabbed the couch cushions and cursed. His thighs strained. Jack kept grinning, even as he wrapped his lips around the head of Ethan's cock and sucked him down.

Later, Ethan was barely conscious, clinging to the couch cushions, his pants around his knees. Jack licked his lips, a wicked smile on his face.

"Not bad for my first time." Jack's voice was hoarse. "Guess the banana practice paid off." He winked as Ethan groaned, burying his face in a mangled throw pillow.

"Mr. President? Time to head out." Welby stood just inside the Oval Office, his tall, lithe build almost filling the doorframe.

Jack's gaze fell to the wide bandage wrapped around Welby's neck. "Did you reschedule your appointment, too?"

Welby hesitated, but nodded once. "Yes, Mr. President."

"Good. There's no sense in you taking personal time to go to the hospital when you're already there with me." He grabbed his jacket off the back of his chair and slid one arm through. Welby helped drape the jacket over his other shoulder and his arm in its sling.

With luck, the doctors would tell him today was the day he could take the damn sling off. It was seriously getting in the way of his love life. Ethan was careful with him, more careful than he needed to be. Jack wanted to let loose, go wild with Ethan in a way they never had. Desire thrummed through him, burning just beneath his skin.

Down, boy. Jack took a careful breath as he followed Welby out of the Oval Office and to the waiting SUV ready to ferry him to Georgetown University Hospital. Since Ethan had come back from the seem-ingly-dead, Jack had been orbiting the planet, hovering somewhere miles and miles above cloud nine. Putting the coup down might have something to do with his happiness as well, but only a small some-thing. Having Ethan back in his arms, and with nothing for them to hide anymore, had lit a rocket under his love... and his libido.

If he could, he'd call in sick to the White House and spend his days in bed with Ethan, memorizing Ethan's body from head to toe. Kiss every inch of his skin.

Grinning, his mind flashed back to the night before. His throat was sore when he woke up. The mark of a great blowjob, Ethan had said. He'd wondered what it would be like when he sucked Ethan off for the first time. A lifetime of social programming had told him that sucking another man's cock was an irredeemable turning point for his masculinity. He'd demolished that programming, though, exam-ining and discarding each nervous hesitation that reared within him. The first, from so long ago when he imagined kissing Ethan back, and then touching his body. Picturing them together, the feel of Ethan around him, over him, beneath him. Fantasizing about making love to Ethan, until his body begged for it to happen.

He and Ethan were well practiced in making out, in kissing until their lips were red and tingling, and in humping each other until the cows came home. Frottage, according to his research. Their bodies pressed oh-so-closely together, sweat-slick skin sliding, kisses every-where, and their breaths shared as they panted, gasping until the end.

He wanted *more*, though. His nerves had warred with his courage until Ethan called him on it. In a tumble of words, he'd flubbed through asking Ethan to be closer. As soon as the words had left his lips, he wanted to take them back. What right did he have asking Ethan for that?

But Ethan had said *yes*. He'd said he wanted Jack in that way.

He'd been elated at the time, and had seized the moment and the opportunity, loving Ethan in a whole new way. Despite what society had programmed in him, he *loved* sucking Ethan, taking him over the edge with just his tongue and his lips. The feel of Ethan trembling beneath him, the sounds he made. God, he loved it. Loved making Ethan fly apart.

What had he gotten himself into, though, with his question? Ethan said yes, said he wanted Jack in *that* way... but what on Earth did Jack know about making love to a man?

What if he was *terrible?*

What if he was so *God-awful* that Ethan rethought their entire relationship?

He had a lot of research to do.

But not now. Jack stared out of the SUV's window, watching DC pass them by. Getting hot and bothered reading up on how to best make love to Ethan was not the wisest choice before walking into a doctor's appointment. He'd probably end up hospitalized for his heart, and that was not a press conference he wanted to have.

He blanked out his mind as they wound through DC, eventually pulling up to the hospital. Welby held the door for him, and then they both headed inside. While Jack had his shoulder examined, Welby's doctor checked the stiches in Welby's throat. He had a Frankenstein stitch running across his neck, as if his head had been severed and reattached.

It almost had. Welby was lucky to be alive.

Jack was given a clean bill of health and told he could remove the sling. He shed it in the doctor's office, balling it up and trying for a basket with the trashcan in the corner.

He missed. The doctor laughed at him.

Welby had to leave his stiches in for another week.

They headed out, and Jack turned his face up to the sky, letting the late autumn sun soak into his skin. For the moment, he was weightless again, buoyed by his hopes and his dreams. Sling-free, what would he and Ethan do that evening? He wanted Ethan so badly, in so many different ways.

Fears gnawed on his fantasies again as they drove back to the White House.

400 | TAL BAUER

"Thinking about Ethan, Mr. President?" Welby's eyes met his in the rearview mirror as they glided through DC's traffic.

Jack's jaw dropped and his cheeks burned. "How did you know?" He tried to surreptitiously look down, checking his crotch. He didn't think that he was sporting an erection.

Welby's smile was tiny, but there. "You have a certain look on your face when you think of him."

Oh. Jack's face burned even hotter, and he looked out of the window, smothering his smile as he bit his bottom lip.

"Is... everything all right?" In the mirror, Welby frowned. The SUV coasted to a gentle stop at a red light. They were running without a motorcade, which meant adhering to the traffic laws. "You look a little concerned, Mr. President."

Damn it. Had Welby seen his terror? He looked down at his hands, laced together in his lap. "Are you seeing anyone, Agent Welby?"

"No sir. It's been a while." Welby's eyes crinkled at the corners, his frown deepening.

"If you started seeing someone again and it had been a while for... you know... would you be nervous about...." He fought for the right words. "Performing?" He cringed even as he spoke.

Welby was silent. To his credit, he didn't laugh in Jack's face. The traffic light changed to green, and the SUV gently rolled forward. "I'd like to think that the person I was with would love me so much that nothing as trivial as that would matter to them." *Just like Ethan loves you* hung unspoken in the SUV as Welby stared at him in the mirror.

Something loosened in Jack's chest. "Thanks," he said softly. "I needed to hear that."

Welby sent him his tiny, barely-there smile. "No problem, Mr. President."

"Do you, um, have any idea how I can get... supplies?" Jack's voice went high on the last word.

Welby's eyebrows shot straight up. "Supplies, Mr. President?"

"You know..."

Welby stared at him, not blinking.

He licked his lips. His cheeks were on fire, God, his whole body was scorching. "Condoms." He winced. "Lube."

Welby froze in the front seat. Jack heard leather creak as Welby's hands clenched on the steering wheel. "Anything you need can be requisitioned through the White House, Mr. President," Welby said automatically.

Jack blew air out of his lips, his cheeks ballooning as his eyes went wide. "Not sure I want that on the official White House record."

Silence.

Welby finally spoke, his voice low. "We could make a quick stop before we get back to the White House."

Jack laughed breathlessly. "Do you have any idea what the headlines would be if I buy sex supplies for me and Ethan?"

"I could buy what you need."

Jack's eyes flicked to the mirror. Welby's eyes practically seared holes through him.

This was a new side to Agent Welby. Nine months ago, hadn't he bemoaned Welby and his jailer-like attitude to Ethan? Had that been the moment, the reason, the cause of everything that came after? Him and Ethan, all because Welby had a stick-up-his-ass?

No boring agent here.

"Agent Welby, I can't ask you to do that."

Welby flicked the turning indicator, and the steady rhythmic beat pulsed through the SUV. "I'm offering."

Could he really ask Welby to do this for him? God, it felt scummy. Was he not brave enough to go out there and buy what he and Ethan needed? What did that say about him? Granted, this wasn't a normal relationship by any stretch of the imagination. He wasn't just Jack Spiers, anonymous attorney who could fade into the background of the thousands of other shoppers buying shampoo and toothpaste and deodorant. He was the *president*. What would a picture of him and a box of condoms in his hand do? What would the reverberations of that become? For a half second, part of him thought about trying to put a positive spin on it. Safe sex, a public commitment to personal safety, health-conscious behavior—

But then he thought about the endless nights of pundits calling him a sex-fiend, saying he was so obsessed with his boyfriend that he personally purchased condoms when he could have been attending an intelligence briefing. Or working with Congress. Or doing a million other presidential things, anything other than buying condoms, or being a man in love.

The SUV rolled to a stop beside the curb. Outside the window, Jack spotted the red and white sign of the corner drug store.

Welby left the engine running. "Mr. President?"

Jack closed his eyes. "You would seriously do this?"

"Yes, Mr. President. Just say the word."

He held his breath. "Please," he whispered. "God, I'm so sorry."

"No problem. I'll be right back." Welby slid out of the SUV and locked Jack in behind the black-tinted windows before he jogged to the store. He had a scarf around his neck, hiding his bandage, and he shrugged into his trench coat as well. He pulled out his earpiece, tucking the coiled wire into his scarf before entering the store.

Jack waited, picking at his nails as he called himself every name in the book.

WHAT THE FUCK *am I doing?*

Welby stared at the long, long line of condom boxes and bottles of lube. Jesus, how long had it been since he'd had sex? He barely recognized some of these brands. What happened to just general condoms?

Ribbed or studded? *Jesus.* What would the president want? Ribbing? Would Ethan want 'gentle studs to provide extra stimulation'?

His mind blanked out, refusing to process the imagery.

He shoved both boxes back on the shelf, sliding them to the back. They skittered away, flung behind boxes and boxes of condoms. Black and blue cardboard screamed at him, neon colors and circular shapes trying to entice his eye.

Flavored? No, he wasn't going there.

Where the fuck was regular?

Finally. Plain, regular latex condoms.

Did Ethan have a latex allergy? He'd never mentioned anything in the twelve years they'd served together. What about the president? He didn't say anything either, but latex allergies were relatively common in the US population—

No. If it was a problem, then the president would have said something. He reached for the blue box, the box of plain, latex condoms—

And hesitated. What size? Regular? Extra-large? ... Magnum?

What did I volunteer for? He grabbed the regular and the extra-large and read the backs, searching for some kind of size chart. A moment later, he tossed the regular back on the shelf.

Extra-large plain latex condoms. That should do—

Wait. There were ultra-thin ones.

It had been a long time, but even he remembered that the thinner the condom, the better the experience. He hunted for the extra-large size, discarding the neon colors and the strawberry flavors until he found them, finally. Extra-large, plain, ultra-thin latex condoms.

On to the lube.

Shit, there were more flavors than he ever thought possible. Who would want coffee flavored lube? They all seemed sticky, though, and syrupy sweet when he tentatively sniffed the top. No.

He'd stick with plain. If Ethan wanted the president to taste like a hot fudge sundae, lemon sorbet, or a banana split, then he could damn well order that online.

Plain came in too many options. Ultra-glide, ultra-smooth, ultra-wet. Latex safe. Water based. Silicone based. *Christ.*

He grabbed the latex safe varieties and scanned the backs of three. Ultra-glide sensations. Ultra-wet for the slickest experience.

How the hell was he supposed to know what the president and Ethan wanted? What was right for two men? He should pull out his phone and call Ethan, but Ethan would no doubt shrivel up and die of mortification as soon as Welby asked, and then the whole trip would be pointless.

He'd do his best. It would get them through until Ethan figured out what to do. The president trying to prepare on his own was sweet, and it touched something in Welby. He'd thought Ethan would be the one to take care of everything, but the president's hesitancy, coupled with his obvious enthusiasm, showed his eagerness. His honest desire. As obvious as Ethan was about his love, the president was the same, in his own way.

Welby never thought he'd be romantic about two middle-aged men falling in love, but there it was.

And here *he* was, buying both middle-aged men sex supplies. He was their condom mule.

White House scandals were born from less.

He grabbed the bottle of ultra-glide plain lubricant and the box of condoms and headed for the register. This was good. It would work. They'd be able to... do whatever they wanted to do. The president could surprise Ethan with his forward thinking. Ethan would be, hopefully, touched. Emotionally *and* physically.

He was a condom mule, and the bearer of sexual happiness. He could live with that.

And he could live with mortifying Ethan for the rest of his life.

———

MINUTES LATER, Welby jogged back to the SUV carrying a small brown bag. He shoved his earpiece back in and ditched his trench coat and scarf, laying both on top of the bag in the front seat. "Mission accomplished, Mr. President."

Jack sighed. "Agent Welby, I'm very sorry. This was incredibly unprofessional of me. I shouldn't have said anything, and I shouldn't have asked you to—"

"Mr. President." Welby smoothly interrupted him, gliding the SUV back into traffic. "I am more than happy to help."

He still felt like shit. "Can I at least buy you lunch? Thank you in some real way?"

"I won't turn down food, Mr. President." Welby turned right, heading down a side street. "I know a good drive through."

"Why don't we run through it and then park outside Lafayette Square? We can watch the White House tourists for a little bit."

Welby nodded. "When we get back, I'll carry everything inside. You don't want to be caught in the West Wing with that."

"Are you sure?"

"I'll take everything up to the Residence."

He was quiet as the SUV hummed along the road, tires rolling over warm concrete. "Thank you. Really. Thank you. I should not have asked you for this, but... it's a big help."

"Ethan is my friend, too, Mr. President. I'm happy he's happy. And alive."

Jack nodded, shivering as fear sluiced down his spine, remnants and shadows of the nightmares he'd had thinking Ethan was gone for good, dead in the backwaters of Ethiopia.

"I've never seen Ethan this way." Welby's eyes found his again in the mirror. "Crazy in love. We used to call him 'the Iceman'." He shrugged, looking back at the road. "Now that everything is out in the open, you two should enjoy each other."

Again, warmth flooded Jack, gratitude and acceptance spreading from his heart and touching all corners of his soul. Ethan was alive, back in his arms. The coup had failed and Black Fox had shattered. They had people in their corner, people who supported them and wanted the best for them. They could *do* this, love each other. *Be* together.

They could really do this.

ETHAN FROWNED at the suspiciously plain brown bag lying on their bed in the Residence.

Jack tried to sweep it away, tucking it into the drawer on the nightstand on his side of the bed.

Ethan wrapped his arms around Jack's waist and kissed his neck. "What's that?"

Caught, Jack tugged open the drawer.

A box of condoms and a tube of lube, brand new, stared up at Ethan.

"Do you know how hard it is to buy condoms and lube when you're the president of the United States?"

"Oh God." Ethan had spent the day at his condo, packing and sorting his belongings into two piles—stuff for Iowa and stuff for storage. He wasn't planning on taking much. Iowa wasn't going to be permanent.

He hadn't been with Jack at all that day. Hadn't been by his side.

And Jack, when he was up to something, was a creative one.

"Please don't tell me you actually bought condoms and lube yourself." He could see the headlines now. The press, already camped outside his condo and the White House, would triple.

Jack tried to keep a straight face, but failed. "Welby got them for me."

A thousand times worse. Ethan groaned, burying his face in Jack's neck. "*Welby?* You had *Welby* buy you condoms and lube? Jesus, I can never look him in the eye again."

"He's actually a pretty good guy." Jack spun in Ethan's hold, wrapping his arms around Ethan's neck. "It was on the way back from the hospital." Jack waved his sling-free arm, grinning. "We grabbed hot wings after. Ate them in the SUV and people-watched the tourists outside the White House. It was fun."

Ethan chuckled. That was Jack, hiding from the spotlight instead of living inside it.

"He smuggled the bag up here when we got back." Jack nudged the drawer closed with his knee.

Ethan stopped him. "Would you like to put them to use?"

He saw Jack's pulse speed up, pounding in his neck. His breaths came faster, hotter, and his eyes burned. "If you're su—"

"I'm sure." Ethan smiled.

Then it was hot kisses and slow stripping, and hands stroking over skin. Jack sucked Ethan hard, until Ethan pulled him off, trembling. He lay back on the bed and beckoned Jack to him, sighing as the warmth of Jack's naked skin stroked across his. Another long kiss, and shared breaths.

Jack knelt above Ethan, his cock rock-hard. "You're so beautiful, Ethan," he whispered. "How am I the lucky man you fell for?"

Ethan didn't have an answer for that. Instead, he tugged Jack down again.

Another kiss, and their bodies slid together, hands tangled overhead, legs entwined, hips rolling. Ethan's fingers ran down Jack's back, over the contours of his muscles and the ridges of his spine. Jack shivered above him, pressing kisses to his neck and his chest.

Finally, Ethan wrapped his legs around Jack's waist and rolled his hips up, catching Jack's cock in the cleft of his ass.

"I want you to make love to me," Ethan breathed.

He wanted Jack inside him. The yearning almost surprised him. But taking Jack was more than just sex, more than fucking, more than just the next step in their growing relationship. It was Jack's love for him, and his love for Jack, made real. It was holding Jack within him, feeling him in a place where he could almost touch Ethan's soul.

And Jack wanted to be inside Ethan—wanted to make love to him —and if there was any deeper symbol of devotion and love, then Ethan didn't know what that would look like. He'd spent decades pounding out raw, physical sex and seeking out men who, like him, just wanted the physical release.

But now, with so many layers of love and desire tangled within this moment, the act was suddenly so much more than just a release.

Jack seemed to sense the change as well. His hands shook as he reached for the condoms and the lube. He had to breathe deeply before he sheathed himself, and he took ten times longer than Ethan ever had—ever—with the prep.

"I did some reading," Jack said softly, when Ethan urged him to hurry up. More of his damn research that drove Ethan over the edge. "The last thing I want is to hurt you. And... I read what this means, too. You know, you doing this. Bottoming, when you normally top."

And then Jack's fingers stroked just the right spot, and Ethan didn't care how long he was taking.

"There's nothing normal about us," Ethan finally said. His fingers tangled with Jack's free hand. "I'm doing this because I want to. I want *you*." He sighed, arching his back. His thoughts, once so profound, so loving, fled. "Jack, now. Please!"

There was pushing, stretching, and Ethan hovered on the edge of pain and pleasure. He tried to remember to breathe, but the look in Jack's eyes made his lungs sear. Pressure filled him until he gasped, his world wavering on the edges of his vision, but then Jack was kissing his eyelids and his forehead, his cheeks and his neck, and babbling about how beautiful Ethan was, and how much he loved him. Every sense snapped, a rubber band ricochet, into perfect clarity. He cried out, his fingers finding the headboard behind them and squeezing tight.

They rocked together, finding a slow, rolling rhythm. Ethan's legs spread wide, and Jack's thighs kept him held back. He was held open, more than he'd ever been before. Lying back, his ass propped up on a pillow, and his legs splayed, Ethan offered himself up to Jack.

Or was it Jack offering his love to Ethan, worshipping his body, every breath and every movement of his hips and his cock meant for Ethan's pleasure?

Deep thrusts made Ethan see stars and had him gasping for breath. Jack had to stop more than once, squeezing his eyes closed and panting, trying to hold back.

Kisses stretched on. Jack's hands tangled with Ethan's on the pillow beside Ethan's head. He gasped when Jack angled just so, slow rolls and long strokes that filled him completely. His hard cock wept against their bellies, sandwiched between their bodies, and he hovered on the edge of orgasm, his toes curling as spots danced in front of his eyes.

Jack's thighs flexed, pushing him impossibly deeper. Ethan reached for Jack, cupping his cheeks, and chanting his name, a mantra he repeated as the world whited out around them. Jack's cock seemed to harden further, and they bounced on the mattress, springs squawking and the frame creaking.

Jack stared down at Ethan, his eyes blazing, and whispered, "I love you," over and over.

He never wanted this to stop. He wanted more, God, so much more. He wanted everything, absolutely everything with Jack, especially this perfect lovemaking. He gasped again, struggling to breathe, and held on to Jack.

Jack groaned, plunged his cock deep into Ethan, and shuddered. His whole body shook, and Ethan felt Jack's cock jerk deep inside him. He watched Jack come apart, his eyes blown wide, gazing at Ethan like he was the answer to Jack's whole life.

Hot bliss lanced through Ethan, burning every nerve, pushing him past every place he'd ever been before. He thrashed, trying to chase the electric zing racing through his veins. His balls clenched, and then he came, bucking against Jack, howling his name and spilling come across his stomach with his cock untouched. Never before, never had that happened before. He gasped, his eyes swimming, and he grabbed on to Jack, trying to cling to reality.

When Ethan could see again, he rained kisses on Jack's face and stroked his back. Wrapped his legs around Jack's waist and tried to hold on to the feeling of Jack inside him.

That had been something more than sex, more than even lovemaking. Jack had reached something deep within Ethan, something Ethan had never before touched, or had even known existed. It wasn't physical. It was something more, something deeper. Something that felt like perfection.

ETHAN WOKE BEFORE JACK, and he slipped into the kitchen in his boxers. He was sore, but the memory made him smile, and he hummed as he whipped up an omelet and a plate of pancakes. He swiped a rose from one of the vases in the hall, and, holding it in his mouth, he headed back to the bedroom.

Jack woke when Ethan entered, holding Jack's breakfast tray and leaning over him with a rose between his teeth and a grin on his face. Jack laughed, and as they ate in bed, Ethan's eyes traced Jack's spiky bed head and his blond hair streaked with flecks of gray, and the kiss-bruise he'd left on his chest from two nights before.

Jack had it all backward. How had he ended up the lucky one, with Jack falling in love with him?

CHAPTER 48

Des Moines, Iowa

DES MOINES WAS A DISASTER, from the very beginning.

"I don't want you here," Shepherd, his new boss, said to Ethan as soon as he sat down. "But headquarters insisted. So, you're here. You will run investigations, just like everyone else, and you'll pull details as required for protectees who visit the area. It's quiet most of the year, but we get a lot of activity when midterms and general elections happen."

He ran financial investigations and tracked down counterfeiters. Made one or two friendly acquaintances with the local cops, but in the Secret Service, Ethan was the office pariah. No one befriended him. Barely anyone spoke to him.

Fridays at three PM, he was on the way to the airport, and he was at the White House by nine-thirty PM. He took the latest flight back, the eleven-thirty PM departure, but it was always terrible. The flights home were miserable, and an ache grew in his chest with each return to Des Moines.

Months passed. Thanksgiving, and then Christmas, came and went. They made headlines over the holidays, in more ways than one.

He missed Jack with a physical ache, something that tried to wear him down, grind him out. The weekends were never enough, and the days without Jack seemed to stretch ever onward, an endless length of barren days and nights without his lover.

Eventually, Jack traveled to the Midwest, gearing up for midterms.

―――――――

ETHAN RAN his sweat-slick palms down the side of his jeans as his eyes bounced over his small, near-empty apartment. Boring brown couch, check. Computer monitor doubling as the TV, check. Card table set up in the empty space he was supposed to erect a breakfast nook in, check. Six new crappy metal folding chairs arrayed around the table, check.

He'd vacuumed—and re-vacuumed— his carpets until tufts of cream fibers stood at almost military precision.

For one night, Des Moines, Iowa—specifically his apartment— was going to be the home away from home for the president of the United States. For Jack.

His chest tightened against the hammering of his heart. His government-issued apartment, more a crash pad for where he slept during the week, was about to play host to not just Jack, but his friends as well. His shitty, bare-bones apartment, barely furnished at all, mostly plain walls and a scattering of functional furniture. He didn't even have a headboard in the bedroom. Just a mattress and box spring resting on a cheap metal frame.

At least his towels matched.

But he still fished his socks and underwear out of two suitcases he'd propped up against the wall in his bedroom months ago and had kept as some sort of modern urban Neanderthal organization scheme. Why buy a dresser? Why invest money in a place that wasn't his home? His home—the condo he owned—was in DC. Not here.

Sometimes, he thought maybe he was starting to make a second home with Jack at the White House, too. At least, every time he visited it felt a little bit more normal to be there.

He never thought, ever, that anyone would visit him in his Des Moines crash pad. Jack was the president—the thought of him visiting was ludicrous. Presidents stayed in secure locations. The White House. Properly screened and vetted hotels. Military bases. Not the shitty apartment of his boyfriend serving an exile rotation in Iowa.

But Jack hadn't met a boundary he couldn't blur—or eliminate entirely—and he seemed to revel in getting every part of the government to twist against their own rules. Work across party lines? Sure thing. Sponsor democratic legislation as a republican president and get it through both houses of Congress? Of course. Work on an honest alliance with post-Putin Russia, and use his new friendship with President Puchkov for good in the world? That was just a Tuesday to Jack.

Date Ethan? Jack kept saying yes to that, too.

So he really should have seen this one coming. Jack had hopped around the Midwest for a week, from Chicago to Kansas City to Oklahoma City, and then back north to Madison and the Twin Cities. He'd stumped for the members of his party who welcomed him, and then stumped for democrats who had worked with him in DC, rejecting attacks coming at him from challengers within his own party.

And then, Friday night during their Skype call, Jack had grinned at him—that bright, sunny smile that Ethan could never say no to— and asked if he wanted Jack to "swing by" the next night. Shirt rumpled, sleeves rolled up, and tie loose, Jack had looked like every one of Ethan's late night fantasies and early morning shower conjurings. He'd breathlessly said yes.

The reality of what he'd agreed to hit him square in the chest, later.

So, Saturday was spent cleaning with all the intensity of a fastidious drill sergeant. He bought more chairs. Picked up and put back a few pieces of wall art. Grabbed some beers for him and Jack, and soda for everyone else. And, at the last second, a pack of cards and some poker chips.

After his maniacal cleaning, all he could do was wait. And vacuum some more.

Scott had finally texted him when they landed at Des Moines airport, and again when they hit the road, driving without the red and blues or sirens on their way across town. Agents from Ethan's own Des Moines Secret Service office had met Scott at the airport, and the expanded detail from DC as well as Ethan's Iowa coworkers were scheduled to stand watch in nearby vacant government apartments and around the perimeter of his gated complex.

His coworkers were going to be standing guard all night while he and Jack—

He'd pay for this on Monday. Shepherd hadn't contacted him, but Scott had relayed how incredibly unimpressed his boss had sounded on the phone when Scott called to brief him on the president's movements through Des Moines. Shepherd was a hard man to pin down, but he seemed to hover just above actively despising Ethan, instead settling on sullen resentment that Ethan had been dropped in his small pond. Out of all the offices, in all the States, why had he been given to Shepherd?

Ethan's phone buzzed in his pocket, and he fished it out, clammy fingers sliding on the case for a moment. A text lit up his screen.

Scott says we're almost there.

Fuck. Panic, and a rush of almost giddy excitement, sizzled down his spine. He had thought he and Jack were going to lose this weekend together. Jack's travel schedule wouldn't give them enough time to justify flying to DC, but this...

[I'm here.]

I would hope so.

Ethan rolled his eyes. It was a wonder he ever managed to graduate first grade, much less become a fully functioning adult, what with the spectacularly intelligent things he said to Jack sometimes. Jack always gently pulled his leg, which, weirdly had him loosening up.

Like Jack knew him or something.

[I'm about to go out of my mind. Can't believe you're coming here.]

Actually... we've arrived.

His head shot up, staring at his plain white door as if Jack was about to materialize through the wood like a ghost. Outside in the parking lot, he heard the slow squeal of SUVs braking and car doors opening and slamming. Low voices, chattering and giving directions. Most of the agents would peel off and head for the command post Shepherd's team had set up during the day. Ethan heard their feet trampling up the nearby stairwell.

Swallowing, he opened the door and stepped out onto his front patio. He had a second-floor apartment, a private stair entrance, and a small patio, all his. From where he stood, he had a perfect view of the parking lot, and Jack's convoy, and of Jack himself, standing outside a black SUV and staring up at the apartments.

Scott saw Ethan first, and he waved before gesturing to Daniels. Daniels sidled up alongside Jack as they fell into place behind Scott, and two more agents followed behind them both, buttoned up in long dark trench coats and thick scarves.

Ethan barely noticed. His gaze was fixed on Jack—beaming, brilliant Jack, staring back at him with that gorgeous smile as he thundered up the steps.

Scott stepped aside, letting Jack up to be the first to greet Ethan.

"Hey." Ethan's hands slotted into the pockets of his jeans and his shoulders rose as he breathed in sharply. Jack always seemed to steal the air from the room, and even outdoors, when there was still snow clustered around trees and bushes and the air was fresh and crisp, Jack made Ethan feel like he couldn't quite breathe right.

"Hi, love," Jack whispered around his wide smile, striding toward Ethan with bright eyes and flushed cheeks. Shameless, his hands found Ethan's waist, found his hips, and squeezed as he stepped close, until their bodies were flush together. He pressed a lingering, chaste kiss to Ethan's lips.

As always, Ethan's brain was two steps behind when it came to being confronted by Jack and his love. He kissed back, standing still for too long, and then finally reached for him, running his hands up Jack's arms as Jack chuckled.

"Nice to see you too, buddy." Scott shouldered past Ethan and into his apartment, winking as he carried a duffel inside. Daniels waited a few steps down, smirking but politely averting his eyes as Jack moved away from Ethan.

God, his entire office had probably seen that. Not that he and Jack hadn't made their way onto more than one front-page headline, but still.

"Going to give me the tour?" Jack rocked on his feet, grinning, His hair was tousled, just enough to be rakish, and his black suit and black overcoat were offset by the sunny yellow scarf he had draped around his neck. That scarf had appeared after Ethan reminisced about the yellow tie Jack used to wear. The scarf looked just as amazing as the tie had.

"It's not much." Ethan held the door for Jack and gestured him inside. Scott had already swept through the place, doing his duty as Jack's lead detail agent and securing Ethan's apartment. Scott was perfunctory and professional, and he slipped out of Ethan's bedroom silently and headed for the tiny kitchen, waiting as Ethan showed Jack around. There was a small living room connected to the claustrophobic kitchen. A miniscule hallway leading to a bathroom and Ethan's bedroom, facing each other across the hall.

Jack smiled through Ethan's quick tour, especially at the pictures Ethan had on his fridge and on his bathroom mirror of the two of them. He poked his head into the bedroom, nodding at his duffel that had been dropped there by Scott, and then sent Ethan a smoldering look, one that went straight to Ethan's bones. His friends were supposed to stay for dinner, but... Would it be rude to just shut the bedroom door and ignore everyone else?

Jack's fingers trailed down his chest, dusting over the midnight blue cotton of his sweater, and settled on his belt buckle. Leaning in again, Jack hesitated just before his lips brushed Ethan's. "Thank you for letting me come."

Ethan shrugged, gnawing on the inside of his lip as he stared into Jack's eyes. "It's just a boring box." He shook his head, almost scoffing. "I can't believe you're actually here."

Jack frowned, tilting his head as a thin line appeared between his eyebrows.

"I should have a nicer place for you if you're going to show up. You should have the best."

Jack finally pressed his lips to Ethan's, sweeping his tongue over Ethan's lower lip as he squeezed his hip. "I'm looking at the best."

Flushing, Ethan cupped Jack's cheek, totally unable to stop his ridiculous grin. Jack grinned right back, and they moved in for another kiss, one that promised to be longer, slower, and downright filthy if Ethan had his way.

"Ethan!" Daniels shouted from the kitchen, and knuckles rapped on the wall in the hallway. "Did you order takeout for us? There's a delivery driver one of our guys stopped at the gate."

"Yeah! Should be Thai!" Sighing, Ethan leaned his forehead against Jack's.

"You gotta confirm the order, man."

"I'm coming, I'm coming!" He kissed Jack as Jack laughed softly against his cheek.

Together, they headed back to the main area after Jack shucked his overcoat, suit jacket, and scarf, and stripped his tie, balling everything up and tossing it at the foot of Ethan's bed. Ethan wrapped his arm around Jack's waist and Jack fit one of his hands into Ethan's back pocket.

The Thai order was exactly what he'd placed, and the wide-eyed driver handed it over to the heavily armed SWAT-like Secret Service agents with shaking hands. Ethan had paid for everything with his credit card over the phone, but the driver needed a signature, so the burly agent had to sign for Ethan, scowling over his balaclava as he shouldered his rifle and signed against the hood of the battered Toyota sedan. Ethan got the scribbled receipt and his bag of food from another agent who ran it up to his door, and when he poked his head out to take it, a part of his stomach clenched hard. There were so many agents in the parking lot. So many police. So many eyes on his tiny apartment.

It wasn't any different, really, then when he was in DC. They were just better hidden there. This felt... raw. Overexposed. All of those agents were going to stay up through the night, securing the apartment, Ethan, and Jack while they—

"Come on, man! We're starving!" Daniels called him back, and Ethan threw his friend a glare as Scott passed out sodas from the fridge to everyone except Jack. Ethan doled out the Thai takeout, setting it all in the center of the card table. He'd put a stack of paper plates and plastic forks out earlier, and the guys dug in as he silently slid Jack one of the beers he'd bought for them both. Jack's favorite, a darker ale from Texas.

Dinner went long as they picked through the containers, demolishing everything. Ethan had bought enough food to feed an Army platoon, but five hungry Secret Service agents and one hungry president made quick work of that.

Scott and Daniels sat across from Ethan and Jack—who had pointedly scooted his chair right alongside Ethan's until their legs were touching from hip to feet—and Welby and Inada sat at the ends. Ethan hadn't seen or spoken to Inada since he'd moved to Iowa, and had only heard through Daniels that his friend had transferred to Headquarters and was working on the intel squad. He'd volunteered to go on the trip to the Midwest as the headquarters intel liaison because the rumor was, he said, that there might be a stopover in Des Moines.

"Just how long were you planning this?" Ethan side-eyed Jack and took a drag from his beer.

Jack shrugged, but his eyes gleamed. "If I'd asked you too early, you'd have worried yourself out of it."

Ethan narrowed his eyes, but under the table, he squeezed Jack's knee.

He and Jack had a few more beers each while the guys stuck to sodas. They were still working, still protecting Jack, even in Ethan's apartment. After the empty cartons and paper plates had been thrown in the trash, Ethan tossed the pack of cards at Scott and told him to deal while he passed out the chips. Daniels groaned, Inada laughed, and Jack arched his eyebrows toward Ethan.

"You suckered me once with pool." Ethan winked. "But you'll be up against some stiff competition here. Texas Hold 'Em is a time-honored tradition in the Secret Service. And Scott has a poker face that a politician would be proud of. Or jealous of."

Inada flushed crimson, his eyes boggling at Ethan's words, as Jack laughed. "I've seen a few great poker faces in my day." His eyes brimmed with laughter. "Can't say that one of them is my own."

"Nope." Grinning, Ethan leaned over and pressed a kiss to Jack's lips. He caught Daniels and Welby exchanging quick looks, Scott's smothered smirk, and Inada's flushed stare down at the tabletop.

"C'mon, let's play." Scott pretended to flick a card at Ethan, but dealt six hands as Ethan laid out chips for everyone. Jack's hand dropped below the table and rested on Ethan's thigh, and Ethan laced his fingers through Jack's, rubbing his thumb over Jack's palm.

Jack lost the first hand almost immediately, and Scott, predictably, won. Groaning about Scott's endless winning streak, Daniels, Ethan, and Inada picked up where they had left off over a year and a half ago, grousing about Scott cheating and counting cards. Welby and Jack shared bemused looks as Scott dealt the cards again.

The game kept going. Scott won and lost, and everyone took turns dealing. Ethan and Jack polished off the rest of the beer, and the world turned softer. Gentler, and warmer on the edges as a ball of contentment sat in Ethan's chest. Surrounded by his friends and next to Jack, it was enough, for the moment, to forget about the rest of the world outside his apartment.

Jack's hand moving over his thigh didn't hurt, either.

Jack had started with a simple touch, just a laying of his palm on top of Ethan's jeans. That turned to a soft caress, and then a gentle kneading. His hand crept higher on Ethan's leg, until his fingers were ghosting over the seams around Ethan's crotch and he leaned sideways into Ethan's shoulder. One of Jack's hands had remained beneath the table for a suspiciously long time, and the angle of his arm could only imply one thing. Ethan's eyes darted around the table, but his friends were either ignoring it or they hadn't noticed. Yet.

He shot a sidelong stare toward Jack. Jack blew him a kiss, slow and saucy.

Ethan shifted.

Jack folded on the next round and laughed himself out of the game, taking a detour to the bathroom while Daniels, Scott, Ethan, and Welby squared off. Ethan raised across from Scott, as did Daniels, while it seemed like Welby was silently laughing at them all. Inada stared down at his phone.

Jack slipped back to the table, but instead of sitting next to Ethan again, he stood behind him, snaking his arms around Ethan's shoulders and leaning down, pressing his cheek to the side of Ethan's face. He kissed him, resting his hands over Ethan's chest.

"Good hand," Jack murmured into his ear. "Might win with that." Hot breath ghosted over Ethan's skin and Jack's lips brushed his hair.

He shivered. He tried to hide it.

Inada cleared his throat, long and loud.

Standing, Jack slowly dragged his hands over Ethan's chest and up to his shoulders, massaging him. A groan escaped Ethan's lips before he could stop it, and his eyes slipped closed as his head tipped forward.

"Raise." Scott thunked down another three chips and stared at Ethan. His lips were quivering, barely suppressing his shit-eating grin that Ethan just knew was on the verge of bursting out.

Jack's thumbs snaked up Ethan's neck, ruffling his hair and stroking over his spine. His breathy whisper filled Ethan's ear. "You going to call or raise?"

He trembled, his head titling both toward and away from Jack's warm lips and throaty words. His thoughts were fleeing him, replaced with the feel of Jack's hands on his shoulders, lips brushing at his hairline and his temples and his skin. Jack's scent, and the heat of his body. "What do you think?" he murmured.

Mistake. Big mistake. Jack kissed the edge of his ear, nibbling just slightly, and breathed, "I definitely think you should go *big*, big boy."

Ethan's spine went rigid, ramrod straight as he dragged in a sharp inhale. Jack's hands squeezed his shoulders again, and around the table, chuckles and snorts burst free from his friends. Welby arched his eyebrow, and Inada seemed like he was about to self-combust what with all that heat pouring off him and the ruby color of his cheeks.

Ethan shoved all his chips into the pot, sliding his sweat-slick palm across the table and messily tipping over the neat stacks he'd built all evening.

Shaking his head, Welby folded. Daniels couldn't keep his smile contained, and he shoved all his chips into the pile as well.

Jack rested his chin on Ethan's shoulder and wrapped his arms around his waist.

Scott and Daniels laid out their cards, and for once Daniels was in the lead. Ethan couldn't tell if he actually had a good hand or not anymore. He tossed down his cards, but then realized he didn't know what to do with his hands anymore. Holding a death grip on his cards had kept him from grabbing on to Jack, but now... He snaked one arm out, sliding it through Jack's legs and stroked over his knee and up the back of his thigh.

Daniels must have won because he started partying in his chair before playfully trying to scoop all the chips toward him, like Scrooge McDuck was about to go diving into the pile.

Inada and Welby stood, almost too quickly, the legs of Inada's chair scraping loudly over the cheap linoleum floor in Ethan's apartment.

Scott gathered the cards, preparing to shuffle as he stared up at his teammates. "What? We leaving?"

Ethan kicked him under the table as the others laughed and headed for the door. They moved fast, not stopping for chitchat as they shared long looks and smothered smiles.

He tried to hide what Jack's flirtatious behavior had done to him. Though, what could Jack expect when he touched him like that? Looked at him like that?

Everyone grabbed their coats and scarves, and Ethan wrapped his arms around Jack's waist, standing behind him. They waved goodbye, and Scott pointed in the general direction of another apartment they would all be sleeping in for the night.

"We'll be back to pick you up at eleven AM, Mr. President," Scott said.

"Yes, Dad." Jack winked.

Sighing, Scott followed the rest of the agents out the door, shaking his head but grinning. Ethan slapped the door shut behind Scott and almost hit him in the ass. Outside, Ethan heard Scott's deep chuckle, and then the stomp of his feet against the stairs.

And then, Jack spun in his arms and walked him backward through his apartment and down the hallway to his bedroom. Their gazes were locked, eyes blazing with heat and lust and so much happiness. Ethan's blood boiled, and his hands trembled as he tried to touch Jack everywhere, wanting everything all at once. He fumbled behind him, opening the bedroom door one-handed while Jack steered him toward his bed. His knees hit the edge of the mattress and he sank down, his eyes darting for the nightstand where he'd laid out a couple of folded towels, a bottle of lube, and a condom. Not that he was presuming. Much. Just hoping. Hoping that Jack would make love to him.

Jack slithered up his body, kneeling on all fours on the mattress and hovering above him. His smile burned brilliant, bright enough to sear Ethan's soul, and he beamed back at Jack as he cupped Jack's face in both hands and pulled him down for a long, deep kiss.

AFTER, Ethan lay boneless and breathing hard, and half on the rumpled towel they had managed to throw across the bedspread. Jack lay on his chest, his head pillowed on Ethan's shoulder, and his fingers traced over his stomach and across his pecs, tangling in his chest hair.

"Thank you," Jack said softly, resting his hand over Ethan's heart.

Ethan squeezed Jack's hand and held on. He pressed a kiss to the top of Jack's sweat-damp hair. "What for?"

"Letting me come here. I sprung it on you without any warning."

"You were right. If I had time to worry about it, I would have chickened out." Thoughts of his coworkers standing in his parking lot curdled in his stomach. He tried to push them away. "My place isn't that great. I'm sorry it's so boring."

"It's not boring." Pushing up to his elbow, Jack leaned in and kissed Ethan. "Your place has everything that I want." He kissed him again, smiling. "Everything that I love." Another kiss. "Everything I need."

Ethan ran his fingers through Jack's hair, curling his hands around the back of Jack's neck and playing with the short strands there. "It's not as cool as the White House."

"*You* are far cooler than the White House." Another kiss, and then Jack slithered out of bed, standing naked and stretching before he padded across the hall to the bathroom. Ethan leaned over, watching him move in and out of the light and shadow as Jack brushed his teeth and splashed water on his face, and then wet one of the washcloths Ethan had laid out to wipe himself down.

When Jack walked back into the bedroom, Ethan had already balled up their towel and kicked it under the bed. He lit a candle, something that smelled like pine and snow-covered mountains and fresh air. It was the best he'd found during the day, and it reminded him of Jack.

Jack took a deep breath and smiled. "That's nice."

Ethan headed for the bathroom and cleaned up, brushing his teeth and shutting the door for a moment as he wiped himself down. His veins were still buzzing, the electric sizzle of their lovemaking swirling through him.

He caught his reflection in the mirror. He was smiling, albeit softly, but it was there. He was just walking around with a sweet smile on his face, plainly happy. Happy with Jack, with their lovemaking, with seeing his friends. Happy, for the moment, being with Jack in his dumpy apartment like they were two normal people and there *weren't* dozens and dozens of Secret Service agents—his colleagues—hanging outside all night long.

Ethan stared himself down in the mirror, bracing his hands on the edge of the simple laminate countertop. *He is worth all of it. All of it. Every single thing.*

He flipped the light switch and headed back for the bedroom, navigating by the shifting twitch of the candlelight playing against his bare white walls. Jack had already crawled into bed, but he was waiting for Ethan with a smile. Sliding between the sheets, they wrapped their arms around each other, and their legs slotted together, their bodies fitting like perfect puzzle pieces. "I'm glad you came," Ethan breathed into Jack's hair. He buried his nose against Jack's temple, kissing his soft skin. "I love you."

HE PAID for Jack's trip on Monday. He was reassigned to the cold cases, the excruciating stack of files that had run into a dead end.

Jack called him out on his mood on Skype later that night. "What's wrong, love"

Ethan shook his head. "It's hard being away from you. And from the guys. This weekend..." Ethan swallowed. "That was really nice." But it had hurt in so many ways when Jack and everyone left. His apartment had never felt emptier, or lonelier. It had seemed like the universe was about to collapse in on him, the silence of his four walls so huge that he thought he'd fallen like Alice into some weird, twisted world. He'd stayed up almost the whole night, clinging to the pillow Jack had slept on and breathing in his scent.

"It's only for three more years, less actually. And then I'll come out there. I'll move to Des Moines. There's got to be something I can do." Jack grinned. "I could learn to farm."

Ethan wasn't in the mood to be cheered up. "Jack... You need to stop saying that. You deserve more than one term. You need to run for reelection."

"And *you* need to stop thinking that you're somehow less important than this presidency. You're *not. You're* my life, Ethan. Not this job. This is *just* a job."

"You're better at the job than most. I want to see you succeed."

"And I want to see you happy." Jack pressed his lips together. "What can I do?"

"We knew this would happen," Ethan grumbled. He stared at the empty walls in his tiny apartment, at the photos of him and Jack he'd tacked on the fridge. At the cartons of Thai food in his trash. "There's nothing we can do. I'm in exile."

Jack was quiet for a long moment as Ethan stared down at his carpet.

"You know," Jack finally said. "There is a position here that is open to you. The White House needs a first gentleman."

Ethan finally looked up. He blinked fast, and he looked away from Jack's gaze. "I don't want to be a freeloader."

"It's important work." Jack tried for humor. "How are you with doilies and table settings? 'Cause they're getting on me about picking out my official state china patterns, and it all looks the same to me."

Ethan chuckled. "I'm actually a pretty shit decorator. I don't fit the stereotype."

Jack stayed quiet, watching him over the screen.

"I wanted to do good," Ethan finally whispered. "I wanted to make a difference. I wanted to be part of something great, something important. I still do."

"You have, God, you have, Ethan. You saved the *world*. You saved my life. Those aren't small things." Jack smiled. "And, I like to think that you *are* a part of something great. *We* are something great."

Ethan nodded. "Yeah." It was getting late. Jack needed to get some sleep, and he wasn't fit for good conversation anymore. "Talk to you tomorrow?"

Jack nodded, sighing softly. "Don't forget to send me your flight information for Wednesday. The guys will pick you up at Dulles. I'll have your tux ready here." It was the annual White House Correspondents' Dinner, and Jack had asked Ethan to accompany him. Shepherd hadn't liked signing the leave request, but he didn't say anything snide about it.

They logged off, but Ethan tossed and turned all night long.

WHEN HE GOT into the office the next morning, he stopped dead.

He stared at his desk, at the cold case files. He stared at his coworkers, all ignoring him. He stared at Shepherd, watching him from inside his office.

He turned around and walked out.

CHAPTER 49

Washington DC

Jack checked his phone for the sixty-seventh time and frowned. No texts from Ethan. It wasn't like them to go an hour without texting. Six hours and nothing? He sent another text, a question mark, as he walked with Irwin to the Cabinet Room.

Later, he and Irwin were locked in conversation, debating China's invite for a conversation over Taiwan and a possible release of the island back to self-governance. They headed into the Oval Office without stopping their conversation, and missed Ethan rising from the couch.

Jack did a double take when he saw his lover. "Ethan! When did you... You're not supposed to be here until tomorrow." Joy made his heart sing, but anxious tension tempered his excitement. Ethan's eyes were wide, and he had that same look that he'd had before he kissed Jack for the first time. Determination, but also panic, and deep within, fractional hope.

Irwin stepped back, heading for the exit.

"I know what I want, Jack," Ethan said carefully.

Jack stopped breathing. He wanted Ethan there with him at his side so badly his teeth ached. He wanted Ethan to be happy, but their love couldn't just override Ethan's life, force him to change everything about himself. He wouldn't make demands, wouldn't put Ethan in the position of having to choose: Jack or Ethan's career.

But he wanted Ethan with him every *single* day. The loneliness suffocated him at times. Still, he loved Ethan too much to pressure him.

Ethan pressed his lips together. He nodded once, a final decision made. "I want to be by your side. Every day. Always. So... I'll take that job you offered. First gentleman."

Jack crossed the office in three quick strides, drawing Ethan close and pulling him in for a deep kiss. Ethan wrapped his arms around him, and the moment, the decision, felt so right, so perfect, to Jack. This was their future, together. They'd make it work. Commitment settled around them in that moment, deeper than what was spoken aloud. *Forever,* Jack's heart whispered. *Forever.*

He didn't notice Irwin's quiet exit, leaving them in silence.

———

THEY PICKED out the state china that night, laughing the whole way through. They were both awful at it, but the beers and the kisses and the giggles made it better. After, they played a game of pool, but that ended when Jack pushed Ethan against the table and dropped to his knees. Later, they both cramped from laughter as they tried to wipe out a come stain from the green felt of the pool table.

———

ETHAN STRODE through Lafayette Square early the next day, wrapped in a wool coat with a scarf around his neck. He'd sent in his resignation to the Secret Service, and for the first time in decades, he was officially a private citizen. The early spring air was cool and clean, and he breathed deeply the smells of DC. Traffic fumes, manicured lawns of the national parks, and dried piss. He smiled. Car horns blared, cars jockeying for space at the traffic circle. Buckled concrete in the road made tires slap and groan.

His phone buzzed, and he expected to see a warm message from Jack, some comment on his first day on the new job, or a joke about him coming on the pool table. Instead, Irwin's number flashed across his screen.

Ethan, this is Lawrence Irwin. I understand you're no longer with the Secret Service.

[That's right.]

I'm not affiliated with the CIA anymore—officially—but I know the agency could use a man like you. Would you be interested in one of the more special programs? Continue to serve your country?

[I won't do anything that jeopardizes Jack. Or means we have to hide. Again.]

Nothing like that, I promise. Just think about it. Let me know if you'd like to talk.

[I have to talk to Jack first.]

Ethan pocketed his phone and kept walking. The bustle of the morning continued on, joggers and dog walkers and mothers with strollers. Businessmen talking loudly into their cell phones. Aides in dark suits running with wild looks in their eyes. The business of Washington DC.

His eyes caught on a man sitting on one of the benches.

A very familiar-looking man.

Ethan stalked to him, glaring.

"I thought I said I never wanted to see you again."

Colonel Song folded his newspaper away. "Is that any way to greet someone who helped you?"

He had conflicted feelings about that help. Colonel Song wasn't technically an ally. That had been a gray area of international relations, and one they'd kept away from the press. "What are you doing here?"

"I came here with a message for your president."

"So call the White House."

"I'm looking for a more direct line." Colonel Song stood. "Remind your president of that old adage, 'the enemy of my enemy is my friend'. Who are his enemies now? And who are his friends?"

"Are you threatening him?"

"No." Colonel Song pulled out a pair of sunglasses and slipped them on. "I look forward to working with you, when you work for the CIA."

A chill settled in Ethan's stomach as he watched Colonel Song walk away.

THEY HELPED each other dress in their tuxes for the Correspondents' Dinner. Jack batted Ethan's hands away and tied his bow tie for him, and Ethan distracted Jack with a hand down his pants as Jack struggled to tie his own. Then they were late to the limo, running down the stairs and trying to smother their laughter in front of Welby and Daniels.

Ethan still flushed every time he saw Welby.

The dinner was fun, the comedian hilarious, but it was the dancing after that was the best part. A live band traded off with a DJ, playing popular covers from the last five decades. Jack and Ethan danced to every song, starting with a loose swing step before drawing close in a slow song.

"Dance stupid with me," Jack said, grinning ear to ear. "It's my thing."

"What, like this?" Ethan busted out a ridiculous disco fever dance move that turned into moonwalking, and Jack tried a one-legged hopping move that had gone out of style the moment it was first tried. They fake tangoed together and then laughed themselves silly doing the worst dance moves of the late '90s.

Finally, a slow song saved the rest of the dancers from their antics. Ethan chuckled, holding Jack close. "I have to turn in my gay card after that."

"Aww." Jack pushed out his bottom lip. "But I just got mine."

Ethan kissed him, full on the lips, and the cameras flashed.

And he didn't care at all.

When the last song played, they were the only ones still on the dance floor, cheek to cheek, fingers entwined, and eyes closed. They held hands the whole way back in the limo, and then up the stairs to the Residence.

————

ETHAN FINALLY TOLD Jack about Irwin's offer as they stripped and readied for bed. He leaned against the bathroom counter, arms crossed, his hip against the sink as Jack watched him in the mirror while he brushed his teeth. "I support you," Jack said, after rinsing. "Anything you want, Ethan. I will always support you."

"I need to think about it."

Then he told him about Colonel Song.

Jack knew the truth of their time in Saudi Arabia. He'd called Prince Faisal personally to thank him for his aid to Ethan, Scott, and Cooper's team. But they couldn't publicize what had happened. Not that part, at least.

Jack flopped onto the bed face first, spread-eagled and taking up the entire surface. He groaned into the down pillows.

"It's a weird world," Jack finally said, flopping like a fish onto his back as Ethan rolled against his side. He kissed Ethan's palm and rested his hand over his heart. "Colonel Song's message means something. But we won't know unless we engage with him."

"So... yes to Irwin and the CIA? And figuring out what the colonel means?"

Jack rolled onto his side, propping himself up on one elbow with his head in his hand. "Well, I'm with you all the way, Ethan. What do you say?"

————

ABOUT THE AUTHOR

Who is Tal Bauer? Tal Bauer is an award-winning and best-selling author of gay romantic thrillers, bringing together a career in law enforcement and international humanitarian aid to create dynamic characters, intriguing plots, and exotic locations. He is happily married and lives with his husband in Texas. Tal is a member of the Romance Writers of America. Check out Tal's website: www.talbauerwrites.com or follow Tal on social media.

What is the best way to stay up to date on new releases and all things Tal Bauer? Follow Tal on BookBub and sign up for his newsletter! Newsletter: https://mailchi.mp/f1fd8baec198/talbauerwrites

BookBub: www.bookbub.com/authors/tal-bauer New releases will always be announced via newsletter, and subscribers will also receive special promotions, excerpts, and exclusives.

BB bookbub.com/authors/tal-bauer

a amazon.com/author/talbauer

O instagram.com/talbauerwrites

twitter.com/talbauerwrites

f facebook.com/talbauerauthor

OTHER BOOKS BY TAL BAUER

The Executive Office Series

Enemies of the State

Interlude

Enemy of My Enemy

Enemy Within

Interlude: Cavatina

The Executive Power Series

Ascendent

Stand Alone Novels

Hush

Whisper

A Time to Rise

Splintered

Hell and Gone